THE WORLD BREAKER

Arc of the Sky, book 3

L.M.R. Clarke

Cover designed by The Gilded Quill

L.M.R. Clarke
Visit my website at www.castrumpress.com/lmr-clarke

Printed in the United Kingdom

First Printing: Oct 2019

castrum PRESS

ISBN-13 978-1-9123273-0-0

CONTENTS

CHAPTER ONE

Bandim-Dorai

As soon as he'd been well enough to travel, Bandim-Dorai had left the rubble of Althemer behind to return to the city of Masvam. The journey took several days on the *Heart of Dorai*, but he dared not use his power to return. It would have been faster and undoubtedly more spectacular to arrive in a swirl of hot bright flame, but had his injuries caused him pain or drained his strength, he mightn't have survived the journey. The Sun Emperor's demise would come only after a lifetime of glory. His death would never be at the hands of the sea. If death came at all, he had mused as the ship cut the water, sailing north. Would death ever come to a goddess?

Though he'd promised them the island, Bandim-Dorai had demanded that both Tesselica and Johrann Maa return to the empire at his side. Neither would have denied him anything. They stayed with him for the whole uneventful sea crossing. Besides, he hadn't granted them any official status; doing so without his Inner Court would make the claim illegitimate. It was in their interests to stay close to guarantee their reward.

While the waves had been tumultuous, tossing even a huge warship like the *Heart of Dorai* with the sea's strength, they'd arrived in the grand port of the city of Masvam unscathed. The scant remains of the Althemerian navy had turned tail and fled south, so he didn't order an attempt to block their route. No doubt they were trying to scrabble together a paltry and pointless defense. It was a futile endeavor. They could never defeat him.

As the city came into view, Bandim-Dorai drew his eyeridges together. The change in emotion since his departure was stark. When he'd left, the prevailing feelings had been joyous devotion from true converts and sharp fear from the liars who clung to Nunako in secret. As he traveled through the city in the back of an ornate royal carriage drawn by six vaemar, anger flared within him. In his absence, rebels had spread their poison.

He grasped one of Johrann's and one of Tesselica's hands to amplify his senses and closed his eyes, willing his mind to focus solely on the currents of emotion. As he squeezed, his companions squeezed back. There was still an undertow of fear, but it floated discordantly alongside the sticky warmth of resentment. There was something else, too. It was a feeling like the sickly give of the skin on overripe fruit under even gentle talons. As they pulled onto the main avenue that led to the palace, Bandim-Dorai managed to identify this feeling. It was a sense of virtue, the misguided emotion of someone who thought to rail against Dorai was holy. It was Nunako's arrogant righteousness.

When Bandim-Dorai opened his eyes again, his face contorted with disgust.

"The followers of my sister's foolishness are trying to rise," he said. He ignored the flicker of confusion from Tesselica as he worked his way through the emperor's meaning. Bandim had no sister, but Bandim-Dorai did. "Perhaps I shouldn't have left to crush the Althemerians after all."

"Forgive my impertinence," Tesselica said, "but I think you were right to go. You broke the Althemerians when no other emperor could. Once Nunako's followers hear of Althemer's destruction, they'll lose all faith in their rebellion."

Johrann Maa nodded. "I agree. Once news spreads that Althemer is all but crushed, those who would stand against you must see their actions are futile."

Their twin reassurances made Bandim-Dorai reach for their hands again. "I much prefer it when you agree with each other. It makes things far more pleasant."

He favored them with a smile as the carriage crossed over the thick redbark and blackblood drawbridge and passed under the dark portcullis. The vaemar slowed to a trot as they wound through the many courtyards and passages in the palace's sprawling grounds. The driver pulled the beasts to a stop near the bottom of the Eternal Tower, where the emperor's chambers were, and as soon as the carriage was still, a swarm of attendants were outside. They spread a carpet for Bandim-Dorai to descend onto, and one offered a posy for the emperor's neck, lest the smell of the panting vaemar offend him. Bandim-Dorai declined it. The stink of animals was nothing compared to the vile stench of rebellion.

He strode toward the elaborately carved doors to his tower. Johrann and Tesselica joined him, she on the right and he on the left. Both stayed a respectful pace behind. Servants and guards and attendants swirled around them in their black livery, embroidered with the glimmering flames of the sun.

"I want to speak to my ministers," Bandim-Dorai said, clicking his fingers at a nearby attendant. "Gather the Inner Court." The male scurried off straight away.

Once inside his chamber, the attendants of his closet set to work stripping, washing, and redressing their emperor. Bandim-Dorai, sitting at his dressing table, cast a sidelong look at Johrann. "Do you sense it?"

One of his attendants gently teased his fronds from their travel-knots as Johrann answered. "Yes, my Emperor. The weeds of discontent have grown in your absence, despite your victory."

"They'll grow whether there is victory or not," Bandim-Dorai replied as the attendant oiled his frond mane handful by handful. "Word will spread of my success in Althemer, but the danger comes from the folk who don't care about anything but the successful return of worship of my sister." Fronds glistening and loose, Bandim-Dorai stood to dress in layers of black silk inlaid with shimmering red and yellow jewels. "They'll accept a return to the Light, and nothing else. They're the ones who pose a threat to my rule."

Tesselica's face reflected in the looking plate. It was tight with anger and, as always, his sincerity bloomed like the most beautiful of flowers. "They're fools to the very last one. They can't see through the fog of heresy the world has raised around them."

Bandim-Dorai let the attendants place supple leather shoes on his feet. "When I made my proclamation to the folk in Merish, I said that if they followed me, they would flourish." *You will not burn but will take your place as righteous stars in my Dark Sky.* He still meant it, though the more Dorai became him and he became Dorai, the more he understood that the idea of Light and Dark was folly. "I've given them time. I've allowed them to keep their religious practices." That hadn't been out of kindness, rather it was part of a clever plan to gain from their belief, but the folk didn't need that knowledge. "It's time I followed through on the rest of my words. I promised death to those who wouldn't submit. It's time to start meting out that punishment."

Turning to his companions, Bandim-Dorai raised his arms to seek their opinion of his appearance. Tesselica clapped his hands, and Johrann Maa bowed her head and said, "You look godly and beautiful."

"Excellent," Bandim-Dorai replied, though he hadn't needed her approval. "I'll meet with the Inner Court and start ripping out the weeds of discontent you speak of."

He glanced at himself one final time in the looking plate before he strode to the door. Tesselica hurried to open it for him. Two of the four guards outside the chamber fell in behind the Sun Emperor as he descended the stair again, leaving another two behind to stand guard. Even when he was absent, he demanded they keep his rooms under the watchful eye of loyal soldiers. It would be too easy for a budding assassin to slip inside an unguarded chamber, and lurk in a dark corner with a blade, or spread poison on his bedsheets.

The Inner Court assembled in the congress chamber. The Masvam Empire had long been too vast for the emperor to rule alone, though the emperor held sway in any argument.

Over them all loomed six huge stained-glass windows, each showing the ciphers and colors of the six great Masvam houses: Yru, Rserra, Vnarr, Gilgram, Armaren, and Tiboli. Each of the five overdukes hailed from one of them, and the emperor represented his own house; though for Bandim-Dorai, the name Tiboli meant as little as a passing leaf on the wind. Eventually he would abandon it altogether.

The overdukes rose as Bandim-Dorai entered. He didn't permit them to sit until he'd ensconced himself in the carved chair at the head of the table. Before he allowed anyone to speak, he took the time to imbibe their emotions. There was much wariness, and a deep pull of fear. *Perhaps it's me*, Bandim-Dorai thought. *They all know, now, what my power can achieve.*

Overduke of the Marches; Koan of House Rserra was the most reserved of them all. His cool head was the reason Bandim-Dorai had promoted him to the overseeing of the Masvam Empire's borderlands. Overduke of the Military; Adzunetsi of House Armaren was alight, with more pride and determination than Overduke of Commerce; Vuvezo of House Vnarr, and Chimou of House Gilgram combined. They were the overdukes of infrastructure and commerce, neither male built for battle or conflict, but their lessened pride reflected more of Adzunetsi's fervor than a failing by the rest. Though he considered them all, Bandim-Dorai spent more time staring at one of the gathered males than the others.

Overduke of Diplomats; Solseo of House Yru was Bandim-Dorai's uncle, his mother's much older brother. Of an age with Braslen rather than Phen, Solseo was the only member of his father's Inner Chamber that Bandim had kept. Solseo, who had the same dark skin and golden armor as his sister, was a male who would be difficult to replace. Under Braslen's rule, he had traveled further into the known and unknown world than anyone else alive. He understood customs and rights and beliefs and societal structures like no other, so Bandim-Dorai had kept him. The rest he'd replaced with those loyal to the crown and to Dorai.

When Solseo met the Sun Emperor's gaze, Bandim-Dorai's throat clenched. Those eyes were his mother's eyes, deep and golden and full of life. Phen's eyes were eyes no longer, instead piles of ash blown on the heretical winds of Althemer. The sweep of Solseo's jaw from ear to neck was much squarer than the slim line of Phen's face but when he tilted his head just so, he was the image of his younger sister.

His dead sister. He wouldn't know, of course. Those who had known of the dowager empress' catatonic imprisonment had no idea where she'd gone the previous Merish. To Solseo, his sister had vanished. Not dead, surely, for if she had passed, they would surely have burned her in the temple. If she was dead and unburned, Solseo was in no position to question the emperor about her whereabouts.

Bandim-Dorai forced away the wedge of guilt that tried to maneuver its way into his emotions. No guilt. No regrets. Phen deserved the fate he had dealt her. Solseo didn't need to know his sister was dead and how she had died, not until Bandim-Dorai decided it was prudent to reveal such information.

He leaned back in his grand chair and shook his head. "In my absence, my Inner Court has been negligent in curbing dissent."

Adzunetsi Armaren bristled at that. His pride bruised like a dropped fruit. "Your Imperial Majesty, we are doing everything we can for you. We root out the rebels with as much fervor as we can."

Bandim-Dorai nodded, his lips a tight line. Adzunetsi was honest, a male who had been loyal to Dorai long before she returned to the world. He'd been one of those nobles in the now-abandoned underground temple who wore a mask and worshiped with every mote of breath in his body.

Adzunetsi's gaze slid across the table to Solseo. "There are certain houses that are less loyal than others, such as House Yru."

Solseo stiffened, and fear rippled from him. Bandim-Dorai rubbed his foreclaw and thumb together, keeping his hooded eyes trained on his uncle. "Tell me more." Adzunetsi opened his mouth but Bandim-Dorai cut him off with a flick of his wrist. "No. I want the overduke of diplomats himself to explain your meaning."

The ripples of fear gave way to a rising tide of indignation. Solseo straightened his back and held his nephew's gaze. "The overduke of the military refers to my son. Your cousin Elsya has left the court, and there are rumors—and I must stress, Your Imperial Majesty, these are only rumors—that he is stirring up hatred for your rule."

Though Solseo spoke with strength, his indignation was peppered with unease, like tiny stones falling through water. Bandim-Dorai kept rubbing his claws together and licked his lips. Elsya Yru, his closest cousin. Five cycles Bandim and Mantos' senior, Elsya had hatched not long after Emperor Braslen had married Phen of House Yru. Elsya wasn't a prince but he was the heir to the Masvam throne. Not that it mattered, for Bandim-Dorai was certain he would reign forever. However, Elsya had always been a brash and headstrong individual, with airs above his station. His familial proximity to the empress ensured his closeness to the throne where other cousins such as Tesselica remained distant, both by blood and by Braslen.

Bandim-Dorai refused to let Solseo from his gaze. "Rumors," he said. "I'm sure you have more knowledge than that, Uncle. Dear cousin Elsya would never leave without telling you his intentions. He's all you've had left since Aunt Siputsuna's death." Siputsuna, a Metakalan noble, had given her son his red eyes, his armor, and his fiery personality.

Solseo bowed under the weight of Bandim-Dorai's gaze. "I don't know where my son is or what he's doing. That's the truth of the matter."

It was. Bandim-Dorai could glean no speck of mistruth in his uncle's words. Elsya Yru had run away from the court and his father, and it didn't take much effort to conclude why he had done so.

Bandim-Dorai's tone was mournful. "You and your son never believed in my power, did you?"

Solseo's head snapped up, and even as his mouth spluttered denials, the room filled with the sour taste of his lies. "We're loyal to the throne," Solseo said. "Both of us. I don't know why Elsya has left the palace, but I can't believe he's stirring up rebellion against you. You're his kin."

"Oh, Uncle," Bandim-Dorai continued. His voice turned pitiful. "You can believe it. I know the truth. You and your son remain staunch believers in the False Goddess despite my showing you the contrary."

Before Solseo could deny it again, the Sun Emperor willed a powerful flame to flare from his left palm and sent it snaking toward his uncle's neck. The other overdukes flung back their chairs and stood, half-terrified and half-amazed.

Bandim-Dorai let the bite of the flame draw in slowly. "I'm no fool, dear uncle. I am the One True Goddess, and I see straight through your lies." The first tendril licked Solseo's skin. The male scrabbled backward but the fire was faster. Solseo remained in a partial crouch as Bandim-Dorai's flaming noose hovered around his throat, not quite touching, but close enough to blacken his armor. "I believe that you don't know where Cousin Elsya is, or what he does, but I don't believe that either of you are faithful to me. The only logical conclusion I can glean to explain why the heir to my throne, a heretical believer in the so-called Light, has suddenly left court, is to stir up dissent. I believe dear Elsya intends to build himself a little army. I believe he'll play on the fears of the idiots who cannot comprehend my true nature as a goddess. I believe he intends to take the throne from me and place my horn jewels on his own head. But I also believe," Bandim-Dorai said, clicking his fingers to recall the lash of fire, "that he discussed none of this with you. I believe you are innocent."

Solseo's chest heaved as he sucked in a relieved breath. Panic seethed from him. "I am, Your Imperial Majesty. I don't know what Elsya intends to do."

With a nod from Bandim-Dorai, the other overdukes took their places at the table once more. The Sun Emperor's expression returned to one of pity. "It's a good thing someone in our family has the wit to see what isn't obvious. I do apologize, Uncle. This isn't what my mother would have wanted but then," he added with a chuckle, "I suppose she didn't want me to kill her either."

The room shifted in a heartbeat. Adzunetsi Armaren's heart quickened with delight. Overduke of the Marches; Koan Rserra gripped the arms of his seat. Chimou and Vuvezo leaned as far back as they could without toppling from their chairs.

"What did you do to her?" Solseo managed, before Bandim-Dorai brought his hands together in a thunderclap and sent a twisting braid of white-hot fire into his uncle's chest. Flame bored through Solseo's torso and the chair behind. The older male sat with his arms raised and his head bent, staring at the smoking hole in his body, before his life's thread burned away and he pitched forward, dead before his head struck the table.

Adzunetsi spoke first. "Your Imperial Majesty is powerful and wise. Solseo Yru was of the old way. The government is better without him."

Though he needed no reassurance, Bandim-Dorai nodded. He met the gazes of each of the remaining members of the Inner Court in turn. Chimou and Vuvezo were dark with fear. Koan remained reserved, the coolness of his pragmatism refreshing against the hotness of Adzunetsi's fervor.

"My dear cousin condemned his father to death when he fled the court with no good reason. I spoke the truth when I said my uncle knew nothing about Elsya's whereabouts or intentions. Regardless, Solseo of House Yru was no longer trustworthy enough to sit on my Inner Court." The living overdukes murmured their agreement. "I intend to use my uncle's body as a message to cousin Elsya. Chimou, I need you to have my uncle's body strung up on the wall above the main portcullis for everyone to see, spread by wrist, ankle, and tail. Showcase the cavity in his chest. And I want a Metakalan word emblazoned on his face." Bandim-Dorai let out a low chuckle. "Elsya will know what it means."

The overduke of infrastructure set to his task straight away. Chimou's daily work lay more in planning roads and viaducts and rebuilding razed towns but he completed this small task with as much methodical action as any other.

Once word of completion had reached Bandim-Dorai, he took a turn around the palace grounds with Johrann and Tesselica at his sides. On his journey, he guided his two companions through the deep stone arch that led to the external portcullis. Together they stood on the interlocking red and black of the drawbridge and stared at Chimou's handiwork.

Solseo of House Yru hung from the wall in exactly the manner the Sun Emperor had demanded. The body hung suspended by the neck, his arms, legs, and tail spread and nailed to turn him into the outline of a star. On his face, in bold chalkwater letters, was the word Bandim-Dorai had asked for.

NOSHO.

Tesselica stared upward with a confused expression. "Forgive my ignorance, my Emperor, but I don't know that word."

Bandim-Dorai grinned. "I'm not surprised you don't. It's a Metakalan word." He turned to favor Johrann Maa with an indulgent smile. "Do you know what it means, my Heart?"

Johrann's emotions were, as always, closed to him. She returned his smile and nodded. "Yes. It's the word for 'cousin.'"

CHAPTER TWO

Bandim-Dorai

She'd seen it all before, Dorai mused as they rode. The royal entourage didn't take the flatness of the direct route to Elsya but kept to winding and lesser-traveled paths, sometimes dipping into the tree line and doubling back for a time. Doubtless Elsya and the rebels would have spies on the road. Bandim didn't need her counsel on the best way to stay undetected. It was he who had spent his life lurking in shadows. Subtlety wasn't in Dorai's arsenal.

A previous emperor, a mortal emperor, might have thought such subterfuge and effort beneath him. A ruler did not go to the rebels. A ruler tasked others to find the rot and decreed the punishment but others carried out the sentence. A ruler sat on his throne and watched others do his bidding. That wasn't the goddess' way; thus, it wasn't Bandim-Dorai's way. However, there was something lingering in the back of Bandim's mind, lurking in the deep shadows there, that made Dorai wonder if, without her, he would have sought to cleave the heads from the rebels by himself regardless. It was the pain that swirled in his darkness, thick and cold, juxtaposed with the hot swell of a desire to prove himself worthy.

Bandim's deep belief that he had to prove himself burned brighter than any of Dorai's blessed fire. Whatever the reason for his choice as her vessel, she was grateful. No one else, she mused, not one other being under the Arc of the Sky, could have more suited her needs. She knew nothing of Mantos but Dorai knew in her heart, in Bandim's heart, that he was not worthy of her. He was a coward, a pest that wouldn't die regardless of how many times they crushed it underfoot, just like Nunako. If the wretched daughter she and Dorai had spawned ever brought Nunako back into the world, Dorai knew Bandim would destroy them both. He would destroy them all.

As expected, Elsya ignored Bandim-Dorai's message on the walls of the palace, and in the following five days, pockets of violence broke out around the empire.

Bandim-Dorai made little work of them. The poor deluded rebels who sought to defy his rule made so many of their futile plans by fireside and candlelight. His reach was wide, and pervaded into their secrets; thus, he put so many of the rebellious acts to the torch before they even began. For most, the rebels' deaths were at the very moment they realized the power of the Sun Emperor was absolute and their defiance was in vain. When the goddess incarnate visited them in their beds, all belief in Nunako fled, but it was too late. Such so-called repentance had covered many a dark heart through the centuries. Lip service wasn't enough. The true way to safeguard against betrayal was death.

As many Tiboli rulers had discovered in cycle upon cycle of rule, the root of the rebellion wasn't as easy to wrench out as the individual blooms. What was it their father had once said about quelling dissent? *You must remove the head of a rebellion to ensure its death.* Until the brain was severed from the spine, the idea would never die.

Elsya of House Yru had so far eluded him. Whether he'd somehow discovered the intelligence that all flames were windows to the Sun Emperor, or whether it had been dumb luck, was unclear. But Bandim-Dorai had gleaned no sign of Elsya by fire. He was the head that commanded the heart, and the heart that commanded the limbs. No matter how many rebels Bandim-Dorai killed, if their leader remained, the Sun Emperor could not triumph. His cousin would seep into his rule like the stain left by a decomposing body. Until he eliminated Elsya, the rebellion would continue.

There were ways of drawing a traitor into the light. This was why the Sun Emperor gave so many rebellious voices a stay of execution as they spoke of rallies and proclamations. But the day Bandim-Dorai rode out of the palace as dawn split the horizon, flanked by Tesselica and Johrann Maa and a scant entourage of black-liveried guards, was the day that stay of execution ended, and the life of Elsya would end.

Once they'd crested the wooded hill and come out into a clearing, the soldier at the head of their party signaled a stop. Bandim-Dorai pulled his vaemar to the commander's side and followed the point of the three-torqued arm. At the edge of the forest, outside the town Dzoicha and cradled in a gathering of rocks, was a village of tents. No smoke rose, for despite the cold, there were no fires. Regardless, there was plenty of activity, and the reason for the gathering was clear. Everyone was armed, male and female alike. They wore mismatched, ill-fitting leather and mail armor but the weapons sheathed at their waists, or leaning in wait, were still deadly; burnished or not. Bandim-Dorai reached out with his power, seeking even the dim glimmer of a single candle, but there was nothing.

"Someone in Elsya's company has realized how I've peered through the fire into their plans," he said. The commander nodded, though Bandim-Dorai hadn't sought to speak to him.

It meant their advantage was only what they could glean from their eyes. The commander called up a subordinate who came armed with a lantern and flint. At the Sun Emperor's permission, the soldier lit the lamp and crouched toward the periphery of the rebel gathering, holding the flame aloft for Bandim-Dorai to better see.

The Sun Emperor joined him in the fire. The noisy crumple of Vhaun-worn grass beneath the soldier's feet was obscene in this proximity. The problem resolved when the figure slid onto his belly and slithered forward, now obscured behind the stones surrounding the camp. While Bandim-Dorai could see nothing but the ground and the wall of rock before him, the rebels' voices became clear. Most spoke with pathetic simplicity, concerned with the welfare of the families they had left behind. None of the voices were familiar. Some who sat and worked at their armor, rubbing a strange substance into the leather, complained of the repetitive nature of the task.

"Cousin, cousin," Bandim-Dorai whispered. The lantern flame shivered with his words. "Where are you?"

Even as the soldier crept to the stone wall and pressed his body flat against it, holding the lantern as high as he dared, Bandim-Dorai caught no sight or sound of Elsya, nor found a fiery foothold further into the camp.

But his cousin was here. The Sun Emperor had heard it with his own ears through his own flames.

Then truth hit him like a scald. They had tricked him. Once the rebels had discovered the truth of his window into their world, they'd laid a trap, and he had fallen horns-first into it.

Bandim-Dorai whipped back from the lantern and into himself, seething with sudden rage. He wrenched his vaemar around and stalked back to his entourage. "Elsya isn't there. This has all been a ruse."

"Not quite, cousin."

Every head turned to face the speaker. Elsya of House Yru, heir to the Masvam throne, emerged from the tree line. He stood a little distance from Bandim-Dorai and the rest. The other soldiers and the commander drew their weapons. Bandim-Dorai turned his vaemar, watching as a circle of rebel faces appeared around them.

Elsya had drawn back his arm, still and strong as steel as he kept an arrow nocked in his bow. His voice was light. "I intended to be here. Just not where you expected. Oh, and I received your message." His voice took a dark turn. "It only made us more certain you aren't fit to sit on your father's throne."

Just like those in the camp, Elsya and the others wore a miscellaneous rainbow of armor. The only unifying feature was the odd liquid sheen every piece had. Even their skin shone. Some wore metal chest plates and helms. Many had splashes of color on their faces, signifying their houses. Tiboli red and orange, Vnarr white and red, Rserra's black and silver, and most prominent of all, Yru blue and yellow. Everyone to the last had their fronds clipped back to the skull.

Still on the back of his mount, Bandim-Dorai's enmity flared with the fire in his palms. "I don't know what you thought you would achieve bringing me here, cousin." He spat the last word. "You've sealed your own fate. Everything burns!"

Elsya kept his arrow solid and true. "I wouldn't be so sure about that."

"Enough!" Wrenching as much strength as he could muster, the Sun Emperor lifted his arms in a huge arc of fire, wrenching the vaemar around. He sent a whirlwind of flame shooting toward the circle of rebels. The forest crumpled under his power, the trees towers of flaming victory before his eyes.

It was Johrann Maa who saw it first. "What?"

Before he could ask her meaning, Bandim-Dorai saw it too. Every rebel stood in the flame's midst, unharmed.

"What?"

Elsya's grin was fierce. "It would seem that not everything burns."

He let his arrow fly.

Slowed by disbelief, Bandim-Dorai braced himself for the shot, but the arrow whipped off-course by a sudden wind. Johrann Maa was by Bandim-Dorai's side, her eyes red and alight with her Uloni power, her hands raised in the echo of her actions. Her body taut and her face bright, she had never looked more beautiful.

Emboldened by Johrann and strengthened by the rapid spread of the flames through the treescape, Bandim-Dorai raised his arms, locked his gaze on Elsya, and went in for the kill.

The rebels outnumbered them three to one. Despite this and their strange flame-resistance, Bandim had Dorai in himself, and Dorai's descendant at his side. They fought through the rebel onslaught, fire and wind whipping together in beautiful harmony.

The more fire Bandim-Dorai sent at the rebels, the lesser their sheen became. They fought hard against the Masvam soldiers, matching them skill for skill. Of course they did, Bandim-Dorai realized. Many of the males were deserters from his army. That thought stoked his fire more, and the Sun Emperor fought harder and harder, sending unending flame at the wall of enemies.

Eventually, under the onslaught, the first caught alight. Bandim-Dorai's lips curled in a smirk. Victory was on his side once more. Whatever it was they had used as their shield, the shining substance, it wasn't infallible. He pushed through the rebellion, power churning and surging, amplified by Johrann's proximity and Tesselica's distant adoration.

"Retreat!"

Elsya's cry carried over the roar of the inferno, and the rebels disappeared into the forest.

The trees were too many and too thick for Bandim-Dorai to pursue aloft with his power, and his vaemar reared against attempts to ride into the flames. Instead, the Sun Emperor's mind darted into the inferno, flitting from flame to flame in pursuit of Elsya. His cousin careened through the undergrowth with his rebel soldiers on his tail, their military training pushing them forward. They moved as one, with a purpose, and Bandim-Dorai knew that this was a planned escape. Unable to kill him, they fled to fight another day. Eventually they slipped beyond the fire and out of Bandim-Dorai's sight.

When he returned to himself, he stood amid a circle of smoldering forest, his body smoke blackened. The bodies of the few rebels who hadn't lived to follow their traitorous leader lay crumpled on the clearing's Vhaun-hard grass.

Something moved in the periphery of Bandim-Dorai's vision, and he snapped around. One of them wasn't dead. Yet.

The Sun Emperor strode toward her and flipped her onto her back with the toe of one boot. The female moaned, her belly run through with a sword, her life pumping from the wound.

"Where is Elsya going?" Bandim-Dorai asked. When the female responded with a laugh thick with spittle, he plunged his heel into her great gash. She screamed. "Where is he going?"

The rebel tried to coil into herself to ward off the pain but couldn't. When her head flopped back, crowned with decaying leaves, she managed a grin. "You don't scare me. I'm already dead."

By the time Bandim-Dorai drove his boot into her wound again and cut her thread, giving her words truth. With his strike, another rebel was dead.

Tesselica and Johrann came to his side, staring down at the body with twin looks of disgust. Bandim-Dorai gave the body one last kick, this time to the head, and strode away, emotions churning.

What burned inside him wasn't anger but shame. He'd ridden into his cousin's trap. He'd allowed himself to be led. If not for Johrann's swift action, Elsya's arrow would have pierced his heart. He imagined he was immortal but didn't want to test it with his life.

Let them run, he thought. *No matter where they go in the empire, my soldiers will pursue them. He can't win.*

He gestured to the litter of bodies around them. "Bring them back with us, and anyone left in that camp. I'll drag their bodies through the streets of the city and hang the mangled corpses from the walls, every single one of them, and show the folk what happens to traitors."

CHAPTER THREE

Fonbir

Despite a love for the sea, Fonbir spent none of his journey to the Kingdom of Khin above decks. Instead, he lingered in his cabin, permitting only few to enter. The ship sailing north was a two-masted daruchon, the *Jox*, which made quick work of the journey north with its new tutel rigging and talented Captain Ako. If his duty had been anything else, Fonbir would have discarded his wretched waist chain, thrown on a pair of trousers, and scaled the rattlins to the gargon's nest on the first day. Ako always indulged him. But on this journey, the desire to breathe the salt air and let the wind whip his short red fronds to a frenzy hadn't come. The only desire Fonbir had was the one he couldn't have: the desire to go home.

He wondered if, had Captain Ako reported his behavior to his mother, she might have been proud of him. Royal seawater ran in their veins, the same in his as in Valaria's or Fylica's. Fonbir snorted. If his mother had been proud, she would have kept it secret. Her outward face was always regal and proper.

Fonbir curled into the thick blanket and buried his head. Whether he would see any of them again was unknown. Valaria had promised to come to him someday, and she might, but Queen Valentia didn't leave the island or the Sea of Souls. She wouldn't come to the marriage ceremony. He was lucky she'd allowed his attendant Othelan to stay.

"Althemerians belong to Althemer," she often said. "We live and die on this island or in its seas."

Fonbir huffed a hot breath. That sentiment didn't extend to princes when the island needed a new ally. *Wasn't he Althemerian? Didn't he deserve to live and die in his homeland?* Unfortunately, he had no such privilege. He was the price paid for Khinish forces; a royal pawn placed where his mother decreed.

Time passed and he remained under the blanket, taking what succor he could from the sea. Waves crashed against the ship's hull as the *Jox* sliced north, rising and falling in symbiosis with the water. Othelan appeared at regular intervals to force him to wash, eat, change his clothing, and to cajole him into taking the sea air. Fonbir acquiesced to all but the latter. When he'd gone below decks, Althemer was still on the horizon. Now it would be gone.

When Othelan appeared again, he wrenched the blanket from Fonbir's back. "Come, Fon," he said. "This time you have to get up."

"Oth!" Fonbir protested, grappling for the blanket. "What are you doing?"

Had it been anyone other than Oth, Fonbir's attendant since he'd been old enough to need one, he would have sent him from his service in disgrace. But Oth was Oth. He could get away with anything.

"It's time to get into your livery," Othelan said. When he saw the drop of Fonbir's features, he nodded. "Yes. We're here."

Fonbir slackened his grip and sat on the edge of his berth. Here, at the end of his journey. The coast of the Kingdom of Khin, where he would remain for the rest of his life.

Othelan held out his hands and helped the prince rise. "I know."

It was all he had to say. In his fur-lined leather boots with their thick soles, Othelan towered over Fonbir. His fine fur cape hung from a peg near the doorway, and instead of robes, he wore a cold-weather garment called a keela. It covered him from neck to foot, though it had wide trouser legs gathered tight at the ankles for ease of movement.

Fonbir squeezed Othelan's hands and jutted his chin upward. "Make me wonderful."

With a proud grin, Othelan nodded. He called out a command, and a deckswab came in with a wide pail of steaming water. Once he'd ushered the swab out, he set to work.

He opened a trunk marked with chalk to indicate it was to stay with the prince. From it he pulled many soaps, unguents, and perfumes, and Othelan scrubbed Fonbir inch by inch. As always, his work was thorough to the point of perfectionism. Once Fonbir was cleaned and perfumed, Othelan bade him step into a keela, then fastened the buttons and straps that kept the garment in place. Though Fonbir protested, Othelan placed the heavy chain belt around his waist. It was protocol. It was his lot as a male.

Fonbir had no looking plate but also had no concerns. Othelan took great care of his prince's appearance and served better than a plate. From another trunk Othelan took a long parchment-wrapped package and laid it on the bed. In it was a hooded fur cape but when Oth pulled back the parchment, Fonbir stilled. It wasn't the cape he expected.

It was an exquisite garment of black fur, lined in silver silk, its front parted in two perfect curves at the neck, silver serpentine fastenings nestling between.

Fonbir smoothed his hands over impossible softness. "This isn't mine."

Oth nodded as he lifted the garment with care. "No, it isn't. It's from your mother. She instructed me to tell you when you wore it that this belonged to your father, His Highness Prince Consort Banti. She said it was His Highness's favorite winter cape, and that she wanted you to have it now."

Fonbir slipped his hands inside to feel the silk interior. He didn't remember this, but he'd been only seven when his father had perished from the Death. Since then, the only trace of him was the serpents Fonbir's mother had named after him.

"This is beautiful," Fonbir said. The beauty was twofold: one, because the garment was precious. Two, because his mother had thought to send it along, a garment he would wear often that had once belonged to his father. A constant reminder of home. His mother might not have seen him sail off, but she had thought of him with love.

After Othelan laced Fonbir into a pair of supple leather boots lined in fur, he lifted the cape. Fonbir turned, and Oth arranged the garment around his shoulders, then asked his prince to turn so he could fasten the front. After that, he was quick to place jewels on Fonbir's talons, and on his horns a fine gold chain that dripped with black diamonds. He slipped matching hoops of gold into Fonbir's ears, all the way up to their pointed tips.

Then he stepped back to admire his work. Though he was of an age with Fonbir, he smiled like a proud parent. "Wonderful."

Fonbir's horn chains tinkled as he looked at himself. He might have looked wonderful, but he didn't feel it. Although, while vulnerability threatened to seep into him, the armor Othelan had wrapped him in gave him the strength of his mother and sister combined.

Fonbir straightened his back and tipped his chin up. "Lead the way, Oth. I'm ready."

After slipping into his own cape, Othelan opened the cabin door. He stopped and shouted, "All hail Prince Fonbir, First Prince of the Island of Althemer!" The cry echoed as it passed from mouth to mouth on the top deck.

Othelan stepped aside to allow Fonbir to pass. Immediately flanked by guards, their cloaks and tunics thick, blue, and fur lined, Fonbir strode up the wooden steps and onto the deck. Fierce cold snapped at him, the wind burned, and his chain clanked but he kept his face stoic as he walked the route lined by his armed entourage. He looked at the coast only when he walked toward it. He bit down on his gasp.

The Kingdom of Khin rose in a jagged line, gray mountains and their snow-capped peaks sailing into the white sky. There was little land at their bases, the foot of the mountains a violent upward stretch. Fonbir pulled his gaze closer and took in the sights closest to him. The port wasn't more than a cluster of customs checks and warehouses. The crew winched a canopied longboat to the *Jox*'s deck by the same harness that had taken Bomsoi, Phen, and Mantos' body on board.

The pang of sorrow at Mantos' memory would have felled him had he been alone. But eyes and anticipation surrounded him, and the weight of Althemer was on his shoulders. He showed no weakness, instead walking still straight-backed to the boat.

Four pale skinned Khinish stood at the oars, and another stood at the side of the boat. Fonbir couldn't tell if the figure was male or female but by their dress, he knew they had power. They held a small pail of snow in one hand.

"Prince Fonbir, First Prince of the Island of Althemer," they said in Althemerian, "we welcome you into our protection." They scooped out some snow and scattered it on the edge of the boat where Fonbir would enter. "From this moment onward, gracious King Khitarian of the Kingdom of Khin pledges to protect you and your folk until their dying day."

Fonbir approached, a crease between his eyeridges. The Khinish noble's Althemerian was poor if they mixed words as they did. When he reached the threshold of the boat that would bear him to the mountains, the noble reached for him with one pale-skinned, silver-armored talon. They anointed his forehead with snow on either side of his first horn, then scattered more in a pathway forward.

"Welcome," they said.

Fonbir bowed. "Thank you. I do not speak much of your language, but I hope that I will learn as our two countries join through the union between myself and Queen Khitarian."

He stepped onto the side of the boat unaided. The snow crunched under his boot. He turned back to see Othelan behind him, ready to climb on board. The rest of the crew and his guard were to remain, and to carry news of his safe arrival back to the island. Once departed, the only Althemerians in the Kingdom of Khin would be Fonbir and Oth.

Fonbir stepped into the boat, and his companion joined behind. When he turned for one final look at Captain Ako and the rest, they all kissed their two foreclaws and placed them on the deck of the ship. Fonbir refused to let one tear slip from his eyes. Instead, he kissed his foreclaws in turn and inclined his head, placing his talons to his lips.

The Khinish noble signaled for Fonbir and Othelan to sit under the canopy as the four rowers took up their positions. With a creak, the crew of the *Jox* operated the winch, and the boat descended to the water. The familiar undulation of coastal waves brought Fonbir comfort. The noble sat across from them, not under the canopy, but protected from the wind and snow by their layers of oilcloth and skins.

"You are most welcome here," they repeated. "I am Ta Emba, sent by Their Majesty to bring you safely to Nowuku, where the palace lies. It is also my duty to educate you in some of the most basic but vitally important customs of our land."

Fonbir bristled. "I have some knowledge of your ways."

"I'm afraid, Your Highness, that it is not enough." Ta Emba ducked their head. "Please don't assume insult where there is none. I only wish to make the path to your union with Their Majesty as smooth as possible. Firstly, our land is not a queendom but a kingdom. We don't distinguish between 'king' and 'queen' here. Our monarch, regardless of gender, is always a king."

Most of Fonbir's pride melted away. That explained the language he'd assumed was a lack of knowledge. Instead, it was his lack of knowledge that had brought the ignorance.

"I see," Fonbir said. "Then, Ta Emba, please educate me as we travel. I wish no disrespect to King Khitarian."

Emba nodded, and Fonbir glanced at Othelan, who gave him the slightest comforting touch just above the base of his tail.

They traveled on, over the glassy ocean and onto the barren mountain, onward into the unknown.

CHAPTER FOUR

Emmy

When they entered the long tent set up as a kitchen, with rows of wooden tables and benches strewn inside for eating on, Emmy motioned for Zecha to bring Charo and claim a place. She crossed to a trestle table and took three stacked cups, a skin of warm wine, and a few bread rolls on a wooden slat plate before joining her friends. Those Khinish, still present at the end of the morning meal, deferred to her by stepping aside and offering to carry the food and drink for her. Emmy shook her head in polite refusal and took her place across from Charo and Zecha.

She decanted the warm wine into the cups. Zecha took one with a grateful nod, and Emmy pushed another across the table. Charo accepted it with a weak smile. Her face was pallid, the work of carrying her egg weighing heavily on her young frame. That was enough to drain anyone.

They'd been in the Uloni village for a week, living on a mountain, surrounded by snow and Emmy's dead ancestors. Her days and nights were filled not with the discomfort and worry Charo experienced but with unending training and pressure. They weren't lingering in the Uloni village because they wanted to. They had to. They couldn't leave until Emmy did what Bomsoi needed, and the greater the pressure, the harder it was to succeed.

Zecha cradled his steaming cup in one hand. He pressed the other into Charo's shoulder, his grip on her firm as he protected the greatest treasure he had.

"How are you today?" Emmy asked.

"It won't be long." Charo's voice was full of a weariness Emmy hadn't heard since her friend was first recovering from being stabbed in the Wailing Woods. "It feels like it'll be soon. I don't know why I think that."

"I imagine it's instinct," Zecha said, releasing his cup to snag two rolls. He offered one to Charo, with no success, and shoved the entirety of the other into his mouth.

Emmy nodded at Zecha's words, trying not to laugh at his stuffed cheeks as she sipped her wine. "I'd say it is. I've heard a lot of females say that just before their laying."

Charo's hands left her untouched cup to rest on her abdomen. Under her layers of clothing, the slight swelling was invisible. "I'm not sure how we'll keep the egg warm when it comes out. We need more shelter than a tent."

Their stay in the Uloni village had been as comfortable and welcoming as the Khinish could make it. Everything they'd been able to provide, they had. It happened that warm houses with wooden walls weren't one of those things. The Khinish garrisoned soldiers in the village to protect what they considered a holy site, living only in tents. Those soldiers lived with the barest minimum of supplies. Even as they sent messengers out for more food, clothing, and shelter for their guests, the caravan of sleds that had rumbled into the village contained no buildings: only wooden frames with canvas and animal-hide coverings.

Zecha swallowed his mouthful with a gulp of wine. "I've been thinking of asking Bomsoi if the Khinish would bring the two of us somewhere else, maybe a village with more permanent structures. There must be somewhere near enough, considering how quickly they've brought in supplies."

A shiver of fear traced up Emmy's back. She didn't want to separate from her friends, especially Zecha. But he was right. She knew it. This village of snow and ice was an echo of death, no place to incubate an egg.

Hands still on her belly, Charo grimaced. "What we need is a fire. A real one that can burn and burn for heat. But that cursed Bandim Tiboli means we can't do that."

"He doesn't know who you two are," Emmy said. "He can't learn anything he needs to know from you, unless you talk about the Uloni or Bomsoi or Mantos. Once you're gone, you can have a fire with no issue. Just watch what you say in front of it."

Charo lifted an eyeridge and groused, "That's one way to make someone feel useless."

Emmy huffed. "I didn't mean it that way, and you know it."

"I know," Charo admitted with a sigh. "That's not even why I feel useless. I want to help you, Emmy. I want to fight with you. We've come all this way together, and I'm not willing to abandon everything now. But right now," —she gestured to herself— "I can't do anything."

Emmy placed a hand on Charo's shoulder and shook her head. "Maybe this is the goddess' way of telling you you've fought enough. You don't have to fight anymore."

"That's another way to make someone feel useless," Charo said, though she smiled. "And anyway, which goddess do you mean?"

Emmy shook her head with a laugh. "Take your pick. Who knows?"

After she finished her morning meal, she parted ways with her friends. Emmy trudged through the snow toward her daily destination. She slipped out of her cloak and overshoes at the door to the Uloni temple. Inside the round building of wood and stone, training proceeded as it always did. They practiced until long after the sun had sunk, and the only light came from moondust lanterns and the wisps of moonlight entering through the open roof.

"Concentrate," Bomsoi said.

Emmy ground her teeth. That word again. There were fewer words she hated. "*I'm trying.*"

"*Try more.*"

She closed her eyes to block out the temple's wood-paneled interior. Bomsoi commanded her to open them again. "*Concentration isn't about blocking out. It's about homing in. You can't close your eyes in the face of your enemy.*"

They'd had this conversation so many times. Forcing her eyes open again, Emmy locked her gaze on the sight in front of her. Pooled in the dim light let in by the open temple roof, she and Bomsoi stood before each other. While Bomsoi was fluid with ease, Emmy stayed coiled, like an Althemerian serpent ready to strike.

"*Reach inside me and find my heart,*" Bomsoi said. "*Find it and stop it.*"

Frustration boiled over, and Emmy grunted. The ground under her feet crackled with new tendrils of ice. That mistake only grew her frustration more. She couldn't do it. She wasn't enough. She would never be enough.

Before Bomsoi could interject, Emmy side-stepped to plant her boots on firmer ground, and forced her mind to quiet. "*No. I can do it. I am good enough.*"

Though she kept her eyes wide open, she looked into herself. She traced the interior of her own body, the vessels that carried her blood and her power, all surging toward her center, her heart. She widened her gaze, transferring the map of her veins to Bomsoi. Though she couldn't see Bomsoi's physical heart, Emmy knew where it dwelled, sheltered beneath bright white ribs and sternum. Coldness pulsed. Emmy reached out, her line of sight and her talons a crossbow bolt waiting to strike.

"Concentrate," Bomsoi repeated.

Emmy loosed the bolt.

Ice shot from her talons toward Bomsoi's chest. Her instinct was to let it strike just as she'd struck Bandim. She fought that instinct, and even as sweat beaded on her forehead to trickle around her horns, she split her ice into the tiniest of shards and buried them into Bomsoi. They passed through Bomsoi's skin, past her bones, and surrounded the beating redness of her life. Without hesitation, Emmy whipped her hand up and commanded the ice to clamp around Bomsoi's heart.

A strangled cry escaped from the Stranger's throat, followed by a burble and a gasp. The horrendous sound continued for a moment, echoing in the emptiness of the temple. Then Bomsoi slumped to the ground, unmoving. She remained on the stone floor even as Emmy called off her ice. At Bomsoi's stillness, a coldness beyond anything she'd known gripped Emmy's own heart.

"Bomsoi, wake up!" The Stranger remained on the temple floor, pooled in a perfect circle of light. "Bomsoi, get up!"

Still nothing.

Emmy dropped to the ground, hands scrabbling to pull Bomsoi onto her back. This shouldn't be happening. Bomsoi had assured her she would be fine, that it didn't matter what Emmy did, as Bomsoi would always be more powerful. That Bomsoi couldn't die. Yet there she lay, with a still heart and no breath in her body.

"*Bomsoi, you liar!*"

Panic spread like a drip of black ink in clear water, the poison of Emmy's mind invading everything. She'd killed Bomsoi. She'd ruined everything. Bandim and Dorai would crush the world under their boots.

No. The strength that had made her plant her boots before returned. Casting aside all doubt, Emmy laid her hands on Bomsoi's chest, searching for the divot in her sternum that signaled the dwelling place of the heart. The map of Bomsoi's inner body blinked into existence again, and Emmy traced the blood vessels, the redness inside unmoving. Just as she'd buried her ice in Bomsoi's chest, she pushed her healing through, bright and hot, and giving. Emmy passed the sensation through every road on the map, from the tiniest peripherals to the thick meat of the veins around the heart.

Drop by drop, Emmy forced Bomsoi's blood to move again, slowly at first, but then fast enough to set the heart pumping and start the bellowing in and out of Bomsoi's lungs. Breath returned to the daughter of gods and at last, Bomsoi opened her gray eyes.

Emmy's first instinct was to slap her, though just like her negative thoughts, she beat down the urge. "Bomsoi! What happened? You said you would be fine."

Bomsoi accept Emmy's offered hand, pulled herself upright, and gestured to herself. "Am I not fine?"

"You are now!" Emmy blurted. "But you weren't. You were dead."

A shadow passed over Bomsoi's face. "I might have appeared that way, but I assure you I was never dead. It will take more than stopping my heart to kill me."

Emmy's expression softened at the sadness in Bomsoi's face. She looked too young, too vulnerable. "Can you actually die, Bomsoi? Rel once told me you couldn't."

Bomsoi cupped Emmy's face in her hand. Her touch bloomed cold. "It would take a mighty force to destroy me. Fear not, my youngling. You alone can't kill me. I was never in danger."

Though the words should have comforted her, Bomsoi's admission left a greasy mark behind. Until now, Emmy had assumed Bomsoi was immortal, no one could kill the daughter of gods. But that wasn't true. Emmy suppressed her shudder.

Bomsoi patted Emmy's cheek once and smiled. "You performed admirably, Emmy. To reach inside and use your power to stop a heart from within shows strength indeed. What was stronger again was that you reached inside yourself and quelled your self-doubt and fear. You are powerful, and you finally begin to accept it."

As if to prove Bomsoi's point, an immediate, "*No I'm not*," swelled in Emmy's mind, only for her to put it down. "I'm trying," she said instead.

Bomsoi made for the temple doors and bade Emmy follow. "That's all you can do. It isn't easy reforming the beliefs you have about yourself. It takes more strength to challenge that inner darkness than to wield any other power. But you'll do it, my dear. I have faith in you."

That brought a wide smile to Emmy's face. "Thank you."

"Thank yourself," Bomsoi replied as she grasped the temple door's carved wooden handle. "You're the one who does it."

The long training day over at last, they stepped uncloaked into the mountainous twilight. Stars blinked between gashes of dark cloud, and a sliver of Rafa peeked through. Moondust lanterns glimmered from poles, casting their eerie light across the village of tents. Emmy stilled and watched. The only cold she felt came from the sharp gusts of wind. Anyone scurrying through the snow wore many layers against the mountain climate, seeking shelter from flurries.

It hadn't always been this way. When the village was the Uloni homeland, filled with her blue and purple kin, no one would have feared the cold. Just like her, they wouldn't have felt it. Emmy's mind populated the sight before her with Uloni walking to the temple, greeting one another, corralling their younglings into some order. Her imagination conjured the huge spheres of pristine ice that Rel had once mentioned, catching the light to banish darkness.

The question was out of her mouth before she realized. "*Do you think my parents loved me?*"

Compassion rolled off Bomsoi in waves. "*I'm sure of it*," she said. "*Younglings are a gift to treasure and teach. Though I don't know the identities of your mother and father, I know that every Uloni egg that hatched was cherished.*"

"*I hope I was, Bomsoi. I really do.*"

When she got her feet to get moving again, Bomsoi stayed at her side.

"*When will I be ready to help bring the spirit of Nunako into Mantos?*" Emmy asked.

Bomsoi showed no shock at her abrupt turn of questioning. "*Now you've wielded power over the heart, you know where to guide Nunako. That means you're ready. The question is whether you and I are strong enough to bring her back. Bandim's Uloni Heart had the Lunar Awakening to help her. All we have is each other."*

"*You could ask your father to help again,*" Emmy suggested.

Bomsoi let out a rueful laugh. "*I've asked him every day since we arrived. I can only hope his presence creates a draw for Mother Nunako. We will soon see. I shall ask the Khinish to pray for our success.*"

"*Will that work?*" Emmy asked. "*They don't pray to Nunako, or even Dorai.*"

"*True. But their prayers are greater for that. They don't pray to my mothers. They pray to my grandmother, the Grandmother of the World.*" At Emmy's scrunched brow, she elaborated. "*I told you once of my origins, that Nunako and Dorai together are my mothers. The Grandmother is their mother, who placed her two littlest talons into two eggs and hatched her daughter goddesses Nunako and Dorai, who in turn hatched me. Because of Nunako and Dorai's closeness to the folk under the Arc and their jealous desire for worship, they didn't spread knowledge of the Grandmother. But I did. The temple*" —Bomsoi turned to face the circular building again— "*is a temple to my grandmother. My folk always worshiped the Grandmother of the World above anything else. They call her Yoyominkos. The Khinish, or Kiseoyan as they refer to themselves, were friends of the Uloni from the beginning. They adopted worship of the Grandmother alongside my folk and have worshiped her since. That's why they preserved the memory of this place and rebuilt the temple. That's why they welcomed us.*"

Emmy's eye line drifted from the temple to the Khinish who passed through the snow. Each of the color-blanched figures was a friend of the Uloni. Some of their elders would have been alive when Emmy's parents still lived.

"*In the same way Nunako and Dorai draw power from belief, so does the Grandmother of the World.*" Bomsoi turned again and crossed the village, toward the sleeping tents. "*The difference is that the Grandmother doesn't desire worship. Mother Nunako and Mother Dorai covet the love of the folk. What Grandmother wishes, I don't know, but she's never walked the lands under the Arc with the desire for folk to love her. My grandmother needs no approval,*" she continued, her tone edged with ominousness. "*I can only hope she hears our cries and comes to our aid in whatever way she sees fit.*" Bomsoi stopped outside Rel's tent and held Emmy's eyes. Emmy's steps faltered under the weight of Bomsoi's gaze. "*We will try in two nights' time when the moons are full. The sooner Nunako is with us, the sooner we can be the counterweight to Bandim and Dorai.*"

Emmy swallowed, unable to nod. The sudden pressure of Bomsoi's announcement chilled her where the snow couldn't. "*Two nights,*" she repeated.

Bomsoi nodded, then opened the entrance to Rel's tent. Emmy knocked the snow from her boots and followed inside.

At their presence, Rel raised herself on her elbows. Though the injuries caused by Bandim's fire were extensive, the swiftness of Bomsoi and Emmy's healing had reduced the damage. While the burns healed well, they traced in a morphing crisscross of bleached white over one side of Rel's face, winding down her neck and under her sleep shirt.

"Serious faces," the Bonebreaker said.

"Serious business," Bomsoi replied. "My friend, do you think yourself well enough to help us? We need your power."

Rel didn't need to ask why. There was only one reason. She pushed herself further upright, winced, and shook off Emmy's concern. "I'm well enough for anything. Is Emmy ready?"

"She is," Bomsoi replied. "Emmy stopped my heart with her power. She's ready to guide Nunako into Mantos."

Rel swung her legs from under her blankets and planted her feet on the rugs that made the floor of her tent. The smile she gave Emmy was brighter than sunrise. "Once you set a boulder rolling down a hill, it picks up speed. You learn just as fast."

Humor quirked Emmy's lips. "Did you just compare me to a rock?"

"A talented rock." Rel stood but faltered. Emmy and Bomsoi were at her side immediately. "I'm all right," she assured them. "I've been in bed too long."

Only when she was sure Rel had her own balance did Emmy pull back. Bomsoi kept one hand on Rel and gestured with the other. "Go and eat. Gather your strength and rest these next two days. However difficult you think this will be, it will be ten times more so."

Responsibility became an iron collar as Emmy stepped back into the jaws of the wind. The collar pulled her down. *You can't do it. You aren't powerful enough. You'll never be Mantos' Heart.*

She forced her head upright with every step. All she could do was try.

CHAPTER FIVE

Mantos

By nightfall, another caravan of supplies had arrived in the Uloni village. Mantos helped to lift and carry bags and crates of food, erect larger tents, and distribute new clothing to everyone gathered in the shadow of the temple. As he worked, snow and moons' light whipped around him, painting him in silver. The flakes fell as a blanket that covered everything. Underneath it, their colors all looked the same.

Mantos accepted a wooden crate from a set of gloved Khinish hands. He took the weight and handed the burden to the next folk in line. They worked in a winding trail to unload the hardy sleds that had made the difficult journey from Nowuku, the nearest settlement and also the Khinish capital. His arms threatened to tremble at the memory, but he pushed onward. Nowuku was where Fonbir was, off to complete his duty to his mother. Mantos denied another tremble. Queen Valentia was dead now, and Mantos' mother along with her, not to mention Fylica. Fonbir had never been fond of his youngest sibling but that would mean nothing now that she was dead.

He swiveled back to receive the next crate. He wanted to be the one to give Fonbir the news. His should be the arms his Nabi sought comfort in. He doubted Valaria would allow it and doubted even more that Fonbir would accept his comfort. Mantos had returned and was now with Bomsoi, waiting for the moment when she decided it was time for him to imbibe the spirit of Nunako but that didn't change things. It didn't erase Mantos' cowardice. It didn't forgive his betrayal.

Mantos denied a third tremble and pushed his muscles to lift higher. Grief and shame would no longer be his masters. He refused to allow them to draw out the path he would follow. Half a cycle ago, he would have buried himself in the mountains rather than face his duty. No more. From within Tero's tight wrap, under the light of Dato, Rafa, and Akata, Mantos had emerged as if hatched anew. Gone was his cowardice. Gone was his selfishness. Their memories pained him, but they didn't rule him. From now on his single dedication was to stop the encroachment of his brother's claws.

Mantos hefted his next burden but as he trudged across the snow something caught his attention. Valaria crossed the dark village. Though swaddled in furs, she still looked regal. There was something in her bearing and the way she carried her head that spoke of her destiny to wear a crown. Her face was still as if carved from mountain ice, her eyeridges pulled low.

Beating back the self-depreciating whiplash about his own head and whether it was worthy of a crown, Mantos deposited the bag of supplies at the back of the cook tent and followed the princess as she slipped through the doors into the Uloni temple. Though she didn't turn to look at him, she held the door open behind her.

"Yes, Masvam?" Her voice echoed in the grand circular structure.

Mantos took the weight of the door and closed it behind them without a sound. As she had spoken her own language, he offered his reply in the same. "You looked troubled, Princess."

"I looked interesting to your greedy Masvam eyes, more like." She strode to the center of the temple, then diverted to the side to sit in a front pew. "You want to learn my business, not my mood."

All Mantos could do was shrug. She was right. He stood a way off from her and waited until she gestured for him to join her. As he sank onto the bench at a respectful distance from her, he remained silent.

"I'm leaving for Nowuku in the morning," Valaria said. Her words swirled in the emptiness. "I received a letter on that supply train. Fonbir has arrived, and King Khitarian tells me my brother now knows of Mother and Fylica's deaths."

Pain swelled within Mantos. "I can imagine how he must feel."

"Doubtless dreadful," Valaria said, keeping her gaze trained forward and not on him, "but my brother is stronger than even Mother understood. However, I don't travel for his comfort. I need to meet with Khitarian to discuss our next steps, if there are any to take. With the loss of our island, Khitarian has no reason to continue our alliance. At best, the king will send us on our way with a ship so I can gather what remains of my folk. At worst, we'll leave with only the clothes on our backs."

Mantos nodded, adding a 'hum' of agreement as Valaria still kept her eyes away. "It's impossible to tell what the Kingdom of Khin will do. Queen Sarkin and King Jaka Narr were elusive enough, but with all the power of my father's scouts and spies, we knew nothing more of Khitarian than that she was the heir."

"Their status," Valaria corrected. "The Khinish recognize a third gender, though I can't say I understand it."

"Ah," Mantos said. "I've heard of it but only in books. But the fact Father didn't know that of Khitarian shows how little we understand of the Khinish and their ways."

Concern bubbled in Mantos' stomach. His lack of knowledge meant there was little comfort over Fonbir's status as the prince of a conquered realm. Would Khitarian treat him well, or would they cast him aside? Would they condemn him to life in a prison cell until his sister came to claim him?

Valaria tipped her head backward to stare at the perfect circle of star-mottled sky visible through the temple roof. "I came in here to pray but now I'm here, I fear I don't remember how. It's so silent in this place. There's no chanting, no praise for Ethay and Apago. This is a shrine to a god I don't believe in." She turned her face to him. "Your brother has killed not only my mother, my sister, and my folk but my belief in my gods. Where were Ethay and Apago as the so-called Sun Emperor attacked Kubodinnu?" Her eyes shone, though her voice remained steady. "With my island gone, where are they now?"

No comforting words leaped into Mantos' mouth, so he remained silent.

Valaria huffed and turned away. "Know this, Masvam," she continued. "When I get my claws on your brother, I will choke him with these two hands. When he's on the cusp of oblivion, I'll release his neck enough to bring one final sweet breath into his chest, and then I will clamp down again until he's dead."

She turned to face him again, defiance shining. Mantos inclined his head.

"I'll not stand in your way." The words formed like sand in his mouth, but he had to speak them. "We must hold Bandim accountable."

Surprise replaced Valaria's defiance for a moment. She turned to face him, her long tail trailing behind her. "What of the rest of his actions? What of the actions of your folk for cycle after cycle? Shall we hold the Masvams accountable for the rest of the destruction your folk have wrought?"

The figure of Queen Ishka of the Selamans flickered in his mind's eye. Mantos' talons flexed at the memory of the queen pressing her own neck onto his blade, drawing the first blood of her own death. She'd remained poised, without even a solitary tremble passing through her thin body. She'd stared him down though she kneeled beneath him, looking at him with a face as brown and gold as his own.

"Rot in the ground, Masvam. May you never burn."

Then he'd done what he'd done, and Selama had fallen.

Mantos pressed his lips together before he answered Valaria's question. "You won't believe my words but they're true. I never wanted this." At Valaria's derisive snort, he nodded. "Whatever you think, I speak the truth. I never wanted to rule. But I did my duty through respect for my father, and to protect the empire from Bandim. I knew that if he sat on the throne, the world would burn." It was his turn to snort. "Unfortunately, Bandim and his Uloni had other intentions for me. If it wasn't for Bomsoi, I would still be dead. If it wasn't for Mother's strange temple novice, I would have been dead long ago. I didn't want to rule. But I've returned to this world death after death. Perhaps," he said, allowing a cool breath to escape his lips, "my destiny is not to rule but to hold my nation accountable for the actions of Bandim, and my father, and all those who came before him. Perhaps," he said again, finding Valaria's eyes in the temple gloom, "my destiny is to end the empire once and for all."

The princess's usual mask of perfect indifference slipped, revealing an open-mouthed and wide-eyed stare. "You can't believe that."

Mantos managed a half-smile. "I said you wouldn't believe me words but they're true. The longer I reflect, the more I think this is my duty."

Turning on the pew, Valaria stared hard at Mantos for some time. He allowed the stare, keeping his gaze steady.

"I never understood why Fonbir insisted on being in love with you," Valaria said, "but perhaps this is why. You're a strange Masvam with strange Masvam words." Her features softened, revealing something of the kindness Fonbir had often written of, though Mantos had never seen it. "I'll bring a letter to him from you if you wish, though I can't guarantee he won't simply burn it on sight."

Mantos' laugh was abrupt. "I couldn't blame him if he did. But I would be grateful if you brought him my words. Even if he does burn them unread, tell him I regret what I did." His throat tightened. "Tell him that I love him."

Valaria harrumphed in response and stood but the softness remained at her eyes. "I will."

Then she left the temple without a further word. Mantos sat on the bench until the doors closed behind her, staring at his hands. He turned them over and traced the creases and folds of his brown skin. They were hands that had killed Queen Ishka. They were hands that had loved Fonbir, that had died and returned from the dead twice. They were hands destined to become Nunako's.

He looked away from them, the worlds inside their cupped palms too great and unwieldy, past, present, and future all swirled together. Instead of looking at them, Mantos determined to put them back to work, and returned to helping unload the Khinish supply sleds.

When the sleds were empty, the Khinish deconstructed them, the wood for use in building. None of it was for fire. Few fires burned in the Uloni village, and those that did were in the single stone oven the Khinish erected. The flame inside, and the eyes that might see through it, could behold nothing more than rising bread or smooth stones heated for warming pans or bags. Bandim would learn nothing from them.

His task completed, Mantos bent into the veil of snow and crossed the village. Before anything else, he composed his letter to Fonbir, written in their secret code, and delivered it to Valaria. She accepted it with a grunt and tucked it inside her padded Khinish tunic, offering no further conversation.

Dismissed by her silence, Mantos went in search of food. He reached a long tent that served as the main eating and congregating area, its many skins stitched together in an unpredictable mass. Mantos entered the first flap and shook the snow from his head and shoulders, then hung his outer cloak on one of the pegs in the little entranceway and placed his gloves underneath it. Then he removed the soaked outer shoe from his boot, leaving it behind to avoid trailing snow melt through the tent. He pushed into the tent proper. Like everywhere else in the village, moondust banished the darkness.

When he entered, there was something satisfying about the lack of attention he garnered. It was understandable. Not just for the last forty days, or more, since he'd left Kubodinnu, not even just since his father had died but for Mantos' entire life he had been the center of attention. At his hatching, they'd hailed him the heir. When he died as a yearling, his mother's actions had brought him swirls of curiosity and awe. As an imperial prince, expectation hung from his shoulders like a stone mantle. His place in the army was a beacon of hope and strength, and his last action before his second death had been a deliberate act to gain attention. Dressed in white, he had waited for the first cry that heralded his father's death and Mantos' own ascendancy.

Now he walked the length of the tent with little attention. A scant few Khinish turned their heads but they didn't look for long. Their lilting conversations were much more interesting than someone who, to them, was just a Masvam. He didn't know how much they understood of his origins, and he didn't care. He didn't want the scorn. To walk among them was like walking at home in disguise. He passed them by as just one more set of footsteps.

Mantos went to the trestle tables set up with food and took a thick trencher. The bread was as hard as the stone of the oven it baked in but when the stew, he ladled into it, did its work at least some of it would be edible. He sat alone at the end of one of the long tables and ate. With his back to the tent walls, he was free to watch the folk as they ate too.

Wrapped in their furs and oilcloth and deep hoods, it was difficult to tell any particular Khinish from another. Yet he had learned that under their many layers, each one was a clear individual. Contrary to initial impressions, there were indeed both male and females present. Though their silver and gray skin and armor gave little distinction between one and the other, their voices lifted and fell in different cadences, and the subtle difference in torso shape and the length of their horns defined them. While their lack of distinction between genders had perplexed Mantos at first, the more he thought on it, the more he considered its sense. Under the Arc of the Sky, some countries decreed males should behave in one way, while the next country over held its males to an entirely different standard. Yet wasn't a male still a male, wherever they came from and however they behaved?

To think on such things inevitably brought his mind to Fonbir. The expectations for him were almost opposite to those placed on Mantos. Mantos, a Masvam, was to be a male of action, of strength and power and control. The expectation for Fonbir, an Althemerian, was to be passive, demure, covered up and chained. But under it all, weren't they both the same? Underneath their clothes, were they not made of the same armor and skin and flesh and bone? They were. Yet, Mantos thought as he spooned the last of his stew into his mouth, the same or not, it mattered little. It was likely they would never be together again.

There was a pull in his stomach, as if his body sought to rise and go to Fonbir, knowing where he was without doubt. It was like an arrow shot sure and true, trailing a rope to bind them. Fonbir couldn't be too far away. With both of them now in the Kingdom of Khin, the temptation to leap atop a vaemar and ride into the undulating white of the mountains was strong. Mantos would find a way, his heart a weathervane pointing with the wind of love. Yet as much as his heart desired it, he could not. It would be a short-term pleasure but Mantos had changed. Short-term desires were now in his past.

CHAPTER SIX

Fonbir

It took two full days' travel to reach Nowuku, the Khinish capital. Their journey into the depths of the Great Northern Range hadn't been by vaemar-drawn cart. Instead, they had traveled in a covered sled, its great silvery running blades smooth on the snow and ice. Two creatures, unlike anything Fonbir had seen before, pulled the sled. They were kemba, four-legged animals that looked more fur than creature. They were sure-footed on the treacherous terrain, even if their progress was slow. Their coats were white, with only a tinge of cream coating their undersides.

The journey was full of information. Ta Emba warned both Fonbir and Othelan not to refer to their folk as the Khin or Khinish, as those were names given to the mountain folk by others, and not the names they held for themselves. They called themselves Kiseoya, which Emba translated into Althemerian as "those who dwell in the grandmother's home." It made little sense to Fonbir. Regardless, he repeated it until he learned it.

His hands never stilled, either. Emba dedicated a whole day to learning the basics of how to communicate with the king, for Khitarian had neither hearing nor speech. Emba had shown Fonbir how to sign common phrases such as "thank you" and "Your Highness," but Fonbir knew it would take some time to learn to converse with the one he was to twine with. That left his mouth dry.

The third unexpected piece of information Emba provided was that Khitarian wasn't female. They weren't male either but were what the Khinish—the Kiseoyans, as they called themselves—referred to as okkum, different-gendered. After trying to comprehend and remember the signs he'd learned, all Fonbir had wanted to know was how not to offend the king. It wasn't difficult, Ta Emba had told him. Respect went a long way with Khitarian.

Eventually the learning was complete, and Fonbir fell into a restless sleep on the last day. He only realized they had reached Nowuku, which Emba translated as 'capital,' when he jolted awake to find the sled at a standstill and the sounds of many voices around it. Ta Emba had left and Othelan still slept, wrapped in a thick blanket. Fonbir slid across the seat to the arched window and peered over the frosting of new snow at its base. He was inside a compound full of the comings and goings of many folk. It wasn't dissimilar to the huge courtyards of his home. Emba had his back to the sled. The face of the female he spoke to was grave. When he turned, his already pale face was ashen. A cold lump of dread pulled Fonbir back onto his seat just as Emba entered the sled.

A light dusting of fresh snow frosted his shoulders and pooled in his hood. The clunk as the door closed behind him roused Othelan. He stirred; then when reality returned, he snapped upright, the blanket falling away.

"We're here?" he asked.

Ta Emba pursed his lips before he answered. "Yes. We're here."

Fonbir narrowed his eyes. "What's wrong?" A thousandfold possibilities raced through his mind. Did the king not want his claws to twine with any longer? Had the alliance between the Althemerians and the Khinish collapsed before it had even begun?

Emba spoke as if reading words in a language he didn't comprehend. "The king will speak to you. Please come with me."

Part of Fonbir wanted to grasp Emba's shoulders and shake him until he gave up the information. Instead, Othelan guided him outside.

They didn't go straight to the king. Emba permitted them and their luggage a detour into empty quarters to wash and change. While Emba waited in the antechamber, Othelan helped Fonbir out of his crumpled traveling clothes and into a fresh outfit in the same style. Fonbir's mind whirled. The haunted look on Emba's face could mean nothing other than bad news. The fact he was unable speak of it brought it from bad to grave.

"I'm not sure I want to know this news," Fonbir said as Othelan adjusted the shoulders of his keela and rearranged the chains and black jewels on his horn crest.

Oth nodded. "It doesn't bode well, Fon. I don't know what to say."

As soon as the prince was redressed Ta Emba guided them, not to a throne room or meeting hall as Fonbir had expected, but to a set of rooms in another part of the palace. The seat of Kiseoyan power was an ancient dwelling, huge and deep-set in the mountainside. The surface of the mountain bathed in reflected snow-white light. Further inside the palace, the light became glowing and green as sun gave way to moondust lanterns. Despite being underground, darkness didn't press upon them. Moondust came from the Kiseoyan mountains, and while it was a rare commodity even for royalty on Althemer, the mountainfolk had it in abundance. They mined it from their great mountains. There were no flames inside. Fonbir was glad for that.

Emba knocked three times on the solid doors. They opened inward, pulled by two servants. Emba motioned for Fonbir to enter first.

The chamber was lit with moondust. Rich flat-woven rugs covered the floor. Tapestries and ancient weapons adorned the walls. There was no fire, but warmth emanated from many braziers filled with red coals. Fonbir looked at the enormous arched window at the far end of the room. Slivers of light cracked the wooden shutters.

A figure stood beside a pair of stuffed chairs. Another lingered a little way off, drawing forward as they approached. Emba guided Fonbir and Othelan toward them and gave a deep bow. When he spoke, Emba's arms and hands moved with a swift grace.

"Your Majesty," he said, signing the words alongside the sounds. "I present to you Prince Fonbir of the Althemerians, and his attendant Othelan."

As he'd been taught, Fonbir first dipped in a formal greeting and gave the two-talon symbol for a respectful hello that Emba had taught him in the sled. Then he allowed his sharp eyes to begin their analysis. King Khitarian was tall, though not as tall as Mantos. Their armor sparkled silver on their pale skin, and the pull of their fronds framed their face like a heart. Their blue eyes were deep-set, glinting green in the moondust light.

Khitarian signed a greeting in return, translated by the second figure. Fonbir felt the first tug of worry when he watched their hands move and comprehended none of the meaning.

"I wanted to give you this news myself," the translator said. Fonbir needed a moment to understand who 'I' was. It wasn't the translator herself. She was giving voice to Khitarian's words. The king signed and gestured to a seat. "I think you should sit."

Fonbir cast a worried glance at Othelan, who tried to smile, but Fonbir saw the worry that lay in his attendant's brown eyes. He sank into one chair, while Khitarian sat on the edge of the other. The king laced their talons together. Ta Emba joined Khitarian, standing a little behind them.

"We received news several days ago." Fonbir kept pulling his gaze from Khitarian's hands to their face. The king stilled their hands, on the edge of a sigh. "I don't believe there's an easy way to say this. The Sun Emperor, as he calls himself, attacked Kubodinnu." Clammy sickness crawled across Fonbir's skin. "The Masvams overwhelmed your forces. The city has fallen."

"No," Fonbir breathed, "that can't be."

Khitarian nodded their head. "I'm afraid it is. But there's more."

Fonbir's sickness turned to dread. "Mother. My sisters. Where are they?"

Khitarian's pale face was a mask of respectful sorrow. "Your mother is dead, as is the younger princess, Fylica. They were inside your great palace when it fell, as was the former Empress Phen of the Masvam Empire. They all perished."

Had Fonbir not been sitting, he would have collapsed. "Destroyed?" He turned to Othelan; whose dark face was colorless with shock. "Am I understanding this?" When Othelan gave the tiniest nod, Fonbir shook his head. "It can't be. Dead? Destroyed? There were hundreds of folk inside the palace. And the city? Gone?"

Khitarian's blue eyes were soft with sorrow. "I'm sorry, Fonbir."

For a moment, Fonbir's whole body stiffened. It couldn't be, yet Khitarian said it was so. Masvams had destroyed his home. His land was now likely overrun by them. Fylica was dead. His mother was dead. Ethay and Apago had abandoned him, his family, his nation. He had nothing. This journey was for nothing.

His numb stiffness gave way to a wave that traveled his whole body. He turned to the door, then back. He opened his mouth, then closed it again. Everything had been for nothing.

When his knees gave way, he expected the hard embrace of the floor. Before he struck the ground, a pair of strong hands had grabbed him and pulled him into an embrace. It wasn't Othelan. It was Khitarian. The warmth and strength of their embrace said everything, and Fonbir pressed his face into their chest. He didn't cry. Fonbir never cried. But in that moment, he was glad for the strength of Khitarian's arms.

When he collected himself enough to draw back again, he swallowed a deep breath. "You told me Mother and Fylica are dead. What about Valaria?"

Khitarian's lips spread in a smile of relief. "Your other sister is alive."

Joy spread through Fonbir, bittersweet in the echo of sorrow. "Are you sure?"

"I am," Khitarian said. "She escaped from the palace before it collapsed, all with the help of the one you call" —they stopped for a moment, grappling for the right sign, and seeking help from Ta Emba.

Emba offered a possibility. Khitarian snapped their talons in victory. "Yes, the one they call 'Stranger.'"

A tide of gratefulness washed over Fonbir. Bomsoi. Ethay and Apago hadn't abandoned either he or his folk.

"Where is my sister now?" Fonbir asked. "I need to see her."

Khitarian gave him another smile. "Your sister should be with us by nightfall."

"Today?" Fonbir asked, his voice pitched high with shock.

"Yes, today." Khitarian's face shifted from the happiness of giving good news to the steely determination of a monarch Fonbir was so familiar with. "Your mother might be dead, but our alliance remains. I gave my word that we would help your folk, and my word is as strong as the very rocks around us. The Masvams may have taken your island but the Sun Emperor will not have the chance to keep it."

Khitarian took one of Fonbir's hands in a gentle grip and placed a kiss on his middle knuckle, above one of his glittering rings. "I promise you, the Kingdom of Khin will fight to the last to take back what the Masvams have stolen."

A strangeness passed through Fonbir at the touch of Khitarian's lips to his hand. There was no rush of feeling, as when Mantos touched him, but the glimmer of determination in Khitarian's light eyes brought a different flutter to Fonbir's chest. There was unabashed truth in them. At the sight of it, Fonbir wondered why it had taken a war for the Khinish to come into the world with everyone else. Or perhaps it hadn't. Perhaps it had taken a war to make his mother look beyond the edges of her own prejudice. He hoped that, now she was in the embrace of Ethay and Apago with Fylica and his father, she could see beyond it now.

* * *

Just as Khitarian said, Valaria arrived under the cloak of darkness. Despite the bitter chill, Fonbir had insisted on waiting for her in the palace grounds, his eyes fixed on the gate. He pulled his father's fur cape tighter around his neck. The silver serpent fastenings glinted in both the moonlight and the glow of the moondust lanterns. Othelan had grumbled about the cold, and stubborn princes catching illnesses, more times than Fonbir cared to count but he stayed by his side throughout.

"The outer sections of the palace have windows, Fon," Oth said, trying another tactic. "You could just wait inside and look, so you'd see when Princess Valaria arrives. Then you could go out."

Fonbir didn't reply, just as he hadn't replied to any of Othelan's other arguments. Instead, he ignored the grumbles and tutting and kept his eyes fixed ahead. While his fur cape and armor kept much of him temperate if not comfortable, his exposed skin burned in the frigid mountain winds. It didn't matter. Fonbir would be the first one to greet his sister. For one wretched moment, he'd thought she was dead. No one else deserved the honor of embracing her before he did. It also didn't matter that the embrace between them would be short, and perhaps even rejected. Fonbir would be the first, whether she wanted it or not.

When the princess and her guards came into view, all riding high on the backs of shaggy kemba, Fonbir did something even he didn't expect. He broke into a run. Othelan's shouts whipped past on the wind as Fonbir launched himself forward, giving no regard to snow or ice or decorum. When she saw him, Valaria did something unexpected too. She leaped from her kemba's sturdy back and sprinted forward, catching him in an embrace so tight Fonbir couldn't breathe. But it didn't matter. Nothing else mattered beyond the touch of his last remaining blood relative.

Fonbir squeezed Valaria back as hard as he could, pressing his icy face into the crook of her scaled neck.

"Fonbir," was all Valaria could say. "Fonbir."

He withdrew his face and placed his chin on her shoulder. "Valaria, I thought you were dead like the rest of them. I thought I'd lost everything."

Valaria's hands were at the back of his head, pressing hard as if she couldn't believe he was real. "I'm here, and you're here. We've still got each other."

The pain of their words was sharper than any cold. They weren't like this. They had never been like this. He knew she loved him. He knew she cared. But there was always a distance, three strides between them. The closest they'd been was when Fonbir had left. That felt like an eternity ago. But now they clung to one another, tight and heavy with the knowledge that they were the last of Althemer's royal blood.

When they pulled apart, Othelan was by their sides. As soon as Valaria turned to face him, he dropped to one knee. "My queen."

Valaria's Khinish guards caught up with them, and a color party from the palace seeped into the darkness, their shadows long and flickering in the moonlight.

When Valaria spoke, it was clear she addressed them all, not just Othelan. "I will not call myself a queen until I have my island back. I'll take my crown among the remnants of my mother's palace, and not before."

Othelan nodded. "Yes, Your Highness."

She bade him rise and took Fonbir's arm in hers. She kept him close as the Khinish guided them into the warmth of the palace, bringing her lips close to his ear. "I have a letter for you."

Fonbir's first instinct was to freeze. Only one individual would send him a message. He pressed past the churn of emotion and nodded. "Oh?"

"You know who it's from," Valaria continued. "You'll be glad to know I didn't read it because I couldn't. It's written in that gods-forsaken code you two insisted on using. He's aware you might not read it, so he asked me to give you a message too."

Fonbir felt the press of folded parchment in his gloved hand. He swallowed, his heart missing half its beats. "What did he have to say?"

"Your Masvam is sorry for everything he's done. He regrets his actions. But above all, he asked me to tell you he loves you."

Fonbir's heart missed all its beats for longer than should have been possible. His chest tightened as fear, hate, desire, and love coursed through him at once. He only realized he'd been trembling when Valaria brought her other hand up to steady him.

"Brother, I've never heard someone say those words with such sincerity," she said as their guide took them through winding palace hallways and into its dark depths. "I think you should believe him."

Fonbir turned to her, his eyeridges furrowed. "You never liked him," was all he said.

"I still don't like him," Valaria said, "but I think I understand why you do. He's an idiot, and he's one of the enemy. But Mantos Tiboli loves you more than I've seen anyone love another. He loves you more than even Mother loved Father." She fingered the edge of their father's fur cape as she spoke, a tired smile drawing across her face. "I thought you should know. Read the letter or burn it; it's up to you. But I know what I'd do."

Before now, Fonbir knew Valaria would have chosen the latter. He would have done the same. But the ache in his stomach and the press of every emotion at once made him clench the note in his fist. He didn't reach for the nearest flame. Instead he slipped the crumpled note into his pocket, then tightened his grip on his sister's arm to steady the tiller of his heart.

CHAPTER SEVEN

Emmy

As commanded by Bomsoi, Emmy filled her trencher with stew and looked for a place to sit. The Khinish inclined their heads and pressed their palms over their hearts as she passed. Their reverence made her hesitant to sit with any of them, not that she could carry out conversation with them even if she did. She spoke none of their language. Her gaze roved for a free, solitary seat. At first, she settled on an empty bench but when she spied Mantos she made for him. Why not? She was to bring the goddess into his heart, after all. He stood as she set her food on the table.

"May I join you?" she asked.

Mantos did as the Khinish did and nodded, pressing the flat of his hand to his sternum. "Please."

When they both sat, the silence between them was filled only by the genial chatter of the Khinish around them. Emmy kept her focus on her food and spooned up the soft chunks of brown meat first, followed by root vegetables. She remained silent as she ate and Mantos mirrored her, waiting for her to speak. He couldn't know how soon Bomsoi intended to bring the goddess into him. The decision was only just made. Her shoulders stiffened with tension. With Mantos' background in fleeing, the thought of telling him filled her with sickly unease. But, she mused, she had to do it.

She was halfway through her meal when she looked up to broach the issue. "I spoke to Bomsoi."

Mantos nodded and stayed silent. Emmy needed no prodding. "She wants us to bring Nunako back into the world tomorrow night."

Emmy watched as fear and anticipation fizzed within Mantos. She imagined it traveling across his skin and armor like spreading cracks on an icy lake. The Masvam nodded again, still saying nothing.

Emmy abandoned her food. "I'm going to guide the spirit of Nunako into your heart. To do that, I must penetrate your body with my power. I've only practiced on Bomsoi, and I don't know whether it will work or whether it will hurt. I wanted to tell you that."

Mantos held her eyes, silver meeting gold. She studied the striations of brown that streaked his yellow irises and the dark band that split them from the whites of his eyes. She widened her gaze to his whole face. She was younger than he, perhaps twenty-one or two to her sixteen cycles. He bound his fronds in a tight tail, pulling his face in a serious, almost strained expression.

When with no warning, Mantos reached for her. Emmy flinched away but she cooled her emotions and allowed his touch. He settled the tips of his talons on the side of her head.

"Tell me about yourself," Mantos said. "If you're to be my Heart, I want to understand who you are."

Emmy pulled away from his hand. This was too intimate. She wanted to retreat, throw up layer upon layer of shields to protect herself, not only from him, but from the entire world. Mantos let his hand fall to the table. Emmy's gaze followed its gentle path.

"I don't talk about myself," she said. "There's nothing to say."

Mantos offered her a mild smile. "I don't understand anything of Bomsoi and your Uloni powers. But my heart knows what my hands will do, and my hands know what my heart desires. They're both part of my body, my spirit. I think if we're to become the Hand and Heart of Nunako, I need to know you, just as my hands know my heart."

Emmy stopped her flinch. When she spoke her words were petulant, but she didn't care. "You tell me about yourself, then. I want to understand the Hand I'm meant to guide."

"A fair point," Mantos said, smiling in the face of her peevishness. Shame rose within Emmy like suffocation. "I'll tell you whatever you want."

"We'll go to the temple," Emmy said. She gathered her half-eaten meal. Her hands went to lift his too, but she stopped. She lifted her long legs over the bench. "We'll have peace to talk there."

She turned her back to him and discarded her uneaten food into a slop's pail. Mantos rose and did the same, then followed her. He threw on his cloak, and together they crossed the snowy flat of the village and entered the Uloni temple.

Despite having spent much time with Bomsoi; the Daughter of Gods, and holding godly blood in her veins, knowing an imperial prince was still intimidating. When Mantos Tiboli held the temple door open for her to pass inside, Emmy's skin tingled. This male was royalty from one of the most infamous ruling houses of the Masvam Empire. Who was Emmy? An apothecary's assistant from the provincial country of

Metakala. She stilled her feet as she corrected that. She wasn't just her past. She was Emmy, blood of Nunako and Dorai, an Uloni tasked with helping to bring balance back to the world. Despite the grand and truthful claims about herself, she still found it hard to meet Mantos' look as he motioned for her to sit in the pool of light.

"What would you like to ask first?" he asked as he sat across from her, wrapping his tail around his legs.

Emmy had many suggestions. She could ask how many lives he had taken. She could ask what his intention would be when he regained the Masvam throne. She could ask whether he believed she was eternally inferior on account of her gender.

She chose a different tactic. "What's your favorite color?"

Mantos' mouth opened with a guffaw. "Really? You ask that first?"

Emmy shrugged, trying to seem nonchalant. "I like blue," she said. "I enjoy looking at a clear sky." It was an odd question to begin with, considering the gravity of what they had to accomplish, but it seemed an easier place to begin.

One side of Mantos' mouth lifted, and his face brightened with a smile Emmy hadn't seen grace his face in the short time they'd been together. "I like white," he replied.

Emmy shook her head, suppressing her pout. "Is that a color?" She thought of the leeching of pigment from skin and armor where Uloni magic touched a body to heal it. "It's no color at all."

Mantos' smile slipped, though he made a valiant effort to keep it in place. "To me it's a color. It's the best color."

His face took on a faraway look. There was something more to his love of white beyond it being 'the best.'

Sensing it best to leave the subject for now, Emmy ventured another question. "What do you like to eat?"

Mantos tapped his chin as he considered. "I like sweet things. I used to love sampling every one of the desserts laid on at banquets, even when my mother told me it would make me sick. It did," he added with a chuckle. His eyes grew soft. "Mother was right about most things."

Phen's crumpled body, the last of her life pumping from her slit throat, flashed in Emmy's mind's eye. She remembered the cloak of red Mantos had worn, a cloak of his mother's blood.

Emmy dropped her gaze to her hands, folded neatly on top of one another. "I never knew my mother," she said. Then, to break the somber atmosphere, she added, "and I've never tasted dessert either."

Mantos gave her a half-hearted smile. "When this is all over, I'll throw a great banquet and I'll ask for every dessert known under the Arc. You can take a spoon and try them one by one."

There was a beat of silence before Emmy responded. "Do you think we'll succeed?"

Mantos leaned back and planted the flats of his hands against the smooth stone floor. His talons glinted in the moons' light that fell on them in a perfect circle. "I believe we will. If we don't, we lose everything. My mother's death, my entire life's purpose, will be a waste. Worse, Bandim will spread his poison, and the world will tip in a direction it might not recover from."

In her head, Emmy conjured the image of the Arc on a set of scales, with Nunako on one plate and Dorai on the other. Too much power from one changed the balance between them. If there was one useful thing Krodge had taught her, it was how to balance the scales.

Her memory brought her back into the apothecary shop, young enough to need to stand on a box to see what Krodge did on the counter. The old crone bent to watch the scales fall even, a weight on one side and the correct portion of powdered arra fruit on the other. Emmy thought of Phen, the Masvam who'd given her life's thread to save her youngling. Krodge wouldn't have lifted a finger to save Emmy, except that in a way, she had. Somehow, a message from Bomsoi had reached Krodge, who had obeyed and protected Emmy all her life. But despite being a good teacher, shrewd in business and wildly intelligent, Krodge had never been a mother figure.

Emmy looked down at her hands. "I never knew my mother. She died when I was a hatchling. The same with my father."

"I didn't know my mother either," Mantos said. At Emmy's raised eyeridge, he explained the circumstances of his hatching, his first death, and his mother's sacrifice. "I got so little time with her." He huffed a thin laugh. "After spending cycle upon cycle wishing for her to come back to me, when she finally did, I was the one who left. Then she died. It's my fault. I squandered the time I had." As if trying to dash away his sorrow, Mantos turned his focus on Emmy. "Tell me about your life. How did your mother die? What was your life like?"

It took her some time to start but eventually Emmy bared her story. The first part of her life, she told as best she could. The familiar sting of Krodge's version came first, followed by the details revealed by Bomsoi of her Uloni heritage, of the fire in the temple.

There was still a gaping hole in the narrative, which Mantos was quick to question her on. "How did you get to Krodge's doorstep? And who started the fire?"

Emmy replied, "No one's been able to tell me. Bomsoi said she willed me to safety but didn't understand how."

The Masvam prince gave a solemn nod. "There are questions about my first resurrection. A 'temple novice' returned me from the dead. I never found out who she was or how she did it." He swallowed. "My mother paid a terrible price for it."

"It must have been your brother's Uloni, his Heart," Emmy said. "Only the goddesses' power could do that. If you're dead, you're dead. That's it."

Mantos' whole body stilled. It was as if time had stopped. Emmy bent her neck to get a better view of his face. His expression changed from hollow and haunted to dark with fury.

"Mantos?"

When he spoke, his words were like broken glass. "Back in Kubodinnu, Bomsoi told me she couldn't save my mother because there was no sorcery in her death. Bandim didn't kill her with his powers. He slit her throat with a blade." Realization came like a dawning. "My mother didn't drop me. If she had, I would be dead. It was her, that 'temple novice.' She must have been Bandim's Uloni. She made this happen." He laughed, the sound like knives. When his eyes met Emmy's, his yellow irises were liquid gold. "How long has that viper been in our midst? Mother wasn't responsible for my death. She thought she'd killed me, and gave her own life to secure my thread, to return me to the world again. But the Uloni killed me with her power. She must have. Now my mother is dead, and she'll never find out the truth. She died thinking she was responsible. All of her sacrifice was for nothing."

Emboldened by his grief, Emmy laid the blue and purple of her hand over the brown and gold of his. "It was for more than nothing." She paused, her words like a precipice. One wrong move and this burgeoning trust between them could collapse. "This Uloni can't have acted with no reason. There must be a motivation behind hurting you, killing you."

Mantos' expression brightened. He turned his palm to press into Emmy's. "The One of Two. That's why she did it."

Emmy's eyeridges folded. "I don't understand."

"In the Book of Divine Tears, the holy book of Dorai, it mentions how the One of Two, 'pushed aside, will rise like flame, and the goddess will inhabit him.' Bandim and I were the Two, and he no doubt feels pushed aside. Bandim's Uloni must have seen us as the 'Two,' and chose this path for us before we even hatched."

Still confused, Emmy withdrew her hand. "You need to explain. I couldn't go into a temple or read the Gospel of Nunako—though I did—never mind the holy book of Dorai. Is it because you're brothers?"

As Mantos spoke, revealing the nature of their double laying and double hatching, Emmy's mouth went dry. "I've never heard of two eggs laid together, not even in stories."

"Not since the time of the goddesses themselves," Mantos said.

Something sparked in Emmy. "Meia, the Grandmother of the World. That's who the Khinish worship and who the Uloni worshiped. She brought two eggs into the world at the same time. This can't be a coincidence. Bomsoi must have some information about this." She pointed at Mantos. "Now you and your brother, hatched from two eggs laid at the same time, will become the goddesses' Hands. It's fate."

"Is it?" Mantos asked. His voice dropped. "Or have we become pawns in someone else's game? If Bandim's Heart hadn't pushed the stone, it might not have rolled this far. If she'd stayed away from us, Mother wouldn't have sacrificed herself. And if she hadn't, Bandim wouldn't have grown to resent me the way he does." He let out a long breath. "This Uloni took it on herself to force us down this path. But why?"

Emmy stayed silent. She smoothed the legs of her fur-lined trousers. "I don't know. I don't know why the Uloni village was destroyed either. Rel said 'unwelcome visitors' did it but who?" She flicked her gaze away. "It couldn't have been the Khinish. They were the Uloni's friends. Was it Masvams?"

Mantos shook his head. "It can't have been my folk. Masvam troops have never encroached on Khinish territory. It's too difficult to traverse and impossible to claim. You'd have to be determined or petty to come into the Great Northern Range. My father maintained the Khinish lands would be the last to fall to our rule. It would take the might of our army and the armies of the claimed lands to overwhelm the mountains."

"So, who was it?" Emmy asked, tapping her chin. "And who rescued me?"

"Two questions we have no answers to," Mantos replied.

Emmy slid onto her feet and rose. Mantos followed. Together they stood in the pool of light, casting long shadows. "Bomsoi doesn't have the answer to my question about my parents," Emmy said, "but I wonder if she knows more about the attack on the village than she says. She was there. She's the blood of the goddesses. She must have some idea."

"Perhaps we should ask her," Mantos said, "though with Bomsoi, straight answers don't come easily."

A memory flickered. Fire, turmoil, screaming, all interspersed with joyous laughter. A mother's indulgence. A child's screams. Emmy's whole body stiffened with intent. "We might not have to ask her. There's something else that might give us answers."

"Something?" Mantos asked.

Emmy was at the temple door before he finished the question. She didn't answer but beckoned him to follow and then plunged into the cold stillness of the night.

CHAPTER EIGHT

Mantos

The prince followed the apothecary's assistant through the darkness like in the plot of a play. Mantos estimated he'd watched more theater than anyone else in the Masvam Empire and had read even more plays than he'd seen. Their ridiculous creep across the Khinish compound, two dark figures crouched and keeping to the shadows, was something straight from the stage and threatened to make him laugh aloud and reveal them.

"Where are we going?" he whispered again but Emmy slashed a hushing hand at him and continued forward.

The apparent secrecy they had to maintain was only part of the farce. The other part was that in the midst of the greatness of threat from his brother and the importance Bomsoi had placed on his shoulders, he was lurking in darkness and moving to the backs of the sleeping tents. Whatever Emmy was up to, he both couldn't wait to find out and couldn't believe it was as important as their goal.

The Uloni was silent on her feet, not making any indentations in the snow. Mantos' feet sank into the freshness of a snowfall that had lain barren for days. Mantos felt a fizz of excitement bubble inside him. It was like he was sixteen again and invading the kitchens to steal a pastry or escaping the palace to explore the city unbeknownst to his father. Though only five cycles before, it seemed an age away.

Emmy reached her destination and signaled for Mantos to be silent. She listened against the canvas and skin walls before motioning him forward. She plucked up the bottom edge of the tent and slipped inside. Mantos followed, curiosity brimming. What was this strange female up to?

When he stood inside, he realized where they were. This was Rel's convalescent tent. The half-Uloni was asleep on her pallet, her chest rising and falling in a soft rhythm. Her face, even in sleep, pulled with as much tension as the scars that warped her skin and armor. Mantos didn't feel like that youngling stealing pastries anymore. His brother had done that to Rel. The worst thing? Rel's injuries were likely the least heinous of all the things Bandim had done.

While he was contemplating, Emmy had kneeled and slid a long, leather-wrapped bundle from the bottom of Rel's bed. Her brow glistened with the effort of moving whatever was inside. By the length and narrowness, Mantos knew what it was. "That's a weapon."

Emmy checked that Rel was still asleep before she unwrapped the leather. Just as Mantos had guessed, it was a long sword in one of the most beautiful sheaths he had ever seen. Tiny lines of different woods made a pattern, some light and some dark, many with a red tinge. The hilt, wrapped in a weave of supple leather, had a huge pommel. At first it looked like a simple sphere, but when he looked closer, Mantos recognized the pattern of marks on its face.

"That's Akata."

Emmy ignored him and stared at the sword, her gray eyes glancing up to ensure Rel was still unaware of their presence.

"The sword is Haelo," she said. "Bomsoi made it with only her power and her hands."

Confusion set in, and Mantos frowned. "How can a sword answer our questions?"

"Haelo isn't just any sword," Emmy replied. "It's so heavy because it only lets you wield it if it knows you. Haelo has a memory. It was there on the night the Uloni temple burned."

Disbelief gave way to realization. "Do you think Haelo can show us what happened?"

"I know it can," Emmy said. Her claws hovered over the sheathed blade. "I've held Haelo before, and I've seen images from its past. Before, I couldn't make sense of them. But I think it was the destruction of the Uloni village. I wonder if now I know what Haelo's trying to show me, I might see the visions better. Maybe then we'll find out what happened, who my parents were and who destroyed the village."

Eyeridges raised in skepticism, Mantos remained standing. "You can barely move it. If the sword won't even let you pick it up, what makes you think it'll show you what you want to see?"

Emmy huffed a breath through her nostrils. "Because Haelo's tried to show me this before but it frightened me, and I didn't want to see. Now I do. Maybe it'll be clearer."

Though his movements were slow and hesitating, Mantos slid to his knees beside Emmy. He took in the details of the weapon, crafted with such skill and beauty. Sometimes it was difficult to remember what such weapons were for. They were bringers of death, not baubles.

"We'll touch the hilt together," Emmy said. "That might mean you'll be able to see what I see. I don't know if Haelo only responds to Uloni touch or not."

Mantos nodded and placed his hand in the air beside hers. "I suppose we have nothing to lose."

They shared one final look. The depth of Emmy's silver eyes, and the faint blue that lingered in their depths, struck Mantos. He counted them in. "Three, two, one."

Together they clamped their hands upon the hilt. With all four sets of claws together, the world lurched sideways, and the ground gave way beneath them.

Then they were falling, falling, falling...

* * *

Mantos gritted his teeth and held tight to the sword. This was familiar. It was the same pitch and fall as when he'd found Bandim on the Sea of Souls. Blue and white swirled around them in impossible streaks, as if they tumbled from a cliff top to a gruesome death below. But instead of losing their lives, the sword brought them to an abrupt stop, planting their feet on the ground.

They weren't in Rel's tent any longer. Sunshine shone through the peaks of the same mountains in the Khinish camp, though snow still covered the ground in a thick blanket. The snowfall lacked the pristine bleakness of what they'd left behind. Instead many footprints pockmarked it, and huge paths were carved through it. There were buildings beyond the temple and dotted around the village where huge spheres of ice, perfect in their roundness, cast an iridescent glow even in the daylight. What brought Mantos' heart into his throat the most was the source of the burble of chatter and laughter. Uloni filled the village.

He glanced at Emmy. Between them they still held the sword, now the weight of an ordinary weapon still in its sheath. Her gaze fixed on the bustle of life before them. Uloni wound from their homes toward the temple. The Khinish had recreated it well but this temple seemed grander in its simplicity. The great roof still had its open center, and the walls were chalkwater white.

A baying call sounded nearby. Mantos looked up as a winged shadow passed over the temple.

The sight broke Emmy's stupor, and she broke her grip on Haelo. "Neiruk!"

As Bomsoi's great beast disappeared into the depths of the mountains, Emmy's gaze snapped back to her hand, no longer gripping the sword that had brought them here. Mantos stilled, and they waited for something to happen, for Emmy to disappear from the vision or the sword to fall into the snow, too heavy to move. Neither happened. Mantos hooked Haelo's sheath onto his belt with a shrug.

"This must be the day the temple was burned," Emmy said. She broke into a run. "My parents are in there!"

"Emmy, wait!" Mantos was quick to catch her and grabbed her wrist. "What if they can see us?"

"What if they can?" she asked, wrenching her arm from his grip. "If you had the chance to see your mother again, wouldn't you take it?"

She had him with that. Mantos would do anything for that possibility. Pressing his lips together, he nodded and set off at a jog. Emmy fell in beside him, and they reached the temple just as the last few Uloni entered. Mantos ducked his head inside. No one had spotted them so far but walking straight into the temple still seemed a poor choice. Emmy did the same.

"There's Bomsoi," Mantos said, keeping his voice low, though he realized there was little point.

Emmy nodded and pointed. "That's Rel near her. They both look the same."

Neither seemed to have aged in the last sixteen cycles. Mantos supposed his surprise was unwarranted. They were both descendants of the goddesses. Perhaps that meant Emmy would stop aging after a point too.

Emmy's head swiveled as she scanned the crowd, her mouth open as she beheld so many faces like her own. Mantos looked at her more than at the past before them. What must it have been like for her to grow up believing herself damned and cursed? Her existence was the opposite of his. Where he received praise, folk reviled her.

Emmy interrupted his musings when she came upon the only non-Uloni face in the temple. "Krodge!"

The odd face in the crowd was a rotund Metakalan female. She was old but not ancient. Her expression was tight with frustration, as if she wanted to be elsewhere.

"Why is Krodge here?" Emmy asked, pushing forward.

Mantos tried to grab her arm again but she slipped away. Mantos followed. Though they shot toward the center of the temple, this time a diffuse pool of daylight, none of the Uloni looked at them. They couldn't see them, which was a blessing, as Emmy flew through the congregation straight to her old mistress.

She skidded to a stop and waved her hand in Krodge's face. "Hey!" The old Metakalan continued to glance over her shoulder and shuffle in place. "Hey!"

When Emmy reached to slap her mistress, her hand traveled through her face, just as Bandim's had gone through Mantos'. Stunned, Emmy recoiled, staring at her hand.

As if nothing had happened, Krodge took one final glance over her shoulder before pushing past the Uloni beside her, coughing.

"Sorry, sorry," she spluttered, covering her mouth with her hand. "I need some air."

When one of the Uloni tried to accompany her, she waved them off. Unseen, Emmy and Mantos followed her into the open air. Once she was a few paces past the door, Krodge slumped against the temple wall and sighed a breath that sent clouds around her face.

"Ugh," Krodge said to herself, though to Mantos and Emmy too. "These Uloni and their constant worship. How does anyone get anything done?"

Krodge pushed from the wall and trudged away from the temple, toward a cluster of little buildings Mantos assumed to be houses. Emmy tried to follow but he stopped her. "We need to understand why the temple burned."

The spell of seeing Krodge broke, and Emmy gave a curt nod. "Right."

Together they ran back to the temple, Haelo growing heavy on Mantos' waist. He was strong, accustomed to wearing armor and weapons day to day, so the weight could only be Haelo's doing. They circled the building as Bomsoi's voice rose inside, followed by the Uloni's chants of worship. The sounds drifted through the open roof.

For some time, nothing happened. The worship continued inside, and Emmy and Mantos stood outside. Despite the cold, he didn't shiver. Like in Bomsoi's vision, the snow had no impact, though he still made indentations where Emmy did not.

When the figure appeared, Mantos gave it no attention. It was an Uloni by the telltale blue and purple of her face, late for the service and rushing to join in. Yet when he looked again, it wasn't. Mantos frowned. The figure wore heavy traveling clothes, stained, and rumpled from a long journey. She wasn't rushing but moving with intense purpose, dragging a long, thick tree limb behind her.

Emmy saw her too. "She's coming home. Bomsoi said she spent a lot of time looking for Uloni who left the village."

Mantos' frown deepened. Somehow, he didn't think that was the case.

The Uloni moved with swiftness. The closer they got to them, the clearer their face was. Mantos squinted his eyes, trying to place the features. It was a female, and the more he looked, the deeper the dread in his stomach became. He knew that face but knew it in Masvam brown and gold. But from where? As she reached the walls of the temple, her intention became clear.

The Uloni barred the door with the huge branch, shoving it between the carved wooden handles to bar any exit. Then she pressed her palms together, and when she drew them apart a perfect ball of fire hung between them. She pushed the first of her flames into the wooden walls of the temple and within seconds, an entire panel was aflame.

"No," Emmy whispered as the Uloni moved onto another section of temple wall.

Mantos watched, mouth and hands impotent. He could do nothing. What could he say? Haelo grew heavier each time the Uloni set another fire. Smoke rose, black against the icy sky.

It didn't take long before the whole temple was aflame, screeches inside rising with the red lick of the fire.

Emmy and Mantos stood still, frozen in time, as the Uloni stepped back and surveyed her work. Mantos watched the slow spread of a wicked smile. He realized hers was the face of a female he had seen in Bandim's company, a fellow worshiper of the Dark. But how this Uloni had a Masvam's face, he couldn't explain.

As the cries inside the temple rose, Emmy spoke, her words bereft. "Why aren't they doing anything about the fire? Why aren't they using their powers? Why is Bomsoi not doing anything?" She snapped from her stupor and ran forward. "Bomsoi!"

Emmy sprinted forward; this time too fast for Mantos to catch. "Emmy!" The roar of the fire drowned his calls, but he knew that even if Emmy had heard him, she wouldn't have stopped. Swallowed in this time shift, she remained between past and present. Mantos pursued her, but the weight of Haelo was so much now, he had to slip the sword from his belt and drag it through the snow. In front of him Emmy flitted around the temple's flaming walls. Her mouth moved in screams Mantos couldn't hear over the crackling flame.

Then he remembered the other Uloni. He swiveled his head to where she had stood but she had fled. He would never forget that face, the same features with different colors. She knew Bandim. Something turned inside him like a wheel jolting into motion. She was Bandim's Uloni, the one who'd forced them all down this path of destruction.

"No, no!"

Another voice broke through the unending crackle and thunder of the fire. Mantos spun around. It was Krodge. The Metakalan female had her hands over her mouth, the expression underneath pulled with horror. Emmy rounded the temple and stopped on her heel when she saw her old mistress. She bolted forward and went to grab Krodge by the shoulders. Her claws slipped straight through Krodge and Emmy stumbled, overbalanced, and collapsed in a heap on the snow-dusted path.

"Do something!" she screeched, tears now streaming down her cheeks. "Do something, you old hag!"

Krodge couldn't hear her. What could she have done? The Metakalan was no sorceress, no blood of the goddess. Mantos went to Emmy and kneeled. Haelo weighed him down so much he knew he wouldn't lift it again. Instead he released the weapon and pulled Emmy's shrieking, sobbing form into his arms. She bucked against him, struggling to get free but Mantos held firm. Krodge dropped to her knees beside them, her hands clamped over her mouth. Through her claws she muttered, "Let one survive. Let me save just one."

The fire blazed on and on.

Then something strange happened. A booted foot kicked through one wall of inferno, sending fiery splinters in all directions. It came again, breaking through the fire. After one final time, it stopped. Beside them, Krodge scrambled to her feet as a pair of gruesome, blackened claws passed a bundle of something through the makeshift exit. The arms pulled back into the blaze. They didn't return.

Emmy sat up straight as Krodge ran to the bundle. Mantos slackened his grip on Emmy as he watched the old Metakalan unfold the wrappings. His mouth gaped when a tiny blue and purple arm reached for her, followed by the high-pitched cry of a hatchling. Krodge re-wrapped the small Uloni and staggered backward, clutching the bundle to her chest.

Another roar erupted from behind them. Mantos wrenched his neck around as another building caught alight. Fire lifted to the white sky, the flame and smoke like bloody, twisting thorns. Then another building burst into flame, and another and another. The Uloni who had done this hadn't fled at all. Within minutes, everything around them was a forest of flame. Krodge turned in circles, eyes wide with terror, the hatchling on her chest screeching and screeching. The Metakalan took a few uncertain steps backward, the fire glimmering in her red eyes, before she turned and ran.

"That was me," Emmy said. "It was just like Bomsoi said. She willed someone to save me. It was Krodge. She brought me all the way from here to Bellim. She saved me."

Mantos placed a comforting hand to her back. "She did."

His other hand sought Haelo. As soon as he touched the soft leather hilt, the world bucked and turned, and swirled. And they disappeared.

CHAPTER NINE

Emmy

They whirled through an abyss, a never-ending tunnel of darkness. Emmy kept her eyes shut tight, and a death-grip on Mantos. The Masvam prince had one hand jammed on Haelo's hilt, the other scooped around her back. His claws felt like immovable rocks. They spun and whirled but the Uloni village remained elusive. Something deep in Emmy's gut told her they weren't returning to Rel's tent just yet.

"Mantos!" she cried. "What's happening?"

His reply was strength itself. "Just hold on! We'll be all right, I promise!"

"How can you promise that?"

Together they spun and spun, clinging to each other until eventually the world began to slow. Haelo guided them downward, and hard ground loomed. When their feet touched solidity, Emmy could breathe again.

She glanced around, her eyeridges drawn low. It was a scene of desolation, somewhere unknown and black, with scorched ground and trees that were nothing more than skeletal shadows. Everything was rubble, dirt, and dust.

Emmy reached for Haelo, touching its hilt with two talons. "Why have you brought us here?" she asked, though as she expected, the sword didn't reply.

The world around them was eerie in its silence. No gargon screeches, no streams running in the distance, no murmur of far-off conversation. There was nothing.

Mantos placed Haelo on his belt once more and took a few steps away. The parched ground puffed like smoke under his boots. Emmy looked beyond him to the skyline. The sky where the arc met the ground was gray as dead flesh, and what had once been fertile land was black. Something landed on her lip, and she instinctively licked it. She winced at the acrid taste. It was ash. More flecks floated by on a soundless wind.

"Where are we?" Emmy asked, her voice irreverent in the stone silence.

Mantos scowled, shaking his head. "I don't know but it looks like my brother has been here."

"Is this," Emmy started, swallowing against the sudden dryness in her throat, "is this what the world will be if we don't stop Bandim and Dorai?"

"I don't know."

A third voice pierced the silence. "You do know."

Emmy jerked with fright and spun around, searching for the speaker. Mantos snapped into a fighting stance, Haelo held aloft and ready to strike.

The motes of ash swirled together, morphing into a shadowy figure, cloaked and crooked and leaning on a walking stick. A hood hid its face; only the tips of ragged claws and a wizened tail stuck out from beneath the hems of its dark robes.

"Who are you?" Mantos demanded.

The figure chuckled but didn't answer. Mantos went on. "What do you want with us? Why are we here?"

Emmy stepped backwards and behind him as the figure drew closer. If it hadn't been for the color of the skin and armor of its claws, by the figure's gait and stoop Emmy could easily have thought it was Krodge. Whoever it was didn't have Metakalan brown and red. Instead, the hues shifted and changed with every step.

The cloaked figure hobbled forward. It chuckled again as, with unexpected swiftness, it pushed the smooth handle of its cane up under Mantos' chin. When its face tilted upward, the eyes were still in shadow, but its mouth became visible. Again, the skin and armor were iridescent and changing.

With a 'humph,' it withdrew the walking stick and batted Mantos on the arm. Instinctively he moved aside, Haelo now held low. It was Emmy's turn to have the cane's head thrust under her chin.

"Emena, isn't it?" the figure asked. "A word meaning 'no one.' What a cruel stroke."

As the figure appraised her like a lump of meat, Emmy scowled. "I'm called Emmy." Then reality struck her. "How do you know my name?"

The figure gave another 'humph' and continued to inspect her. "You can't really call it a name." The more the figure spoke, the more its voice sounded female. "But if you must, you must. Why do you assume I shouldn't know it?"

Emmy stepped out of the walking stick's reach and clenched her fists. "Who are you?"

The female's mouth, still visible, broke into a crooked-toothed smile. "Ah, Emmy. You are truly one of the best things to come from Bomsoi. Perhaps the best of all her work." With her free hand, the figure pulled down her hood. Pearly eyes blinked from an ancient face. "I am the one they call the Grandmother. I am from Beforetime and Aftertime. I have always been. I always will be."

Shock strangled Emmy. "You're the one the Khinish worship," she squeaked, "the one the Uloni worshiped. You're the mother of the goddesses."

"The who?"

The Grandmother turned her sharp gaze on Mantos. "I expected you to be more intelligent."

Mantos' mouth gaped. In the surprise of the moment, a laugh escaped Emmy's mouth. She clamped her hands over her face, but her shoulders still shook with mirth. This was impossible.

When Mantos finally managed to start an utterance, the Grandmother held up a wizened hand for silence. "Despite your apparent lack of memory, you do know who I am. Bomsoi once told you of me, Meia, the Grandmother of the World. Nunako and Dorai are my children, and Bomsoi, their child."

Emmy saw the flicker of memory dart across Mantos' eyes as he whispered, "Of course."

The Grandmother grunted and waved a hand, conjuring a chair for herself from dust and light.

"Why have you brought us here?" Mantos asked, stepping toward her.

The Grandmother fell into her chair with a grateful sigh. "You think I brought you here? You've come here yourselves. I live in the past, the present, and the future. I am always. You brought yourselves here. This is the future in your minds."

For a moment Emmy's eyes met Mantos.' Haelo hung on his waist again, but Emmy could tell from his slight bend, that the sword grew heavy once more. They didn't have much time. This was the future that lay before them, a burned land bereft of life, all because of Bandim and Dorai. With his power unchecked and unchallenged, everything under the Arc would be reduced to nothing but ash.

"If you didn't bring us here, why are you here with us?" Mantos asked.

The Grandmother waved a hand. "The past, the present, the future. Tell me, young Masvam, which one of those do I not inhabit?" Mantos clamped his lips shut, and the Grandmother laughed. "Your ability to close your mouth when you have nothing to say suggests you aren't as stupid as I thought you were. I am everywhere."

"Is this a vision?" Emmy asked.

The Grandmother gave a curt nod. "It is a distinct possibility."

Emmy's stomach lurched. "Grandmother, please, tell us what we need to do."

The Grandmother laughed again, the sound hollow. "If things don't change, this is what will happen to the world Nunako and Dorai grew together, a world that brought them the greatest of joy." Her voice wavered. "This is all wrong."

Mantos' back was further bent by Haelo's weight. "How can we stop this from happening? We want the world to be safe. I think I must kill Bandim but is that enough? Will that stop Dorai's power?"

The Grandmother sighed. The sound was a rattling wheeze, as if the weight of the entire world pressed on her chest. "Life is not simple. You need to discover that for yourself, as I did."

Her words sent Emmy's mind into a spin. "I don't understand. Please, Grandmother, tell us what we should do."

The Grandmother stood, and her chair swirled back into nothingness. Clouds of dust swirled at her feet. When she spoke again, her words were those Emmy had heard before. "What is made cannot be unmade but what has been made can be destroyed."

"What does that mean?"

Emmy's head snapped to the side. Mantos had asked in tandem with her.

The Grandmother's body flickered and faded. Haelo brought Mantos to his knees.

"Return balance to the world and all will be well." The Grandmother's voice was half-lost in the ether. "Whatever it takes, you must do it."

Then she disappeared.

Mantos kept one hand locked on Haelo's hilt and reached for Emmy with the other. "We're out of time. Grab onto me."

Just like the Grandmother, his body shimmered, and patches of him disappeared. Heart in her throat, Emmy dived forward as Mantos blinked out of view, colliding with the dusty ground. She'd missed him. It was too late. Had she stranded herself here forever?

Then a set of claws grasped her wrist and ground the bones, and the world pitched into darkness once again.

* * *

When they reappeared in Rel's tent, the injured healer wasn't their only company. Bomsoi sat cross-legged at Rel's bedside, her face impassive. Haelo tumbled from Mantos' grip and lay on the folds of the rugs, glinting in the moondust lantern. Emmy slumped backward, her tail curling around her drawn-up knees.

"It would seem nothing is private any longer."

Emmy swiveled toward the sound. Rel sat upright on her cot, her lips pursed with disapproval. Emmy went to speak but found she hadn't the words to describe everything that had happened. Krodge had been in the Uloni village. It was an Uloni who'd burned the rest of their kin to death. They had seen the Grandmother, and the desolate future that lay before them if they did nothing to stop Bandim and Dorai. The world was sharper than ever before.

"Rel, I'm sorry," Emmy managed at last. "Mantos and I were talking, sharing our stories."

"There were questions," Mantos added, sounding more scolded student than imperial prince, "about how Emmy's mistress came to care for her, and who set the fire that killed your folk."

"I had the idea that we could use Haelo to find answers." Emmy pulled herself into a kneel. "Bomsoi, why didn't you tell me Krodge was in the Uloni village? She slipped out of the temple before the fire. She saved me."

Bomsoi's impassive mask cracked, and she managed an abashed smile. "To my shame, I never learned the visitor's name. I didn't even see their colors. It shouldn't have been beneath my notice, yet it was." Her face grew hard. "Did your Krodge start the fire?"

"No!" Emmy said, more defensively than she intended. "No, it wasn't Krodge. But she did save me. Someone, maybe one of my parents, got me out of the temple. Krodge lifted me from the snow."

"As I willed," Bomsoi said. "If she didn't start the fire, who did?"

Emmy's voice failed her again. Mantos stepped in. "It was an Uloni," he said.

Bomsoi's response was swift, harsh, and cold. "No. You're wrong."

"Haelo showed us," Emmy said. She glanced at Rel, whose face was paler now with shock on top of her weakness. "We saw her come into the village. She was dragging a huge bough from a tree and used it to bar the temple door."

Mantos continued, "Then she used her power to set each panel of the temple wall alight."

Before either Rel or Bomsoi could respond, Emmy shook her head. "Why didn't you use your powers to stop the fire?" she asked. "There were so many Uloni in there. You could have quelled the flames."

When Rel spoke, her voice was low and grim. "We tried, to the last of us. Something stopped us. Only Bomsoi could wield any power, and even then, it was such a meager amount. That's how she saved the two of us."

Bomsoi had closed her eyes. "Something dampened our powers. It had never happened before, and it has never happened since."

"Was it the Uloni who started the fire?" Emmy asked.

Rel shook her head. "It couldn't have been. No Uloni is stronger than Bomsoi. We all come from her. But I cannot believe one of our own would destroy us."

Mantos frowned. "As soon as I saw her, I knew there was something familiar about that Uloni. I'd seen her face before, though she wore Masvam colors. She was one of those Bandim kept close to him through his worship of what they called the Dark."

A flash of realization shot through Emmy's mind. She knew what Mantos would say before he spoke the words. "It was Bandim's Uloni. His priestess of the 'Dark' is one of your folk. She's the same so-called temple novice who made my mother think she'd dropped me. She can't have. If she had, the Uloni couldn't have revived me.

You said it yourself, Bomsoi" —his eyes met hers— "that you couldn't bring Mother back to life because Bandim hadn't killed her with his power. I realized earlier that my mother dropping me couldn't have caused my first death. If she had, the 'temple novice' couldn't have brought me back to life. Why this Uloni has interfered in our lives for so long, and why she destroyed the rest of her folk, I don't understand. But she's the same one in all these events. She must be."

There was silence in the tent after Mantos spoke. Bomsoi sat still as stone, her gaze locked on the floor. Rel broke the silence with a soft, "Bomsoi?"

The daughter of gods said nothing. Instead she rose and slipped out of the tent. Emmy jumped up to follow but Rel snagged the tip of her tail to stop her. "Leave her be," she said.

Emmy flopped onto the edge of Rel's pallet and shook her head. "I can't believe it. Bandim's Uloni is the one who destroyed my parents, and everything Bomsoi made."

"Not everything," Mantos said. At Emmy's quizzical look, he clarified, "You're still here. The Grandmother called you 'one of the best things to come from Bomsoi.' She said you were the best of Bomsoi's work." His eyes flicked to Rel. "No offense."

Rel shrugged. "I am only half-Uloni, only part Bomsoi's kin." She raised one eyeridge. "The Grandmother? What else did you see on your surreptitious journey?"

"The Grandmother spoke to us in a world she called a potential future. Bandim and Dorai burned everything. And she used a phrase I've heard from Bomsoi before. 'What is made cannot be unmade but what has been made can be destroyed.'"

"She's said that to me," Mantos added. "Do you understand what it means?"

Rel shifted on her bed, reclining as weariness encroached on her again. Emmy's heart ached at seeing her strong friend so weak.

"Bomsoi has spoken that phrase to me many times," Rel said, "and sometimes I hear her murmuring it to herself. I don't understand its true meaning. I wonder if it's connected to 'balance.' By bringing Dorai into himself, Bandim has made something dangerous. It cannot be unmade but it can be destroyed."

Mantos shifted. "By the same logic, bringing Nunako into my body would be dangerous too, something else to be destroyed." He sighed. "Then again, if I die for this, it wouldn't even be my first death. Which," he added with a grim smile, "is what I've suspected from the start. It was part of the reason I ran before." He dropped his head, ashamed. "I was afraid to die again. When I died the first time, I don't remember what happened. When I died the second time, there was nothing. No Light. No peace. Just nothing." He lifted his head, his eyes afire with determination. "But I won't run again. If I have to die, let the third time be the last."

Emmy did something then that she couldn't account for. She grabbed Mantos' hand and gripped it in her own. His eyes widened, then he blinked, and then he squeezed her talons in return.

"Whatever it is, we'll do it together," Emmy said. "We've just met, but after everything we've just been through, I feel like I know you."

Mantos nodded. "And I know you."

From the bed, Rel chuckled, drawing both of their attention. "Perhaps your excursion was less furtive and more integral," she said. "It would seem our Hand and our Heart have connected in a way they weren't before."

Emmy pressed her lips together before she nodded. "We are."

"Then for certain," Rel added, trying to rise again, "the time has come."

CHAPTER TEN

Emmy

The Khinish made the temple ready for the night's miracle. Emmy sat on the floor of her tent, grateful for the soft warmth of the rugs that cocooned her from the freezing ground. When she'd entered her tent, she'd been full of determination. It shone from her brighter than the moondust lantern hanging from the tent's central pole. Her meeting with the Grandmother, the goddess Meia herself, had filled her with a confidence and a purpose that swelled her heart. But as she stripped off her day's clothing and replaced old skins and furs with new, the gnaw of self-doubt crept in, insidious as the first tendrils of smoke that had risen when Bandim's Uloni burned her entire race of folk.

That self-doubt became more, swirling through Emmy's memory to form a figure, stout and hunched, and leaning on a cane, but with more strength and speed than an old crone should have.

Krodge's lessons played through her mind again and again.

"*What are you?*"

"*I am a Moon Rogue.*"

"*And?*"

"*I am an inconvenience.*"

"*And?*"

"*I am truly grateful for all you have given me, Madame.*"

The switch would come down hard, once on each palm, reliable as the tides or the rise and fall of the suns and moons in the sky.

"*Don't forget it.*"

You needn't worry about that, old hag, Emmy thought. *I'll never forget what you did to me.*

Even as hatred for Krodge roiled within her, the image of a younger Krodge, no cane or stoop in sight, came unbidden into Emmy's mind. How could the female who wept over the massacre of the Uloni treat her with contempt? How could the hands that had plucked her from the snow as nothing but a youngling, and cradled her like her own offspring, have brought the switch down so hard on her innocent skin? Emmy looked at her palms and the faint scars that remained from the last lessons Krodge had taught her. The old crone who had treated her as little more than a slave, who had beaten and mocked her, had taken pleasure in Emmy's pain.

"*Once I'm dead, there'll be no one left to protect you!*"

Emmy folded her claws into her palms and closed her eyes, willing Krodge to leave her mind. That wasn't true. She had Bomsoi and Rel, and Charo and Zecha, and Mantos Tiboli now. She had the Khinish. She had Neiruk. Krodge was, among other things, a liar. Emmy wasn't inconsiderate. She wasn't an inconvenience. She was more than the vile insults that Krodge kindled about her in others, not tainted, or pathetic, or evil.

She was Emmy, one of the last of the Uloni. She would help Bomsoi bring balance to the world at last. If that made her a Moon Rogue, she would wear that title like a crown.

The moondust lantern dimmed as its coals cooled.

A dull scratching caught Emmy's attention. A pair of deft claws made little work of the ties that held her tent flap in place, and in a gust of cold, Bomsoi slipped inside. She took care to retie the flap before she turned her attention to Emmy. When she spoke, both her words and her expression were warm.

"How do you feel?"

The answer was too complex for words. Instead, Emmy shrugged her shoulders and looked down again. Bomsoi knew how she felt. She could feel everything Emmy felt as keenly as she did herself.

Bomsoi lowered herself to the floor and took up Emmy's hands. "I have total faith in you, my daughter."

"But what if I can't help bring Nunako into the world?"

Before Bomsoi could answer, the tent flap opened. Another figure stepped in, leaning on a cane.

"What if the moons fall from the sky? What if the trees uproot themselves and walk away?"

Emmy leaped up at the voice. "Rel!"

She was at her friend's elbow in an instant, though Rel eased herself from Emmy's grip.

"Should you be out of bed?"

"No," Bomsoi answered. "She should still be in bed, but she refuses to listen."

Fatigue pained Rel's burn-scarred face, but it didn't stop her from drawing herself to her considerable full height. "I'm no invalid, nor a youngling who needs told what to do," she said, trying to sound stern. Her smile betrayed her. She settled herself on the low edge of Emmy's pallet bed and leaned her cane on the hip where Haelo often sat. "Even if I was, I'd still be here."

"You're still recovering," Emmy began but Rel stopped her with a raised claw.

Bomsoi slid across the floor and tugged Emmy back onto the rug. "Peace, daughters. We do need Rel's power."

Emmy took up her place at Bomsoi's side again. Her eyes trained on Rel's ravaged face.

Rel turned her soft gaze on Emmy. "I'm fine. Stop fretting. My concern lies with you and you only. What we ask of you tonight isn't easy."

Emmy nodded, lowering her head. Krodge returned to her mind unbidden, and Emmy batted her away again. "I don't know if I can do it."

Rel nodded, her smile gone. "I understand that well. If I could bear this burden for you, I would. But we know I can't."

The washed-out blue and purple of her half-Uloni complexion seemed dull, like the bloom on liquid wax cooling on a cold surface.

"*Please don't fear, Emmy,*" Bomsoi said, switching to their Uloni communication. "*You've come a long way from the frightened young thing Rel met in the Althemerian camp, and even further from the youngling trodden upon by your mistress. All you need to do is trust in your friends, your family, the Grandmother, and most of all, yourself.*"

Emmy's mind cycled through the faces of those Bomsoi had mentioned. Zecha and Charo, her dear friends, who'd stayed by her side through everything, though they could have fled for a better life. Rel and Bomsoi, her sister and mother, kin she never thought she'd ever have. Meia, the Grandmother of the World, who had called her the best of all Bomsoi's work.

And herself, the Moon Rogue, rare as a dark night. Not an inconvenience but a gift.

"*What about Mantos?*" Emmy asked. "*He left once. What's to say he won't leave again? What if he changes his mind?*"

"*He cannot reconsider,*" Bomsoi said. She placed a talon on the center of Emmy's chest and pressed between the divots of two plates. "*You are his Heart. You will guide him. He, as the Hand, will protect you. He's one of the most fearsome warriors under the Arc. There is nowhere safer than in his care. Together, you'll do what you must.*"

Emmy leaned against the edge of the bed. "But what if I can't? What if Mantos can't? What if we fail and Bandim kills us all?"

Rel took up her cane and rose. Emmy flinched, anticipating a hit until sense caught up to action and she realized Rel wasn't Krodge. Leaning on her stick, Rel unhooked the moondust lantern from the middle of the tent and lowered it to the ground. Its light was paltry, and when Emmy touched the metal base, it was cool enough to hold with bare skin.

"Open it," Rel said.

Emmy glanced at Bomsoi, who sat back with a strange mixture of pride and intrigue painted on her face.

"Listen to Rel," Bomsoi said. "Do as she asks."

Emmy did as Rel told her and unscrewed the temperate metal. The ridges creaked, revealing the coals inside.

"You could take up one of those coals and bring the warmth back into it, if you put your mind to it." Rel said. "I can't. My blood limits my power. Yours does not."

Emmy's long-learned instincts kicked in. "I'm not as powerful as you think I am." She stared at the dim sparkle of the coals. "I can't."

Rel's voice cut across her with a stern sharpness Emmy had never heard her use. "No more of this 'I can't' and 'I'm not,' Emmy. Pick up a coal and will it to burn. You can, I promise you."

Emmy's first instinct was to contradict. She'd done nothing with her power beyond wielding ice or willing sickness to abate and healing to occur. She'd never even considered manipulating heat. That was the domain of Bandim. But instead of giving in to her thoughts, Emmy swallowed and nodded.

She reached into the bottom of the lantern. Her hand enclosed on a coal, and when she opened her claws, it lingered in a dark pool of shadow and soot. Heart in her throat, Emmy concentrated, her eyes fixed on the black mass. *Burn*, she thought. *I can do this. I command you to burn.*

At first there was nothing. No cold track through her veins. Then she realized there *was* something: not the fractal cracking of ice climbing through her limbs, but a hum of warmth that began low, then burst into flame within her. The hotness swirled around her arms and rushed to the tips of her talons. She closed them around the coal once again. Warmth swelled in her hand, and smoke rose in coils from the slits between her fingers. When she opened her talons again, the coal glowed bright and red.

"I did it," she whispered.

Rel slid to the floor in an inelegant slump and wrapped an arm around Emmy's shoulders. "Of course you did, Emmy. You're more powerful than you know."

Emmy beamed at the pride in Bomsoi's eyes. Bomsoi reached for the coal and returned it to the lantern bottom. Screwed back into place, the green light of warm moondust illuminated the tent, casting long shadows on its canvas and hide walls.

"I told you to listen to Rel," Bomsoi said. "She knows well how belief in yourself can help you. Once, I sent her to sea during a storm in only the smallest of boats. While the waves capsized all others, Rel's stayed afloat because she believed in her own power over the winds. She knew she wouldn't drown, and she didn't. You're ready, Emmy." Her words became thick. "How far you've come and how close we are to putting everything to rights." Bomsoi sat on Emmy's other side and placed an arm around her too. "I need to know one thing. When the time comes, will you do what you must?"

Emmy's answer came without hesitation. "Yes, I will."

With a gentle squeeze to her shoulder, Bomsoi smiled. "I can ask nothing more. Now come. Tonight is the night we welcome Mother Nunako back into the world."

CHAPTER ELEVEN

Mantos

Mantos tucked his chin deeper into the thick layers of fur and closed his eyes. He'd climbed a little way up the mountain, keeping the Uloni village in view. His exact purpose? Unclear. Perhaps he hoped the chill Great Northern Range winds would clear the fear from his head. Perhaps he needed to be alone as he stood on the precipice of his life changing forever.

It's not my life I'm worried about, he thought. *It's what I do afterward. I've proved myself a coward more than once, despite the great warrior I'm supposed to be. What happens if Nunako rejects me? What if I reject her? Or, if we come together, we're worse than Bandim and Dorai could be? The unknowns stacked up like stones, a prison wall building around him.*

No. Not a prison around me but a building to protect me. The distinction was little but important.

Mantos glanced up. Clouds encroached, blocking the moons and the stars, and brought a darkness more profound than words could describe. He kept his head tipped back and stared. Perhaps it was a poor omen. Tonight, when they needed the moons' light, Nunako's gift, more than ever before, she withheld it from them. A new chill rattled through him. He couldn't think like that. He shouldn't. But it kept coming back.

The same fear that had propelled him into escape back in the Althemerian palace returned. The soles of his feet itched with a deep-rooted desire to leave. If he ran, he couldn't fail.

Yet if I run, I do fail. If I'd stayed before and faced this terror, my mother might be alive. This could be in the past. He cursed his past self for being craven. He cursed his present self for the urge to flee again. He feared for his future self, perhaps cursed, and doomed for the rest of his life. If there was a rest of his life. With Nunako's arrival, it might mean his end. At least this death would be different.

For a moment, the mountain winds stilled. Then the moment stretched. Mantos looked back at the camp. Something stopped him, keeping his attention on the sable clouds. They were moving, not in the slow flow of weather across the sky, but in a swirl. What started as a slow twist soon developed into a vortex, the clouds whipping in swift circles. A tether of whipping wind grasped them. With a flick, the swirl of clouds disappeared to the horizon, leaving the brightness of three moons and countless stars gleaming on a background of deepest black. Mantos followed the direction the tether had come from. Three figures stood outside the temple, their colors obscured by night, all except the six pinpricks of blue that shone from the three Uloni, looking straight at him. Bomsoi, Rel, and Emmy had cleared the skies, revealing Nunako's three faces once again. Mantos licked his lips against the cold and willed steel into his spine. He turned to the moons, Rafa, Dato, and Akata, and did something he hadn't done in longer than he could remember. He prayed.

"Goddess Nunako, Lady of Light, tonight I pledge myself to you in a way I never thought I could. Please forgive my weakness and accept me as your servant and your vessel. Use me to bring balance back into the world. Please," his voice stumbled, "help me avenge my mother and stop my brother. I don't want to kill him, but if I must, I will. I won't falter again."

The goddess' beloved moons spread across the sky, peering down like another three faces and six eyes fixed upon him. Nunako gave no reply, but the sight of her moons staring unblinking and unstoppable brought strength to Mantos' heart. Under their eyes, he descended the mountain, chest plates and neck scales fluttering, ready to meet his goddess.

The moons stayed above him for the whole short journey, separate from each other but gleaming among the tiny silver stars. The clouds now created a circular keep around the village. They hung like gray sentinels, watching. By the time he reached the village, the temple teemed with life. Everyone else, Emmy's companions and the Khinish folk, had taken up a place inside the hall. Mantos remained outside at Bomsoi's bidding, the doors closed against him while everyone else lingered inside.

That thought made Mantos' skin prickle. Thanks to Haelo, he had witnessed the Uloni's destruction behind the facade of the old temple. He'd heard their screams, seen the flames lick up and up, felt the impotence of being unable to save them. Mantos stared in the direction the arsonist had come from, the one who wore Bandim's priestess' face. Bandim's Uloni. Did he know she'd massacred her own folk? If he did, did he care? Did it endear him to her even more? The likely answer made Mantos' stomach twist.

He pulled his gaze back to the doors. Mantos traced the wood with his gloved talons, imagining the thick bough of a tree shoved through the carved handles, blocking any attempt to exit. The doors were of dark wood inlaid with lighter panels, the design more mosaic than carving. A coldness washed over Mantos. It reminded him of the complex mosaic of the grand receiving hall in the palace in Kubodinnu.

Kubodinnu reminded him of Fonbir, which brought a whole new aching layer of cold. Snatches of their last conversation came back.

"All I know is that Oatutkubis, the Demon Who Rides the Sky, is upon us," Fonbir had told him. His expression was one of fear but overriding that was such a beautiful, pure hope. "But I have faith. Faith in Ethay and Apago. Faith in Bomsoi. And most important of all, faith in you." Fonbir's voice cracked. "You are good and loyal, Mantos. I know you'll do what is right."

And how had Mantos responded to this unbreakable faith and loyalty? With bitter, bitter words: "Then you are a fool."

Much as he wanted it to stop, the memory continued.

"Mantos, I—" Fonbir began.

Mantos, so full of his own self-hatred and despair, hadn't even allowed his love to finish. "No. Don't. I think you should leave."

Worst of all was the fury in those dazzling white eyes. "As you wish."

Then Fonbir had left, and Mantos had never seen him again. He chastised himself with a scoff. Whose fault was that? His and his alone. Fonbir had believed he could do what Bomsoi needed. Fonbir had believed that under all Mantos' life's layers, his conquering Masvam heritage, his bloody hands, was something good. Something loyal.

Mantos straightened his back and flicked out his tail, pulling himself to his full height as he faced the closed door.

"I'll do it for you, Fonbir," he said. "I will never let you down again."

The inlaid doors swung inward. The temple was lit by green moondust lanterns and balls of floating, ethereal blue light. Bomsoi stood in the doorway, framed by the congregation behind her, and bowed. "Please, come in, Mantos of House Tiboli."

Mantos shook his head. "Not any longer," he said. "I'm just Mantos now."

Bomsoi inclined her head and rephrased, spreading her arms in welcome. "Then come in, Mantos. We're ready for you."

He crossed the threshold, toward Bomsoi's open arms, into the maw of the Uloni temple and the moment that would change him forever.

The Khinish congregation was silent and pale as bone, their eyes tracking Mantos as he followed Bomsoi to his fate. The pool of light at the temple's center was ethereal, brighter than anything Mantos had seen. Emmy stood just outside it, the toes of her boots touching its circumference. Rel sat beside her on a low stool, leaning on a cane. Just beyond, in the first circle of onlookers, he saw Emmy's two companions. The male, Zecha, held a comforting hand around the scarred female's back. Charo wore the same pained look of an upcoming laying that Mantos had seen on the faces of servants before their confinement.

His eyes slipped upward, staring at the circle of sky above. The Uloni temple was similar enough to the Temple of Light in the city of Masvam that he felt like he'd been here before. But unlike in the temple at home, there were no swirling designs of burning candles. There was no great pyre. Instead there was the dim green glow of moondust, and a simple circle of light.

As Mantos and Bomsoi reached the others, Emmy's mouth bent in a smile. On the surface it welcomed him, but her lips wavered with tension. Mantos inclined his head to her and laid his hands flat, palms upward and tilted toward her. She wouldn't know the gesture's true meaning, but he hoped she would glean some peace from it. It was a Masvam sign for hope, love, and good fortune.

Bomsoi gestured for Mantos to come forward. Doing as she commanded, Mantos looked to her for his next instruction. His heart's flutter became a smith's hammer beating in time with the rush of blood in his head.

Bomsoi pointed to the pool of moonlight. "Onto the floor, please. Kneel."

Mantos obeyed, face flushing as he dropped to his knees. He was too hot, too cold. His hands trembled, his tail was unruly, and his heart still thundered. When he looked up, he found Emmy's eyes. This time it was she who signaled to him. She inclined her head and pressed her two foreclaws to her lips. She must have learned it on Althemer, for it was something Fonbir had taught him. For a moment, it wasn't Emmy who looked with compassionate yet fearful eyes. It was Fonbir.

He blinked, and the sight disappeared. He dropped his gaze to his hands, resting on his lap. Fonbir wasn't with him, yet he was. Despite everything he had done, abandoning his Nabi to dwell in his own selfishness, Mantos' mind still went to Fonbir for help and protection. For hope. *I won't let you down again.* As Bomsoi began to speak, Mantos lifted his chin with the confidence Fonbir had always given to him.

"Today," the daughter of gods began, her voice ringing clear and bright in the temple's silence, "in the sight of all those present who love and worship Meia, Grandmother of the World, we gather here to ask for her gracious help. Friends, we are here to bring about the greatest good we can. We face the greatest evil to threaten everything under Meia's Arc of the Sky."

Bomsoi placed the heels of her hands against Mantos' forehead, one on each side of his horns. Her touch was ice. "Mantos, your actions today are noble, and we thank you for your sacrifice." She dropped her voice so only those close to her could hear. "I thank you, more than you will ever understand." Before Mantos could ask what she meant, she withdrew her hands and lifted her voice again. "Bandim Tiboli, the self-styled Sun Emperor, has meddled with powers he does not understand, but today we strike back. He has brought corruption to the world by imbibing one goddess but today we counter that. Mantos, forever joined with his brother, will, today, become the vessel of Nunako, to counter Bandim's Dorai.

"Today is a great day in history," Bomsoi went on, circling outside the light and speaking to the crowd. "We bring Nunako back to the world. While Dorai returned through the gift of the Lunar Awakening, we have no such power on our side.

However, in the Grandmother of the World's sight, and in the love of each other" — she held out her claws, gesturing for everyone to do the same — "we will welcome Nunako as Dorai's counter, and we will start down the path to restoring balance to the world."

Mantos' ears quirked as the temple filled with the sound of arms unfolding like flower petals. The Khinish lifted their pale palms to the light. Among them, Zecha and Charo did the same, their hands dots of color in a sea of white. Closest to him, Rel did the same. Emmy remained still, a beautiful statue on the edge of the light.

"With the will of the goddess and the power of my folk, we will succeed. Emmy, step forward."

The Uloni did. Bomsoi continued. "Emmy, my daughter, whose veins run thick with the blood of the Grandmother, today we need you to become the conduit through which Nunako will return. Do you accept this burden?"

There was no hesitation. "I do."

"Then kneel."

Mantos' heart swelled with pride for this young female he didn't know, yet part of him knew her. Emmy did as Bomsoi commanded and slipped down in front of him. She reached forward with one hand, but before she could place it on him, Mantos grasped it in both of his own.

"I believe in you," he whispered.

Emmy's throat bobbed as she swallowed. "I believe in you, too."

Mantos nodded. "Let's bring about the beginning of the end."

He released her hand and allowed her to press her talons to his chest, just over the plates covering his heart. For a long moment, everything was silent. After a while, Bomsoi spoke.

"By the goddess, the Grandmother, Ethay and Apago, all names of the gods, please listen to us today as we pray. We beg of you, Nunako, take this mortal as your vessel. Cleanse him of his failings and see him for what he is: good and honest. Guide the goddess into his Heart, Emmy, and help us bring about the balance this world needs."

Mantos closed his eyes, his mind weaving through memory as Bomsoi's words washed over him. There were distant flashes of his time as a youngling, playing with Bandim and Valaria and Fonbir as their monarch parents tried to find some way to hold their tense alliance together. There were clearer memories of lessons with Old Master Abe, his intoning voice, Bandim's bored sneering. He remembered every letter he had written to Fonbir, their connection deepening with every coded quill stroke. Most of all, he remembered his mother; not as the ragged waif in the tower, not even in the crumpled form of her slit-throat murder, but as a strong and striking creature bedecked in Yru blue and yellow. She reached for him, power glittering around her like jewels.

"I believe in you, my son. The Grandmother is with you."

Mantos' eyes snapped open. That was no memory. The entire temple trembled as a fierce wind whipped. Emmy was in front of him, her eyes glowing blue and focused on the hand laid on his heart. Mantos looked up. Every set of eyes looked at him. Every set glowed blue.

"Emmy, I—"

His words died in his throat as a freezing power penetrated him. He gasped for breath, chest contracting as if there was no air. Ice formed along his skin, tracking like chains. Every part of him threatened to shatter under her power. The entire world shook. Mantos couldn't breathe. Emmy had stopped his heart. She was killing him.

His movements jerky and not his own, Mantos clamped Emmy's hand. As soon as his hand touched hers, a thousand cycles passed in a second. Mantos' eyes rolled back as every thought and hope and fear the young Uloni had ever possessed streaked through him. Every slap to her face, every blow to her body, struck him. Every insult, every rejection, every tear she had shed came to him. He gritted his teeth against cycle upon cycle of anguish and hate. It whirled around him like an ice storm, shards of glass pummeling his body. *She's experienced such pain.*

The Uloni's voice sounded in his mind, as clear as Althemerian temple chanting. "*So have you, Mantos. I think in some ways, we're the same.*" Her words became soft. "*Are you ready?*"

Mantos, no breath in his body, nodded in reply. "*I am.*"

Emmy nodded and raised her gaze to the sky. Mantos followed, every star glimmering silver and bright above them. Neiruk swept across the open circle of sky, baying into the wilderness.

"Nunako!" Emmy cried aloud. "Accept this vessel!"

There was a deep *clunk* from everywhere and nowhere. Dust shook from the rafters, and a resonant *boom* erupted, echoing out into the mountains. Around them the Khinish called out in their strange language. Neiruk crossed the sky once more. That was the last thing Mantos saw.

White-hot light exploded around him, banishing everything from sight except for one figure. Emmy stood before him, clothed in brightness. She lifted her hands and placed them on Mantos' face, cupping his chin in her coldness. She leaned in, pressing her icy lips to his cheek.

That was the moment everything changed. Something Mantos couldn't understand moved from her into him. His back arched, and his limbs jerked. Pain and pleasure, light and dark, the brightest happiness and the darkest fear all moved within him. Mantos shuddered as the world fell away.

"Do not fear," Emmy whispered. "All will be well."

CHAPTER TWELVE

Bandim-Dorai

One of the many benefits of being a goddess was that much daily experience was akin to what one had experienced before. Dorai hadn't affected the world for some time but little had changed in the interval. Folk were much the same. That being the case, she had plenty of recommendations for the Sun Emperor to deal with his little rebellion.

Bandim's immediate thought, as his immediate thoughts always *were*, was one of violence. Dorai knew from experience that violence didn't bring everyone in line. To string up the broken bodies of put-down rebels would be effective against those ruled by fear. Where a grotesque sculpture of rotting flesh would deter some, for others it would only bring insurgence, declarations of "This is why we stand against the Sun Emperor!" Bandim, young and desperate as he was, couldn't see such things. His reasoning always ran thus: violence upon violence, until all succumb. What he didn't realize was that the goddesses hadn't made all their folk the same. When the wretched Nunako had molded them from the earth, shaping their forms like clay on a potter's wheel, she hadn't imbibed them with such sameness. That might have been enough for Nunako, whose thirst for devotion was as unquenchable as Bandim's. But it wasn't enough for Dorai, who had instructed Nunako on all the differences to make. Why create a race of beings who looked the same, did the same things, and believed whatever they were told?

In retrospect, Dorai thought as she planted the seeds of her idea in Bandim's mind, manipulating the thoughts lying within, it would have been easier if they were all the same. If the folk they had wanted to worship them had been single-minded and stupid, perhaps they would have never failed in their devotion. But neither Dorai nor her sister could change the past. The Grandmother had kept the power to move between past, present, and future all to herself. Another good idea, Dorai had to admit. Had she been able to go back in time to smash her sister goddess' egg before she hatched, she would have done so long before.

As all seeds needed time to germinate, so she allowed her suggestions to flourish in Bandim's mind. She could force him to do as she commanded. She could have forced him to do anything from the moment she entered his body. But that was Nunako's style, not Dorai's. Where was the fun in that? It didn't take long for the Sun Emperor to decide that displaying dead corpses wasn't the best way to put down the little rebellion. Dorai sat back, basking in the same happiness that Bandim felt in his mind. His pleasure was a gift.

* * *

By the time he returned to the palace, Bandim-Dorai's ire had cooled, if only a little. While he wanted to hang the rebel corpses from palace walls, something told him not to, yet. Instead, he sent the bodies to the icy morgue in the depths of the underpalace, a winding warren of cells and crypts in the palace's foundations and retired to his chambers. An idea blossomed in his mind.

Three days later, he sent out the heralds. A week later, on the appointed day, the city of Masvam was bursting with folk all come to celebrate, despite the bitterness of the middle of Vhaun.

The corpses were on the walls now, frozen in straight lines from their time lying on slabs of stone. The Vhaun chill kept them stiff and strange, discolored, pale, and bluish but the bodies had become more curiosity than abject deterrent. Those ruled by fear would keep their claws and thoughts in check, not wanting to end up on the walls. However, that wasn't the reason many folk had battled the barren roads and frigid winds to come to the capital when no one traveled unless they had to.

The speaker's bowl brimmed with nobles and commoners, workers and merchants, gathered to hear the Sun Emperor speak. They came to the capital because of his promise, disseminated through the empire by gargon and vaemar and foot alike.

As Bandim-Dorai stepped onto the grand balcony, the herald called out his name.

"His Imperial Majesty, Sole Ruler of the Masvam Empire, Protector of the Realm, Conqueror of Heathens, Scorcher of Souls, the All-Powerful, All-Wise, and All-Beautiful One True Goddess incarnate, Emperor Bandim-Dorai!"

This time, everyone to the very last cheered for their emperor-goddess.

Dressed in fine robes with jewels dripping from his horns and the flames of Dorai painted on his face, he strode straight to the balustrade and raised his hands in greeting. Every torch in the bowl exploded into light, in harmony with the snapping banners of Dorai's flame on a field of purest black. The crowd's jubilation rose to a fever pitch. Bandim-Dorai gave his best benevolent smile as their devotion filled him from the claws of his toes to the crown of his horn crest. They loved him. They loved

Dorai. Behind him, on either side, Johrann and Tesselica loved him too. How beautiful it was to see a nation change for the better, all under his watchful eye.

"My dearest, dearest friends," he began. As his voice carried around the bowl, the crowd's fervor eased. "Your presence, my true citizens of the Masvam Empire, warms my heart more than any flame ever could. I welcome you here, and I thank you for coming out in such incredible numbers during what is the harshest point of the cycle."

His breath escaped in white clouds, though with his power he felt no cold. The gathered folk did. Underneath their adoration was layer upon layer of fear. Fear they wouldn't survive the season. Fear their younglings might starve. Fear that rebels might pillage their scant Vhaun larders or, even worse, burn them. A barrel of wizened arra fruit might mean the difference between survival or starvation for the poorest of them, who were also the most vulnerable to rebel attacks. Elsya and his rabble may have thought rebellion benefited the masses but that could never be the case if their actions brought destruction. In Masvam history, all rebellion brought destruction, and the poorest suffered the most.

This was Bandim-Dorai's foundation. Dead bodies were one deterrent, but this was much better.

"When I spoke upon this balcony last, I promised you land, riches, and bounty. Already I've gained for you the Island of Althemer. The riches from the heathen queendom's ruins have come to us at last, and the bounty of their nation is about to become yours." Another cheer rose. "I have granted some of you estates, but for those of humbler ranks, I promise, there is land aplenty for you to work and claim on the island. There will be ships sailing for the island in the coming Merish, at the beginning of planting season. I will pay your passage, so anyone who wishes to go may do so. If you wish for your own land, a place to put down deep Masvam roots into the island, you will do me a wonderful honor by conquering the island. To you, I will always be grateful."

The next cheer tinged with disbelief and knife-edge delight. Some folk couldn't have their own land. By taking their place in the newest part of the empire, not only would they drive the Althemerians further out and put them in their subordinate place, but they would drive Masvam claws hard into the island. The Althemerians would never reclaim their homeland. It was Bandim's now.

"However," Bandim-Dorai went on, quieting the crowd again, "waiting for the closing cusp of Vhaun to touch the opening cusp of Merish will be long and difficult, and I hope none of my true citizens suffer. That's why I've called you all to me today. I, Emperor Bandim-Dorai, pledge to do everything I can to help my folk survive this dark time, and all dark times to come. When the sun is at its apex, the bounty of Althemer will open to you. Everyone shall receive enough food to survive, courtesy of the former Island of Serpents. From this moment, Althemer shall die, and in its place will rise the Island of Promise, for I promise you that under my reign you will survive, succeed, and thrive!"

The crowd erupted, and Bandim-Dorai drank in their adoration. He held his hands up for all to see, laid flat with palms upward and tilted to the crowd to signal for them hope, love, and good fortune. "We will from now on know this day as the Thanks of Vhaun, for I thank you for your undying belief. Go now, my dear friends. Feast on this day and take your fill to ensure every one of you eats every single day of Vhaun. Remember that your goddess loves you. I will always protect you."

Bandim-Dorai left the balcony on a crest of unending cheers and the congratulations of his overdukes. He accepted each compliment with a gracious nod, the delight of the folk washing over him like ripples. His plan had worked, not that he had doubted himself.

The Sun Emperor strode into the receiving chamber off the balcony. Attendants took off his horn jewels and the outermost layers of his ceremonial clothing. They helped him to a chair by the hearth and drew two further seats to the fireside. Bandim-Dorai permitted Johrann and Tesselica to sit, then turned a benevolent smile to the cupbearer who approached, pushing a little wheeled tray laden with cups and a steaming carafe of hot wine. She kept her head down.

"Dearest Yameteth," he said as the young female took up the carafe and poured him a generous cup, "how are you, my kin?"

Yameteth curtsied at the emperor's kindness, still holding the carafe. While once all she had felt for him was terror, now her prevailing emotion was gratitude. "I'm well, Your Imperial Majesty."

She ventured a glance at him, and Bandim-Dorai gave her another smile, motioning for her to fill the cups of his companions. "I'm very glad to hear it," he said, and he meant it.

His distant cousin's cheeks flushed as a cloud of pleasure rose around her. Her task completed, she set the carafe on the wheeled tray once more and retreated, leaving the tray behind.

Bandim-Dorai plucked up the cup and inhaled the spiced scent before taking a long sip. "That went as well as expected, don't you agree?"

Tesselica responded with his usual enthusiasm. Johrann Maa gave an approving nod and said, "It did, My Emperor. Your actions are a stroke of genius."

The tiniest sliver of golden approval slipped through her emotional wall. Bandim-Dorai fell into his old ways, finding himself preening at the praise. The next step of his old ways followed, like the left foot sweeping after the right. Hot rage welled in him, and his hand ached to strike her for making him feel like a fool, but he stopped it before his talons so much as twitched. He was the Sun Emperor, no longer the second-rate spare of Braslen Tiboli. He needed neither to seek praise nor to flagellate himself for enjoying it. Whatever he desired was what he had the right to receive.

Tesselica brimmed with pride. "Bringing in the stores from Althemer—the Island of Promise," he corrected himself, "is inspired, My Emperor. The rebels can't feed the folk, but if you show that you can, their loyalties will always lie with you."

"The folk are an easy sort when you get to their bones," Bandim-Dorai said. He swirled the spice-laden wine in his cup, tracing the play of firelight on the tiny waves. "They wish to survive the barren season, so I'll help them survive. It won't take long for them to realize that if you scorch the hand that gives you life, your life won't be worth living."

Hanging traitors to show what fate awaited further rebellions would have been enough for some. The seeping creep of fear that wound from the palace's outer walls like tendrils was palpable. Many folk didn't care much, beyond the survival of their own families, about who sat on the throne and what goddess they worshipped. Those issues paled compared to the real darkness that was the starvation of your ailing mother or your tiny hatchling. More than crowns or temples, those folk coveted food. It ruled them more than the emperor could. Thus, Bandim-Dorai had realized, why not use it?

Dead bodies were one deterrent, but this was much better.

CHAPTER THIRTEEN

Nunako

The first thing Nunako did was have the vessel remove his shoes and run through the snow. Life was a joy. She stopped short of having him strip to his armor and skin and disappear into the mountains. The Goddess Nunako had left the world for more cycles than she even knew but she remembered her folk. What a waste to return to walk among them only for her new body to freeze and die on the first day.

The second thing Nunako did was to bring Mantos, former Prince of the Masvam Empire, to his tent. Alone, they sat together as Nunako examined every part of him. She took in his gold armor and dark skin, the ripple of his neck scales, the length of his dark fronds, the blunted tips of his talons, the play of muscles in his flesh. The one thing she couldn't see was his face. Was her vessel handsome? Were his features sharp and wily, or dull like a boulder, or were they small, rounded, and perfect? How Nunako ached for a handplate.

Dorai had always been fond of lambasting Nunako for her concern with looks. Why did it matter, Dorai had so often asked, when the truth of folk dwelled in their hearts? Her sister never took the chance to understand. Instead, her sister-goddess who knew everything condemned Nunako to vanity and disregard. As Nunako turned her vessel's hands over and back, examining the patterns of his scales, she sighed. Dorai understood nothing she didn't make or decide herself.

* * *

Mantos

The disconcerting feeling of being in symbiosis was different to anything Mantos expected. His greatest fear had been that once the goddess moved within him, he would cease to be, but this was not the case. He retreated to his tent after the ceremony, with a bootless detour through the snow he knew was not his own bidding and found himself in deep consideration of his own body. This, too, must have been Nunako's doing. Mantos cared little for his appearance, yet he examined every hill and valley of himself.

Through all of this, though, he never lost his sense of self. Mantos was still Mantos, a Masvam with two arms and two legs and a tail. He moved those limbs under his own power. He had his own thoughts, his mind not supplanted by another being. Even the actions he completed under the goddess's command weren't so much commands as suggestions. Requests. Nunako asked of him, and he complied. Mantos was still there. The only difference was a low-pitched hum in the back of his mind that told him he was no longer alone.

Nunako was like a rumble: not thunder, but the movement of the earth beneath him. Under her influence, Mantos pulled aside the many rugs and sheets that protected him from the cold freeze of the ground. He placed his hands flat upon the barren soil so she could feel the earth again. The hum of her power inside him grew louder, a constant shift and grind of rock and soil. It slipped down from his head and swirled along his arms. It became a thrum of something powerful passing through his veins, pooling in the tips of his fingers and disappearing into the frozen land that once was the home of the Uloni, the folk of Bomsoi's blood. His blood.

Nunako's blood, Mantos thought as he pulled his hands back. *Not mine.* His blood ran thick with generations of Masvam rulers. The Uloni were not of him. They were of Bomsoi, who was of Nunako and Dorai.

Mantos sat back on his heels, leaning on his tail. *I need to get used to this.* The feeling was, for the briefest moment, a sincere belief. Mantos shivered as the coldness of the ground permeated his fingertips. He was still himself, yet he was Nunako as well. He hadn't lost himself, but when he'd touched the earth, Nunako bloomed within him like the bounty of Decos. Her memories. Her emotions. Her connection to the land.

Fear came like weeds among Nunako's flowers. This was how he would lose himself. It was to be a slow slippage, Mantos supplanted by Nunako part by part. The low-pitched hum returned, bringing a wave of comfort. No. He was himself but changed.

Mantos went to his knees once more and brought his hands to the ground. Fear gave way to duty. His main concern was for the world, this place under the Arc that Nunako cultivated. He had a role to fulfill, even if it meant he ceased to be. He touched the ground once more.

The hum became a thrum, which became a rumble. *Nunako, I'm yours. Do what you must.*

The ground cracked beneath his touch. His claws sank into the hard earth as if it was sand. Something flowed through him, a power that connected his mind to the ground. He reached downward, into the seams of metal beneath his touch, into the unmistakable flow of molten rock. Then he wasn't just touching it. He was the rock, the red-hot dance and swirl of the world beneath. The more it was him, the more power he had. The more power he had, the stronger his connection to the world.

A tremor ran from his spine down his tail and into the ground, or was it from the ground up into him? Whatever happened, the tremor became a quake, and the mountain itself jarred and shifted under his touch.

The ground broke underneath him, splitting into the mouth of a chasm that would swallow the world.

Mantos snatched his hands away and held them aloft, as far from the start of the fissure as he could. He did that. He'd cleaved the earth beneath his tent with only the power of his hands.

No, he thought. *The power of Nunako.*

Mantos stumbled into the cold and shielded his face from the snow flurries. When his vision cleared, he stopped cold. The crack in the earth spread outward from his tent in a jagged line, bisecting the Uloni village like an axis. Some Khinish folk helped each other up, the force of Mantos' power having knocked them from their feet. Others kept their gazes fixed on the mountain slopes that rose around them, poised to run in the face of an avalanche.

"Mantos!"

A voice cried from behind him. Emmy ran toward him, her feet making no imprint on the snowfall. Bomsoi strode along behind.

"Was that you?" Emmy asked when she reached him. When she clutched his arm, her talons tightened like vices.

"It was," Mantos replied. "Or at least, it was a part of me."

When Bomsoi drew up beside them, she gave a tight smile. "Mother Nunako is flexing her talons, I see." A far-off rumble like thunder sounded, signaling a dangerous shift in the snow. "Perhaps this isn't the best place to exercise those skills."

Mantos nodded, bringing his hands up to stare at his palms. They were dirt-streaked and frozen, and he didn't care. He lifted his head to say something in reply but stopped. Khinish circled around them, whispering, and staring.

One of them called out, "Keyëyñopo?"

Bomsoi nodded in return, sending a new flurry of whispers through the group.

Emmy frowned. "What did they ask?"

In reply, Bomsoi clamped a hand around Mantos' shoulder. There was coldness at her touch but something else now. Mantos traced the line of her arm all the way out to her own shoulder, then up to rest on her face. Something connected them. Mantos knew nothing more about Bomsoi now than he had before he'd taken Nunako into his body, yet he knew more. In a way, she was his daughter.

"They asked who he was," Bomsoi said, her hand still on Mantos' shoulder. "They call him Keyëyñopo. It means 'The World Breaker.' From the looks of it, they've given Mantos an apt name." She managed a chuckle. "Mother Nunako always enjoyed her mastery over rock and earth."

She released him, but Mantos' hand snapped up and grabbed hers before she could let it fall. He kept his gaze on hers and narrowed his eyes, searching her face for something he wasn't sure he even knew.

"You've grown, my child," he said, though the words came without his bidding. "And you're hurting."

He raised his other hand to press it against Bomsoi's ribs, but she twisted out of his grip and cleared some distance between them. She started to speak but clamped her lips together, pressing them until the skin grew white.

Mantos regained mastery over his tongue. "Bomsoi, I didn't mean to say anything."

The daughter of gods, his daughter and yet not his daughter, gave the tiniest shake of her head. "I'm aware of that."

She pushed through the crowd of Khinish and disappeared. Mantos turned to Emmy, his arms hanging loose with helplessness.

"She'll be fine," Emmy said as she took his elbow to guide him away from the crowd.

"Will she?"

Emmy ushered Mantos away from the split in the earth he had caused and toward the long tent, where soon the next meal would arrive. "Maybe."

* * *

Nunako

There was pain in her daughter's eyes, more pain than Nunako had seen linger in the gray before. Bomsoi had shown no pain when she'd betrayed her and fled to the mountains. Fear, yes. Anger, yes. But no pain. Her willful daughter had been single-minded in her actions. On reflection, Nunako understood the keen sharpness of what they had done. She and Dorai had placed the weight of all their hopes on one back. They'd brought Bomsoi into the world for the purpose of fulfilling their desires. They never wanted her for herself, and they had never accepted her for who she was. Bomsoi had the strength of a god, and the weakness of flesh, but one could overcome the weakness of flesh. Why else be a mother? Bomsoi had two, yet she had none.

Nunako slipped into the dark recesses of Mantos' mind. She filtered through memories of his mother and everything she had done for him. Phen, of mortal flesh, had hatched two younglings together, just like Nunako's mother Meia had, and Phen had given her offspring everything she could. Even her life.

What had Nunako and Dorai given Bomsoi? A curse.

What has been made cannot be unmade but what has been made can be destroyed.

CHAPTER FOURTEEN

Emmy

The village was a whirl of activity as they prepared for their departure. Now that Nunako had inhabited Mantos, they could leave the village. They were to travel to Nowuku, the Khinish capital, though what would happen when they got there, Emmy wasn't sure. With traveling came the need for breaking down camp, packing bags and loading sleds. Once she'd taken care of her own few belongings, Emmy had found herself more of a hindrance than a help.

While the Khinish took everything in hand, Emmy retreated to the solace of the Uloni temple. Inside she was alone, and an immediate silence fell as the door closed. The only noise was her footsteps, which echoed as she approached the temple's center. There was no bright circle of light in stark contrast with surrounding shadow. Instead, there was a diffuse pattern of gray on the floor, seeping from the open roof above.

Emmy kneeled and touched her talons to the ground where the goddess, the Lady of Light herself, had taken her first mortal steps. And it had been Emmy who'd made it happen. She'd reached into Mantos' chest and guided Nunako into his heart. The goddess had touched her. Emmy had imbibed her power.

She'd done it.

Emmy's neck scales bristled, and she didn't understand why. Accomplishment was a strange companion, and she'd shared its path too few times in her life for comfort. She spread her hands wide on the cold stone. Gray light washed over them.

"What next?" she asked the silence. "Now that Nunako's returned to the world, is my purpose complete?" The great fissure in the earth Mantos had wrought with the goddess' power cracked in her mind. "I can't help with grand plans for battles and destruction, so do Mantos or Bomsoi or Nunako even need me any longer?"

Silence was her reply. Emmy sighed. She'd expected nothing else, yet the disappointment was still sharp.

"*A Hand always needs a Heart to guide it.*"

Her head snapped upward at the voice, seeking the speaker. But she was alone in the temple. No one had entered before her, or after.

"Hello?" Emmy's response echoed along the temple's curved walls. She wracked her mind for answers. The voice was familiar. She was certain she'd heard it before, though perhaps only once, but where and when she couldn't recall. She called out, "Speak to me!"

But there was only silence again. Emmy pulled herself to her feet and peered into the temple gloom. It was clear she was still very much alone.

"I'm hearing things," she muttered, though not even an inch of her believed that. She'd been through too much since Middlemerish to dismiss this strangeness.

Emmy padded back toward the temple doors, intending to join the others and make ready to leave. Just as she laid a claw on the handle, a clear footstep sounded from the opposite end of the temple.

Emmy spun on her heel. "Who's there?" But for the third time, only silence met her.

As she turned to leave once more, something dark flickered in her periphery. This time there was more than nothing. When it happened, her chest tightened. The benches in the temple filled as, one by one, smoky figures appeared. The remains of the horrific fire snaked around them like translucent vines. Underneath the cloak of gray, faces and hands flashed red and black. Their features were wreathed in smoke, their skin and armor in constant flux between perfect and beautiful, and the wet blood and black of charred corpses.

Emmy's mouth went dry as two figures stepped toward the center of the temple. They stood in the darkness, waiting for her. The first was tall and slim, long dark fronds bound in an old style of braids, its face obscured. There was gold amid the scorch of its skin. The second figure stood beside it, Uloni tall with something familiar about its stance, but again Emmy couldn't see its face. Purple flashed within the black.

Emmy seized her courage and broke into a run to reach the figures before they disappeared. The weight of every burning gaze around her fell hard on her back. Emmy stopped short as the figures' eyes, one pair of gold and one pair of silver, blinked at her from their burned and unburned faces, underneath their veils of smoke.

When the one with golden eyes spoke, Emmy recognized her. "Please take care of my son."

It was Phen, Mantos' mother. Tendrils of smoke writhed around her, an echo of the gruesome fate her body had received, her neck bearing the slice of Bandim's dagger. Despite the cracking of her burned skin that revealed a sickening slide of flesh underneath, her expression was firm. Brave. Unyielding, just as she had been in the face of death.

As Emmy opened her mouth to ask how Phen was here, the other figure spoke. "Take care of yourself, my daughter," the Uloni said, for the figure's heritage was now clear. "Your mother will always be with you."

"Mother?"

Emmy's voice was an inelegant squeak. She reached out, a sudden desperateness coursing through her. This was her mother, the one who had saved her from a fiery death at the hands of Bandim's wicked Uloni. This was the female who had used her last strength to force a break in the burning temple wall to deposit her youngling into the safety of the snow. This was the female Emmy had longed to know her entire life.

Her mother reached for her. Just as the tips of their talons met, Emmy's mother's hands dissipated like smoke caught by a high wind. Within moments it took the rest of her and captured Phen in its grasp, swirling the two figures upward and out of the open temple roof. The rest of the burned figures followed in their wake, disappearing into the sky in a thin haze.

"No!"

Emmy's cry echoed into the emptiness of the temple. Phen, her mother, the rest of the Uloni, were gone. Once again, Emmy was alone. She stared at the flat gray of the Vhaun sky, wishing the flecks of her mother would come back to her and form into something tangible she could touch, a figure she could talk to or, at the very least, thank. *Mother saved me when even Bomsoi couldn't save her folk, whatever the reason might have been. I wish I could tell her how grateful I am.*

For she was. Despite how intolerable life had been with Krodge, she'd been safe. She'd been alive. The only other Uloni who had that privilege was the one who'd killed their kin. No matter what Krodge might have done, Emmy was thankful for that.

No matter how long she stared at the sky, the smoke that had been her mother and Mantos' mother didn't return. Pulling on the threads of her courage, Emmy burst from the temple, determination driving her steps rather than fear. Mantos needed to know what had happened.

She flew into the blinding whiteness of the village, dodging around Khinish folk loading sleds. Emmy closed her eyes and took a moment to find her center. She sensed the direction she needed to take. As if pulled by a hook in her chest, she found Mantos just as the central pole of the eating tent came down in his strong grip.

The Masvam's expression was almost serene as he worked. Since Nunako had come to him, much of the creased strain of worry had gone from his face. Emmy stopped short in a moment of hesitation. Should she tell him? She didn't want to ruin his peace.

Mantos eased the pole onto the ground. When he noticed her, he gave her an easy smile. It faltered when he saw her face. "Emmy?"

"I saw your mother," she blurted out, "and mine. They came to me in the temple. They were so burned, and I know they weren't there, but they said to remember they would always be with us."

Mantos' expression was a mask, and guilt coiled in Emmy's stomach. She'd robbed him of his serenity by reminding him not just of his mother's untimely demise, but the gruesome nature of it too.

As Emmy went to apologize, Mantos stopped her with a smile. "Deep down, I knew my mother would never leave. It's good to hear that she's with me. You saw your mother, Emmy? How are you?"

This wasn't what she'd expected, and the sense of imbalance it gave her shook her core. She knew she'd had a mother. She'd seen hands that were so likely her mother's save her from a fiery demise. To see her mother so close, so almost there, had been like ice in her heart, constricting its beat. "I..."

She couldn't finish but Mantos seemed to understand. He touched her head, rubbing his thumbs over her temples. "I know."

Before, Emmy would pull away from touch. She would have shrunk in on herself and rejected any comfort, only to flee and cry alone in the safety of her little room off the kitchen in the apothecary shop. Now, in Vhaun, there were no tears. There was no pulling away. She straightened her spine, imbibing Mantos' strength, and nodded. "I'm fine."

Mantos ran his palms down the side of her face and pushed her fronds over her shoulders. "Let's get to work."

* * *

Once again, Emmy was astride a vaemar. It was the beast that had brought their little group to the Uloni village what seemed like an age before. Since their arrival, the two vaemar had lived with the Khinish's sturdy fur-covered kemba and had recovered from their hard journey. Her mount was strong and sure-footed in his oilcloth paw bindings, and Emmy struggled to keep him in check in the winding tread of the convoy of Khinish. Charo and Zecha were snug in one of the covered sleds and Rel was in another, despite protesting she was well enough to ride. Instead, as Bomsoi took her place on Neiruk's back and sped ahead of the rest, Mantos took up the saddle of the other vaemar.

They rode side by side through the narrow mountain passes for three days, the Masvam lost in his thoughts. The silence and the monotonous tread of their long journey lulled Emmy into her own mind, and she wasn't even sure what day it was when Rel's voice entered her thoughts.

"*You seem somber, Emmy.*"

"*I'm just thinking.*"

"*About?*"

Though she didn't want to share her thoughts, she sighed and answered anyway. "*I'm worried. I'm worried about whether Mantos and I will be any match for his brother and his Heart. Bandim's had his power from Dorai for far longer than Mantos with Nunako, and Bandim's Uloni's been using her power for*" —she suppressed a laugh— "*longer than I've even been alive, if she's the one who brought Mantos back to life when he was a youngling.*"

There was a pause, and Emmy could imagine Rel's solemn nod. "*The timing isn't ideal but at least Nunako is here and we can return the balance to the world as Bomsoi wishes. Try not to worry about Mantos. There's great power within him. He'll do the right thing.*"

"*It's taken me so long to learn to use my powers,*" Emmy continued. "*Mantos has had no time at all.*"

"*But the goddess moves within him in ways she does not move in you or me,*" Rel countered. "*It isn't the same. We're blood of the goddess but Mantos is the goddess.*"

Emmy's mouth opened in a soft 'o' of understanding. "*I hadn't thought of it that way. That makes sense. I mean, look at what he did to the ground so soon after Nunako came into him.*" Her heart lifted, the knowledge making it a little lighter. "*Perhaps I shouldn't be so worried.*"

Rel's voice disappeared, and Emmy turned her thoughts to herself once more.

"*I appreciate your concern.*"

The interjection of the new voice made Emmy jump in her saddle, sending her vaemar into a skitter. Mantos grabbed for the creature's reins and smiled at her with kind eyes. The voice had been his.

"*How can you speak like this?*" she asked, though as soon as she'd uttered the words, she grimaced.

Mantos chuckled and kept his gaze focused on those ahead of them. "*I started hearing your secret communication as soon as Nunako came to me. It didn't take long to master.*"

Emmy's lower lip jutted out. "*Well, it wasn't easy for me. Maybe everything is easier when you're a god.*"

Mantos laughed aloud. It was a hearty sound Emmy hadn't heard before. It was genuine, the laugh that comes from deep inside. "*I'm not a god but I suppose I'm close. The goddess moves within me. There are so many things I can do now I never dreamed possible, like speaking without speaking.*"

A pang of regret crossed from Mantos to Emmy. Images of coded letters flashed through Emmy's mind.

"*You could have used this to speak to him, couldn't you?*" she asked.

Though they'd never spoken of it, Emmy knew the 'him' was Prince Fonbir. They'd shared all of themselves as the goddess used Emmy as a conduit.

Mantos licked his lips. "*If we'd had this strange communication, we'd have been even closer than we were. Being able to speak to Fonbir every day, if not see him, would make my heart sing.*"

It did. Emmy could feel it. Then the joy disappeared.

Emmy mirrored the sorrowful crease of Mantos' eyeridges without meaning to. "*You're worried about seeing him again.*"

Mantos nodded. "*I am. What if he rejects me?*"

"*I'm afraid I can't give you any advice,*" Emmy said. "*I don't feel for folk the way you and most others do. All I can say is that the ones closest to me my whole life, like Zecha, have never abandoned me, even when I've been less than a pleasant friend.*" She smiled as Zecha's wide grin came unbidden into her mind. Mantos smiled too. "*I think Zecha would say if he loves you, he'll always love you. Charo lied to us about her whole life before Zecha found her in the Wailing Woods, bleeding to death, but it didn't change how he felt about her. She tried to keep their egg from him, but he didn't hold it against her. He loves her no matter what.*"

"*I love Fonbir no matter what,*" Mantos echoed. "*I can only hope he's as good as Zecha.*"

One side of Emmy's mouth lifted in mirth. "*Zecha's especially good. I don't think anyone else is as good as him.*"

Mantos managed a chuckle. "*Then I hope Fonbir can be almost as good as Zecha.*" His smile shifted as his focus turned inward. "*I hope he can forgive me. It's like there's so much potential in me. I want to show Fonbir that I can be better. It's like I'm just an egg again and I'm hatching all over again as something new.*"

Emmy managed a genuine smile at that. "*I know that feeling. It's how I felt when I found out everything about my folk, my home, and how I came to be with my mistress.*"

Mantos' next words were friendly, but the mood shifted as the winds turned. The convoy halted as the lead Khinish held up a hand. A scout had returned. A runner came through the sleds, spreading the word.

"*Wanukëks,*" the Kiseoyan said, eying Mantos.

"*Rel,*" Emmy asked, "*what does that word mean?*"

There was a pause before Rel answered. "*I don't know many of their words, but I know that one. It's a word for an enemy. It's the Khinish word for Masvam.*"

CHAPTER FIFTEEN

Mantos

The mention of his folk made Mantos' neck scales flare. *Masvams in the mountains? We don't venture into the Great Northern Range. Why are they here?* The Khinish broke from their convoy and fell into military formation, wielding swords and pikes and shields. They kept their shoulders together and their backs to the sleds, facing outward in a tight flank. Everyone was ready. Even the most inexperienced bore their weapons with a hard set to their pale faces. Zecha's Metakalan brown and red shone bright among the gray, his eyes as deadly as the arrow nocked in his bow. The only folk Mantos couldn't see were Rel and Charo. He squeezed his talons around his vaemar's reins. All he had was the hope they would stay safe. In the mountains, only the strong survived.

Beside him, Emmy's power surged as she conferred with Rel. Mantos forced his focus inward, dulling their clipped conversation, then pushed his concentration outward to the encroaching forces. At first there was nothing; then came a vibration in the ground no one else noticed. Mantos felt the sets of feet thundering toward them. There was something discordant about it. Something strange.

He called out in recognition as the Khinish raised their weapons. "They're coming from two directions!"

A pack of Masvams on vaemar were careening from due south. Another pack, powered only by their legs, came from southwest. They were on a collision course; the point of meeting was right where the Khinish convoy was, deep in a mountainous narrow.

The Khinish commander shouted orders Mantos couldn't understand. Emmy's vaemar, sensing the tension, shuddered, and huffed out steaming breaths, its wrapped paws dancing from side to side.

"There's something wrong," Mantos said.

"There are Masvams in the mountains," Emmy said as she calmed the vaemar into stillness, "that's 'something wrong.'"

"No," Mantos said, the firmness of his tone echoing against the ice and rock around them. "They're not coming for us."

He couldn't answer Emmy's unasked question, because as soon as her lips parted, the world erupted. An onslaught of Masvams exploded into the narrow pass, followed by another. Everything was chaos. Mantos' vaemar skipped to the side as Masvams broke through the Khinish line like cannon fire. Then another line of Masvams shot behind them but they were different. The mass was of soldiers in thick cloaks, his brother's black livery flickering from underneath the dark fur. Mantos' gaze flicked to the first Masvams. They didn't have a uniform, didn't wear the colors of Bandim and Dorai.

Tiboli red and orange. Vnarr white and red. Gilgram greens. Rserra black and silver. Armaren pink, red, and green. And most prominent of all, Yru yellow and blue.

Mantos' words disappeared in the din of battle, so he used his new voice. "*Emmy! Rel! My brother's soldiers are the ones in black with the fire cipher. The others aren't our enemies!*"

"*They're all Masvams!*" Emmy answered.

"*The others are rebels!*" Mantos replied. "*They must be. They're wearing their own house colors, all working together. We have to help them!*"

"*What?*"

Emmy's disbelief disrupted as her vaemar fought and bucked and unseated her, catapulting her upward in an arc. Before Mantos managed to twitch his reins to go to her, she had wrenched a twist of ice from the narrow mountain walls to control her fall. She fell into the battle, and Mantos lost sight of her, but he felt her spirit.

"Traitor!"

The word came with a blow levied toward Mantos' head. He ducked away, almost coming off the saddle, and whirled his vaemar to face his attacker. It was one of Bandim's soldiers, seething with controlled and deadly rage. Dressed in anything but his brother's livery, it marked Mantos as an enemy. A rebel.

Mantos held up a hand. "The true traitor is the one who sits on the throne."

He swept his hand downward, then pulled up. His muscles burned as he wrenched the ground underneath the soldier, ripping it apart, sending him jolting to the side and downward. Another Masvam clad in the colors of Dorai came for him, but Mantos cast him aside in the same way. There was a shudder as the whole pass trembled under his power.

"*This might not be the best place to use your powers!*" Emmy said. "*You'll bring the whole pass down on us!*"

"*You're right, you're right!*" Mantos dove from the saddle and snatched up a discarded Masvam scimitar. The weight was comfortable in its familiarity, yet it didn't seem right. It was an enemy's weapon.

In the near distance, flashes of ice shot across the passage. Emmy's actions were strong, but even under the chaos of the battle, Mantos heard her internal monologue. Terror overwhelmed her. She knew she couldn't do this, yet she fought, and she did. From within came a double pang of pride. One was from Mantos himself, the other from Nunako. *She's—I'm—so proud of who Emmy's become.*

The moment ended as a sword came for him, wielded by another Masvam clad in black and flame. Mantos stepped beyond its reach and parried the next blow, sliding the soldier's blade from his own. Masvam upon Masvam came for him, but even as he held Nunako's pulsing power at bay, they were no match for him. They might all have trained but no one in the empire had trained harder than Mantos.

As two soldiers came in tandem, Mantos snatched another discarded weapon from the crimson snow and fought them both back. Nunako's rage rumbled inside him, her power aching within his limbs. She wanted to come out. She wanted to fight. *Not now*, Mantos thought, though whether he spoke to himself or Nunako or both, he wasn't sure. *We'll do more damage than good.* Nunako twisted within him, flustered, but pulled away from the tips of his talons. Mantos gave her silent thanks and set his jaw as more soldiers came for him, and he put them down one by one by one, forcing himself further into the maw of the battle.

Emmy fought with glittering ice, and the darkness of Bandim's forces swirled with the gray of the Khinish, interspersed with the patchwork colors of the Masvam rebels. A flicker of yellow and green flashed in the corner of Mantos' vision. He knew only one folk with those colors. His fear for Charo and her unlaid egg rose hot and heavy, and he turned in the wrong direction. His head snapped back as one of Bandim's soldiers lunged for him, frothing with rage. Mantos knew he wouldn't parry in time.

An arrow shot from above, piercing the Masvam through the temple. He fell, bringing fresh red to the blackening snow. Mantos followed the line of the shot. Zecha, from a miraculous perch on the icy pass walls, gave him a salute.

Mantos grinned. One of Bandim's finest felled by an untrained Metakalan. Glorious.

Despite the save, Mantos was unwilling to need help again, and returned to the fray. A group of rebels had backed against the pass wall, outnumbered though they fought hard. Mantos swung toward the soldiers, felling one, then another. The rebels' eyes flashed at him, uncertain which side he was on. He wasn't one of them, but he wasn't one of Bandim's.

Then one of them spoke. "Mantos?"

He knew that voice. He knew the slight lilt, the almost provincial accent that marked him as someone brought up in the court, but not born there.

For a moment, everything stopped. There was no sound. There was no movement. In the still quiet, Mantos recognized the face before him, the face that looked like his mother's, but red where hers was gold. The face painted with Yru yellow and blue.

"*Elsya?*"

Time started with a jolt, and the battle continued. Mantos' mind whirled. Elsya, his cousin Elsya, whose father was Solseo of House Yru, his mother's brother. Mantos would have given anything for the power of the goddess to extend into Elsya's mind to seek answers. Why was Elsya here? Was he a rebel? A thought clanged in Mantos' head as a sword crashed against his. Elsya was the next in line for the throne after Bandim. Not knowing Mantos was alive, Elsya would have believed himself the heir. The true heir. Elsya was the leader of the rebellion. Elsya was good, kind, and noble. He would never allow Darkness to reign in the empire.

Not 'Darkness,' Nunako corrected without words. *The evil of arrogance. The evil of hate.*

Mantos thrust his sword into the chest of another foe, and as a live enemy replaced the dead one, Elsya called out to his rebels, "Protect this Masvam! He's one of us!" At that simple command, they surrounded Mantos with loyalty, and the surge of power that flowed through him thundered to the tips of his talons. He quelled it as best he could, but he had suppressed Nunako for too long.

The narrowness of the pass filled with the fallen, both Masvam and Khinish, rebels and forces of the empire alike. Though thinned, the fight went on, the mountain filled with the clang of metal, cries for mercy, and the stench of blood.

Enough, came a thought. Mantos wasn't sure if it was his or Nunako's. He raised his hands as they pulsed with unplanned power, then brought them down to the ground. A ripple went through the pass, knocking everyone from their feet, regardless of creed or colors. The living toppled onto the dead and for a moment there was silence, apart from the low moans of the wounded.

"Hear this!" Mantos called, his words echoing against the sheer rock walls. "Tell your Sun Emperor that his reign is ending. Tell Bandim Tiboli, or Bandim-Dorai, whatever he calls himself, that the true heir is coming. Tell him that Mantos will wear the crown, and if I have to break the world in two to wrench it from his heathen hands, I will!"

Khinish whispered. The only word Mantos recognized was "Keyëyñopo."

The World Breaker. Him.

The rebels stared at Elsya, then at Mantos.

"Mantos?" one asked. "Mantos Tiboli? But he's dead."

"Yes, Mantos Tiboli," Elsya replied, clamping Mantos' shoulder. "Not dead but very much alive. The rightful heir to the Masvam Empire."

Through the thin distance, a Masvam voice returned. "Long live the Sun Emperor!"

That broke the peace, and the battle erupted again. The rebels were equal parts confused and enthralled, and fought back harder than Bandim's thinned forces could stand. Some of these folk would have seen him on the balcony in the speaker's bowl, dressed in white, would have heard the cry go up, "*The emperor is dead*!" They would have seen him fall, crumpled and dead. They would have seen him laid on his funeral pyre, ready for his journey to the Light.

But Mantos wasn't dead any longer. He was alive and vibrating with the belief of the surrounding folk, the Hand of Nunako pulsing with the power of her Heart. His talons tingled in anticipation of bringing Nunako's greatness forth once again.

"*Mantos, be careful—*"

Emmy's voice in his mind stopped, like a head cleaved from a neck, and Mantos couldn't feel her any longer. Without her, Nunako's power dimmed like a half-lidded eye.

"*Emmy?*" No response. "*Rel?*"

There was panic in Rel's tone. "*I can't feel her anymore!*"

At the far end of the mountain pass, a figure stood silhouetted against the brightness of a snowy sky untainted with blood. Mantos could make out no details of its face, but it was clear it was carrying a burden: a tall, drooping burden with a slack tail.

"Emmy!"

The figure, and its burden, disappeared.

"No, no, no!" Mantos cried, his neck scales pulsing.

Elsya stared, dumbfounded, but there was no time for clarification. All Mantos wanted to do was careen through the tightness of the pass, the snow slick and thick with blood, and grab Emmy back from whoever had taken her. But he couldn't. He needed her, but the others here and now needed him too. Though his power drooped like a parched flower at the end of Decos, he couldn't go after her. He'd never make it, and even if he used what remained of Nunako's might, it wouldn't be enough to get him through. Either that, or the slightest tremor would kill them all.

Mantos returned his attention to the other Masvams. Unlike Emmy's captor, they weren't retreating from the mountain, but stayed to fight on. His Heart might have been stolen, he thought as he raged through the enemy, but that didn't mean they would lose the battle.

They fought long and hard until the pass was still, darkening as night fell. They gave mercy to the wounded who wouldn't make it from the mountains alive. Charo and Zecha came to him, both flushed with battle and without serious injury, their gazes flitting around him.

"Where's Emmy?" Charo asked.

They hadn't seen. They didn't know.

Mantos' face darkened. "She's gone."

Zecha paled. "Gone? But we need her. Bomsoi needs her. You need her." Charo touched him with a bloodstained hand, but Zecha refused to calm. "Emmy can't be gone. We have to get her back, now."

"We'll get her back," Mantos said, the tone of his voice taut with the strength of his father's conviction, the conviction of an emperor who saw everything. "Now we need to get to Nowuku."

"But Emmy," Zecha said, his eyeridges upturned and his mouth pleading.

"Emmy's strong," Mantos said. "She's the strongest of all of us."

Those words were no platitudes. It was, as far as Mantos knew, the absolute truth.

CHAPTER SIXTEEN

Mantos

It was a murky dawn when they arrived in Nowuku. A party of King Khitarian's advisers, attendants, and a thick ring of soldiers met Mantos and the rest. They raised their weapons at the band of unknown Masvams who had arrived with the Kiseoyans.

In their midst was Bomsoi, whose face was ashen when she spoke. "Where is Emmy? I can't sense her."

As the Khinish whirled around them, Mantos shook his head. "She's gone. One of Bandim's soldiers took her. One minute I could sense her, and the next, I couldn't. I glimpsed her on the shoulders of a Masvam before he disappeared with her. The battle wasn't over. We couldn't save her."

"I'll find her," Bomsoi said, with more panic in her tone than Mantos had ever heard. Before Mantos could object, pointing out the vastness of the passage of time, Bomsoi shook her head. "I have Neiruk. I'll find her."

Mantos' every instinct told him that Bomsoi's search would be in vain, but another part of him remained silent. If it Fonbir was missing, Mantos would turn over the world to find him. Bomsoi could only feel the same for Emmy.

"Good luck," was all he responded with.

Bomsoi disappeared, emerging a few minutes later from the ragged mountain astride Neiruk. The Prago shrieked, and they disappeared into the gray morning.

A soft cough caught Mantos' attention and when he turned, an officious noble was standing before him. He spoke in Masvam. "You are Mantos Tiboli."

The name made Mantos grit his teeth. "I am only Mantos now. I no longer use my house name."

The noble ducked his head. "Mantos, then." He pulled a small pail of snow from inside his robe and touched some melting whiteness to either side of Mantos' first horn. "My name is Ta Emba, and with Their Highness King Khitarian's authority, I welcome you to our capital."

The words caught Mantos off guard at first, but stories told to him by Khinish of their ways returned. Their monarch was always a king, and Khitarian was neither male nor female.

"King Khitarian is gracious in their welcome," Mantos replied. Old Master Abe would have been proud of his deportment. "I hope the same welcome will extend to my fellow Masvams." He gestured to Elsya and his rebels. "These folk are our allies. They were fleeing from my brother's army. They stand toe to toe against him, not by his side."

The Khinish who had traveled from the Uloni village confirmed the message, but they didn't lower their weapons until Ta Emba gave a nod.

"As long as these Masvams are friends, they're welcome to take sanctuary here," he said, speaking loud enough for all to hear. "But know that King Khitarian deals with traitors in a swift and brutal fashion. There will be no mercy."

Elsya stepped forward and dropped onto one knee, placing his fist in the snow. "We accept your offer of sanctuary with humble thanks."

Ta Emba raised an eyeridge as his gaze flicked from Mantos to Elsya, then onward to the other Masvams. "You look so different from one another. Your Masvam Empire is strange."

"Our Masvam Empire is large," Mantos said. "Not all Masvams are alike."

No one lost the weight of his statement. When Elsya rose, he gave Mantos a tight nod. "Too true, cousin."

"Cousin?" Ta Emba asked, his other eyeridge joining the first. "By blood?"

"My mother and his father were siblings," Mantos said.

Ta Emba's face darkened. "So both of you are blood of the Sun Emperor."

"We can't help blood," Elsya said.

The razor edge of his tone grazed against Mantos, but he couldn't deny his cousin the anger. Elsya must have noticed, for he placed a brief touch above the base of Mantos' tail and said, "We have much to discuss."

With the Khinish weapons lowered, the atmosphere changed, and they welcomed the Masvams inside for shelter. Under Ta Emba's guidance, the soldiers went in a different direction from Mantos and the others. Elsya tried to insist on going with the other Masvams, but Ta Emba's clear love for protocol overruled him.

"We treat the blood of royalty with respect, regardless of whose blood it is."

As Elsya tried to splutter an explanation as Emba led them into the palace, that his father had only been an overduke and not a prince, Mantos raised a hand to quiet him.

"If we stay together, we'll have more chance to talk. And my uncle was an overduke?" Was?"

A deep darkness passed over Elsya's face that struck Mantos like a discordant clang.

"Your brother murdered my father," Elsya said. The muscles of his jaws tightened with his rage. "He burned a hole right through his chest and strung him up on the walls of the palace for all to see. I swear, Mantos, if I get the chance, I'll kill Bandim with my claws alone."

Mantos shook his head. "I'm sorry, Elsya."

They walked in step with one another as they slipped deeper into the carved interior of the palace.

"It's not your doing, Mantos. You needn't apologize for your brother's idiocy. You did that enough in our youth. He's grown enough to be responsible for himself." Elsya threw a sideways glance. "You do need to explain what happened to you. Like everyone else in the empire, I thought you were dead. Where have you been? And how in the name of the Lady of Light did you shake the earth?"

The title *Lady of Light* lit something within Mantos' belly, kindling the power that had been deadened since Emmy's capture.

"It's a long story," he said, "and one I'll tell you. Later, though. For now, we attend to other matters."

Ta Emba deposited them in adjoining chambers. He instructed them to wash and rest, and that he would send an attendant when King Khitarian was ready to receive them. When Elsya disappeared behind his door, Mantos' power dropped away again. Disappointment bloomed.

He slipped into his own plush chamber. A haze of steam carried him into an antechamber, and his jaw dropped in delight. Sunk into the floor was a bath lined with ornate tiles, filled with fragrant hot water. How long had it been since he'd had a bath? How long had it been since he'd had any form of comfort?

That word sent his thoughts skipping through all the luxuries he'd left behind but stopped at the foot of a memory that made Mantos' heart ache. The greatest comfort he'd ever received was lying in the arms of his beloved. Fonbir was here, and he might've read Mantos' letter. He might've accepted his apology. Mantos might even get to see him.

Mantos' momentary joy sank like a boulder tossed in the sea. No matter what happened, whether Fonbir forgave him or not, his love was to marry King Khitarian. A cold sorrow permeated Mantos, and the water didn't seem as inviting. As he tried to convince himself that Fonbir would never forgive him for his selfishness anyway, that it didn't matter, Mantos stripped down to his skin and armor and stepped into the bath. At first it scalded, but after a moment was glorious. The cold inside him abated. It didn't matter what might or might not happen between the two princes. There were more pressing matters at stake. He had an empire to reclaim. He had a goddess to vanquish.

Though he knew all that, not even the hot water could relieve Mantos of the deep-set ache left by Fonbir's absence. Despite the pain and the worry about what was to come, Mantos slipped into a half-sleep. At first his mind filled with visions of Fonbir's smile, the sound of Fonbir's laughter, the sight of his beautiful handwriting in their coded letters. Then the pleasant memories jerked away, replaced with the sight of Uncle Solseo and the gaping, smoking hole in his chest.

Then it wasn't Solseo, but his mother.

Mantos jerked awake, sending water cascading around him. As his breathing calmed, his determination rose. He wrenched himself from the still-steaming water and strode into his chamber. He would stop Bandim no matter what, even if it took Mantos' third and final death.

* * *

The king summoned Mantos and Elsya after what couldn't have been enough time to rest. When the attendant pushed open a set of heavy doors into the meeting chamber, Mantos saw something he didn't expect. In his own palace, and in the palace of Queen Valentia, meetings of royals happened around huge wooden tables, the gathered folk sat on straight-backed chairs. The Khinish did things in a different way.

There was no grand table surrounded by chairs. Instead there was a sunken, circular hollow carved into the floor, illuminated with moondust. Within the hollow were benches plush with pillows of metallic fabrics, offset with the occasional flash of ruby or sapphire. He exchanged a wide-eyed look with Elsya. Though he'd never had personal business in the congress chamber, his father had been one of Emperor Braslen's overdukes. Elsya would have known well that this wasn't close to the Masvam way. At the top of the sunken circle sat a Khinish figure resplendent in silver and white, flanked by two figures regarding Mantos with cool blue eyes.

King Khitarian wore a circlet of silver atop their head, with clusters of moonpearls set on either side of their first horn. Their heart-shaped face glimmered opal and silver in the ethereal light. Then Mantos flicked his eyes left. His throat tightened at the sight of the beautiful white-eyed figure sitting on Khitarian's right.

Fonbir.

Though he wanted to rush forward and seize his love into an embrace that would never end, Mantos kept hold of his restraint as if letting go would kill him. The attendant ushered him and Elsya forward, down into the circle and within steps of the king.

"Your Majesty, I present to you Prince Mantos, heir to the Masvam throne, and Elsya of House Yru, his noble cousin."

Though Mantos had given up his house name, it rang bare compared to his cousin's full title. At the king's side, Fonbir shifted and pressed his lips until they lost all color, but he remained silent.

Khitarian's mouth stayed closed, but their hands moved. The figure sitting on their left was Khinish and seemed to interpret the king's gestures and turn them into words. Realization came to Mantos. Khitarian couldn't speak, or couldn't hear, or both.

"You're most welcome in my kingdom, Prince Mantos and Elsya of House Yru." Mantos took a moment to pull his eyes back to Khitarian. When he managed, he glimpsed a burning stare from Fonbir. "Everything under the Arc of the Sky seems turned around. But we Kiseoyans welcome change. We would not have our mountains if we did not have the great quakes that build them."

Beside him, Elsya tensed, not understanding. Mantos knew what Khitarian meant. He'd read the same knowledge passed down through cycle to cycle, the great shaking that came from within the ground and pulled up mountains. The thought of it brought an echo of power trembling within him. The mountains were Nunako's doing.

"The world is not as it was when my father still lived," Mantos replied. "It feels as though his death was cycles ago, but we haven't even seen one full turn of the seasons."

"The good thing about a circle," Khitarian said, "is that it always turns. There is no beginning and no end. Bandim Tiboli isn't the end. Even as he rises and we fall, he will fall as we rise. Such is the way of things." Mantos nodded his reply, saying nothing in the face of such truth. "So tell me, are the reports of my soldiers true? Have you gained the powers of the one you call Nunako?"

He should have felt a buzz of power at his goddess,' his name, but Mantos felt a dark nothing. "It's true, but I've lost my Heart. I'm not sure what that means for me."

"There's a story here you must tell," Khitarian said, "but we'll wait for everyone to arrive. I don't know about you, but I hate to repeat myself."

When the rest arrived, Mantos and Elsya sat on plump cushions not too far from Khitarian and Fonbir. Across from them, Princess Valaria sat, shooting alternating looks of concern at Fonbir and viperous anger at Mantos. While she'd said before she understood a little of why Fonbir loved him, her fury at his actions had resurfaced now that she saw them both in the same room.

Ta Emba joined them, followed by other Khinish of consequence. The last to arrive was a still-weak Rel, flanked on either side by a harried Zecha and a weary Charo. Mantos shot a look at Khitarian, expecting the king to send the common folk away, but they didn't. Instead, they gestured for all three to take seats.

The king must have expected no one else, for once Rel, Charo, and Zecha settled, they turned to Mantos. "You have much to tell us, so please, tell us."

Mantos pushed his tongue into the warm softness of his cheek, grappling for the best place to start. Bomsoi was best placed to start this story. She would have known what to say. But as he looked at the figures gathered, all eyes on him, the bereft emptiness without Bomsoi and Emmy pushed his voice into action. He owed it to them, to Emmy, to be strong and tell what he knew. So he did.

By the time Mantos had given up his knowledge—about himself and his cowardice, about Bandim and Bomsoi and the Uloni and the Grandmother—his throat rasped with the effort. Throughout his tale, Khitarian's face had remained as still as the rocks of their palace. Perhaps that was what earned them the title 'Mountainess.'

She spoke with her hands. "It must seem like all this happened over many cycles, not within a mere two seasons. We Kiseoyans have long kept our distance from the rest of the world, and it would seem we've had good reason to do so. Things are different in our mountains. Calmer and perhaps simpler." Her brows dropped low, her whole face darkening. "However, I warned my aunt and uncle that a change was coming. You might worship other gods, but we in the mountains cling to the Grandmother of the World as the one who rules over everything under the Arc."

Khitarian stood and paced forward into the center of the sunken circle. Every head swiveled to follow them, except the translator, who moved to ensure she could see their hands at all times. Mantos glimpsed Elsya in the corner of his eye. His cousin had broken from watching Khitarian to send a strange glance Mantos' way. The emotion was too mixed to understand. There was awe. There was horror. There was fear.

The king continued. "The Grandmother came to me when I was a mere ten cycles old. She told me I would bring a great change to this world. She told me I would be okkum, what you might call a third way of gendering, and not to fear it. She told me Kiseoyan ways must change, and that if my uncle could not listen to what she had to say, then I would be the one who would need to act on her behalf."

Khitarian cast a look at Ta Emba that was half-sorrowful, half-grateful. "She must have gone to my dear uncle, the late King Jaka Narr, and also told him what she needed. Alas, his mind was not strong enough for her, and he descended into madness. He killed my aunt, and before he plunged the blade into his own neck and caused such a great red flood, he turned it on me."

Dread coiled in Mantos' belly. Family members bringing death to one another was painful and familiar.

"Before killing himself, he tried to force the blade into my throat. Though I couldn't hear what he said, I remember well the words that passed his lips. '*You cannot hear, and you cannot speak. You will not rule behind me.*' Many folk in my life have tried to tell me I 'cannot.' None of them have been right. I heard the words of the Grandmother. So I stepped away and allowed my uncle to take his own life. His death heralded the change in our Kiseoyan ways."

Khitarian turned to face Mantos, their face as hard and beautiful as an icy mountainside and their hands graceful in communication. "We Kiseoyans will not stand by and allow Bandim Tiboli to destroy the Grandmother's world. We lingered here too long when our actions may have helped prevent the fall of Althemer. We will linger no longer. When I leave this world to face her and prove my worth, I must be able to hold my head high and prove to the Grandmother that I deserve her love. Thus, Mantos, formerly Tiboli and now blood of the Grandmother, the power of the Kiseoyans is yours." The edge of her mouth quirked in a sudden smile. "A daughter thinks she knows better, but a mother always knows more. Dorai will fall. It is the Grandmother's will."

Khitarian's words brought a bloom of power into Mantos' chest, and he stood. "Thank you, King Khitarian. Your trust and your belief will make us all strong. On behalf of all who seek to throw off the shackles of my brother and Dorai, I thank you. The Grandmother," he said, though in his mind Nunako whispered, *my mother*, "chose you for a reason, just like Bandim and me. We are all marked. Together, we'll do what we must to return balance to the world."

Something else sparked power within him. From his side, Elsya's face had lost its fear and was lit with awe and pride. There was something even more. Mantos flitted from face to face, and strength came from all of them, even Rel in her pain and exhaustion. Still, that wasn't it. Mantos came upon the source.

His eyes met Fonbir's, and everything was clear, bright, and white.

CHAPTER SEVENTEEN

Fonbir

The sight of Mantos elicited so many emotions at once, Fonbir couldn't decide whether to laugh or cry to fall into a blazing rage. Khitarian drew him aside after the meeting. The king, along with their ever-present translator Tima, ushered him to an enclave to the side of the main meeting chamber. It was lit with moondust lanterns set into the wall. When they sat on a plush bench, Fonbir's chain weighed him down.

When they spoke, Khitarian's expression was unbearably soft. "*Tell me.*"

Fonbir bit his lower lip, the roil of emotion inside threatening to spill over. What could he say? That Mantos, formerly of House Tiboli, was the one Fonbir had been in love with since they'd gendered? That he was his best friend, the one who'd always been waiting for him in a ciphered reply? The one Fonbir would do anything to comfort? To support, to live to die by. How could he say any of this to his betrothed?

Khitarian placed a gentle hand around Fonbir's jaw and turned his face toward them. "*Tell me*," they repeated.

Fonbir's eyes flicked to Tima as she translated his words. "It's very complicated."

Khitarian caught the look and smiled back. "You know by now my Tima is trustworthy. Don't add that worry to your already substantial pile. Now, tell me."

Though he tried to speak, no sound came. Fonbir's tongue refused to form the words. His hands twitched, wishing as he did every time he spoke to Khitarian that he spoke their language. How much easier it would be to explain this himself, directly to them. With a sigh, he faced Khitarian and made two signs with trembling hands. It was the best he could do.

Masvam.

Love.

Fonbir couldn't sign 'Mantos,' if a sign even existed for the name. Khitarian's eyeridges closed together in thought before they smoothed in understanding.

"You're in love with the Masvam," they clarified.

There was no tone to Khitarian's language, but they needed nothing oral to convey emotion. Fonbir braced himself. He'd expected derision, fire and earthquakes, punishment, and scorn. Instead, Khitarian's blue eyes bloomed with compassion.

"I see." They reached to take up one of Fonbir's hands, cradling his dark talons in their pale ones while signing with their other hand. "How long?"

Fonbir opened his mouth to speak but stopped when another sign came to him. He raised his free hand and swept it in a slow circle.

Forever.

After a squeeze, Khitarian withdrew their touch. "When did you see him last?"

"On Althemer," Fonbir said aloud, his knowledge of signs failing him. "I saw him just before he fled."

Something must have passed across his face, as Khitarian frowned. "You're angry with him."

"He left me," Fonbir blurted, adding the cross-handed symbol for betrayal to his words.

"But you still love him?"

Fonbir's back curved as his body deflated. His chin hit his chest and his tail went limp. He signed, "Yes."

Khitarian hooked their thumb under his head and tilted it back up. They passed a comforting stroke across his cheek. Fonbir tried to turn away from the compassion staring at him, but Khitarian's touch became firm, their expression fierce.

"Go to him," they signed with their other hand. "Love is love."

"But our alliance. Us."

Khitarian released his face, relaxing their expression into kindness before a wave of something else passed over it. It looked almost like guilt.

"I will tell you the truth, because you deserve it," Khitarian said. "The alliance between our folk doesn't depend on our marriage, and it never did."

Relief and a strange form of sadness twisted in Fonbir's gut. "It doesn't? It didn't?"

Khitarian dipped their head in a tiny nod. "It doesn't. I offered my hand because that's the way folk do things outside these mountains. The Grandmother of the World set me on this path, and that is the reason I help Althemer. Not because we are, or were, to marry."

Were. Fonbir sat back, blinking. "Were?"

Khitarian tucked a stray frond behind Fonbir's ear and smiled. "Love is a sacred thing. It shouldn't bend or break, not even for a king. Now go to him." Their smile widened, and Khitarian's face became the most beautiful sight in the world. "Love is love."

"But my sister," Fonbir started.

Khitarian pressed a talon to his lips and shook his head. "Our alliance doesn't depend on our marriage," they repeated. "I will explain my position to Princess Valaria. Whether she approves of your love is a different matter. I can't help you with that. I can only hope she'll understand."

Fear gave way to a hope as fragile as the first blossom in Merish. Anger pulsed in the background, but anticipation at seeing Mantos again, of being with him again, of not having to hide or worry, pushed aside all else.

Fonbir leaned forward and enveloped the king in an embrace. Khitarian was like something from a storybook. They were the moral and loyal king who always did the right thing.

"Thank you," Fonbir whispered. Then, realizing, he pulled back and signed the phrase so Khitarian could understand. The king passed an affectionate hand over Fonbir's cheek.

"Love is love."

* * *

It took both a moment and an eternity to reach Mantos' chambers. Fonbir went to knock on the door but paused, sucking in a deliberate breath to calm himself. He'd rushed straight from Khitarian with such speed he hadn't stopped to reflect. He'd considered nothing other than going to Mantos, but now, as he stood in front of the dark door to his chamber, possibilities spread before him like ink in water.

Nothing would be the same after this. Whatever happened once he stepped across the threshold into Mantos' rooms, he couldn't undo it. What would he do? What should he do? Fonbir cursed his haste, wishing he'd gone to seek Oth's council beforehand. A small part of him knew that no matter what Othelan had suggested, Fonbir would have done what he wanted. But at least having the conversation with his loyal attendant would have given him time to contemplate.

His throat tightened. His fists clenched. The chain about his waist weighed as heavy as his thoughts. What did he want? Everything and nothing. He desired Mantos but wanted all the events of Merish and Decos and Vhaun to disappear, to never have happened. His talons twitched at the idea of touching his love again, just as they had in the brief interlude between Mantos' resurrection and his disappearance, but they also flexed in a desire to strike him hard enough to leave a bruise.

Would what they could have now be enough? Would Fonbir ever be able to look at Mantos again without feeling the punch of betrayal in his stomach? Would he ever be able to show his love without the sour taint of anger?

Whatever the case, Mantos decided for him. The latch clicked from the inside and the door swung open, revealing the Masvam prince, framed in the arch and painted with surprise.

"Fonbir." His voice was breathy. "I—"

The moment took on its own momentum and Fonbir jerked out a hand, pushing Mantos on the chestplate and propelling him backward into the chamber. He thrust the door closed behind him so hard he was sure the sound resonated through the entire mountain.

With a little distance between them, they stared at one another. Fonbir wrestled with his breathing, forcing it under his control again. As his own emotions roiled, he studied the play of feelings on Mantos' handsome, wicked face. There was confusion tinged with affront, though it delighted Fonbir to see an edge of fear lingering too. *Good. He should be afraid.*

As soon as Mantos parted his lips to speak, Fonbir snapped his hand up to stop him.

"Don't. Don't you dare speak. You will listen to me and you will not utter so much as a squeak until I'm done. Understood?"

To his credit, Mantos answered with a silent nod.

Fonbir drew in one steady breath to center himself before he began. "I've spent so much time hating you, Mantos." The other prince flinched at the words, but Fonbir refused to give in to compassion. He needed to speak the truth. "I thought I knew you. I thought you cared for me, that we wanted the same things. I thought there was a chance, even a tiny one, for us to be together." A laugh escaped him, curt and sharp. "But then you left. You ran away like a coward, ignoring all your responsibilities. You abandoned your mother. You abandoned me."

Fonbir paused for a moment, waiting for Mantos' ire to overflow into conflict. It never came. Mantos stood still, his back straight and his tail still, his eyes round with sorrow. Though his heart lurched, Fonbir again refused to give in, willed the welling tears to stay unshed, and continued.

"You placed your own desires above everything else. I never believed you were like that. I'd never have dreamed you could be so thoughtless. Through all the cycles we wrote to one another, and the times we saw each other, you were always so compassionate, so aware of the needs of others, of my needs. You spoke about your father's conquests with such understanding of how folk suffered under the machine of war that I thought, I knew in my heart, you'd do whatever you could to stop Bandim from doing them same." He dropped his voice low. "But then you didn't. You. Ran. Away. You abandoned us all. You refused to help. And so many folk have died, Mantos." The tears that had threatened escaped, tracing his skin in soft arcs. Fonbir cursed them. He never cried. "My mother died. Fylica died. We don't know how many Althemerians have perished under Bandim's boots. And I can't help but think if you'd just stayed with me, with us, and did what Bomsoi wanted you to do then, that they wouldn't be dead. That my home would still be there."

Fonbir dashed the wetness from his face with the back of one hand and shook his head. He kept Mantos' gaze locked in his own. He plunged his other hand into his Khinish clothing and pulled out a folded piece of parchment. When Mantos saw it, the recognition brought fresh misery to his eyes. "You sent this letter to me via Valaria. At first, I wanted to throw it straight into a brazier and watch it burn. But you can thank Valaria for the fact I did read it. Can you imagine what she said?" Mantos managed a tight shake of his head. "She said, 'Mantos Tiboli loves you more than I've seen anyone love another.' That made me wonder what had changed. You didn't show me love when you abandoned me. 'Love' is not a word that's ever passed your lips for me. But Valaria never liked you, and she doesn't speak if she doesn't mean what she says. If she believed you loved me that much, I had to give you a chance."

The letter, so well-read its folded edges had weakened into tears, crackled as Fonbir unfolded it. Mantos' throat bobbed in anticipation as Fonbir read aloud.

My dearest Nabi,

I write this knowing that you'll never read it, and I accept that. I deserve no more of your time or your love, but I've committed these words to ink and parchment because they need to be said.

I'm sorry for everything. I'm not going to dress my actions in fur robes and a crown of golden sorrow. I'm not going to defend myself, as there's no way to defend what I did. I was a coward. I betrayed everything, but above all, I betrayed you. If you read this, I expect nothing back from you. I want nothing, no forgiveness, no love. All I hope is for you to believe me. I'm not the same Mantos that you once knew. Or maybe I am, and I've found who I was before I became so lost.

Please understand, I love you. I have always loved you and I always will love you.

Your Toketa.

By the time he finished reading, Fonbir's talons trembled and wet circles smudged the ink. He folded the letter and replaced it in his pocket as he took two steps forward. As the distance between them closed, the air grew still. Mantos made no sound.

"Did you mean what you said?" Fonbir asked. "That you love me? Because you never said it before. Not even in a letter."

Mantos remained obedient and silent, nodding. This time the action was slow and fluid, and he dropped onto his knees. Mantos looked up and reached for Fonbir's hands. At first Fonbir remained stiff and resistant, refusing to break. Then he reached out, allowing Mantos to take his talons. Mantos kissed each of his knuckles, moving from one hand to the other.

"Tell me now," Fonbir whispered into the stillness of the moment. "Tell me. I need to hear it."

Swallowing, Mantos remained on his knees as he brought the words of his letter to life. "I love you. I have always loved you and I always will love you."

Fonbir's strength left him and he slipped to the floor, his chain clanking. Mantos caught him and eased him downward, cradling Fonbir's head against his chestplate, keeping him safe in his strong arms.

"I hated you," Fonbir said. "*Hated* you. But I always loved you too, and I always will."

In that moment, he knew he'd made his choice. Whether it was the right one, Fonbir didn't know. He couldn't. But something within him changed, as if his heart began stitching itself back together. Mantos was here, and he loved him. After all their cycles together, it had to be worth trusting him one final time.

They stayed on the floor for some time, wound around each other, existing in their warmth. It was cold in the early evening, the hot coals doing what little they could to bring scant warmth. Mantos urged Fonbir onto one of the long couches nearest the largest brazier.

When they settled, Fonbir frowned at Mantos' drawn face. "What's wrong?"

Mantos shook his head, tracing the raised edges of Fonbir's facial armor with a gentle talon. "I was thinking about what I said in the letter, about how I'm not the same Mantos I was before, or perhaps I am, and I've learned from my errors. I wonder how much I've changed again, now Nunako is within me." He let a mirthless chuckle escape. "And I was thinking about Bandim." That name jolted a spike of fury from the tip of Fonbir's tail. "I wonder how much of his cruelty comes from within, and how much from the goddess he's imbibed."

Fonbir grasped Mantos' hand, his grip firm and comforting. "I can't say how much you've changed or haven't, but I knew from the moment I read that letter you were the Mantos I remembered. That's why I'm here now because I knew you'd come back to me. The real you. Whether that's growth or your goddess or something else or nothing at all, I can't say. As far as Bandim is concerned, even when we were younglings, he was cruel. He tormented us when we visited you or you visited us, all in the name of what he called 'fun.' But it wasn't fun for the rest of us. Much of his cruelty comes from a cracked heart within."

Sudden anger set Fonbir trembling. Mantos gripped his arms in comfort. "Your brother is Oatutkubis, released by the sun and the moons and the corruption of hearts, just as predicted. Ethay and Apago haven't walked with us for a thousandfold cycles, but" —Fonbir moved to face Mantos, throwing the weight of his meaning into his words— "Ethay and Apago, Nunako, the Grandmother, whatever you want to call it, is within you." He pressed both hands to Mantos' chestplate. "Bandim might be the Demon Who Rides the Sky, but you're Mantos, and I believe in you."

Mantos slid his hands up to rest on top of Fonbir's, pressing his left temple against Fonbir's right.

"I don't deserve you, but I'll try my hardest. I'll do everything I can to live up to your belief. Bandim might be at fault for the destruction in the world, but it's my responsibility. Now that Nunako is with me, I have to do everything I can to stop him." He pulled back and slid his hands from Fonbir's hands to his arms. "I love you, Nabi. It will crush me to see you marry Khitarian. I dreamed that when this was all over, if you had forgiven me, that we would be together forever."

Fonbir couldn't help himself. He laughed. The confusion and hurt that crossed Mantos' face only made it worse.

"Oh, Toketa," he said around his mirth. "I have something to tell you."

CHAPTER EIGHTEEN

Bandim-Dorai

News came from the mountain that his troops had not only spotted rebels, but someone who called himself Mantos as well. A lone soldier who hadn't been in pursuit of Elsya had clattered into the city, co-opted by a survivor of the battle, to bring not only that news, but more. The survivor was bringing a gift of something the Sun Emperor desired above all else. Bandim-Dorai had an idea what it was. It delighted him. There was only one thing the Sun Emperor wanted beyond his brother's head, attached, or severed. Bandim-Dorai walked to his throne, Tesselica and Johrann Maa following just behind, the room cleared of everyone else other than his guards.

Bandim-Dorai grinned and climbed the dais to settle himself on his throne. He left his companions standing below.

He glanced at Johrann. "This little gift is what I thought, isn't it?"

Johrann's unreadable mask slipped and, for a moment, her face pulled with dread. "Yes, My Emperor."

Her dread spoke volumes. Only one thing could threaten her like that. When he received this gift, Johrann's uniqueness would be no more.

The grand throne room doors opened. Bandim-Dorai sucked in a breath. It was too loud, but only Tess and Johrann could hear his excitement. A battered, limping soldier entered, flanked by two gilded palace guards. Chained between them was a stumbling figure dressed in the rags of the Khinish, a sackcloth bag on her head to conceal her face. But her hands gave away her heritage, gleaming unusual in the flickering throne room light.

"On your knees!" the battered soldier commanded.

His prisoner railed against him, and he was too travel-weakened to force her. His shame bloomed hot, but the two guards shoved the female to the ground. The crack of her knees on the stone floor echoed into every corner. She did not whimper.

The soldier's hand trembled as it grabbed the sackcloth on her head, and he dared a tiny look upward for his emperor's permission. Bandim-Dorai nodded, his grin splitting his face, and the soldier yanked off the hood.

There, kneeling before him on the floor of his throne room, was Emmy. Mantos' Uloni. The wretch who had beaten Bandim-Dorai back in the Althemerian camp. The one he had vowed to claim for himself.

"Well, well," he said, not deigning to rise, "this is a pretty bauble before me."

The Uloni tilted her chin as high as she could and spat. The arc of the globule was noble but pointless, and even before the spittle landed on the floor some distance from the Sun Emperor, one guard smashed his gauntleted fist against the side of her head. Emmy fell hard, though still would not whimper. Unlike Johrann, Bandim-Dorai could feel her emotions. Terror coursed through her, this young thing far from anyone who cared for her. There was a deep tether to her fear, something that traveled to her core. Bandim-Dorai noted that for future use, and the fact there was no doubt now that Johrann was hiding things from him. It wasn't a default of her Uloni heritage that kept her emotions from him. Beside him, even now, she was a thick shell, giving no sign of her feelings about seeing this other member of her folk. But Bandim-Dorai remembered her flash of dread.

"Get her up," he commanded. The guard wrenched Emmy to her knees again, a smear of blood on the floor where her head had been. Her body wavered, though her hate did not. "You've had a long journey, my dear. I'll forgive your behavior on this one occasion."

Emmy blinked the glassiness from her eyes. She tilted her chin up again, but this time she looked away from Bandim-Dorai and straight at Johrann. Interesting.

"I wasn't spitting at you," she rasped. "I was spitting at her."

Very interesting.

Johrann's composure cracked. Something slipped through that Bandim-Dorai couldn't place. There was anger and disgust, but also an edge of fear. *Why should my Johrann fear this waif?*

"I see I missed one," Johrann said, clawing back her stony mask. "Perhaps that was my true error."

Anger flashed hot in Bandim-Dorai's throat, nearly escaping in vitriol. Johrann's one error, as laid out in the Book of Divine Tears, was in returning Mantos to life. To suggest otherwise was blasphemy. Regardless, Bandim-Dorai wrenched back his control to watch the interchange between the two Uloni. He could deal with Johrann later.

"Missed one, my Heart?" he asked.

Johrann pulled the strings of her control and knitted her composure. "For much of my life, the One True Goddess guided me to bring about your glorious return. One instruction the goddess gave me was to destroy the rest of the Uloni, so I did."

Emmy tried to struggle to her feet but found herself shoved back down. "You murdered all of our folk," she hissed. "You burned them to death, to near the very last one!"

While Bandim-Dorai kept his expression clear, Tesselica flicked his gaze from Johrann upward to his emperor. Unwilling to give away his surprise, Bandim-Dorai's response was nothing but silence. He didn't know what was more surprising: that Johrann believed her instructions were from Dorai, or that her actions had brought about a genocide. *Dorai ordered nothing of the sort. The goddess would have given me this knowledge long before now if it were true. It wasn't, which raised the ugly question: from whom had Johrann received those instructions?*

Bandim-Dorai knew she believed what she said. If not from Dorai, who? There were few possibilities, and he appreciated none of them.

This wasn't the time for contemplation. Instead Bandim-Dorai allowed one side of his lips to curl in a smile. "It would seem you've always had a penchant for flame then, my dear."

Tesselica flashed with jealousy at the term of endearment. Bandim-Dorai ignored him.

Johrann nodded, her own mouth quirking. "It's always been a favorite, my Emperor."

Emmy struggled upward only for a guard to shove her down again. "How can you make light of this? You killed my parents. You killed *your* parents. You killed the parents of every Uloni under the Arc of the Sky. You doomed the Uloni. Apart from you and me, they're *all dead*."

"I never knew my parents," Johrann said. "They abandoned me. And anyway, that was rather the point."

Johrann's scathing honesty rippled along Bandim-Dorai's back in a wave of pleasure. Johrann had believed Dorai sent her to kill every one of her folk. Even if it wasn't the case, the fact she'd done it and had no regrets made power and desire stir low in Bandim-Dorai's belly. She'd killed them all to please him, and he had dared to suspect her loyalty.

The Uloni spat again. "*Murderer.*"

For the third and final time, she attempted to fight to her feet. This time when the guard put her down again, Bandim-Dorai flickered into flame and glided to the ground in front of her. Before she could react, he jerked out his hand and clamped it around her slim neck, wrenching her upward.

"Johrann Maa is my beloved Heart," he said, pulling her face so close to his she recoiled, "and I will not have her disrespected by a disgusting wretch like you."

Emmy flinched under the pressure of his proximity and his words, so he kept pressing. Considering what he knew of the difficulties Johrann had faced in her isolated youth, rejected by everyone because of her colors, it wasn't a long stretch to assume the same was true for this other Uloni. Folk were easy to read when you knew how. It wouldn't take much to rip this creature apart.

"You're nothing," he said, dropping his voice to a whisper. He kept the pressure on her neck strong enough to immobilize her but not tight enough that she couldn't breathe. "I can see it in your eyes. You're nothing, and you've been nothing your whole life." He twisted his tone into something akin to pity. "You poor thing. And now, just like everyone else in your life used you, my brother has used you too, hmm? Manipulated you for your power, convinced you to help him in his noble cause?" He tightened his grip and his prey choked. "But it's too late now, isn't it? I've got you, and Mantos can't use you to bring Nunako into this world. Without a Heart and without the Lunar Awakening like I had, he can't stop me."

Some odd emotion flickered in the battered soldier. Bandim-Dorai slackened his grip enough to allow Emmy a whooping breath and her feet to settle on the stone floor. He turned his attention to the male he had forgotten was there. The soldier, still encrusted in dirt and blood, didn't look victorious any longer. Abject terror filled him.

"What are you not telling me?" Bandim-Dorai asked. When the soldier's lips moved without a sound, the Sun Emperor commanded, "Speak!"

"There was another just like you." The soldier's words tumbled over one another. "It must have been Prin—I mean, Mantos," he stammered, horrified that he had almost given the former heir his proper, now-stripped title. "A Masvam, he looked just like you."

Bandim-Dorai brought his talons tight around the Uloni's bruising throat again, wishing it was the soldier's neck instead. "I know my brother was there. Why are you wasting my time?"

"It wasn't just that!" the soldier blurted. "He could manipulate the ground. He caused tremors, ripped up the rock and stone. He did *magic.*"

A strangled gasp came from his victim, and when Bandim-Dorai returned his attention to her face, she was grinning underneath her suffocation.

"Nunako," she choked. "Back."

Power and rage swirled inside him, shooting to his talon-tips. How was that possible? He and Mantos had joined before, had visited one another in their minds across an ocean. Bandim-Dorai had assumed that if anything so powerful as the return of the wretched Nunako would occur, he would feel it. But he hadn't. How could this happen without his knowledge?

As soon as her skin and armor began to smolder under his rage, the smug Uloni wasn't grinning anymore. Bandim-Dorai's entire body shook with unadulterated rage. Flame coiled. He knew what to do. Emmy would soon sport a hole in her abdomen to rival Solseo's, and he would hang her corpse on the walls, her face a fixed mask of pain.

"My Emperor!"

Johrann's voice cooled his ire just as the jolt of flame reached his hands. Emmy's neck smoked. Her face was a patchwork of soot and tears.

"Don't kill her yet," Johrann said. Her tone was strange and soft.

His grip now strong but cool, Bandim-Dorai turned his face to Johrann. She was an emotional blank. Tesselica, behind them, thrummed with fear and hate and desire.

Johrann continued, "Remember why you wanted her, my Emperor. You wanted to use her to make yourself even stronger. If you kill her now, you won't have the chance to try."

Though Bandim-Dorai didn't want to admit it, Johrann was right. The capture of Emmy had been an Arc-high order, something he'd expected no one to achieve. His soldiers hadn't even been looking for her or Mantos. They'd been in pursuit of Elsya and his rebel band. This second Uloni was a blessing, not something to destroy without thought.

He released his grip, and Emmy collapsed like a boneless carcass. She pulled herself into a tight ball and clutched at her neck, clawing at the fresh burns as she sucked in desperate breaths.

Bandim-Dorai peered down at her without tilting his head. "Take her to the cells," he said to the guards. "Keep her in darkness and give her no food, and just enough water to keep her alive. I don't think she'll come to me of her own will, but it's easy to break those who are already weak."

The guards swung into action, looping their arms under her, and dragging her away. Her hoarse pants grew quieter until they pulled her through the chamber doors and out of sight.

With the guards gone, only the battered soldier remained.

"What is your name?" Bandim-Dorai asked.

The soldier went to his knees. "Szuya of House Rserra."

"You've done a great thing for your goddess," Bandim-Dorai said, reaching out to him. "Kiss my hand and I'll tell you what you've earned."

Terror and joy mingled in a strange marbled emotion as Szuya shuffled forward to press his lips to the Sun Emperor's knuckles.

"Where do you come from, Szuya? You're House Rserra, so toward the eastern reaches?"

"Yes, Your Imperial Majesty. Givu Province."

Bandim-Dorai raised his hand to lay it on top of Szuya's bloodied fronds. "Consider the entire province yours."

Despite his tremulous respect, Szuya's face snapped up, showing his youth and earnestness. "Your Imperial Majesty?"

Bandim-Dorai petted the side of Szuya's head. "Yes. That's good pastureland, no? The farmers and their herds all answer to you now. Keep them there if you choose or turn them off if you wish. There's land for them on Althemer if they object to my wishes. But you've earned it, Szuya. Enjoy what gifts your emperor gives and tell everyone about the wages of loyalty."

The soldier's emotions exploded in grateful tears, and Bandim-Dorai turned to Tesselica.

"Tess, be a dear and help this young hero of the empire. Arrange chambers in the palace for him until he's ready to travel back home. Make sure he's looked after."

As loyal as Tesselica always was, he showed no arrogant pride at being asked to perform a servant's task. Instead he preened under the responsibility. "Yes, my Emperor."

Grateful to escape the overwhelming surge of emotion coming from Szuya, Bandim-Dorai motioned for Johrann Maa to fall in step with him to leave the chamber. Guards flanked them as they walked through the palace.

Bandim-Dorai threaded his arm through the crook of Johrann's elbow, eliciting a spark of surprised pleasure. "Take a turn in the gardens with me. The cold will clear my head. And we have much to discuss, dear Heart. You didn't tell me there are no Uloni other than you and this waif because you killed them all."

"Yes, my Emperor," Johrann replied, her joyous spark lengthening into a satisfied thrum. "I did it for Dorai."

This would be a tale indeed.

* * *

Dorai listened with Bandim's ears as Johrann told the parts of her story she had until now withheld. She had always maintained to Bandim that she was the last Uloni and Bandim, being Bandim, had never questioned why. Dorai had wondered, though until now it wasn't of much importance. Her daughter Bomsoi's treacherous creation of her own folk, instead of helping her mothers regain the love of those already under the Arc of the Sky, was a mark of Nunako's selfishness. Any blood of Nunako was treacherous.

Bomsoi had proved that, and Johrann Maa proved it again.

As Bandim and the Uloni walked arm in arm through the bitter frost of the garden as it slept in Vhaun, something uncomfortable coiled within Dorai. Johrann was adamant that Dorai was the one who had come to her in the desert, had saved her and spoken to her and set her on this path to return Dorai to the world.

The truth was, it wasn't true. Dorai spoke to no one, for she had no power. She had been impotent in the world. If not Dorai, then who?

There were a handful of possibilities. Dorai didn't trust the intentions behind any of them. Someone had orchestrated her return to the world, and with her return would always come Nunako's. She had tried to convince Bandim he could prevent it, but it had been a lie. Nunako always followed like a stink. The explanations sat upon Dorai's consciousness like stones.

What has been made cannot be unmade, but what has been made can be destroyed.

CHAPTER NINETEEN

Emmy

Not once in Emmy's sixteen cycles had she been chained. She had been beaten and threatened and abused by her mistress, locked in a cage on a Masvam slave ship, but never chained.

Sixteen cycles? Is it seventeen now? Emmy moved her feet, trying to shift her weight on the slanted block beneath them. Her hatching day had passed. It was at some point in Vhaun. But then, she realized as she shuffled again, trying to relieve the pain in her shoulders, what she knew as her hatching day couldn't be accurate, considering Krodge wouldn't know when the day was. Not that it mattered. It wasn't as if Krodge had ever allowed her to celebrate. Zecha was the one who'd remembered to bring Emmy some birthday bread, a small loaf covered in glorious icing that had tasted obscene in its sweetness.

Emmy shifted again, parting her cracked lips. No matter how hard she tried, she couldn't stand in a way that wasn't excruciating. Whether they had chained her in this cell for hours or days, she couldn't tell. There was no light, no window, and she couldn't tell whether she was above or below ground. For all she knew, she might be in a tower or a dungeon. Bandim had only called it a cell. Emmy huffed a curt laugh through her mouth, which was as arid as a desert. It didn't matter where she was. All that mattered was that she hurt.

Not content with throwing her into a room of pitch darkness, the Sun Emperor had ordered her to be chained. That in itself wasn't cruel enough. Instead of slapping manacles on her wrists and ankles to stop her moving but allow her to slump in a corner, Bandim had ordered her held upright, the chains from the ceiling just high enough that her shoulders burned with the continual effort to prevent her arms from wrenching from their sockets.

Yet even that wasn't enough. Not content to allow her to have her feet on the ground, instead, once the guards stripped off her Kiseoyan boots, they placed her feet on a slanting wooden block. That left Emmy with two options: try to find purchase enough to bear her weight on her feet or swing by her wrists until her shoulders dislocated. Emmy had tended to too many injuries in her time to allow herself the agony of having her arms pulled out of their joints.

Worse even than the pain, as much as she tried, she couldn't muster any strength or power from within. She was too exhausted, too beaten. Even if she'd been able to, she wasn't sure what good her ice would do her. Thus, no matter how hard it became, she forced herself to perch on the block. Pain in four limbs was better than agony in two.

For the first time in her life, Krodge didn't seem like the worst individual Emmy had met. She barked another brief laugh at that. *I wonder, old crone, what you would say if you saw me now. I wonder if you'd admire this punishment and wish you'd used it yourself as one of my 'lessons.'*

It was less than a cycle since Krodge had last brought her switch down on Emmy's bare palms. Above the manacles, Emmy flexed her hands, remembering the sting of the flexible wood across her soft flesh. Somehow it seemed longer ago. An age, even. In her mind, Krodge had become a figure dead and long burned, yet it wasn't long ago. Nothing was long ago.

The only long thing was her time on the block, chained and on the verge of losing the use of both arms. Krodge would've certainly approved.

Minutes, hours, days, weeks, whatever length of time passed, Emmy's focus remained on the block. She understood why she was being kept and hadn't been killed outright. Bandim and the Uloni he'd called Johrann Maa had made the reason clear. Bandim wanted to use her to strengthen himself, as if being an Uloni made her into an easy conduit for his own strength. How could he wear the mantle of a goddess and be so lacking in understanding? He'd made it clear he understood little of Emmy, too.

"You're nothing. I can see it in your eyes. You're nothing, and you've been nothing your whole life."

Emmy shifted again, giving a third laugh. If he imagined he was the first to tell her that, he was a fool.

"I don't think she'll come to me of her own will, but it's easy to break those who are already weak."

That was further evidence of his idiocy. But Emmy had no further time to consider it, for there was an almighty creak as the cell door opened, and a flood of light entered. A figure stood, dark against the brightness, before entering and plunging them into darkness once again.

The next light that rose was hot and red and swirled from a pale blue palm. It was Johrann Maa. Had Emmy any saliva in her mouth, she would have spat at the other Uloni again. There was a long moment of silence, broken only by Emmy's grunts of discomfort and the cracking of the flame in Johrann's palm.

"What is your name?"

Emmy almost laughed. Bandim hadn't told her. Perhaps he didn't remember from the time when she'd stopped him in the Althemerian encampment. Emmy stared through the firelight and into Johrann Maa's eyes. "No one."

Johrann laughed in disbelief. "How fitting, considering that's what you are. Now, what is your name?"

"No one."

A flicker of frustration bloomed on Johrann's face. "What is your name?"

"No one," Emmy replied. "My mistress called me Emena. It's Metakalan."

Johrann's frustration gave way to a wry hilarity. "Metakalan for 'no one.' Your mistress had a sense of humor."

Emmy resisted the urge to roll her eyes and said nothing.

Johrann tilted her head to the side. "I want to know, No one, how you survived." Her voice was soft, the slide of a serpent over stone. "I was sure I got everyone in the village. Unless you weren't in the village, of course. But I think you were."

Emmy couldn't reply through the dryness of her mouth, but after Johrann thrust a rough-hewn cup to her lips, she responded. "My mother saved me," she rasped.

Johrann's face was impassive in the flickering of her palm's flame. "My mother damned me," she replied. "And my father, whoever they were. They abandoned me, condemning me to a life of being an outcast. Your mother didn't 'save' you. She did the same to you as mine did to me."

Precious water dripped over the armor of Emmy's chin. "My mother saved me," she repeated.

Johrann's laugh was hard. "Did you have a wonderful life, then, No one, full of love and contentment and a caregiver who gave you a meaningful name?" A flicker must have crossed Emmy's face that betrayed the truth, because Johrann laughed again. "I didn't think so."

Unwilling to drop her eyes from this other Uloni, unwilling to show any weakness, Emmy forced herself to keep Johrann's gaze in her own. Johrann was older than Emmy by cycles. However, there was something about her that made the time between their hatchings stretch to the edge of the Arc. Emmy had seen it before, in the faces of those who'd lost scores of loved ones to the Lurking Death. It was an expression that said, *I cannot bear another loss.* It was aging through devastation.

"I had a hard life with my mistress," Emmy said, though her throat was drying again, "but it wasn't all bad. I had a friend. Now I have a lot of friends."

This time it was something that flashed across Johrann's expression that gave her truth away. Emmy's words, for the briefest of moments, affected her like a strike to the mouth. But then Johrann's pain disappeared, replaced by wicked spite.

"You've got no one, No One," she said. "All you have is pain."

With a flick of her hands, Johrann Maa sent a twist of fire to curl at Emmy's feet. The flames licked against her skin and armor and consumed the block. Though Emmy tried to keep the cry from bursting from her mouth, there was nothing she could do as the fire snapped closer and hotter and more brutal, and she had to bear her weight on her arms alone.

Her screech echoed in the small cell, as loud as a cannon volley.

"There's much worse to come," Johrann said with that serpentine smoothness. "And look at you, already screaming. Save yourself the agony and submit to Dorai. She's your blood, your family. *We* are *family*. Stop this willfulness and join the One True Goddess. Give the emperor your power."

As if to prove the point that joining Bandim would cease her agony, Johrann Maa clicked her talons, and the fire at Emmy's feet disappeared. Her toes scrabbled for grip on the smoldering wood.

"Everything will be comfortable once you give Bandim-Dorai your Heart's power," Johrann continued, bringing her lips right to Emmy's left ear. "The Sun Emperor will give you anything you wish for, and you'll never come to harm again. No one will torment and abandon you. You'll have everything you desire."

Something sparked in Emmy's chest, and she stiffened. Sensing victory, Johrann Maa pulled back, grinning as she waited for the successful submission of her victim.

Emmy lowered her gaze, staring at the blackened wood beneath her feet. She sucked in a breath, then thrust her chin upward as high as it could go. "I had everything I desired before they brought me here," she spat. "I had friends. I had a family. I don't need your so-called Sun Emperor to save me or fix me or pamper me like a pet. I don't need anyone to protect me from anything. I'm not what he thinks. I'm not weak. So, torture me until you kill me. I'll never, *ever* become Bandim's Heart."

The strength of her words came like another slap to Johrann's face. She pulled backward, aghast, with something that might have been fright lingering behind her eyes. Realization came to her. *She's afraid of him*, Emmy thought. *She's afraid of what he'll do.*

"You don't need him to look after you," Emmy said. "You're an Uloni. We can look after each other."

The words came from a deep pool of understanding that welled from Emmy's insides. Just like her, Johrann was an outcast. In the same way Krodge had tormented her, other folk must have made Johrann Maa's life a misery. How many times had Emmy looked at herself in the still surface of a water barrel or in the stiff shimmer of a polished plate and felt disgust, fury, at her own reflection? How many times had she cursed herself for being a Moon Rogue, a freak?

For being wrong.

"It doesn't matter what you've done," Emmy continued, her own compassion surprising her. Johrann stood before her, mouth slack. "You don't need *him*."

Johrann reared back and caught Emmy's cheek with the flat of her hand, sending her sprawling and swinging on her creaking chains. White-hot pain seared through Emmy's shoulders and shot down her arms.

"You don't understand what I've done and what I'm doing." Johrann's words were as sharp as her strike. "You don't understand why I've done what I've done. It's not all for him."

Her voice broke on the final word. Emmy caught herself on the remains of the block. "Then who is it for?" she ground out through her agony.

"Dorai," Johrann said, "who came to me in the desert when I was a youngling and saved me, who gave me a purpose and a life and a reason to survive."

Though she didn't mean to, Emmy choked out a laugh. "How do you know it was Dorai? How do you know it wasn't just a dream?"

"Because she told me!" Johrann snapped. She lifted her hands, and Emmy flinched away from another strike that didn't come. Instead, Johrann Maa snapped her talons, conjuring more flame. She moved with deliberate care, bringing the fireballs closer and closer to Emmy's throat. "You're arrogant. You are a being of little consequence. You have no right to question me. The One True Goddess has never come to you."

Victory sparked in Emmy's chest. "The Grandmother of the World has, though."

Johrann narrowed her eyes. Her tone was dangerous. "Lies."

"Truth." Viciousness drove Emmy's next words, all compassion gone. "You're not as special as you thought you were, are you?"

Her reward for that comment was a ball of flame licking at either side of her throat, not quite touching but burning, regardless.

"I don't care about the Grandmother, and I don't care about Nunako," Johrann ground out. "All I care about is serving the One True Goddess, the one who's given me the only love and kindness I've ever experienced in my entire life."

Fear swelled within Emmy, followed by the sudden return of her power. Coldness filled her until ice bloomed from her neck scales, forming a protective collar against Johrann's flame. The coldness spread and grew, traveling up her arms and coiling around her wrists, eating at her manacles until, with an impossible *crack*, the metal sheared.

Emmy collapsed to the ground, the ice at her neck shattering. Johrann stepped back, her palm-flames dimmed.

"A dainty trick, 'No one'," Johrann said, though her words wavered. "I'll leave you with your lies for now. When I return, things won't be as pleasant as this encounter."

She took a step backward, snuffed her flames, then must have turned in the darkness. The next thing Emmy saw was her back silhouetted against the light from outside the cell. Then darkness surrounded her again.

With what strength she had remaining, Emmy willed her coldness to heal the pain and injury to her limbs and feet and neck. *Whatever Johrann Maa thinks is right, she's wrong. The Grandmother told us we needed to restore balance to the world, and what Johrann seeks is one-sided power. She's wrong.*

Now freed from her chains, Emmy crawled into a corner of her cell and curled into a ball, wrapping her tail around herself. She'd summoned some power despite her exhaustion. Perhaps with some rest, she could find more strength to fight back, escape, get back to Bomsoi and Mantos.

As her eyes fluttered closed, it wasn't either of them she thought about. Her mind lingered on Zecha and Charo and their impending laying. *Let them be okay*, Emmy thought as she slipped into a dreamless sleep.

CHAPTER TWENTY

Mantos

A rising tide of excitement heralded Neiruk's return. Mantos lingered at the edge of the sunken meeting chamber, peering into the white courtyard below. The strange creature descended like an iridescent gale, its great wings pushing snow and folk back in equal measure. Lowering its long neck and leaning to the side to allow its sole rider to climb off, Mantos pursed his lips. He'd known Bomsoi returned alone, since the Stranger had told both him and Rel as soon as she could, in their secret way. That meant Emmy was still lost. She might even be in his brother's clutches. Cold sorrow pooled in his belly. He wanted her back not for her power, but just to know she was safe.

Khitarian called them all together again to hear the rest of Bomsoi's intelligence. Having been away from the kingdom for two weeks, she'd doubtless learned something of value. Valaria was long gone too, having left to gather what remained of Althemerian forces just before their arrival. She would plead with the Mellul too, desperate for their ships and weaponry. Mantos held little hope for that. Ally of the Althemerians or not, there was little to gain from open conflict with Bandim.

As Bomsoi tracked across the snow and disappeared into the palace, Mantos turned. He kept his arms crossed, held tight to his chest. Khitarian sat in their place of honor, Fonbir to their right. They were conversing in sign, or at least were trying. Even as Fonbir fumbled, his frustration at not being perfect on the first attempt so familiar to Mantos, Khitarian's corrections were gentle and loving. Though the king had relinquished Fonbir from their marriage pact, the thought hovered in Mantos' mind that Khitarian might be a better match for Fonbir. Khitarian could keep him safe. It was clear they loved him. Mantos didn't even have a house name any longer, never mind the means to be the husband Fonbir deserved.

A bloom of power rippled up his spine, and Mantos keenly felt the surrounding possibility. He had command of rock and earth, and they were in a palace carved from the same. *Understood, my goddess*, he thought. Nunako, within him and part of him yet still somehow separate, sometimes sent him reminders that he was worthwhile, especially when self-doubt crept in like the start of a stain.

The flare of power served a second, less palatable purpose. It was strong, no doubt. Since regaining Fonbir's trust, his love's belief had made his strength soar. But it still wasn't enough and didn't bring the surge of robust force that Emmy's presence had. Without her, he was so much less, and now Bomsoi had returned without her.

He turned as the door opened, expecting the Stranger, but seeing Zecha, Charo, and Rel. The weight of circumstance was heavy upon all of them, Charo most of all. It wouldn't be long until her laying. Mantos stood watching the door. He waited for it to open again, but nothing happened. With a sigh, he descended into the sunken pit and took up a seat beside Elsya.

His cousin quirked an eyeridge. "Everyone seems impatient for this Stranger to appear."

"And impatient for news of our friend," Mantos added.

"I'm impatient to move against the False Emperor," Elsya replied. "We've stayed here too long."

While he nodded, Mantos held out a placating hand. "I know. The sooner we can remove my brother from the throne and stop his madness, the better. However, we can't do it alone, not even with the might of the Khinish. Khitarian is right to wait on news from the Mellul."

Elsya couldn't stop the scoff that escaped his mouth. "The Mellul were no help to the Althemerians, and they were allies. What makes you think they, or the Belfoni or the Va Chressans or any of the rest, will rally to the call of the Mountainess?"

Mantos let his hand drop. "Valaria has gone to petition the Mellul and gather what she can of the remains of the Althemerian navy. Her presence as uncrowned monarch of the island will give much weight to the call. Also," he added, dropping his voice, "I think my brother's conquest and this dark power he wields will have shaken every monarch on every throne. He destroyed Althemer in one swoop. They all know, and fear he'll do the same to them."

The door opened a second time and this time it was Bomsoi, dressed in a clean tunic. She approached Khitarian and dropped to one knee.

"Your Highness," she said and signed, "please accept my apology for my absence these past weeks. I should have sought your permission to leave, but my daughter's disappearance was more pressing than sense."

"You need not apologize, nor bow to me," Khitarian replied, gesturing for Bomsoi to stand. "But by your solitary return, we can only assume you did not find her."

Bomsoi shook her head. "I did, Your Highness, but I couldn't get to her."

Mantos stood, his body alight with worry. "Where is she?"

"Emmy is in the Masvam palace," Bomsoi replied. "I couldn't speak to her, but I know she's there. She's weak." Her voice cracked. "We need to free her."

Before either Khitarian or Mantos could reply, Zecha had leaped to his feet and was brandishing a talon in Bomsoi's face.

"Why couldn't you get to her?" He sounded betrayed. "You're a goddess, or at least have the power of one. You should be able to overpower everything, or sneak in and rescue her. You should have brought her back!"

Rel had risen and forced Zecha's arm down again. Bomsoi was gracious in accepting his ire.

"And what if Bandim-Dorai, had discovered us?" she asked, her voice unbearably soft. "I can't raise a hand against my mother. What would I have done in the face of her power, alone? In trying to free Emmy, I could have killed her. The Sun Emperor would slaughter her just to see the pain it would cause."

Zecha's expression turned barren, and he allowed Rel to usher him back to his seat beside Charo. Mantos shot him a sympathetic glance, though the Metakalan didn't seem to see it.

Bomsoi turned back to Khitarian. "We need Emmy. Without her, balance cannot return to the world."

"We will rescue her," the king replied. "The latest intelligence I've had suggests that Bandim is in the Masvam palace also, so that will be our target."

Discomfort coiled within Mantos. "The city is large and the palace well-fortified. It has never fallen."

"We don't need the city to fall," Khitarian replied. "Our forces can engage the Masvam army in battle, but they need not reach the palace itself. We can lure Bandim Tiboli out into open conflict, or if he remains in his palace, you can go in after him. It only takes one stroke of a sword to cut a serpent's head from its body." Fonbir stirred at that comment, and Khitarian gave him a small smile but didn't apologize. "You lived in that palace all your life, Mantos. You must know at least one way of getting in without detection."

"He does," Elsya said before Mantos could reply. "Mantos was famous among us younglings for escaping the palace without detection, and his father never found out."

Mantos winced at the title and the memory. "I can do that, Your Highness. It won't be a problem." He turned to Bomsoi. "I have to confront him, don't I?"

The Stranger nodded. "Yes. I need Bandim and his Heart, and you and yours, together. Only then can we finish this forever."

Mantos swallowed. "Is there no way to return balance without death?"

Bomsoi shook her head. "There's no way. There's a price to pay for balance, a price of blood."

Khitarian interrupted the silence that followed. "Tell us what you learned on your journey. Your intelligence will help us plan our next moves."

With each piece of information Bomsoi shared, Mantos' heart grew heavier. She reported of thousands of his folk, perhaps more than thousands, fleeing the cities and heading for the Marches. They were loyal to Nunako, afraid of Bandim and what they still called Dorai's Darkness.

She told them also of the bands of Elsya's rebels, ebbing and flowing in attack and retreat, unguided and rudderless without their leader. Mantos cast a glance at his cousin, noting the dark cast of his face.

Perhaps worst of all was the spread of the Death. Sickness pervaded the empire in twisting tendrils, following the routes of rebellion and fear.

"Many interpret it as punishment," Bomsoi said, her voice low with sorrow. "Some say it's retribution for Bandim's worship of Dorai. Others, likely perpetuated by the emperor himself, believe it a punishment for disloyalty to the throne."

"What do you believe?" Khitarian asked.

"I believe it's neither," Bomsoi said. "I believe it to be an unfortunate circumstance that exacerbates an already difficult life for so many innocents. The Death was spreading even as we traveled into the mountains." She paused, taking the time to look at Mantos. "I believe it's a sign that we can delay no longer. We can allow no more suffering."

Mantos nodded and stood. "We must gather every soldier we can. Elsya and I will rally what force we can from the rebels and those loyal to the old Masvam ways."

Elsya touched his elbow. "If they rallied to me, even more will come to you when they realize not only that you're alive, but that Nunako lives within you."

Power fluttered with Elsya's belief.

"The might of the Kiseoyan army is with you," Khitarian said. "We might choose to remain within our borders, but those borders have stood strong and impenetrable for hundreds of cycles for good reason. And news will come within days of Valaria's efforts to rebuild Althemerian forces and her plea to the Mellul. We can only hope she has been successful."

A smile flitted across Fonbir's face. "My sister can be very persuasive."

Khitarian gave him an affectionate smile, then turned their attention to Mantos and Elsya. "You will leave tomorrow. How long will it take to spread your call to action?"

"Too long," Mantos said, trying to keep his voice level, "and there's no guarantee the folk will answer the call."

Elsya replied. "Don't underestimate how many folk are loyal to Bandim only through fear. The crown's forces may turn their coats back to red and orange. The Masvams will come to you, Mantos. You're the true heir, and now their goddess."

Bomsoi's face became steel. "Elsya can go with his soldiers on foot, but you and I will ride. Neiruk will bear us across the whole Arc faster than anything else. With your powers, upon his back, no one will doubt Nunako's return."

A moment of stillness settled. The room filled with silent determination.

"We have our plan," Khitarian said at last. "Leave the rest to me."

* * *

The day passed in preparation. By the time night fell and the palace was lit by moondust, Mantos was weary. He knew no rest would come, however, and he found himself in Fonbir's chamber rather than his own.

When Othelan opened the door, Mantos received a look colder than the great icy mountains outside. However, the retainer stood back to allow Mantos entry, bowing his head in respect. "Your Highness."

The words sounded clipped, but Mantos ignored them. Othelan had long been Fonbir's closest attendant and had never approved of Mantos.

"The prince is bathing," he said. "I'll let him know you've arrived."

As Othelan disappeared into the side room, wisps of steam escaping as he opened the door, Mantos took a seat beside the largest of the braziers. He watched the coals as they glowed, red eating into the black. It had been weeks, maybe longer since he'd seen a flame. Part of him wondered if he'd ever be able to look at a flame the same way again, as before his brother had wrought such destruction.

Nunako turned within him, bringing up similar feelings about Dorai. Her memories were flickers in his peripheral vision, unclear but definite.

"Do you think you can ever repair your relationship with your sister?" he asked, his words unbearably loud.

A coldness bloomed at his fingertips, and ice formed. Mantos took that as a solid 'no.'

It wasn't long before Fonbir emerged from the bath, his scales shimmering like obsidian. While he had a wide smile for Mantos, Othelan scowled over his shoulder. The expression was mild enough it might be mistaken for a dour resting face, but Mantos had seen it too many times to think it was anything other than veiled disdain.

"Oth, you can take some time to yourself," Fonbir said as he sank into a chair opposite Mantos.

Othelan's nostrils flared, and it seemed to take all his self-control to prevent his distaste from escaping. Regardless, he obeyed and slipped from the room.

Mantos shook his head. "Othelan will never approve of me."

Fonbir chuckled. "No, he won't." He reached across for Mantos' hand. "But I do."

They passed some time in front of the brazier, enjoying being in each other's company. As time went on, the weight of unsaid words fell upon them. The nearest moondust lantern dimmed, and Mantos released Fonbir's hand. He took one of the hottest coals from the middle of the brazier and switched it for the cool one inside the lantern's base.

"I don't want you to go again," Fonbir said.

Mantos hung the lantern again and dropped to his knees in front of Fonbir, touching Fonbir's legs. "I wish I never had to leave your side again," he said, "but if we have any hope of a life beyond exile inside this mountain, I have to go."

Fonbir reached out to cup Mantos' face. "I know you do, but that doesn't mean I want you to. I don't want to lose what we've clawed back."

"We won't," Mantos said, pressing his cheek into Fonbir's hand. "I promise. I'll get back my empire and I'll reclaim your island for you."

Fonbir chuckled at that. "I have a feeling Valaria might achieve the second part before you do. But," he added, "you'll have to do the first part yourself." His next words were harsh, but his tone was soft. "Come back an emperor, or don't come back at all."

So much came with that statement. Mantos nodded, bringing a hand up to place over Fonbir's. It wasn't that he couldn't come back without victory. It was that he wouldn't, because if Bandim succeeded, it would mean Mantos' death. This time there would be no coming back.

"I won't let you down," he said. "I'll never let you down again."

CHAPTER TWENTY-ONE

Mantos

Mantos watched as the rebel Masvam troops gathered under Elsya's command. Clean and well-fed, they stood as tall and strong as any soldiers Mantos had known. The Khinish repaired and supplemented their patchwork armor, and on their faces, they once more wore the colors of their houses, though when Mantos looked a little closer, his chest tightened. On one side they wore their house colors. On the other, no matter the house, were two bright stripes: red and orange. House Tiboli.

Elsya caught Mantos off-guard and clapped him on the back. "I told them you'd renounced the house name, cousin, but that didn't deter them. They know you as a Tiboli and they're proud to wear the colors of your house. Perhaps," Elsya added, wisdom in his tone, "you should reclaim your name."

"Perhaps," Mantos replied.

Should he? What would taking on the mantle of House Tiboli again mean? Mantos had abandoned that name long before. He'd left it behind in the chamber in Kubodinnu. When he'd clambered from the window into the pelting rain, he'd become Mantos, the one the Metakalans had called No one.

Khinish troops bolstered the band of Masvams. Their numbers alone were too small for safe passage beyond the mountains. Elsya pulled off a glove and placed his thumb and foreclaw in his mouth, letting out a high-pitched whistle that grabbed everyone's attention. Instead of his cousin addressing his troops, Mantos found himself on the receiving end of a knowing look from Elsya.

"Speak to them," he said, low enough for only Mantos to hear. "Give them reason to lay down their lives."

The world was loud and silent. Mantos swallowed, trying to control the motion and mask his sudden nerves. Why did he feel trepidation? He'd given many rousing speeches to Masvam forces in his time, a Tiboli rousing Tiboli troops. Perhaps, he wondered, it was because this time he was a rebel.

No, he thought. *I am no rebel. I'm the heir to the throne. Bandim is the pretender.*

Mantos steeled his resolve, took one deep breath, and spoke.

"You came to these mountains under the command of Elsya of House Yru, a male who is loyal and true. You leave these mountains still under his command, but with a greater purpose. Before, you fought against the tyranny of Bandim Tiboli, who has destroyed the name of the house in fire and drowned it in innocent blood." He looked at each face. He pulled in another breath before speaking again. Once he said these words, he would commit to them. "Now you fight not only against that tyranny, but to reclaim the house name, *my* house name, and to help me reclaim my rightful place on the Masvam throne. I am Mantos Tiboli, first of my name, and I am the rightful emperor. My brother may have tried to kill me, but I am stronger than that. He might try to force all those in the empire to bend to his will, but he will fail. I have the power of Nunako within me," he said, and the ground trembled under them all with his power, "and we will succeed. Go now and gather every willing rebel you can to fight for our cause. We will force the so-called Sun Emperor from the throne. We will put to rights everything he has done wrong. We will return the empire to the bastion of strength that once it was. We will triumph!"

A chorus of determination rose from the rebels, and even the Khinish shook their fists in the air and cheered. Elsya tipped him a salute.

"We'll make you proud," he said.

"I know you will." Mantos smiled. "I already am."

The Masvams and their Khinish allies marched out of the palace complex and into the mountains with their heads held high. A strange loneliness descended on Mantos as the last of them disappeared from view. Speaking to them had rallied them, but it had stirred something dormant within himself too. He was a Tiboli, their emperor, and with that title came responsibility and desire in equal measure. He had never wanted to gain the crown, its weight like an impossible burden. Now he felt different. It wasn't a burden. It was a privilege.

A cry sounded from above, and a shadow passed over them. Mantos glanced upward to see Neiruk descending into the open space the Masvams had departed from. The great beast bayed as he planted his feet on the ground, the snow turned to slush under the tromp of many boots. Bomsoi slid from Neiruk's back, her face half-hidden in the fur-lined hood of her Khinish cloak.

"Are you ready to depart?" she asked.

Mantos nodded. "As ready as I can be."

"Word has arrived from Valaria. She's had success in gathering what remains of the Althemerians. They see it as a miracle from Ethay and Apago that she's alive. However, the Mellul are reluctant to come to her aid. They fear Bandim Tiboli and his power."

"Then the first place we fly is Mellul," Mantos said. "Together we can give a compelling alternative to hiding from my brother. They might think themselves safe south of the Sea of Souls, but no one is truly safe from my brother."

Nodding, Bomsoi touched the leathery flat of Neiruk's snout. "We fly south, my friend." The Prago gave a whine and pressed his head into Bomsoi's touch. "You'll rest soon. I promised you, didn't I?"

Not for the first time, Mantos wondered why the Prago needed rest. The creature had slumbered in the mountains for many cycles. What did Neiruk need to rest from? He didn't ask, as a figure with a stilted walk approached them. Rel's pale gray eyes peered from the midst of her hood. She wore a long sword on her hip. Haelo.

As she reached them, Rel undid the fastenings of her belt and held the sword outward. Bomsoi stared at it, her face impassive, but it wasn't an easy expression. It was as if she worked to keep all emotion from her face.

"You should take this," Rel said. It was clear she meant Mantos, for she didn't look at Bomsoi. "You might need Haelo's strength."

As he accepted the sword, Mantos saw Neiruk recoil. Bomsoi stroked the sides of his head with both hands.

"*It's all right*," she said. "*There's nothing to fear.*"

It took Mantos a moment to realize she hadn't said the words aloud.

"*Why does he fear the sword*?" Mantos asked in the same way, buckling the belt at his waist.

"*He fears what it means*," Bomsoi replied. She turned her attention to Rel with no further explanation. "Are you sure you won't come with us?"

Rel shook her head. "I'll be no use to you." Her tone edged on mournful. "I'm no use to anyone any longer." She stepped back to break the conversation and dipped her head. "I wish you both luck."

With a bow, she turned and trekked back across to the safety of the palace, saying no more.

Bomsoi mounted Neiruk at the base of his neck and reached for Mantos. "Come on. It's time."

Mantos couldn't stop himself from taking one last look at the palace. Deep within the mountainside, Fonbir was watching. Though he couldn't see him, Mantos knew he would be. *I'll make you proud*, he thought in an echo of Elsya's last words. Then he accepted Bomsoi's hand, and they disappeared into the white swath of freezing sky.

They flew for seven days, resting only when Neiruk needed it. Chilled and soaked through, Mantos' teeth chattered as they descended through the layer of cloud that had masked their progress. From above, he recognized nothing of the landscape. They came down too close to make out the jagged outline of the coast. If he'd seen it, Mantos might have recognized its shape from maps. Neiruk's great claws ground into the earth as he landed heavily with exhaustion, sending clumps of soil churning around them. Then the beast was still. The silence of the clearing was vast.

"Where are we?" Mantos asked as he slid from the Prago's back.

"We're on the southern tip of Althemer," Bomsoi replied. "One more day will take us to Mellul, but I thought it best to stop here. We can bring Valaria with us for further clout with the Mellul."

Mantos' neck scales fluttered. "Isn't being on Althemer dangerous?"

Bomsoi chuckled. "Isn't everywhere? It is, but the south of the island is where Valaria is gathering what remains of the Althemerian forces. Here they've carved an enclave of control."

"Is Valaria nearby?" Mantos asked, though he felt foolish. How could Bomsoi know?

"Possibly," the Stranger replied, "although I know for certain one of my folk is near. Or at least, one of my blood."

Her eyes flashed blue, and she stilled. Mantos closed his eyes, sensing her power. Bomsoi was reaching outward, trying to locate someone. One of her folk? An Uloni? Mantos didn't know of any others in existence.

It might not be an Uloni, he realized. It could be a part-Uloni, and he knew one of them, all right.

Bomsoi pulled back into movement and gave him a nod. "I couldn't speak to them, but I know they're not too far off."

"At the coast?" Mantos asked. "Perhaps even on a boat?"

Bomsoi narrowed her eyes. "I suspect so, yes."

"I think I know who they are."

As Neiruk took shelter and rested, Mantos and Bomsoi headed south. Mantos told Bomsoi of Jishu and her powers, how she was the reason The *Water Prago* was the fastest ship on the Sea of Souls. As she listened, a strange look came over Bomsoi's face. It was at once wistful and pained.

"I don't know how many like Jishu are in the world. I can only sense them when I'm nearby. I worry for them, for what will happen."

A coil of worry twisted within Mantos too. It took a moment for him to understand it was Nunako's presence. The goddess felt concern.

"Jishu learned to mask her colors," Mantos said. "If others did too, they'd be safe."

"What of those who can't? What of those whose masks slip?" Bomsoi answered.

Nunako twisted within him again, and Mantos had to bite down on the words she tried to make him say. *You shouldn't have done what you did. You should have done what your mothers asked of you.* The unsaid words were sour on his tongue.

"I'll offer them refuge in the Masvam Empire," he said instead. "It's the least I can do to safeguard my—Nunako's—blood."

Bomsoi's laugh was soft and sorrowful. "If you can find them, and they can get into your borders."

"Masvam borders are vast," Mantos offered, not knowing how to comfort the Stranger's sadness. "Perhaps many of them will already be inside."

Bomsoi didn't respond to that.

They walked in silence for the rest of the way, winding through a thick band of trees. As they neared the other side of the forest, the noise of camped soldiers rose in the distance. They proceeded with more caution, falling silent, trying to keep their footfalls inconspicuous.

He sensed the approaching sword before he saw it. Mantos threw up a wall of rock between himself and the attacker, Nunako's power coursing through him. It wasn't as intense as when Emmy was nearby, but Bomsoi's presence acted as a worthy conduit. The Stranger herself struck out with her power, locking a second attacker's arms within columns of ice.

"We're here to see Princess Valaria," Bomsoi said.

The command in her voice and the strange colors on her face made the two Althemerians jolt. Mantos allowed the wall of rock to fall, and Bomsoi banished her ice.

The one who had come for Mantos nodded, his face pasty with shock. "Come with me."

As they entered the Althemerian encampment and wound through its tented barracks, every set of eyes stared. The air filled with excited whispers of "The Stranger!" and more sinister expressions, "That's a Masvam." Their attackers-turned-escorts brought them to a larger tent in the middle of the makeshift city. One spoke to a guard posted outside, who disappeared inward.

The figure that emerged wasn't the guard. It was Valaria.

She wore armor that bore the scars of battle, and her face spoke of recent skirmishes. Atop her head she wore something Mantos had never seen: a makeshift crown wrought of twisted and charred metal that glinted in the growing moons' light.

"So," she said, crossing her arms, "my brother didn't kill you, then?"

Despite everything, Mantos laughed. "No, he didn't kill me."

Valaria grunted at him, then inclined her head at Bomsoi, two fingers to her lips. "Stranger, it's good to see you again."

"And you, Your Highness. Should we address you as 'queen' from now on?"

Valaria entered her tent and motioned for them to follow. It was full of trestle tables filled with maps and plans, and the many hard-faced soldiers inside rose at her entrance.

"I've vowed I will not become queen until they can crown me in Kubodinnu." There was a murmur of assent from her retinue. "For now, I remain a princess, but I am in command of this island and her armies."

She gestured for them to approach the largest map. It covered a whole table. Mantos stayed silent as she talked them through their progress, how the Althemerians had rallied to her call, the impressive number of troops she'd gathered, a new alliance with what remained of the Selamans and the Metakalans, a gift of supplies from the Belfoni, and the unfortunate stalemate in negotiations with the Mellul.

"We need their ships and their weapons," Valaria said, planting a talon on the map between the southern coast of Althemer and the northernmost tip of Mellul. "We've gathered what remains of the Althemerian fleet, but it's not enough to transport all our combined armies to Masvam soil, not with the Masvams prowling the Sea of Souls."

Mantos folded his arms across his chest. "Where do you intend to land in the Empire, once you have the vessels?"

Valaria slid a narrow gaze toward him. "Khitarian will march south and attack the city of Masvam from the north. We will land south and march north, leaving a contingent on board ships to storm the city from the coast."

"Numbers alone will not break the city," Mantos said.

"Then it's a good thing we're not working on numbers alone, Masvam," Valaria snapped back. "You recall I mentioned a gift of supplies from the Belfoni? They're too far east and beyond too many mountains to send troops, but the Oligarchy know well that if we don't stop the Masvams, Belfon will fall. Eventually they'll cross the mountains. It's only a matter of time. They've gifted us with more Belfoni explosives than Bandim Tiboli could dream of." Her face slid into a vicious scowl. "We'll blast him to pieces, if that's what it takes."

A surge of sickness rose in Mantos' chest, but he banished it. He had to.

"That," Valaria continued, returning her attention to the map, "along with support from Mellul and the siege weapons they can bring, and your little Masvam rebellion, will give us the best chance we have to break the city. Once we break the city and kill your brother, the war is over."

Your war is over, Mantos thought. *Mine never will be.*

Bomsoi must have heard his thoughts, for she responded, "It *will* be, Mantos. I promise."

Valaria missed the look that passed between them and jabbed the map on the thick inkblot that marked the city of Masvam. "Once your brother is dead, I don't care what you do. But I will have my island back. And I'll plant Bandim's skull on a spike right on the site where I'll claim my crown."

"First, we need the Mellul," Bomsoi said. Mantos was grateful she turned the conversation away from his brother's severed head. "That's why we're here. Neiruk has flown us this far, and Mantos and I will continue on tomorrow to visit Queen Tayu. If you consent to join us, I'd like you to come as well. Together, we hope to convince them that coming to Althemer's aid is vital. And to show them we can win."

Valaria trailed her claw down the map to the jutting outline of Mellul's north coast. "So far, they've listened to nothing I have to say. But I'll come with you if you think it useful, Stranger."

With talk of battles and plans at an end, Valaria arranged to billet and feed Mantos and Bomsoi. As soon as he was able, Mantos slipped away, winding his way to the sea's edge. A forest of masts, ships of all sizes, crowded into the safety of a wide bay. Before he found the vessel he sought, a tap on his shoulder made him spin around.

"Well, well, well. If it isn't Mantos Tiboli."

Mantos' face split with a grin. "Chaata."

"That's 'Captain' to you," the Linvarran female said, with a smile to match Mantos' own.

"What are you doing here?" Mantos asked.

Chaata shrugged with feigned nonchalance. "A little smuggling here, a little trading there, and then the new queen of Althemer wants your ship because it's fast, and you end up running explosives from Belfon for her."

Mantos reached for her arm, squeezing it. Chaata allowed the touch. "I'm glad you're safe."

Memories of the last time they had seen one another, back before Kubodinnu and the whole of Althemer fell, crashed over him. A new wave of grief threatened to overwhelm him. It hadn't just been Valentia and Fylica and his mother who had died. It was everyone in the palace, including two younglings who shouldn't ever have been in danger. Tero's ashes would never rest.

Chaata cocked her head to the side at his sudden sadness. Then it was her turn to touch his arm. "Come with me. The crew will want to see you, Jishu in particular. She still talks about how handsome you are. I don't see it myself, but that one has strange tastes."

Mantos allowed the captain to take him through the thickening crowds of sailors and soldiers. Warding off the vicious looks he received as a Masvam, Mantos tried to push his grief away. Chaata led him to a little rowboat and took up the oars, navigating them through the traffic of the bay and to the hull of the *Water Prago*. Chaata signaled, and the crew lowered hooks on ropes and, with strong pulls, lifted the rowboat to the deck.

As soon as Mantos' head was above the rail, all strength left his body. His eyes were drunk with fatigue. It couldn't be. This was impossible. They were dead.

"Uzet!"

As Mantos' voice crossed the deck like a whip crack, the ungendered youngling turned. Their eyes widened in recognition. "Mantos!"

Mantos leaped from the rowboat and scooped the miracle in his arms, swinging Uzet around until the youngling shrieked with joy.

"How?" Mantos hugged the little thing close. "I thought I'd lost you."

Chaata's boots clomped on the deck as she jumped on board. "They never left the *Water Prago*. The older one, Zrazashi, asked if they could stay. I should have declined, but something stopped me." Her expression darkened. "I'm glad I said yes, considering what happened next. If they'd gone with the Althemerians, they would have been dead."

As Mantos placed a giggling Uzet onto the deck, Zrazashi appeared, his arms crossed but a small smile on his face.

"Zrazashi," Mantos said, opening his arms to invite the other male into an embrace.

The other of Tero's younglings hesitated before flinging his arms around Mantos' waist.

"I can't believe you're both alive," Mantos said, holding Zrazashi at arm's length. "Why didn't you leave the ship?"

Zrazashi pulled back and shrugged. "I asked myself what Father would have done. I decided he wouldn't have wanted to go with the Althemerians, so I asked Captain Chaata if we could stay on board. I like to think," he continued, a thickness coming to his words, "that Poi was looking out for us."

Mantos' own throat grew tight. "I like to think that too."

As the evening drew into night and the moons rose, it was with reluctance that Mantos left the *Water Prago*, rowed back to the shore by Chaata herself once again. His face ached from smiling at the miraculous turn events had taken. Perhaps this was the start of good fortune. Perhaps they would win. He looked up, grinning at Nunako's three faces.

Chaata noticed his light heart. "You care for those younglings very much. Why?"

"Their father saved my life, in more ways than one," Mantos replied. "It's the least I can do to honor his memory."

"Grand words," Chaata said over the steady back and forth of her arms as she rowed. "You're always full of grandness. And now godliness, I believe. You succeeded?"

"We did," Mantos replied, "though only in part. There's still some way to go. Things are about to become very dangerous. You shouldn't stay."

Chaata nodded. "The *Water Prago* isn't a military ship. We can't help in a battle. I've agreed to move troops, but once that's over, we'll take our leave."

"Keep them safe for me, please."

"That's what I've been doing this whole time," Chaata replied as they neared the water's edge. "I won't let them come to harm."

"Thank you, Chaata. Captain," Mantos added with a smile. "I owe you much."

"Don't forget your old friends when you're an emperor," she retorted.

CHAPTER TWENTY-TWO

Bandim-Dorai

It had been days. The wretch still hadn't broken. After yet another report of Johrann Maa's lack of success in pulling Emmy apart, Bandim-Dorai could take no more. For her continued failure, Johrann had received a strike to the face that split her lip into a red blossom, and Bandim-Dorai had become determined to take matters into his own hands.

Retreating to the darkness of the underpalace would be a welcome respite from the rest of his duties. A god he might be, but even a god could grow tired of reports of rebellion and plague. The Lurking Death was spreading through the Empire like nothing seen before, following the routes of cowardice as folk fled for what they saw as the safety of the Marches. They seemed to think the further from the capital they could run, the further they would be from disaster. The Death had other plans, and Bandim-Dorai saw it as fitting. *Their disloyalty is the real plague. The more that perish, the better. I only want those loyal to me in my midst.*

As he delved deeper into the underpalace, with its warren of winding corridors, some of the Sun Emperor's worries eased. The darkness had always been comforting in its coolness, its simplicity. Perhaps in its embrace, even as he worked at pulling at every thread of this stubborn Uloni's life, teasing until the fibers unwound, the next steps in Bandim-Dorai's campaign would become clear.

It was only a matter of time before the rebels returned in force, and his brother would be in their midst. But, Bandim-Dorai thought with a smirk, he didn't have a Heart. Bandim-Dorai knew a Heart such as Johrann, as useless as she might be in some ways, was a necessary anchor and amplifier. Without Emmy, Mantos could never match the power of Bandim-Dorai. And with Emmy and Johrann together, nothing could stop the Sun Emperor. Nothing.

Bandim-Dorai stopped outside the thick cell door. The guards, nothing like the resplendent upper palace soldiers, wore not fine black leather inlaid with red, but uniforms more rags than livery. When they saw the robed and jeweled figure of their emperor, the weak bend of their backs became ramrod straight, their weapons snapping upward to attention.

"Your Imperial Majesty," the older of the two males said in a tremulous voice. "We didn't expect you."

Bandim-Dorai flicked his gaze up and down the guards' dress. It wasn't filthy but was threadbare, as if they'd worn the same clothing on their backs from the day they'd taken up their positions. "When did you last receive a new uniform?"

Dread dripped from them, uncertainty seeping like fog. "Your Imperial Majesty," the oldest one said, "never."

"Unacceptable," Bandim-Dorai said. "You'll receive new uniforms by tomorrow. Those under are as important as those over."

Delight and relief burned off the fog like the midday sun. "Thank you, Your Imperial Majesty."

The conversation over, Bandim-Dorai turned to the door and composed himself before he entered. He wasn't afraid. How could he be? Intimidation was an art form, not something to rush into. He reached out with his power, tendrils sneaking through the thin cracks around the door to seek Emmy's truth.

As much as he probed, surprise welled within him. There was fear, of course. Locked in a cell with nothing more than water for days, of course she was afraid. But where Bandim-Dorai had expected a dark maw of terror, there was a pool of serenity. Emmy had such strangeness within her.

It wouldn't take long to drain it. Of this, he was certain.

"Open the door," he said, and the guards obeyed.

Stale air tinged with the odor of body and waste escaped, but Bandim-Dorai paid it no attention. It was nothing compared to the stench of cooking flesh, and he had smelled that more times now than he could count. In the thin light carried from the narrow passageway outside, he spotted the wretch huddled in a corner, the remains of her clothing torn upon her frame from whatever means Johrann had used in her unsuccessful attempts to gain her cooperation. Instead of stirring to look at him, Emmy's body went still, but he saw the wet slide of an eye flickering toward him through the thick strands of her fronds, coming undone from their braids.

"Are you hungry, my dear?" She met his words with silence. Bandim-Dorai gave a light laugh. "Of course you are." He turned to the guards. "Bring some bread and water and close the door behind you when you leave."

As he spoke and as they carried out his orders, Emmy remained still as a corpse. Bandim-Dorai could sense her, though: the pulse of blood through her body, the steady in and out of her breath, the cycling flicker of emotion passing through her. Fear. Defiance. Loathing. Serenity. So it went.

The door closed, plunging them into darkness. It didn't matter. Bandim-Dorai's vision was as clear in the dark as in the light, just as he'd always wanted. Dorai had given him everything he ever desired. He picked up the wooden plate that held a single slice of stale bread and the cup of lukewarm water before hunching down in front of the Uloni. Emmy refused to move, but her heartbeat rose with his proximity. At the scent of the bread, stale as it was, her stomach growled.

"It isn't my wish to punish you, my dear," Bandim-Dorai said. "You're my blood, you know. Daughter of my daughter, my power lives in you. I don't want to hurt you. I don't want you to starve. I simply want to talk to you."

He sensed her lurch forward before it happened and tipped backward out of her reach. He chuckled at the way she bared her teeth and strained against the new, thicker chains that bound her. Ice bloomed at her wrists, but the reinforced metal held.

"I admire your tenacity, little one," he said as he straightened. "That's a nicer name than No one, don't you think? That's your name, isn't it? You told me it was Emmy when we first met, but you told Johrann it was 'Emena.' No one. But Little One is more flattering. I'll call you that instead." He set the plate aside and held the cup toward her. "Drink, Little One, or you'll die. I don't want you to die."

Through her matted tangle of fronds, the Uloni's eyes flicked from his face to the cup and back again. Her tongue darted out in a futile attempt to wet her cracked and bleeding lips. Desire and anger and fear twisted like a rope. With deliberate slowness, Bandim-Dorai brought the cup toward her, tilting it toward her. Though she flinched at first, Emmy's resolve broke and she parted her mouth to drink. Water spilled down her chin. Deep within Bandim-Dorai, a strange sensation rose. It was more than compassion. It was care.

"There, there," he said as he withdrew the cup, eliciting a whimper. "Do you understand, Little One? I don't want to hurt you."

Emotions roiled again. Fear. Defiance. Loathing. Fear. The serenity vanished. Good.

Bandim-Dorai set the cup aside. It made a hollow clunk on the stone floor. He touched the side of Emmy's face, sliding her chin upward so she met his gaze.

Her lips moved, and she croaked, her voice part-moistened, "What do you want?"

"I want you," he replied, sliding his thumb across her cheek.

A burst of revulsion exploded within her. The fallout from it was more fear, sharp and barbed, and angry. He felt her plumb for that well of serenity again, but also felt her failing.

"I was right, wasn't I?" he cooed. "When I said you'd always been nothing, I was right. Oh, my dear. I can see right through you."

Emmy said nothing, her whole face trembling in his grasp. Just as before, he sensed the well of power within her before it happened. As her wrists and hands tracked with ice, fractal patterns tracing up her skin, Bandim-Dorai held fast, undeterred.

"I was also wrong about you," he said, strengthening his grip to stop her shaking. As his power grew, so did his, heat tracking to the tips of his talons. "I thought you were weak, but you're not. You can't be weak. You're blood of mine. Dorai's power, my power, flows within you. I can sense it, see it, feel it burn, even as you use this infernal ice. You have power, Little One. You have courage, though you've heard so many lies throughout your life."

He probed through the dark corners of her memory, imbibing all the feelings, and hearing all the taunts.

Useless.

Unwanted.

Pointless.

Freak.

Moon Rogue.

Demon.

He searched further, filtering out old memories and focusing on more recent ones. Perhaps he could reach inside, try to glean what his brother and his rebellious compatriots were planning. Bandim-Dorai's mouth stretched in a grin as everything came to him.

Mantos.

Bomsoi.

Nunako.

Balance.

Dorai.

Destruction.

And there it was. All of his brother and Bomsoi's plans. Their great desires, their schemes to return balance to the world. All of it spread before him like the scenes embroidered on his father's fine bedspread, the bedspread that Bandim-Dorai had burned to nothing but ash. They were in the Khinish mountains, but the intention was to come here, to destroy the foothold he'd hacked from the earth.

They might try, but they would never succeed.

Bandim-Dorai pulled back from her memory, the tips of his talons hot but not burning.

"My dear, dear Little One," he said. "Even if you do nothing else for me, you've already done enough."

Fear. Loathing. Fear.

He released her face. He was winning, and it felt glorious. Now to strike the blow that would shatter her. He'd come across one particular part of her past he knew would bring her to her knees, and he dealt the killing stroke.

"Tell me who Krodge was. Tell me what she did."

Emmy's eyes sharpened. Fear. Fear. Fear. There was no surprise at that. He had brushed past enough memories of the Metakalan to understand the nature of their relationship.

Bandim-Dorai gave an affectionate chuckle. "Tell me what she did."

Lower lip trembling, Emmy shook her head. "No."

"Such insolence," Bandim-Dorai said, though there was no malice in his tone. "I already know. I was right that you were mistreated. I simply didn't understand how much. Put it into words, Little One. Tell me."

Had she enough saliva, he knew she would've spat. "No."

"She beat you," Bandim-Dorai said in his softest voice. "She tortured you. She cut and cut and cut away at you until you were nothing but flayed bone. That's why Johrann's ministrations haven't worked. You don't fear bodily pain." He traced a finger across the hollow of her throat. "I could cut your neck from ear to ear and you wouldn't fear it. You might even accept it. That's the way things were for so long. But then, things changed for you, didn't they?" He squeezed her shoulders. "This Krodge died. You got away. Thanks to me, it would seem," he added with a grin. "See? I was already helping you before I even knew you existed." He tamed his expression into solemnity. "Once you escaped, you found something new, didn't you? You discovered more than your little friendships. You found acceptance. You found love."

Emmy's whole body trembled under the weight of his hands.

"Well," he continued, dropping his voice low, "let me tell you what will happen if you don't obey. If you don't submit to me and allow me to use you as a conduit for my power, everything will proceed as it would otherwise. Mantos and his little army, wherever he gets it from, will travel down from the mountains. They'll come here and try to take the city. And they'll fail. But if you submit, here's what won't happen. I won't unseam your friend Zecha from throat to stomach. I won't smash your friend Charo's egg in front of her, then crush her head between my hands. I won't finish what I started with your friend Rel and burn her until she's nothing but blackened bone. And I won't make you watch me do all of this. I'll spare them, and I'll spare you from it all."

Bandim-Dorai pulled back and stood, stepping toward the shut door. "Submit, Emmy. I'll give you some time to think about it."

He knocked the door, and it opened, flooding the cell with a faint light. Bandim-Dorai didn't look back as he left. He didn't need to see her face.

Her fear gave way to abject horror and twisting distress.

Terror. Terror. Terror.

Good.

CHAPTER TWENTY-THREE

Emmy

In the dark, Emmy trembled from more than the temperature. Her visit from Bandim had been the only time he'd come to her. It was still once too many. His words echoed in her mind again and again. What rang truest of all was the sincerity in them. He would kill every one of her friends without question or hesitation. Emmy could do nothing to prevent it but submit.

Bandim's visit had been days ago, and it was longer since Johrann Maa's last. The emperor was good to his word and had left her plenty of time to consider her actions. The last water she'd drunk was the small amount Bandim gave her. Since, no guard had entered to give her more. She knew it was just another way to break her. She also knew it was effective. Days blended into night the same way above and below ground had become unknowable. Her worry weighed on her heavier than any lesson Krodge ever taught her.

The cell door flew open. Emmy flinched away. She knew who it was before she saw their face. Johrann Maa appeared in the cold light of her lamp, casting deep shadows under her eyes.

"You stink," she declared.

Had Emmy the energy, she would have snorted. Johrann planted her lamp on the ground and jabbed the toe of her boots under Emmy's chin, forcing her head upward. The desire to lash out, grab Johrann's ankle, and freeze it until the bones snapped was strong, but Emmy's exhaustion stopped her. She tilted her head away. She was too weak.

"Have you had enough time to consider the One True Goddess' words?" Johrann asked. "It shouldn't have taken long to decide what's your best choice."

When Emmy didn't answer, Johrann planted her boot on her chestplate and sent her hurtling into the wall behind her. Chains clanked and bit at her raw wrists. Emmy willed herself to rise, but her body wouldn't obey.

"I should kill you now," Johrann said. She loomed above Emmy and tipped her onto her back with one foot. There was an almost healed cut across her lips. "The emperor would never find out."

With a sliver of courage, Emmy rasped, "You wouldn't do that. You're too afraid of him."

Whether it was emotion or the flickering of the lantern, Emmy couldn't tell, but something changed in Johrann's expression. She repaid Emmy's honesty with a swift kick to the ribs.

"You should be the one who's afraid. It's cooperate or condemn all your friends to death. Don't doubt it, he'll do as he said. He'll make it agonizing."

The dark, burned circles on Johrann's neck pulsed as she spoke. Emmy dragged herself upright, tottering on unsteady feet. Now she understood what those strange marks were.

Though she hadn't seen them, she knew she bore similar marks on her throat from Bandim's flaming grip. "Just like he did to you?" she asked, reaching for the other Uloni's neck with a trembling hand.

Johrann smacked Emmy's hand away, the force of it sending her and her chains back into the wall. "Shut up."

"It doesn't have to be like this," Emmy continued, her claws digging into the mortar between the stones. She wasn't sure where her tongue was leading her, but desperation drove her on. "Why do you need his approval? Why do you let him hurt you?"

Her blow hit home, and Johrann flinched. "I don't need his approval. I'm not doing this for him. I'm doing it for Dorai. I told you before, my whole life has been for the One True Goddess. She saved me, then sent me on this path to bring her back into the world. Everything I've done, I've done for her. Not Bandim Tiboli, but the goddess Dorai."

"And your goddess allows him to burn you?" Emmy asked. With each word, she watched Johrann wind tighter. "Is this how she repays you?"

"Shut up."

Johrann went to strike her again. The blow came but didn't hurt. Instead, the moment her hand touched Emmy's skin, something happened. Everything lurched.

And they were falling.

Emmy woke on the hard ground with the smell of smoke in her nostrils. She sat up, every one of her bones aching, and stared. It was like it had been before. Everything was desolate. Destroyed.

A moan made her turn. Johrann Maa pulled herself upright, pressing a hand to her head.

"Where are we?" she asked. Her confusion made her sound almost friendly.

"This is the future the Grandmother of the World showed me," Emmy said, rising onto unsteady feet. "This is the future where Bandim Tiboli and Dorai win."

Johrann's face warped with a snarl. "Impossible. Dorai doesn't bring destruction."

"No," said a new voice. "But Bandim will."

Emmy whipped around. "Grandmother."

The Grandmother of the World stood before them, stooped yet steady, a dark cast to her face. Johrann shot a glance from Emmy to the goddess and back again, her eyes narrow.

"Impossible."

"Nothing is impossible, child," the Grandmother said. "Improbable, but not impossible."

Stepping back, Johrann's eyes widened. She lifted a trembling hand to her mouth as something like realization washed over her in waves.

"I recognize that voice." Her words were uneasy.

Emmy watched as the Grandmother approached her, both arms outstretched. All she said in reply was, "Yes."

"It was you in the desert," Johrann said, her voice hitching. "It wasn't Dorai. It was you."

Emmy's chest tightened as a wave of despair rolled off the other Uloni. Johrann had been so sure Dorai had come to her, had seen the goddess as her savior. But if it was the Grandmother who had saved her from death in the desert, then nothing Johrann believed was true.

The Grandmother clamped Johrann's elbows, her strength far beyond what her frail frame suggested. Johrann tried to struggle back, but the Grandmother held firm.

"Deception is a powerful thing. You know that well."

"You lied to me. All this time I believed the One True Goddess had come to me, had chosen me for a special purpose. But it was a lie."

"It was no lie," the Grandmother said, still holding her in place "You've served the One True Goddess all these cycles. Me. You've done my bidding, carried out what I needed you to do."

Something lurched within Emmy at that. She drew her eyeridges low. "What do you mean?"

The Grandmother ignored her, instead turning Johrann Maa and forcing her to survey the surrounding scene. "This is what will happen if I don't succeed. Everything under the Arc will burn."

"What do you mean?" Emmy repeated. Her voice echoed across the barren wasteland.

At last the Grandmother turned to her. There was disappointment in her eyes. "You still believe what you want to believe. The world is not black and white, Dark and Light. I hoped you would learn that."

Before Emmy could respond, Johrann asked in a wavering voice, "You're the One True Goddess?"

"Yes," the Grandmother replied. "Nunako and Dorai and all things come from me. I am the beginning and the end: the past, the present, and the future."

"You saved me," Johrann continued. "You took me from the desert. You guided me to the Masvam Palace and the One of Two. You compelled me to destroy the village."

Emmy's vision blurred with betrayal as she glared at the Grandmother. "It was you who made her kill them all. My parents, the other Uloni. It wasn't Dorai. It was you."

"It was." The Grandmother's voice was steady and remorseless. "It had to happen."

Emmy pressed on. "Didn't you want to save the world? To right all the wrongs?"

"I do," the Grandmother replied. "I still do."

"But what—"

Johrann Maa cut across her. "What do you need me to do now, my Goddess?"

The Grandmother's touch became gentle, and she reached to touch Johrann's cheek. "Hands and Hearts, all together. There's one thing left to do. She knows how to proceed."

At that the Grandmother released her. The familiar smoke that heralded the goddess' departure began to form. Emmy leaped forward, but Johrann grabbed her by the waist. Her grasp fell short of the Grandmother's disappearing form.

"What is made cannot but unmade," the Grandmother said once again, "but what has been made can be destroyed."

"No!" Emmy cried.

But it was too late. The Grandmother disappeared.

* * *

She came to on the floor of her cell, once more chained and filthy. The sob erupted from Emmy before she could stop it. The sound was obscene in the silence of the lightless chamber.

Nothing made sense. Before now, Emmy had trusted the Grandmother. She and Mantos were doing what was right by her words. They would stop Bandim Tiboli and Dorai, countering his power with Nunako's. How could the goddess' intentions be good? Now Emmy knew the truth. The Grandmother had sanctioned the Uloni's destruction, descendants of her own blood. She'd called herself the One True Goddess, but how could that be the case? How could a murderer be true?

And Johrann, where was she? Panic rose in Emmy's throat. What if she had gone to Bandim and told him everything? Something stopped that thought short. Emmy forced herself to relax against her heavy chains. Johrann's voice when she'd asked what the Grandmother wanted her to do next was assured and clear. She wouldn't go to Bandim, not if she believed Dorai was no longer the One True Goddess. In the short time she had known her, Emmy knew Johrann was loyal. She had to be, to endure his apparent violence. But Johrann had been loyal all this time to Dorai, not Bandim. Now that she understood it wasn't Dorai but the Grandmother, Emmy understood her allegiance would have shifted in a heartbeat.

Another sob rose in Emmy's throat. This wasn't what she'd believed. It wasn't what Bomsoi had told her. Who had the Grandmother had referred to? Was it Bomsoi? What did 'she knows how to proceed' mean? Somehow, Bandim's threats were pale compared to the earthquake in her mind.

The Grandmother's last words rolled over her again. *What is made cannot but unmade, but what has been made can be destroyed.* Did she mean the Uloni? Did the Grandmother aim to kill them all? Why hadn't she done it already, if she'd already sanctioned the murder of so many of her folk?

The cell door swung open on heavy hinges, and Emmy flinched away from the light. Two sets of heavy boots trooped in. There was a clank of keys, heavy on a ring. It sparked a memory of her own apothecary keys, back when things were simpler. Someone released her wrists and ankles, and two sets of hands hauled her onto trembling feet. Palace guards.

"What?" was all she rasped.

"You're to come with us by order of the Emperor," one voice said.

Emmy's bare feet dragged through the murk that was the cell floor as they pulled her into the stone hallway, past the sneering faces of her jailers. They now wore uniforms as clean as the ones of the soldiers dragging her away.

Perhaps this was it. Bandim would bring her to her knees in front of him, order her to submit or else have all her friends killed in front of her. A small part of her wondered, did it even matter any longer? Despair weighed heavier than her chains. Did anything matter any longer? She'd thought she and Mantos were part of a grand plan to restore balance to the world. But the Grandmother had lied. Had Bomsoi lied? If she based her beliefs on deception, how could she trust anything?

Questions whirled and whirled until she could think no longer, and she allowed the palace guards to drag her to her fate.

CHAPTER TWENTY-FOUR

Bandim-Dorai

At the Sun Emperor's request, servants bedecked the Great Hall with a splendor to amaze the gathered lords and nobles. Bandim-Dorai sat on the dais at the top of the hall, grinning into his cup as a procession of his loyal subjects approached, bowed, and pledged their undying support to the One True Goddess. The seat to his left remained empty. He had no empress, and Johrann was absent, for now. Tesselica sat nearby, reveling in the attention and finery his proximity to the emperor brought. Bandim-Dorai imbibed the other male's pleasure as much as the wine from his cup.

There was no occasion for the grand feasting, no Vhaun festival or important date in the cycle. What there was, however, was a purpose. Bandim-Dorai allowed another simpering lord and his lady to kiss his rings and speak pretty words to him. These were the folk who controlled the provinces and reaches. These were the folk who could curb control of those disloyal traitors who were fleeing, or worse, were turning their tails and their colors to Elsya's rebellion, or worse yet, to Mantos. This grand hall, filled to the brim with beauty and the plunder of the Sun Emperor's latest acquisitions and victories, was a reminder to his lords of what their loyalty got them.

Bandim-Dorai needed all the loyalty he could muster. He knew what went on outside his palace walls and the borders of his vast empire, both from within Emmy's memory and from outside intelligence. He knew about Valaria and her pathetic attempts to rally the remains of the Althemerians. He knew the rebels were creeping from their hiding place in the Great Northern Range. With them might come a rabble from the Kingdom of Khin, though if the new queen Khitarian followed the form of her ancestors, the mountainfolk would never cross their own borders.

No matter how much those who stood against him might try, they would never defeat him. This little feast would secure most his loyal force. No traitors or foreign armies could stand against that.

As the last of the lords bade him well and the all the gathered took their seats, the hall fell silent. Tesselica turned his face upward, beaming with pride as the Sun Emperor stood.

Bandim-Dorai knew he looked like the goddess he was, resplendent in sweeping robes of black and red silk, with a grand jeweled headdress on his horns and flames painted upon his face. He raised his hands, pulling on the power he gleaned from Tesselica's belief, and dimmed every flame in the Great Hall to a low ember. He lowered his arms.

"My most loyal friends," he said in a voice that carried into every corner of the hall, "I thank each of you for coming to celebrate with me today. As we all know, the world outside this palace grows darker, thick with the taint of traitors and the diseases they spread." There was a murmur of agreement, low and threatening. "However, those within his hall are a representation of the wondrous loyalty this empire has. You are the best of my folk, those that I hold closest in my esteem, and to my heart." He slid his gaze toward Tesselica, giving him a lingering look. Power bloomed within him again. "No matter what happens, no matter what those who seek to move against us try to do, we will prosper. The One True Goddess will prevail!"

Bandim-Dorai thrust his arms into the air again, sending every candle, lantern, and hearth fire into an unbearable torrent of flame. The gathered nobles erupted into cheers and shouts, clapping their hands, and hammering their feet against the hard floor. As the Sun Emperor sat, the feast began in earnest, with servants bearing platters swarming into the room.

Course after course came, each one announced by a herald, with care taken to emphasize where the ingredients came from. The descriptions featured every plundered port and overthrown city. Even through food, Bandim-Dorai wanted those in the Great Hall to appreciate the strength of his power and the length of his reach. Anyone who stood with him would share in his bounty. Those against him would feel his wrath.

There was a lull in proceedings before they served the sweet courses. Bandim-Dorai had made these arrangements long in advance, though still reached out to ensure the attendants were ready. Satisfied, he rose and dimmed the flames again, plunging the Great Hall into darkness. Everyone fell silent. At that, the doors swung open and Johrann Maa proceeded through the walkway amid the tables, a chain clanking as it hung behind her and her other hand stretched forward, a flame lighting their path. On the end of the chain, leashed by the neck like an animal, was a figure that made Bandim-Dorai's face split with a grin.

Johrann walked with grace, while Emmy strode with a stiff gait. She'd been scrubbed from the cell's filth and was now dressed in a simple shift. Her feet remained bare.

Bandim-Dorai stepped out from behind the table, but stayed high on the dais, waiting. Whatever happened next, he would make the best of it. An emperor planned for all outcomes.

"Here, before you all, I present the key to my success. This female, brought before you in chains, is just like my beloved Johrann Maa. Just as Johrann was the conduit through which I regained my power, this one has the chance to aid me too. She must make a choice before you." Johrann pulled on the chain to bring Emmy in line with her, then forced her onto her knees. Bandim-Dorai stared down, giving Emmy a hard stare. "So, make your choice before them. Before me. Do you submit to the power of the Sun Emperor, Bandim-Dorai?"

Before Emmy answered, he took a moment to feel. There was sharp fear, restless anticipation, the beauty of Tesselica's delight, and then a deep blankness from Johrann. And from Emmy? Cool resignation. She had made her choice.

Emmy looked up, meeting his eyes with a steady gaze.

"I submit."

Her voice echoed across the hall. Bandim-Dorai chuckled with glee as the room again exploded with applause and approval. He sent the flames into a frenzy once more. Either way would be a victory, but submission was sweeter than any death.

He led the applause for a little while longer, then reached for Johrann. She gave the chain to a guard and ascended to the dais. A ripple of jealousy came from Tesselica, but he kept his face adoring. Bandim-Dorai knew he wanted to be where Johrann was. He wanted his hand in the emperor's grasp, rising to the highest place by his side. Tess was sweet, loyal, and beautiful, but he couldn't serve the same purpose as Johrann.

Signaling for quiet, Bandim-Dorai kept a firm hold on the blue and purple hand in his grasp. Johrann was still shuttered, her inner secrets beyond his senses, but that didn't matter.

"My loyal friends, you have seen before you today the supplication of this creature of power. Perhaps one day she too will come to love me, just like my dearest Johrann Maa." A wave of revulsion rolled off Emmy, but it only made him smile more. "Without Johrann, I could not have returned to you, powerful and corporeal again. Without her unfailing determination to bring me back into this world, the lies of Nunako would still yoke us. That's why today, in the sight of all of you, I declare this: Johrann Maa will become empress of the Masvam Empire!"

There was a beat of shocked silence. Johrann turned to him, her eyes shimmering, her stone resolve falling enough to allow a crack of terror to show. She closed her vulnerability as Bandim-Dorai brought a hand to caress her face. As he moved, the room filled with jubilation once again. There was a different edge to it this time: a definite undercurrent of fear.

"Don't worry, dear Heart," he said, brushing his fingers down her neck to the scars he had put there. "You needn't fear anything. Together we're stronger than anything under the Arc, Hand and Heart together. And now I've taken Mantos' Heart for myself, it doesn't matter what so-called power Nunako grants him. No one can stop me, and I have you to thank for everything. You deserve the elevation as my empress, and I want you at my side always."

Bandim-Dorai guided her to her rightful seat, high on the dais beside him.

"My Emperor," Johrann breathed, clutching the arm of the ornate chair. She trembled under his touch. "I don't deserve this. I don't deserve you."

The surrounding hall settled into conversations about the news, pockets of happiness and fear swirling as the sweet courses began. In the corner of his vision Bandim-Dorai glimpsed Emmy, still chained, disappearing through a side door.

"You deserve this," he said, pressing a kiss to each of her knuckles. "Without you, I would never have returned to the world. All of this is because of you."

A sudden shudder passed through her, though she kept her guard in place. "Thank you, my Emperor. I am nothing without you."

Bandim-Dorai leaned in to press a gentle kiss to the side of her head. "And I am nothing without you."

No matter how much Dorai thought, she couldn't understand the path of Bandim's thoughts. Marriage to Johrann? His cruelty toward her knew no limit. He didn't need that to secure her loyalty. He already had it. So why? Dorai had tried to influence him against this choice. Better to use his marriage the way other rulers and leaders did. He could have fortified an alliance with Sinomi of the Linvarrans. But as had become clearer with each passing day, Bandim wasn't interested in anything other than Dorai's power.

More than the contempt she felt for the foolishness of his choices, Dorai had nothing but sympathy for Johrann. Bandim didn't love her. He used her, abused her, never kept her best interests at heart. Such behavior reminded Dorai of only one other creature: Nunako. She knew too well what it was like to be lied to, tricked, used for another's selfish purpose, yet Johrann seemed oblivious to if all. More fool her.

Bandim's plan for Johrann wasn't the most concerning of things. As she watched from behind his eyes, Dorai had wanted to weep. The sight of one of Bomsoi's younglings, chained and led like an animal by another, had cut her like a sword. That was her blood. Her own power ran through the female's veins. To see a being of the goddesses reduced to nothing was heart-wrenching. Though half the blood was Nunako's, half was Dorai's. This wasn't what either she or her sister had desired when they'd made Bomsoi from their littlest claws. They'd never intended to create more than Bomsoi. Their purpose was singular and simple: restore balance.

Now this creature had submitted to Bandim. What would that mean? The longer Dorai stayed inside this creature's body, the more she wanted to escape it again. But she couldn't. She was at this mortal's mercy. Without him, she would disappear from the world again. She would never regain her purpose, the love of the Younglings. That was all she desired.

But this? This wasn't the way things were ever meant to be.

CHAPTER TWENTY-FIVE

Emmy

After her humiliation at the feast, the guards deposited Emmy inside a chamber lit by many candles, with a bright fire burning in the grate. The door closed behind her, and they drew a bolt from the outside. She was still a prisoner, after all.

First, she snuffed all the candles. She tried to use her power, but she was still too weak, instead smothering the flames with coal, reducing them to nothing but glowing embers. Now he wouldn't be able to see her. Not that he was looking, Emmy thought as she wrapped her arms around herself. Bandim was too busy playing the Sun Emperor among his preening subjects.

Her bare feet were heavy as she dragged herself to the bed. Still dressed in the plain shift, Emmy crawled under the thick Vhaun blanket, desperate for rest. If she would ever escape this place alive, she needed it.

* * *

Emmy jolted awake as the bar on the door slid open. Moons' light streamed through the window, the shutters wide open. Emmy clutched the blanket to her chest as a figure stepped inside.

Johrann Maa's footfalls were silent as she approached. Emmy went to stand, but Johrann held up a hand to stop her. She lowered herself onto the edge of the bed. "Stay where you are."

Silver edged her face and picked out the glinting stitching in her beautiful robes. Emmy waited in the silence, unsure what she could say.

"Did you know," Johrann began in a voice softer than Emmy had ever heard her use, "until earlier today, becoming empress was my most secret desire. I spent so long, cycles, transforming Bandim Tiboli into what the goddess wanted him to be, the One of Two, the vessel of Dorai." She gave a small self-deprecating grunt. "After all my work for the One True Goddess, I wanted a crown as my reward. I held that desire so close to my heart I dared not speak it. I wanted to show the world I was worth something. To prove them all wrong. I thought Dorai chose me. But it was all a lie."

Her voice dropped away to nothing.

"You've always been worth something," Emmy replied.

Johrann gave her a tiny smile. "Perhaps once that was true. You did well in the Great Hall. Bandim has no suspicions."

Sucking in a breath, Emmy nodded. Her spectacle before all the Masvam nobles had been necessary. For her survival, she'd had to lie. A refusal would have brought much death. At least now they had a chance to live. Her friends had a chance to live.

Johrann faced Emmy, her eyes gilded in the moons' light. Part of Emmy whispered. *Don't trust her. Run, flee, escape.* This was the female who had killed her parents. Johrann had murdered so many folk, brought Mantos back to life only to kill him again, had by her own admission manipulated Bandim into bringing Dorai back into the world and set him on the path that brought so much more destruction. Johrann was a traitor to the Uloni, to Bomsoi. Yet she wasn't. All that she had done, she'd done through a sincere belief that it was what the goddess wanted. Emmy didn't doubt about that. She couldn't bring herself to agree with Johrann's choices. Who could murder innocents, even at the behest of a god?

Emmy reminded herself it hadn't been Dorai. It had been the Grandmother. What did that mean?

Johrann's voice pulled her from her thoughts. "Emmy?"

Emmy answered with a shake. "Sorry. Everything is just..."

"Complicated?" Johrann asked. At Emmy's nod of assent, she gave another small smile. "I know that too well."

"I can't understand any of this. Why did the Grandmother order you to kill the Uloni? Why would she want to destroy everything Bomsoi had made? Bomsoi came from Nunako and Dorai, who came from the Grandmother herself. Why?"

Johrann shrugged one shoulder. "When the voice was Dorai, I believed it was for revenge. Dorai—the Grandmother—always told me she hated Nunako and everything they had shared. She told me that Nunako was evil, that it was she who had destroyed everything they'd worked for. Nunako corrupted the Younglings, which meant they stopped worshiping. With no belief, the power of the goddesses waned. That was why Dorai wanted me to sow the seeds of her belief. Folk had returned to their love of Nunako. By calling her the Lady of Light, that meant Dorai's name became associated with the Dark. I worked all these years to build up belief in the truth of the One True Goddess again, including choosing the One of Two who would champion Dorai in the world again." She paused as if the next words pained her. "I knew Empress Phen's two eggs were the Two, so I worked my way into the temple in the city of Masvam to get close to her. When Mantos toppled to his death, I saw that as my chance. By bringing him back to life, I could show him Dorai had chosen him as her vessel to return to the world."

Emmy drew her eyeridges together. "Wait. You wanted to choose Mantos?"

"Not because he was any different from his sibling, but because I saw my chance and took it. Then, as the two younglings grew, I realized Mantos wasn't the One I wanted. It was Bandim. He was so full of rage, of hate, when he realized what his mother had done. Or at least, what he imagined she had done. Phen did nothing. It was me. She didn't ask me to save Mantos. I offered to do it and she took the chance, even though she knew it would kill her in every way but physical death."

"You allowed him to believe his mother favored Mantos' life over his," Emmy said.

A glimmer fell from Johrann's downturned eyes. "I didn't just allow it. I encouraged it. Once he had a seed of hate in his heart, I cultivated it, all in the name of Dorai. Or," she added with a scoff, "what I thought was Dorai. It never was."

Cold disgust curdled Emmy's stomach, yet she tried to push it away. Johrann's actions had been horrific, but Emmy kept reminding herself that the Grandmother had told her to commit them, pretending to be Dorai. The Grandmother had manipulated Johrann as much as she had manipulated Bandim. The whole situation was repulsive. And, like with an infected scab, the urge to scratch at it and keep digging was too much to resist.

"When did the Grandmother tell you to murder the Uloni?" Emmy asked.

Johrann flinched at her phrasing, but Emmy refused to say it any other way. That was what it was.

"It was around five or six cycles after I brought Mantos back to life. It had become clear that Bandim would serve the purpose as the One of Two, so I received further instructions from the goddess. I was to travel to the Great Northern Range. She would guide me to the temple, tell me what to do when I arrived." Johrann shut her eyes, sending more tears glimmering onto Emmy's blanket. "She told me to wait until they were all in the temple, to bar the door, and to use my powers to set the place alight." The suddenness of her look made Emmy flinch. "I didn't agree to it straight away. I asked her why, but she reminded me that these were not my folk, that we might share colors, but they had abandoned me and left me vulnerable to abuse and death. Then I was glad to do it. The Grandmother said she would help me, would stop them from escaping unharmed, but that I needed to set the fire myself, that she couldn't raise her hands against her own."

Emmy licked her lips. "Just like Bomsoi can't hurt Bandim." At Johrann's confused look, she clarified, "Bomsoi can't fight back against Bandim. She can't harm him because he's now of her blood through Dorai."

Johrann nodded, slow and solemn. "I barred the door. I set the fire. I watched them burn. Listened to their screams, believing it was what Dorai wanted." She squeezed her eyes shut again as if warding off the memories. "But it wasn't."

Emmy, without realizing what she was doing, touched Johrann's shoulder. "You did what you thought was right. You did what the goddess commanded."

"It was still wrong." Johrann trembled beneath Emmy's talons. "Nothing will ever make it right."

Emmy withdrew her hand. "I don't understand how Bomsoi allowed it to happen. She was inside the temple. Why didn't she stop it?"

Johrann tilted her head to the side. "Perhaps that was the Grandmother's doing. She might be unable to raise a hand against her blood, but maybe she somehow stopped Bomsoi and the others from using their powers to protect themselves."

"But why?" Emmy asked, blowing out an explosive breath. "I don't understand any of this."

"I thought I understood before," Johrann said, "but it turns out I was wrong." Something new glinted in her eyes. "But I must go on. We have to continue what the Grandmother started. She's still a goddess. She has to have her reasons. All these cycles I've done what she asked, and I will continue to do what she asks of me. I can't stop now, so it doesn't matter that we don't understand. We have to keep going. Bandim believes I'm still loyal to him, and that you're now loyal to him as well."

Emmy swallowed around the lump in her throat. They'd discussed this so far, but the next steps were unknown. In the short period before Bandim had called for her appearance in the hall, they'd decided she would pledge allegiance. What came after that was unknown.

"What do we do now?" Emmy asked. "Do we escape?"

Johrann shook her head. "No. We stay here. That's what the Goddess wants. Hands and Hearts together. There are three of us here. We only need one more."

"How will Mantos know to come here?" Emmy asked. "Perhaps the Grandmother will tell him."

"She won't have to. Mantos is already on his way. He's bringing an army."

Thoughts flying back to her friends, Emmy gave another hard swallow. If Mantos was coming and bringing an army, she knew all those Bandim had threatened would be on his tail, perhaps except for Charo. Zecha wouldn't stay behind. Rel, though injured, would insist on coming. They'd be walking right into Bandim's threats. Far away in the Kingdom of Khin, at least they were beyond his grasp. If he found out her deception, he could do nothing to harm them. But if they were in his palace, all he would need to do was strike out and bring upon them the destruction he had promised.

"What then?" Emmy asked.

Johrann's resolve faltered. "The Grandmother said 'she' would know what to do, though I admit I don't understand who the Grandmother means. I can only hope that's the case."

"It's Bomsoi," Emmy said. "The daughter of Nunako and Dorai, the one they made together with their littlest claws. I've been following Bomsoi's word, her commands. She used me as a conduit to bring Nunako into Mantos."

"Just as I used myself to bring Dorai into Bandim, on the Grandmother's instruction."

They looked at each other in the darkness, neither blinking.

Emmy blew out a long, controlled breath. "Have you heard what the Grandmother said to us before, that phrase, 'What is made cannot be unmade?'"

"'But what has been made can be destroyed'," Johrann finished with a nod. "Yes, I've heard that from her before."

Dread pooled in the pit of Emmy's stomach. "Whatever the Grandmother wants, it will bring pain. But then she said she wanted to stop the destruction Bandim will bring if we don't stop him." She squeezed her eyes shut in confusion. "I don't understand."

This time it was Johrann who touched a comforting hand to Emmy's arm. "Perhaps your Bomsoi will know what to do."

"I hope she does," Emmy replied, but it brought her little comfort.

CHAPTER TWENTY-SIX

Mantos

They arrived in Mellul before dawn. Neiruk descended outside the capital, Pempeng, in a flurry of wings. Travelers on the beaten road winding into the city scurried aside, fleeing from the wind whipped by the Prago's wings. The garrison both outside and upon the walls snapped to attention, heralding their arrival with shouts and the clanking aim of cannons.

"Identify yourselves!" the lead guard commanded. She attempted to keep the tremble from her voice at the sight of mighty Neiruk. "Do so or we will fire!"

The three of them stepped forward together, Valaria pressing a hand to her chest as she spoke.

"I am Princess Valaria of Althemer, soon to be crowned queen." She gestured to her companions. "This is Bomsoi, whom we call the Stranger, a being of the goddesses. And this," she said after a pause only Mantos knew the true meaning of, "is Mantos Tiboli, the true heir to the Masvam Empire."

The lead guard barked a laugh that rattled across the grassy plain that stood between them and the city walls. "Absurd! Mantos Tiboli is dead. Do you take us for fools?"

Valaria's retort came as harsh as a whip crack. "I take you for a fool for speaking to me in such a manner. Take my message to Queen Tayu. I will speak no further with you."

She said the last word with a venom Mantos had only heard her direct toward Masvams. The guard bristled, but relayed the message to another of her troop, who took off at a trot into the capital.

When she returned, it wasn't just with a message, but with an escort of ten soldiers.

"You're to meet the queen," the lead guard barked, jerking her arm for them to fall in between the soldiers.

Mantos suppressed a smile at the meager escort. Ten soldiers were nothing to Valaria, never mind the power both he and Bomsoi could wield.

They trooped under the high archway into the city of Pempeng. Mantos pulled the moist air into his chest. Mellul was far south, even farther from the Empire than Althemer, and relations between the countries were never close. Even in Vhaun, the country was warm. Returning to that warmth brought a rush of memory back, of the one solitary trip he had taken to Mellul with his father. He remembered the brightness of color, the twisting sweep of vines that covered every surface, and the heady scent of unknown flowers. That was at least twelve cycles and two queens before. He knew little more of Queen Tayu than that she had ascended the throne three cycles before and had married a Belfoni lord.

The escort of soldiers ushered them into the back of a closed carriage. Inside was stifling in the heat, and it moved at the guards' pace. A black covering prevented any light from entering. In the darkness, Mantos glanced from Bomsoi to Valaria.

"Do you think the queen will be more receptive to your pleas in person?" he asked.

Valaria shook her head, unsure. "Tayu was never as staunch a supporter of us as her mother, and Bandim's threat has frightened her more than she'll admit. Perhaps," she added, though her tone was dubious, "your special influence will bolster her courage."

The 'special influence' was clear. The Mellul worshiped Nunako and the Light. Something odd sat within Mantos at that. Nunako nudged him from within. It wasn't their love for her that troubled him. It was the Light. More and more, Mantos knew that term troubled Nunako too. There was something strange about it, something that made the goddess uneasy.

"Queen Tayu might not believe the truth," he said, jolting off the seat as the carriage hit a rut in the road.

Bomsoi passed her thumb across her talons, brightening the dark inside with icy light. "When she sees what you can do, she will believe."

Mantos slumped back in his seat. "And what if it's not enough? I don't have Emmy, and I don't have Fonbir. His presence helped because he believed in me, or at least in Nunako's power. Though I admit, it was nothing compared to the power lent to me by Emmy's proximity."

"You need not shake the ground beneath us," Valaria snapped. "All you need to do is prove your worth." There was a pause. When she spoke again, her tone was softer. "As much as I don't like you, and as much as I might not call what lies within you Nunako, I know your strength is from the gods, just like Bomsoi's. So I believe in your power too. If that knowledge is of any help, use it."

Nunako twisted and surged within him, and a rush of power flowed to Mantos' fingertips. The whole carriage rumbled as he brought her influence under control.

"I said you need not shake the ground beneath us!" Valaria said, though the edge of her lips quirked upward. "Save that for the battlefield."

They trundled into the winding bowels of the city and another familiar sensation came over Mantos. The smell of running water, clear of debris and sewage, entered his nostrils. The road beneath them changed from stone paving to the clatter of wood, and Mantos knew where they were. Their carriage was on the bridge that crossed the Kut Ngakong, the great river that sliced through the center of Pempeng. The palace nestled in one of its widest arcs, isolated from the rest of the city by enough distance to protect it from long distance attacks. In his mind, Mantos saw the beautiful engineering of the bridge that spanned it, a wooden passageway set upon stone arches. Upon it were seven sets of gates, a contingent of soldiers manning each. On this occasion, as on Mantos' last visit, the carriage didn't stop, but traveled through the gates. He wondered if openness was a good omen or not.

When their journey ended, Mantos winced at the invasion of brightness as a guard opened the carriage. He blinked against the light and composed himself before he stepped outside, so that when his boots hit the ground, he looked more emperor and god than stumbling foreigner.

The sun beat down upon the bright stone palace, hovering behind to create a halo of light. Unlike the sprawling complex of the Masvam palace, this structure had been a controlled build of walls and terraces that rose upward like a stairway for a giant. The palace in Pempeng was ancient. Mantos had read all about it, thirsty for the knowledge of how folk had built it so long before.

"Come with us."

A guard's voice broke through Mantos' thoughts, and he realized that while Bomsoi and Valaria had walked ahead, he had remained still in his admiration. The princess glowered at him as he caught up, and guards escorted them not into the palace, but into one of the beautiful gardens that surrounded it.

This place was close to perfection. The air filled with trills and chirps, and the scent of a thousand flowers hung in the warm air. Perhaps this was why Tayu was reluctant to help. Why risk the safety of a paradise?

They reached a high wall covered in twisting vines adorned with pink and purple flowers. The guards bade them wait until the queen permitted them entrance. When their admission was granted, Mantos lost his breath to the surrounding magnificence.

The Garden Throne Room nestled within an explosion of color. Every leaf, twig and vine were plucked and positioned with purpose. The contrast of careful control and the riotous spectrum swirled before Mantos' eyes. At the center of it all sat Queen Tayu, resplendent on a high seat of flowers under a canopy of delicate fabric. Her brown skin and red armor glinted bright among the foliage. To her right, on a throne of equal beauty, sat a Belfoni male of green armor and pinkish skin: former

Lord, now Prince Nannu. To her left was a smaller throne, upon which a third figure sat. It was their son and heir, Prince Zuzuidza. They all wore matching outfits of light material, trousers under embroidered tunics, with crowns of equal delicacy upon their heads.

"Come forward."

Tayu's words filled the high-walled clearing and permitted no disobedience. Valaria strode forward, followed by Bomsoi and Mantos. They formed a line beneath the twin thrones and bowed in unison.

"Your Majesties," Valaria said. As she straightened, her many bracelets jingled. "Please forgive our intrusion, but matters are pressing enough that I hope you will understand."

"A grand intrusion indeed," Tayu said. "Such a creature as the one described to me by my soldiers only existed in stories until today."

Valaria cast a glance at Bomsoi, who spoke next. "That is Neiruk, one of my oldest companions. He has become known in legend as the Prago."

"And who are you?" Tayu asked. "Someone of your colors, I confess, I have never seen before, though I have heard of your kind. There have been a scant few tales of strange folk with odd powers traveling our lands."

"This is Bomsoi," Valaria said. "She is the one my mother and I call the Stranger."

"Ah," Tayu said. She rose from her throne to descend onto the grass below, her tail sweeping behind. "So, this is the Stranger the late Queen Valentia spoke of. I've heard much about you." She reached to grasp Bomsoi's upper arm, affording her a sparkling smile. "Well met, Stranger. Or should I call you Bomsoi?"

"Call me what you wish, Your Majesty," she said, bowing her head. "It is of little consequence."

Tayu turned her smile to Mantos, though the sparkle turned to a glint like that of a sharpened blade. "And this, if I am to believe your words, is Mantos Tiboli. Your colors are Masvam, but your royal heritage is questionable. Mantos Tiboli is dead."

Drawing in a sweet-scented breath, Mantos gave her another bow. "If you'll permit us to tell you, there is an entire tale behind this."

Tayu regarded him for some time before she rose onto her throne again.

"What do you think, dearest princes?" she asked her husband and son. "Shall we listen to this little band?"

Prince Zuzuidza, younger than Mantos though not by much, regarded them with a cold stare. His heritage was mixed, giving him red Mellul armor and pinkish Belfoni skin. His father, Prince Nannu, tapped his chin, seeming to consider for a moment before he waved a hand. "They've arrived on the back of a beast of legend. I think we should give them a chance to explain."

Tayu snapped her talons. "Chairs for our storytellers, please. I think this will take some time."

The morning had long since turned to afternoon by the time Bomsoi, Mantos, and Valaria had each told their parts. Nannu had called for tea and food in the story's midst. The remains of the repast now lay scattered on trestle tables. Mantos laced his talons together, grateful for the sunshades attendants had brought as the temperature rose. He kept his gaze on Queen Tayu's face, which had remained impassive for most of the story.

"This is why we need your help, now more than ever," Valaria said. "It's bigger than an old alliance with my folk, or a fallen island, or a former twining promise."

Tayu inclined her head in respectful sorrow. "I was sorry to learn of the deaths of your mother and your sister."

"Thank you, Your Highness," Valaria replied. "We need your country's help despite such losses. Nothing is as simple as we once supposed."

Tayu's expression was careful and still as she turned to Mantos. "You would have us believe you are Nunako reborn."

"In a way," Mantos replied. "Nunako lives within me."

Tayu's response was clipped. "Prove it."

Mantos closed his eyes and rose. He had known this was coming, had known he'd need to prove to her that a godly power rested within his mortal body. Nunako pressed into him, giving him everything she could, and Mantos reached out for Valaria's belief. Power rose within him, soft at first, but growing with the rumble in the ground. Mantos concentrated, controlling the movement of rock beneath their feet. Instead of cracking the surface, he willed hidden boulders to splinter underneath them and wrenched them upward. They broke through the glass like the jagged points of a crown, encircling them all.

The Garden Throne Room filled with cries of disbelief and the clink of weapons drawn in defense of the monarchs. Tayu rose from her seat once more and gestured for her guards to stand down. Nannu rose beside her and they descended, hand in hand. Zuzuidza followed, his expression still set but his eyes wide. Tayu, a head shorter than her husband, stared upward with a face of steel. Nannu regarded him in silence.

"You are Nunako, Lady of Light," Tayu said.

Mantos gave them another bow. "I have mastery of rock in the same way you've heard Bandim has mastery of flame. My power comes from Nunako, and his from Dorai. I will not call myself Nunako the way my brother claims his goddess' name, but she lives within me."

Tayu, Nannu and Zuzuidza dipped in a simultaneous bow, holding themselves low for longer than Mantos felt necessary. Nunako prodded him to speak.

"Rise, please," he said. "I don't require your supplication, only your belief. And your troops."

Tayu lifted her head again, her face once more resplendent with her beautiful smile. "You will have it, Nunako. Mantos Tiboli," she corrected before he interjected. "Mellul has never come to the aid of a Masvam. But if the Lady of Light has chosen you as her vessel, I must accept that you are a force for good."

"Your brother, on the other claw," Nannu added, "thus cannot be. It is our duty to protect this world. We must move against him."

Bomsoi sighed. "It isn't as simple as that, but it's a place to begin, at least. We must stop Bandim Tiboli before he destroys everything under the Arc. After that, there is more to do."

Mantos shot Bomsoi a curious look but said nothing. Instead, he spoke again to Tayu and Nannu. "Thank you for your support."

"You will have everything you need," Tayu said. "Ships, troops, siege engines, supplies. Everything we have, we give to you." She turned to Valaria, her joy turning to apology. "I'm sorry we didn't come to your immediate aid. My mother's ashes will never forgive me for my cowardice."

"Not cowardice," Valaria said with more kindness than Mantos expected. "You acted with the best interests of your folk at heart. I'm not sure if I would risk everything for someone else's lost island either. But as it is my island," she continued, the steel returning to her tone, "I have no choice."

Tayu nodded. "Thank you. I will see you crowned, my friend. We will avenge them all, in the name of Nunako."

Within him, the goddess stirred. Mantos tried to quell her.

"How long will it take to muster your forces?" Bomsoi asked.

"To gather what we need, two days," Tayu said. "To sail to the city of Masvam, twelve days more."

"Fourteen days," Mantos said, "until we stop my brother's destruction once and for all."

Tayu, Nannu, and Valaria voiced their approval and strength, but beside them, Bomsoi closed her eyes in silence.

"Bomsoi?" Mantos asked.

She waved him off. "Nothing. It is nothing."

CHAPTER TWENTY-SEVEN

Bandim-Dorai

The Sun Emperor stroked the front of his shimmering metal armor and traced the outlines of the embossed and enameled flames that trailed his chest. He stood in his chambers, outfitted in splendor for no one but himself.

His enemies were converging on all sides, but Bandim-Dorai had little care for that. The Khinish from the north, the Althemerians and Mellul from the south and west, and the rebels had gathered and pressed in from the east. But it didn't matter. He had his city, and he had his armies, and most of all, he had his own power and two Hearts to amplify it. Every queendom under the Arc could sacrifice every soldier they had, but it would never be enough. Nothing could counter the power of Dorai.

When he called for his attendants, two entered straight away. Together they slid the armor off his limber frame piece by piece, replacing it on the wooden form it had hung from before. Then, in silence, they dressed their emperor in soft evening clothes before disappearing again. Bandim-Dorai lowered himself into the chair by the roaring fireside. On cue, the door opened once again and his cupbearer entered, bearing him wine.

"Thank you, my dear."

But as the presence approached, he realized the footfalls were not those of his little cousin, and the emotions were missing. He turned in the chair, eyeridges furrowing as he saw Johrann bringing the drink and two goblets. "Where is my cupbearer?" he asked.

Johrann made no sound as she placed the goblets on the table. The wine sloshed inside the cups as she poured. "I'm afraid, my Emperor, that Yameteth Tiboli has contracted the Lurking Death."

Bandim-Dorai froze in genuine sorrow. "No."

"The healers confirmed it," Johrann said. "She's gone from your service for the safety of those around her, you in particular."

Bandim-Dorai waved off the offered wine and stood. "No. I will go to her and take this illness away."

Bandim-Dorai reached for a robe hanging from a hook near his bedside, but Johrann took his hand as it closed around the material. Bandim-Dorai shrugged off her touch and narrowed his eyes.

"My Emperor," Johrann said, her voice soft, "healing is not something Dorai can gift you with. Please recall that we have tried before."

The robe swung around Bandim-Dorai's frame, and he went to bite back against Johrann's implication that he wasn't perfect and that he wasn't the goddess herself, but he stopped. She spoke true. On more than one occasion, he had tried to exert power to heal the sick and the injured but had never been successful. Johrann had performed some healing actions, though she'd never been able to banish something as profound as the Death. She was too close to Dorai, too distant from her other godly parentage. Had it been within her power, Bandim-Dorai would already have sent Johrann to spread her ability wide, to show the populace that while the rebels spread the sickness with their disloyalty, the Sun Emperor could lift it if he so chose.

Bandim-Dorai's lips parted in a slow smile. Johrann might not be able to do it, but now he had someone else who might. Someone else whose power came not only from Dorai.

"I'll not go to Yameteth tonight, my dear Heart," he said. He brought his hand up to cup Johrann's face, "but I have a plan for tomorrow. And you will make sure it happens."

Johrann's mouth curved in a smile to match his own, though he couldn't sense her joy. As always, Johrann was a void.

"Yes, My Emperor."

* * *

The servants carried out his plans with as much ceremony as possible at short notice. Bandim-Dorai reclined on his throne high on the dais, Tesselica on a grand chair below, watching the crowd of nobles mill and talk. Soldiers stood at intervals, poised to regain control if the gathered lost their nerve when the Sun Emperor's intentions became clear.

They had pushed aside most of the long dining tables, leaving only one in the center of the room. They had cleared all the chairs, forcing the lords to stand and watch. As yet there was nothing to see. That wouldn't last long. Anticipation was part of the plan.

When he could sense that poor Yameteth was outside the closed doors, borne on a stretcher from her sickbed, Bandim-Dorai rose. The Great Hall fell silent.

"My friends," he said in a voice that carried into every corner, "today I intend to show you the benefit of my new Heart. With her proximity and my power, she will bring forth a miracle before your eyes." They needn't know the healing had nothing to do with him, and Emmy wouldn't tell. He grinned and reached to the door. "Bring them in!"

Four guards in polished armor carried Yameteth inside. Emmy entered afterward, herself followed by another two guards and Johrann Maa. Though Emmy had pledged her submission, there was still a chance she might revolt. No amount of power from Nunako would allow her to recover from a sword through the heart and another through her throat, which were the commands he had given her guards. If that didn't kill her, between himself and Johrann, Bandim-Dorai knew they could end her life for good.

As the guards laid Yameteth on the table, her condition became clear. The gathered nobles recoiled from the sight of the Death, covering their mouths with their bejeweled hands.

"Fear not, my friends," Bandim called over the din. "This young female, my dear cousin Yameteth, will have her sickness cured, all because of my second Heart."

Emmy flicked her eyes up to him. Something burned within them. It tasted of hate. That was fine. She didn't have to love him. She just had to use the power she gained from Nunako and do what he wanted. He nodded, gestured for Johrann to join him, and took his seat on the dais once again, waiting for the show to begin. Below him, Tesselica leaned forward in his chair, his anticipation and delight winding like a plait.

As Johrann sat, void of emotion, Bandim-Dorai leaned into her. "Will she behave?"

"Yes, My Emperor," Johrann replied. "I guarantee it."

The room was so silent that when Emmy began to draw upon her wretched power, Bandim-Dorai heard the crack of gathering ice before he saw the first fractal form. Coldness swept from the tips of Emmy's talons, coiling through her, and when she looked at him again, her eyes glowed blue. None of the fear he had expected materialized. Something within him had thought that in the presence of Nunako's power, he would recoil. It was the opposite to him, ice against his fire, every inch of negativity Nunako created against the goodness and might of Dorai. But it didn't happen. Instead he watched, as enthralled as the rest, while Emmy set to work.

Her hatred for him dissipated, replaced by concentration as pure as clean water. She undid the sick female's tunic and laid her hands upon Yameteth's prone frame, saying nothing. There were no incantations, none of the flourish that Bandim-Dorai had expected. Nunako had always relished the show, the game. But Emmy was silent as she worked, pushing her power into Yameteth. Icy trails tracked across the young female's skin and armor, her body steaming as Emmy's coldness met the hotness of the Lurking Death in her body.

With a jolt, Yameteth shot upright, her eyes wide and blinking and blue. Emmy withdrew her hands, and the glow faded, as did the icy trails. When it was all gone, Bandim-Dorai saw the strange mark on Yameteth's chest. Emmy had left behind two handprints, pristine and white. Healed, Yameteth stared at the gathered crowd, bewildered, but all traces of the pallor of sickness had disappeared.

Before them all, Bandim-Dorai had brought them a miracle. The gathered broke from their stupor and erupted into applause and shouts of joy. Loudest of all was Tesselica, as always.

The Sun Emperor rose and called above them all, "My friends, today you have seen something miraculous! This illness that could not be cured has been cured before your eyes! I now ask you to leave this place and spread the word throughout the palace, the city, and out into your towns and villages. Make sure word spreads that the cursed rebellion has brought rot and death, but that the Sun Emperor brings health and life! Tell them what you've seen here today and tell them that anyone afflicted by the Lurking Death can come to my home for healing." Emmy gave off a flash of panic, but Bandim-Dorai continued. "My second Heart will cure them all, through my power. All I ask is for your loyalty. All I ask is for your love."

The joy that had quieted during his words rose into a wave of devotion. The gathered crashed out of the hall, and Bandim-Dorai grinned as belief in him spread like an unending tide. In the middle of it, Yameteth sat on the table, turning her hands over to stare at her now healthy skin.

"That proceeded as I wanted it to," Bandim-Dorai said.

Johrann nodded, placing a tentative hand upon his arm. "As I knew it would. Emmy will do whatever you ask."

"You seem so certain of that, dear Heart," he replied. "Did I frighten her beyond her wits?"

"You did," Johrann replied. "She's full of Nunako's weakness. She won't dare move against you. She fears for her friends too much."

The guards remained a pace away from Emmy as the crowd thinned. When all the lords and nobles had gone, Bandim-Dorai descended from his dais and walked past Tesselica to Yameteth, keeping his arms wide in welcome and happiness. His young cousin slipped from the table and kneeled before him; her head bowed.

"Thank you, Your Excellence," she breathed.

Bandim-Dorai raised his hand for her to kiss. "Anything for you, my dear. After all," he added, sliding his gaze to Emmy, "friends and family are the most important thing in the world."

"Thank you," Yameteth repeated.

Bandim-Dorai caught her under the chin and tilted her head upward. "It was my pleasure. Now, run along and return to your duties once more. I expect my cupbearer to attend to me when I am in my chambers this evening."

Yameteth leaped to her feet and bowed low before sprinting away. The door closed behind her with a resounding slam.

"You did well in your first task, Emmy," Bandim-Dorai said. He watched his second Heart suppress a flinch as he spoke her name. She didn't respond. "Keep doing well and everything will stay calm. Everyone will stay safe."

Emmy jerked a nod and Bandim-Dorai clicked his tongue. "Come now, show more respect than that. Say, 'Yes, my Emperor.'"

Emmy's face contorted, and bitterness bloomed from her. However, she managed to speak. "Yes, my Emperor."

"What a good little one," he said. Then he turned to Johrann. "Return her to her room and ensure she remains obedient. I'll call for you later, my love."

He pressed a kiss to the side of Johrann's head, then motioned for them to depart. When he turned, he favored Tesselica with a wide grin and opened his arms once more.

"Oh, my dearest Tess, I've been neglecting you. Yameteth isn't the only cousin I care for."

Pleasure rose from Tesselica even as he shook his head. "You never neglect me, my Emperor."

"But I have," Bandim-Dorai said, threading one arm through the crook of Tess.' "Come. We'll spend a little time together this afternoon, just you and I."

"I'm honored, my Emperor."

"As you should be," Bandim-Dorai replied.

They exited the Great Hall arm in arm, the ever-present guards following at a respectful distance. Hope and pleasure emanated from Tesselica like the joy from an obedient vaemar kit toward its master. Bandim-Dorai didn't need Tess any longer. He'd served his purpose as an object of jealousy for Johrann Maa. But deep within, a strange feeling stirred for this male who held such unconstrained belief in Bandim-Dorai's power.

He patted Tesselica's hand and guided him toward his chambers. Perhaps, he mused, the feeling was love.

CHAPTER TWENTY-EIGHT

Mantos

He could have chosen any ship to travel upon, but Mantos chose the *Water Prago*. Despite its size and lack of weaponry, there was no one he'd rather sail under than Captain Chaata. He'd considered flying into the city on Neiruk's back, but that option gave no opportunity for stealth. Bandim would see him coming from miles away, even shoot him out of the sky. So instead of risking that, he'd opted for the sea.

Only a small band of Althemerians sailed on the Prago, and one lone Metakalan—Zecha—but the small schooner was tucked within an armada of Mellul warships. Mantos grasped the side rails as the freezing salt air whipped through his fronds. The weight of Haelo on his hip was comforting, the sword no longer bearing down on him. Perhaps he had gained its trust.

It was nearing the end of Vhaun, and soon the weather would turn back toward the growth of Merish. As he glanced at the gathered troops around him, he held a silent hope that as many of them as possible would live to see it. Within, Nunako turned, and he knew she hoped for the same.

At least Zrazashi and Uzet would be safe, or as safe as anyone could be when the Arc had fallen into war. Tero's younglings remained behind in the south of Althemer, surrounded by the contingent who had stayed to defend their foothold. *When this is all over, I'll bring Zrazashi and Uzet to the palace and give them a new home. It's the least I can do to honor Tero's memory.*

"A bickle for your thoughts?"

Turning at Chaata's voice, Mantos smiled. "I'm thinking dangerous things, Captain, about what I'll do when this nightmare has ended."

Chaata shrugged and leaned against the rail. Even with her face turned toward the wind and spray, she didn't flinch, but only smiled. "You've got to have hope, otherwise why else would we do anything?"

They swayed as the ship bucked on the water, and Mantos nodded. "Wise words."

"Ah, I sometimes have them." The young captain pushed off the rail and folded her arms. "How do you rate your chances?"

Mantos' smile slipped. "I have to get to the city, providing that's where my brother stays. There's a lot of sea and land to cut through before we get there."

"Weren't you able to sense your brother's proximity before?" Chaata asked. "I seem to recall a rather impressive fainting spell. Why not try to sense him now?"

"That's," Mantos started, releasing the rail, "a very good idea."

Chaata grinned. "I sometimes have those too."

Unsure how to begin, Mantos closed his eyes and reached to Nunako for help. When he'd experienced the strangeness of his encounter with Bandim on the Sea of Souls, he'd had no control over it. They'd connected through no effort on his part. Whether Bandim had done anything, he didn't know. Nunako encouraged him to probe outward with his mind, seeking anything unusual.

He sensed the far-off presence of Bomsoi, riding Neiruk high above, ready to send back news of Masvam ship movements and whether their chosen places for troop landings were still safe. Other than that, there was nothing. No Bandim. No Emmy. His brother wasn't on the sea.

Mantos opened his eyes again to see Chaata staring.

"Well?"

"Nothing. He isn't nearby, as far as I can tell."

"He's stayed in his palace," the captain offered, "nice and safe behind his walls and battlements."

Mantos worried his bottom lip. "That doesn't sound like the brother I know who gave a grand performance as he attacked Kubodinnu."

"That time, he was attacking," Chaata said. "This time he's defending. Perhaps he'll bide his time and wait for you to come to him. That's what I'd do."

Mantos gave a small nod. That's what he'd do, too, if faced with an invasion. He'd fortify the city, force the attackers to break his lines. He'd stay inside and wait. It was always harder to attack a city than defend one. Regardless, the city of Masvam wasn't Mantos' true goal. He needed to break into the palace and take on his brother face to face. Elsya was right when he'd said Mantos would have no trouble gaining entry. He knew all the palace's secrets. Getting there was the hard part.

If they could at least make it to the coast south of the city, Chaata and her crew could sail back to safety. By now Khitarian's army would have landed north, and Elsya's rebels would move in from the east. Bandim couldn't fight on all fronts. Somewhere would break, and Mantos had to be at that somewhere. Mantos felt no longing to be at the battlefront, though the responsibility weighed on him. He should be there, leading the Masvam force. But it wasn't to be.

They weren't too far from their landing point when, still standing on the deck, Mantos' head rang with sudden strangeness.

"*Mantos, a huge Masvam flotilla is sailing south in your direction,*" Bomsoi said without speaking. "*Tell your captain. There's no way your fleet can outmaneuver it.*"

Reaching out, Mantos placed Bomsoi and Neiruk. She was coming toward them fast.

"*I will, Bomsoi,*" he replied.

He bolted straight to Chaata, and at her command the whole crew leaped into action. Tiny but fearsome Koli climbed onto the upper deck and placed herself in front of an enormous bell before she rang out a code. Within seconds, the warning message about incoming Masvams had traveled to the Mellul warships, and the whole sea came to life with the clamor of an impending attack.

The *Water Prago*'s crew guided the ship into formation, on the curving left-hand side of a great crescent, protected by Mellul's great ships at each end and through the middle. Mantos mustered with the rest, doing what he could to aid them, though he was no sailor. In the distance, Masvam ships loomed tall and dark against the frost-white horizon, prowling on the dark sea. While Mellul's ships were well-equipped with cannon, all were smaller than the bulk of the Masvam fleet. But they were fast and maneuverable, capable of outrunning the enemy ships.

It wasn't long before they were within firing distance and the first deafening shots rang forth from the Masvam fleet. The Mellul ships couldn't fire back, the range of their weapons falling far shorter than the enemy's, but this was part of the plan. They remained windward, and several of the warships broke formation to draw Masvam fire. Others remained to cover the *Water Prago* and the other non-combat ships.

Mantos listened to the far-off explosions of cannon fire, watched as Mellul broadsides caught the first of the Masvam ships and lurched sideward. Fast-moving Mellul vessels ducked close, drew fire, and shot back before slipping out of range. Most made it to safety. Some did not.

Then things changed. All at once, six infernos erupted on the water. Mantos' chest tightened, and he reached outward, expecting to feel the looming presence of Bandim bearing upon him. Nothing happened. It wasn't his brother. The Masvams had deployed fireships, unmanned vessels set ablaze and on a collision course with the enemy. They forced the Mellul to scatter, and Chaata screamed orders for the *Water Prago* to make a tight turn starboard. Mantos gripped the nearest rigging as the ship lurched and sea spray battered his face. He longed to do something of worth, of value, but he couldn't feel the earth and rock far beneath the body of the ocean, and the water wouldn't obey him.

One fireship drew ever closer, as if it was Bandim's talons coming to close around their throats. It collided with one of the supply ships close by, sending it into a torrent of flame. Mantos sprang from the rigging as the Prago still turned and leaped toward Chaata, screaming above the noise of the battle.

"Get Jishu to use her power! She can blow the fireship off course!"

Chaata gave him a curt nod and shouted for the half-Uloni crewmember. "We need you! Send that ship back toward the Masvams!"

"Anchor me!" Jishu cried.

Two fellow sailors dropped to the deck, clamping their hands around her ankles. Without thinking, Mantos did the same. As Jishu gathered her power, Mantos realized he could add more than just his strength to keep her boots rooted. Though he'd never done it before, it must work both ways. If he could draw power from Emmy as his Heart, perhaps he could offer power to an Uloni as the Hand of Nunako.

Mantos sensed Jishu drawing on the well of power within herself. It was different from Emmy's power, nowhere near as strong. Instead of pulling it into himself, Mantos reversed the process and started to push power out from himself.

Jishu jerked, held in place only by her crewmates, and in a flash, silvery-blue swirls covered her skin and armor. With a grunt and a cry, a surge of power rose through Jishu and as she jerked her hands outward, an enormous gale exploded forward. The fireship crumpled under its strength and went under the water, the flames dead. Even more, the whole sea roiled and bucked, shockwaves of air careening over its surface and pulling great waves upward. The chaotic water pummeled the Masvam ships, the Mellul fleet churning on the edges of the turmoil. In one push, Jishu disrupted the entire Masvam force, countless vessels disappearing into the tumultuous darkness.

As her crewmates rose, steadying her as the traces of her power dissipated, Jishu locked eyes with Mantos. "What was that?"

"An action that's turned the battle," he replied as he clambered to his feet. "Are you all right?"

Though her chest heaved with heavy breaths, Jishu nodded. "Never better."

A strange quiet followed. Not a silence, but the noticeable lessening of the battle's clangor. Chaata called out orders as the *Water Prago* regrouped with the Mellul fleet, taking up her position in the left-hand curve of the crescent once more.

An idea flashed through Mantos and as he ran to the captain, his feet slammed into the deck boards. Chaata caught him as he threw himself toward her at the helm.

"Captain." He clamped his hands on her arms. "I know how we can get to the palace, fast. Stealth be damned. But," he added, some of his enthusiasm dampening, "you won't like it."

"Am I going to like it more than myself, every member of my crew, and you dying?"

Mantos released her. "I hope so. But it'll still hurt."

He ran a hand over one of the ship's sea-worn beams, and it became clear what he meant. Chaata tensed, the cords of her neck straining in stark relief for a moment before she waved a talon in Mantos' face.

"You better win the throne, because you'll owe me an enormous debt only an emperor can repay."

With the Masvams regrouping, they had time to prepare. The *Water Prago* drew alongside one of the smaller Mellul ships, and some of the crew disembarked by a gangplank slung between. Not as many left as Mantos wanted. Zecha remained on board, staunch in his resolution.

"Emmy is my best friend," he'd said. "I'm going with you." That was the end of the conversation.

Chaata refused to stay behind, though Mantos understood her motives. Many of the Linvarrans stayed on board, unfailing in their loyalty to their captain and their ship. Jishu remained, the integral part of the plan, but she found it no sacrifice.

"I'd give anything to have those hands on me again," she said, tipping Mantos a filthy wink.

Koli jammed her elbow into Jishu's ribs, but it did nothing to quell her leer.

As soon as the Mellul ship withdrew her gangplank, Mantos turned to the little band before him: a crew of Linvarrans, a half-Uloni, and a Metakalan, all with determined faces.

"None of you need come with me," he said again, though added, "except for Jishu, of course. But I thank you for doing so."

Koli grunted. "Someone's got to stop Jishu from pawing all over you."

"And this is my ship, Masvam," Chaata added. "If the Prago must die, I'll be on her decks as she does. Anyway, you don't know how to work our special sails."

Mantos agreed to that with a shrug and a grin. "True."

"We're with you to the end, Mantos," Zecha said, and there was something in the male's sincerity that made Mantos' power bloom.

"All right, let's do it."

With those words, he sealed the *Water Prago*'s fate. The rest of the crew sprang into action, and just as they had so long before, back when Mantos was still just Mantos with no Nunako, back before the fall of Althemer, they set about bringing down the Prago's flying sails.

Jishu planted herself in place, sucking in a deep breath.

"Are you ready?" Mantos asked her.

"As I can be," she said, her cockiness gone. "I've never brought the Prago as far as you want me to go. I don't know if I'll be able to do it."

Mantos shook his head. "We have no room for doubts. I'm here with you. We'll do it together."

Jishu grinned as she waited for Chaata's signal, then held her hands aloft. The familiar power rose within her, and Mantos placed his hands on her shoulders, willing Nunako to come to their aid. Willing her to send him home.

He gave Jishu everything he had.

In a whirl of winds and furore, the *Water Prago* built her speed, sails billowing as she cut through the saltwater as if it was nothing. Then she rose from the sea for the last time, torrents of sea splitting and crashing around her as she cut up into the sky.

CHAPTER TWENTY-NINE

Emmy

Bandim might have released her from her physical chains, but he'd chained her again with her new duties. He'd kept her healing in the Great Hall long into the late evening for eight days straight. She'd laid her hands on sick folk upon sick folk. Most came with the Death and left healed, two purest white handprints on their chestplates the only signs they had ever been ill. Others came with different ailments, wilted limbs and sightless eyes, and Emmy touched them all. The leeching of pigment from their skin and armor had made the first recoil, but by the time Bandim permitted Emmy to finish for the evening, needing support from two guards to hold her upright, no one cared any longer.

The guards deposited her in her chamber, at least having the courtesy to bring her to the bed, and Emmy knew nothing until Johrann appeared at her side in the dead of night.

The other Uloni brought a cup of water to Emmy's trembling lips. "How do you feel?"

"Exhausted," she croaked around sips of water. "Healing so much is difficult."

"It is," Johrann replied. "In some ways I'm glad I was never good at it. I know Bandim would have abused my power if I'd been more able."

Emmy drained the cup and wiped her face with the cuff of her shift sleeve. She still wore the same clothing from earlier, stinking from the endless parade of sick folk brought before her.

Johrann took the cup from her. "Bandim is most pleased with you."

"He can be as pleased as he likes," Emmy huffed, flopping back onto the bed. "I don't care."

Johrann shifted to sit closer and passed a soothing hand across Emmy's head. Emmy wanted to flinch away, considering what this female had done, but as time passed, she found she hated Johrann less and less. She'd only done what she thought was right. Wasn't that what Emmy, Bomsoi, and Mantos were trying to do? So instead of recoiling, Emmy allowed the touch.

Emboldened by exhaustion, she asked, "Why didn't you live in the Uloni village? Why were you an outcast?"

Johrann's hand stilled. Emmy heard her open her mouth, but there was a pause before she spoke. "That's a question I don't have an answer to. I don't understand why I was abandoned in a Masvam wood, but I was." Her hand started its stroking again. "I can't have traveled all that distance on my own. I always thought I cast out by my parents for being a Moon Rogue. Evil."

"Your parents might have left the village and died," Emmy offered. "Bomsoi told me she spent a lot of time looking for her folk, because some had gone wandering, even before she was looking for me. There are half-Uloni folk, like my friend Rel. Her mother was Uloni and her father Belfoni. She has power, though not as strong as ours."

Johrann withdrew her hand. "I suppose it says much about my character that I assumed my parents cast me out. I always played the little victim."

The self-loathing in her voice made Emmy sit up again. "How can you be sure those were your own thoughts? It could have been the Grandmother making you think that."

"I'll never be sure," Johrann replied, her voice pained as she stared down at the blankets. "I feel like I understand nothing anymore. Everything I thought was right was wrong."

Emmy ventured one hand to lay it on Johrann's arm. "When I found out what I was, Bomsoi shattered everything I thought I knew. I always thought I was a freak, a Moon Rogue, something strange and unwanted. I never realized I had any power, though now that I look back, I was healing with my Uloni abilities before I knew I was doing it. I spent my whole life in cruelty, believing I was worth nothing, and then I find out I have a heritage, a place where I came from, and a purpose beyond anything I could have dreamed. None of that is because I'm unique. It's something we both share because it comes from our being Uloni." Johrann looked up from the bedspread. Emmy pressed on. "Bomsoi doesn't need me because I'm me. She needs me because I'm a full-blooded Uloni, just like you. If she'd found you instead of me, you might have been the Heart of Nunako."

Johrann nodded. "In another life, you might have been the *Heart of Dorai.*"

"The goddesses aren't good or evil," Emmy continued. "They're the same as each other. We're the same as each other. The Grandmother and Bomsoi have steered us down this path, and we're meant to be together, along with Mantos and Bandim. I don't know how we'll do it, but the four of us together will return balance to the world. At first, I thought it would be the triumph of Nunako over Dorai, but it's not. We need to curb Bandim's power and raise Mantos' up so they're equal once more, both goddesses the same. Just like we're the same."

"Two Hands and two Hearts together," Johrann said, an echo of the Grandmother's words. Her tone shifted, becoming solemn. "But we're not the same, Emmy. We can't be, not unless you do something heinous."

Emmy reached through the darkness and wound her claws between Johrann's. She didn't need to say what she was about to say. She didn't need to offer this female comfort. Johrann didn't deserve it. Yet Emmy took a steadying breath and spoke, regardless. "If it makes you feel any better, I forgive you. For killing the Uloni, for killing my parents and for forcing me into a life that for sixteen cycles was unbearable." Johrann tried to pull away, but Emmy held on. "I do forgive you, Johrann Maa. I think you've suffered just as much in your life as I have in mine."

Unable to speak her thanks, Johrann raised their clenched hands together and kissed the back of Emmy's talons.

Weariness overcame Emmy, and she slid onto her back again. The effort of healing upon healing had milked her of all her power. She ached all the way down to her bones. Johrann passed her hand across her head again.

"Sleep. Bandim will expect more of the same from you tomorrow. You need your rest."

"What I need," Emmy said around a yawn, "is Mantos. Once he's here, all four of us will be together. And Bomsoi needs to be here too. She can tell us what to do. We can finish the Grandmother's plans."

Johrann hushed her into silence, and Emmy pressed the side of her face into the feather pillow, her mind flooded with thoughts of Bomsoi, of Nunako and Dorai, of Mantos and Bandim, and how in the name of everything under the Arc they could get him through seas and fields and a city soon to be slick with battle and blood, into the Masvam palace.

* * *

The next day proceeded like the last. Whitened prints of her hands were upon countless bodies now, and it seemed like the procession of illness would never end. By afternoon she was more than ready for the break the guards afforded her. They guided her into an antechamber off the side of the Great Hall, and a server brought her food and wine enough for two. Emmy glanced upward, waiting for the trick to be pulled, but nothing happened. The guards stood by, holding their pikes, and one even smiled from under his helm.

Her hunger got the better of her suspicion and Emmy dug into the delicious repast before her. For the briefest of moments, she even forgot about the circumstances she was in, until a voice in her head sounded loud and clear.

"*Emmy, can you hear me?*"

Startled, Emmy dropped her cutlery with a squeak. The guards snapped into action, ready to leap at her or whatever had caused the upset. Emmy waved them off with an excuse she wasn't even sure contained coherent words, then forced another load of meat and sauce into her mouth.

"*Bomsoi? Is that you?*"

"*Yes, my dear, it's me.*" Though she was only a voice, her relief was clear. *"I'm nearby, circling above the clouds with Neiruk. Mantos and I will be with you soon, and we can end this for good.*"

"*Is Mantos there too?*" Emmy asked, trying to keep her face as impassive as possible. The guard who'd stared before now looked with a strange curiosity. "*I can't sense him.*"

There was a pause before Bomsoi answered, and when she did, there was definite levity in her words. "*No, but he's on his way. You'll know it when he arrives.*"

"*Bomsoi?*" Emmy asked, but received no clarification.

She chewed another mouthful and swallowed, the food no longer of any interest. Bomsoi was near. Mantos was coming. Then all four would be together. Two Hands, Two Hearts, with the Stranger to guide them. Emmy needed to get to Johrann and warn her, but how?

An idea came to her. She took deliberate care not to drop her utensils and reached for a cup of wine. She placed it to her lips, giving her an excuse to close her eyes as if savoring the taste, though it was in concentration. She hadn't tried this before. It might not work with Johrann if it was a gift from Nunako rather than Dorai, but Emmy had to try.

Just as she did when speaking to Rel or Bomsoi or Mantos, Emmy reached out with her mind, seeking another with her power.

"*Johrann? It's Emmy.*" There was nothing. Emmy pretended to take another long gulp of wine and pressed her lips in a firm line, trying again. "*Johrann, it's Emmy. Mantos and Bomsoi are on their way. We'll be together, all four of us.*"

A sensation passed through her like a hand passing through water. *"Emmy? How is your voice in my head?*"

Emmy bit her lip to suppress her sigh of relief. *"It's something Bomsoi taught me. All Uloni can do it, and Mantos.*"

The pause that followed brought sick fear to Emmy's stomach as she fretted. Had she lost Johrann?

"*Could Bandim?*" came Johrann's reply.

Emmy's fear ran to dread. "*Perhaps. Is he with you?*"

"*No*," came Johrann's reply. "*I'm alone in my chambers. But that doesn't mean he hasn't overheard. I shield my mind from his to stop him sensing my emotion, but you don't. With his powers, who knows what he's capable of without even knowing it?*"

Emmy jerked to her feet, jostling the table, and setting cutlery and plates rattling. The guards tensed once more.

"I want to see Johrann Maa," she blurted. "Now!"

There was safety in numbers, and they needed to be together for whatever it was the Grandmother wanted to achieve. If Bandim had heard her and managed to separate them, they might never carry out her plans.

The guards shared a look. The friendlier of the two shrugged. The other shook his head, but the first gestured to the door with his pike.

"We'll bring you," he said, "but if you make one wrong move, we'll kill you."

I'd like to see you try, Emmy thought, but said instead, "I know. I mean no harm. I just need to see her. Now."

Emmy set a quick pace and escaped the antechamber, flanked by her guard. Though she'd asked them to take her, it was clear she was leading them. Emmy had never walked the halls of the Masvam palace before but ignored the guards' protests for her to slow down, and her burning instinct to break into a run. Johrann's rooms were in one of the towers, and Emmy followed her senses toward a winding stair that climbed upward and upward without end, too narrow to be for anyone but servants. There were no windows or even arrow slits to allow a sliver of sun, so Emmy conjured a palm light, painting the black stone blue.

The two guards clattered behind in their armor, their pikes cumbersome in the tight space. Once they were high enough up and half the distance between two tower exits, if Emmy's stair-counting had been accurate, she stopped. Feigning exhaustion, she slumped against the stone. The guards' chests moved in tandem.

With no warning Emmy extinguished her palm light, plunging them into darkness. Before they could cry out, she pulled on her power and whipped two thick ropes of ice toward them, binding them together, their pikes clattering from their hands. The light of her power lit their faces, showing the shock of the smiling guard and the fury of the other.

"Sorry," Emmy said, and then she was hammering up the stair once more, turning and turning beneath the light of her palm.

When she reached the top and burst through the servants' entrance, Johrann was waiting for her outside her chamber door. She didn't look at Emmy, but at something beyond, out through one of the grand arching windows. Emmy followed her line of sight, blinking to clear her eyes of the dust from the stairwell, because what she saw couldn't be possible. It *wasn't* possible.

Bomsoi's words returned to her. "*He's on his way. You'll know when he arrives.*"

"By the Goddess," Emmy breathed.

Coming straight for the Masvam palace, sailing high above the city on impossible winds, with impossible sails, was a *ship*.

CHAPTER THIRTY

Bandim-Dorai

The strange sensation started in his head in the middle of a meeting with his overdukes. In the congress chamber, Bandim-Dorai flicked up one talon to silence Overduke Adzunetsi's report on Masvam military forces. Something flickered in his mind. No, not flickered. More like sounded. It wasn't an emotion, and it wasn't Dorai. The harder Bandim listened, the clearer the noise became. Then he understood it wasn't just noise. It was words.

"Emmy."

That sounded like Johrann's voice, but not her tone. She should have been colder, angrier. The voice faded, and there was nothing but silence and Adzunetsi's brief attempt to question what was happening, but Bandim-Dorai bade him be silent again.

"Bandim?"

Once again, that was Johrann, this time speaking his name. Something twisted inside him like the sickening lurch of illness.

"*... doesn't mean he hasn't heard.*"

Heard what? he asked, though there was no response. Bandim-Dorai pressed his lips in a firm line and rose from the table, possibilities running through his mind, none of them good. Johrann was speaking to Emmy. She didn't sound like herself. She said his name, mentioned him hearing something with an implication that she didn't want him to. Lies. Betrayal. *But not Johrann*, he thought as the sickness in his stomach turned cold. *She couldn't do that to him.*

Could she?

Before he could speak, an attendant clattered into the congress chamber, begging forgiveness by bowing low in front of the power before him.

"I'm so sorry for intruding, Your Imperial Majesty, My Lords," he panted, "but I was sent with an urgent message."

"Spit it out," Adzunetsi said, though his gaze kept flickering to Bandim-Dorai.

The attendant shook in his boots. "I swear, before I say it, this is the message they gave me, Your Imperial Majesty. It's not a lie." He took a gulping breath. "There's a *sailing ship* flying right toward the palace, coming in from the southwest. I swear, I *swear*, that's the truth."

Adzunetsi scoffed and rose, reaching for the dagger at his belt. "That is impossible. Your incompetence knows no bounds. What's your name? I'll gut you for your insolence and lies!"

Before the terrified attendant could respond, shock and awe rose from outside in sound and feeling. As soon as the wave of emotion hit him, Bandim-Dorai knew what the attendant said was true to the last word. He rested against the table for a moment, the colors of the six stained-glass windows spreading over his skin and armor. He closed his eyes, trying to wrap his thoughts around what was happening. Typical Mantos, typical Nunako, selfish and never playing by the rules. He should have come with an army. But neither Mantos nor Nunako ever did as they should.

And Johrann. The one who'd gifted him his power. The one who'd granted him his every wish, every desire, the one he wanted to marry. Had she betrayed him? But how? Why? No, it couldn't be. But everything pointed to the suggestion that she had. The pain of treachery was like a sword driven through his skull.

He shoved the sensation aside for now. Bandim-Dorai reached outward into whatever flame he could find, and without leaving the council chamber, saw what the attendant had described. A small sailing ship coming from southwest, a strange contraption of sails slung across its hull. Something strange hummed within it, whatever power it was that Mantos had reined to make it fly. It grew closer and closer, dipping downward in an arcing collision course with the palace itself. Bandim-Dorai started to pull back from the flame, but something caught him, stopped him, wrenched him forward.

"*Brother, dear brother.*"

"Mantos," he ground out through clenched teeth.

"*I told you I would find you.*"

"It's not finding me when you knew where I would be," Bandim-Dorai spat, unsure whether he was speaking aloud or in his head or both or neither. "This is *my* home."

Mantos ignored the emphasis. "*Meet me in the speaker's bowl. We'll finish this today, once and for all. Brother to brother, goddess to goddess.*"

Bandim-Dorai went to respond, his tongue sharp, but found himself propelled backward out of his flame, out of his mind, until he was in the council chamber again with his overdukes staring at him, slack-jawed.

"Your Excellence?" Adzunetsi asked.

He didn't respond to the question, or to the confused silence of the others. He turned his back to them, pausing to collect his thoughts. This wasn't how he'd envisioned his encounter with Mantos, but it didn't matter. Regardless of how his brother tried to rig the game, throw him off balance, he would never succeed.

Before any of his overdukes could react, the Sun Emperor broke into a sprint straight at one of the grand stained-glass windows and jumped.

Tiboli orange and red exploded in shards around him. Bandim-Dorai lit his power beneath him, propelling himself upward in a blaze of fire. Growing closer and closer was Mantos' flying ship. Bandim-Dorai willed his power to send a blast of flame toward it and kill them all before they arrived, but the ship's great curved hull dropped as though whatever power kept it aloft had disappeared. It careened downward into the speaker's bowl, figures leaping from its doomed decks, and collided with the white stone in a deafening explosion of beams and boards and flying debris.

One of those leaping figures had been Mantos. Bandim-Dorai's lips curled in a snarl as he shot downward to the chaos of wood that had destroyed the bowl. The remnants of tattered sails settled over the wreckage and dust billowed upward, blocking his view. But Bandim-Dorai knew where his brother was, and Mantos didn't try to hide from him as he climbed onto the highest point, what used to be the prow of the ship.

"Bandim," Mantos called, his voice carrying around the bowl, "let's end this. Leave the rest of them. It's just you and me."

A handful of other green figures clambered from where they had landed, appearing through the wreckage. At the same time, Masvam soldiers poured into the bowl, though none moved to attack. The four-torqued commanders gestured for them to wait, and Bandim-Dorai knew they waited only for his word to attack. One nod from him and Mantos' little band of Linvarrans, *females* of all things, would be dead to the last.

Bandim-Dorai remained high in a twist of flame and shook his head. "It's never been 'just you and me,' Mantos. It's always been you. You demanding. You getting. You controlling. So no, I won't leave the rest. I won't do your bidding. I am the emperor of the Masvam Empire. I am Dorai, and I submit to no one!"

He jerked his head in command to his soldiers, and the entire bowl burst into havoc. Soldiers charged from all entrances, filling the bowl with blackness. Bandim-Dorai remained high for a moment as he watched the green of Mantos' Linvarrans scatter. Mantos remained on the prow for a moment, hanging onto the sculpted figurehead, staring upward. He dared to look angry. He dared to look betrayed. Ire rising, Bandim-Dorai shot downward, intent on taking off his brother's head. Mantos didn't deserve those feelings. Nunako didn't deserve those feelings. They were both liars, and both deserved nothing but death.

It was time to see the extent of his brother's power. Bandim-Dorai summoned a burst of flame, and sent it forward to engulf his prey, but Mantos reached downward and pulled. A huge barrier of the bowl's paving stones and rocks from under the ground shot upward at his command, and Bandim-Dorai's fireball burst against it. The Sun Emperor gritted his teeth and propelled himself over the makeshift wall, sending another blast of fire at the smashed ship's figurehead, but Mantos disappeared.

Bandim-Dorai cursed and reached out to feel his brother's direction, but the clamor of emotion all around clouded his senses. If Johrann was here, no doubt he could use her to clarify his power. He didn't know where she was. Could he ever use her again? Trust her again? Cursing once more, Bandim-Dorai resorted to flicking his gaze from point to point, until the whole speaker's bowl shuddered under something unnatural. Bandim-Dorai whirled around to see it wasn't just the bowl. The whole palace was shaking and quavering, towers jerking and tilting, windows shattering as the ground quaked.

"Bandim, leave this to us and us alone!" Mantos cried above the din. "Leave the rest!"

"*Never*," Bandim-Dorai ground out, still seeking his brother.

Mantos revealed himself by rising on a plinth of stone, his eyes blazing blue, rocks orbiting his body, swirling around his hands. Bandim-Dorai dove forward, turning in circles and dodging sideways as Mantos shot projectiles at him. It was a feeble gesture. Bandim-Dorai drew on the pulsing belief of those around him who were witness to the Sun Emperor's, the goddess Dorai's power, and summoned a torrent of fire. He sent it from his fingertips, a wave of braided and whipping tongues licking toward his brother, intent on roasting him alive, destroying everything Mantos was, what he had once been, what he intended to be.

His brother threw up another rock wall, sending the palace heaving again, toppling Masvam soldiers from their feet.

"You can't win!" Bandim-Dorai called out as he sent more burning weaponry outward. "You can try and try but you'll never best me."

He swooped in low as Mantos parried every one of his massive blasts with obstacles of stone. Bandim-Dorai kept his feet off the ground to avoid losing footing under Mantos' wretched earthquakes, lit his fists and swung for his brother's head over and over. Mantos, unable to wrench up barriers fast enough, ducked backward and away from the blows, his boots slipping on the uneven ground and refuse of the destroyed ship. All around them the sounds of fighting filled the bowl. Whoever they were, Mantos' Linvarrans were putting up more of a fight than expected.

"Haven't you learned by now?" Bandim-Dorai caught the side of Mantos' head with a blow and sent him reeling and stumbling. "Won't you ever learn that you'll never be as good as me? Or do I have to teach you that lesson through death, just like I had to teach our mother?"

Mantos straightened as fast as a crack of lightning and before Bandim-Dorai could see him move, he'd drawn a great sword from an ornate scabbard at his belt. It was an enormous blade with a deadly pommel on the end that looked like one of Nunako's cursed moons. Mantos thrust it outward, forcing Bandim-Dorai to retreat and sweep out of reach.

"It's you that needs to learn a lesson through death," Mantos growled. "If you can't learn from the death, you're bringing all around you, I'll teach you by killing you myself. Father wouldn't want this. It's not what the goddesses want either."

Bandim-Dorai jerked his arms upward and brought a hail of fire down on Mantos' head, forcing his brother to throw himself under a jutting beam for cover. The wood burst into flame.

"You speak to me of what the goddesses want when I am one of them?" he said, sending another barrage downward. "Typical Mantos, thinking he knows everything. Typical Nunako, always assuming her opinion is the one we both should share. But it's not!" The last word exploded from his chest with the wrath of Dorai. Every flame in the palace, all the fires he had started in the speaker's bowl, erupted in columns that snaked to the sky. "You don't know everything!"

Mantos rolled across the wreckage of the ground just as the beam above him collapsed. He discarded his sword and clapped his hands together. As he drew them apart, a great boulder grew between his palms. He sent it flying forward but Bandim-Dorai was too fast, flitting aside before it could strike him.

"I'm one of the goddesses now too," Mantos replied, pulling himself to his feet, "and I know it's not what Nunako wants. It's not what the Grandmother of the World wants either. The only one who wants all this destruction is you, Bandim. Just you."

The mention of that name made Bandim-Dorai jerk backward as if it had struck him. The what? That term was strange, yet it wasn't. Dorai knew it. It was the name of her mother, the goddess who'd created the Arc of the Sky, then Nunako and Dorai, sending them forth to shape and populate the world and split everything between them, equally. But it had never been equal. Dorai had shown him everything, how Nunako had created all the life under the Arc, and how the Younglings loved her for it. How they praised her and ignored the love and care that Dorai gave them. Nunako might have wrought them from the earth by her hands but it was Dorai who had done everything to nurture and protect them, even wrenching off one of her own arms to protect them.

But the Younglings came to see her as demonic, as evil, as death, and Nunako had done nothing to stop them, setting herself up as the Lady of Light to counter Dorai's so-called Darkness.

Now, Nunako had even taken Dorai's Heart if his suspicions were true. His *Johrann*. The only one who'd remained loyal through all these cycles. It had to be Mantos' doing. It had to be.

Something broke within Bandim-Dorai. He screeched and channeled all his fury, all his hatred, into the power coursing through his veins and into his hands. This would end. Now.

Bandim-Dorai summoned every last mote of power, locked eyes with Mantos and sent everything he had toward his brother, his sister-goddess, his mortal enemy. He would kill them once and for all.

A cold blueness shot upward, casting his flames aside. Mantos peered through a wall of ethereal ice, his face warped.

Bandim-Dorai screeched again.

CHAPTER THIRTY-ONE

Mantos

He'd known any attempt to convince his brother to confine the fighting between them would be futile, but he also knew he had to try. Twice he tried to reason with Bandim, and twice Bandim had rebuffed him.

Sweat drenched Mantos' brow as he fought back against Bandim's fiery onslaught again and again, pulling on every thread of power he could. His brother kept forcing him backward, sending him flying into the debris of the *Water Prago.* The thought of the ship made him think of her crew, of Zecha, now in a sea of black as the Masvam forces fell upon them.

"You speak to me of what the goddesses want when I am one of them?" Bandim said. "Typical Mantos, thinking he knows everything. Typical Nunako, always assuming her opinion is the one we both should share. But it's not! You don't know everything!"

When his brother's fury turned every lick of flame around them into a blaze, Mantos flung himself under part of the ship's wreckage. Haelo clattered across the tortured ground. He clapped his hands together, not knowing what he was doing, but Nunako guided him as he drew his hands apart, conjuring a huge boulder and sending it hurtling in Bandim's direction.

His brother jerked aside, the projectile sailing past, a cruel grin on his face. Mantos struggled to his feet.

"I'm one of the goddesses now too," he said, "and it's not what Nunako wants. It's not what the Grandmother of the World wants either. The only one who wants all this destruction is you, Bandim. Just you."

His brother's body snapped backward as if something had struck him, and his face morphed with sudden despair. Something Mantos had said had wounded him, or perhaps Dorai, deep enough to cleave a chasm of hurt. The despair disappeared, replaced with snarling fury, and Bandim screamed, the veins and tendons of his neck pulsing, his scales flaring, and he sent a blast of fire toward Mantos so strong it was clear he intended to kill him.

Mantos was unafraid. He sensed her before she was there, felt the cold rush of her power before the sheer wall of ice erupted between them, blocking Bandim's fire and sending it careening in every direction except at Mantos. Through the distorted texture of the ice, Mantos watched Bandim, the play of emotion on his face. Anger. Betrayal. Fury. Despair. Then determination.

As his brother shot upward, Mantos retreated, catching sight of not only Emmy, but the other Uloni too. Bandim's Heart.

"No time for extended introductions," Emmy said, breathless. "Johrann, this is Mantos. Mantos, Johrann."

The other Uloni jerked her head in greeting before skipping backward, her steps lighter than they should have been, her eyes glowing red with her power. Red, like Bandim's.

"*Is she an ally?*" Mantos asked as Bandim dove the near side of the ice wall, consumed by flame.

"*We're all on the same side,*" Emmy replied as she shot icy tendrils at Bandim, trying to slow his descent, "*except Bandim.*"

"*Clearly.*"

Mantos pulled up a shield of rock to protect himself and Emmy from Bandim's onslaught, but he sailed past them both, coming to a halt a distance from Johrann.

"I never expected this from you," Bandim said to the other Uloni. Mantos winced at the sound of betrayal in his tone. "Johrann Maa, the one who stood beside me all these years, the one who gave me everything I ever wanted. Johrann Maa, the one I would have married." His voice broke on the last word. "How could you?"

He hovered in the air above her, but Johrann rose upward in a swirl of wind, meeting his gaze. "All these cycles I was true to you," she said. "It was me who was betrayed."

"What?"

Johrann's voice was thick. "I thought the one who saved me was Dorai. The voice told me it was. But it wasn't. All the things I've done, things I thought I was doing for Dorai, I wasn't. I've been lied to every day since I can remember. But don't doubt the truth of what I did for you. I made you the One of Two. I brought Dorai into you. I killed your brother, delivered you your crown, just like you wanted."

Any sliver of sympathy Mantos had for her froze as cold as Emmy's ice. His neck scales pulsed. Before he could speak, Emmy's voice broke through.

"*Just as we thought, Johrann was the one who brought you back to life as a hatchling. She was the priestess your mother turned to. A voice claiming to be Dorai told her to save you. But it wasn't Dorai. It was the Grandmother.*"

"*And now we're on the same side? How?*" Mantos asked, his eyeridges low with a scowl. "*As far as I'm concerned, you don't kill the folk who're on your side.*"

Johrann continued her tirade at Bandim. Tears slid down her armored cheeks. "You knew it wasn't Dorai who'd spoken to me in the desert. You had to know. Yet you didn't tell me."

When Bandim replied, there was something like sorrow in his voice. "I only realized when you spoke about the killing of your folk. I never lied to you, Johrann." The sorrow in his words disappeared, replaced once more by fiery anger. "You're the liar. Not long after this other Uloni arrived," he said, jerking a talon at Emmy, "I started to suspect you were keeping something from me. It wouldn't be the first time, would it? After all the hiding you did from me, keeping your emotions shielded away. But I never, ever expected you would turn your tail on me."

Bandim lit his hands and Mantos tensed, ready to strike, but Emmy stopped him with a cold touch. "Wait."

Johrann closed her eyes, schooling her emotions. "I haven't turned my tail on you. All my life I've been working for the Grandmother of the World without even knowing it. I'm still working with her now, just in a different way. I don't understand what she wants but she needs us to come *together.*" She gestured down at Mantos and Emmy. "All four of us."

Understanding his brother better than anyone else under the Arc, Mantos saw it a split-second before the others. The idea of Mantos and Bandim together lit Bandim's rage once more like a Belfoni firework. He lashed out with flaming fists, spinning toward Johrann. Before he collided with her, Mantos' pillar of rock struck him, sending Bandim spiraling off. Johrann flitted backward and down, hovering a step above the ground.

"I knew that would happen," she said, "but it was worth a try."

"You can't reason with Bandim," Mantos replied.

He took in the female's face. This was the one who'd killed him. Twice. She was older than Emmy, though how old he couldn't tell. Her gray eyes seemed shadowed, and cycles of stress had puckered her fine features.

A glancing shot from Bandim destroyed Mantos' moment of contemplation. It was wide enough that he knew his brother hadn't meant for it to strike him.

"Johrann Maa is mine," Bandim said, whipping new flames between his palms, "not yours, Mantos."

Brow creasing with confusion, Mantos ducked down as Bandim sent another shot at him. This time, ice didn't deflect it, but an enormous burst of wind from Johrann's hands.

"This Uloni doesn't belong to anyone," Mantos called above the noise of the melee. "The only one we belong to is the Grandmother of the World!"

Bandim arced upward, a dark swirl of fronds and robes against the sky, before diving back down again, white-hot and enraged.

"How wrong you are!" he bellowed, and Mantos had to pull a great arch of rock above his head to shield him from the immensity of Bandim's power. "I belong to no one, and everyone under the Arc of the Sky belongs to us. We made them, Dorai and Nunako together. Except you stole them from me!"

Mantos had to scrabble on top of his arch of rock, avoiding Bandim as he attempted to ram him into submission. His chest heaving, Mantos reached out to Emmy, seeking power and succor. Bandim was so strong. Dorai was so strong. Mantos knew which was speaking then.

"You turned the Younglings against me," Bandim went on, speaking with the goddess's tongue as he dove back at Mantos again, "and made yourself into the goddess of virtue in charge of their 'Light.' Ha! You've always been and always will be a selfish creature, Mantos. And Nunako." His voice grew low as he drew back, poised to strike again. "Especially you, Nunako."

Mantos went to respond but something within him stilled his mouth. It was Nunako, nudging him and shaking her head. No.

No?

The goddess writhed inside him. She closed his eyes and played out the many memories of the time she walked the Arc, a thousand cycles before Mantos ever existed. Dorai and Nunako together, crafting and caring for the world. The Younglings as a new life, seeking guidance and reassurance and protection from their goddesses.

A slam hit Mantos' stomach, but he knew it wasn't physical, even as he bent double under its strength. The split within the Younglings, the power struggle between the two goddesses. The great storm that neither of them created that threatened to kill everything they'd made. Dorai wrenching off one of her arms, soaking the soil in her blood, all to protect the Younglings she loved, not just from the danger of the storm, but from the danger of Nunako's arrogance.

Then Nunako taking the glory. Nunako imbibing the praise. Nunako condemning her sister, claiming the storm was the work of the Darkness of Dorai. The start of everything that had led them down the path they now stood at the end of.

Bomsoi; the One of Balance.

Her betrayal.

The loss of power, Nunako and Dorai retreating from the world.

And now this.

When Mantos regained his senses, Bandim, Emmy, and Johrann stared at him. He reached upward, feeling the warm wetness on his face. Nunako's tears.

"Dorai," he whispered. She whispered, staring at the tear-stained hands of this mortal body she inhabited. "This is all my doing. I'm sorry."

Bandim released another howl of abject rage. Mantos snapped back to himself, Nunako releasing control of his body once more just in time for him to leap aside and cocoon himself in the safety of rock. Nunako had shown him the truth. She'd turned on her sister, stolen all the love of the Younglings for herself. Nunako had cast Dorai as a demon, just like the one Fonbir and the Althemerians called Oatutkubis, the Demon Who Rides the Sky. It was Nunako who had done this, Nunako who had destroyed her sister's reputation and cast her as one of the Dark.

"*How could you?*" Mantos asked her but he received no reply.

Mantos burst from his stone protection in time to see a blast of fire meet a crack of ice above him. Bandim and Emmy faced off, the pain of exertion on their faces. Johrann was at Mantos' side, helping him onto his feet.

"Nunako turned against Dorai," he said. "All of this is because of her."

Johrann's face was dark. "That's something I've known for cycles. The one who I thought was Dorai told me so. For a thousand cycles, they've demonized Dorai."

"But she did nothing wrong," Mantos finished.

Johrann nodded. "The Grandmother of the World knows too. I think that's why she wants us together. We can put things right at last."

Hope shimmered in Mantos' mind. *Put things right?* Perhaps not just between Nunako and Dorai, but between Mantos and Bandim too. *Perhaps... perhaps both of them could live.*

That hope died and Mantos cried out as Bandim bellowed, feral and betrayed, and forced more power from himself. His neck scales flared and flexed, and his tail whipped as his fire encroached on Emmy faster and faster. Emmy's arms trembled under the weight of her exertion, but then Mantos was with her, holding onto her arms, lacing his fingers atop hers and willing whatever power he could into her body.

"Mantos!" she cried, bewildered, but then she could speak no more as the power of Nunako's Hand and Nunako's Heart combined.

"*We need to end this,*" he said.

"*Yes,*" Emmy replied.

"*Yes.*" This came from Nunako.

He felt everything at once, saw everything at once. Every emotion, every memory that Emmy and Mantos and Nunako had experienced, all the combined cycles of their lives, their weaknesses, their strengths, coming together.

They pushed it all into their power, forcing Bandim's fire back, back, back, until the ice reached him.

And he screamed.

CHAPTER THIRTY-TWO

Emmy

The storm of Bandim's power was unending but she couldn't see Mantos. For a dreadful moment, Emmy thought he was dead. Then, with a crack, he emerged from the stone he'd protected himself within, and relief flowed into her.

At the same time, Bandim released a howl of rage that spoke of cycle upon cycle of pain and betrayal and punishment, a sound Emmy herself might have made at Krodge if ever she'd had the courage. With the sound came an explosion of blazing fury that rampaged forth, and before she knew what she was doing, Emmy threw herself in front of Bandim's flames, forcing his power back with her ice.

In their minds, they were back in Hutuketshu Encampment at their first meeting. Haloed in flame, flickering in and out, Bandim had hovered before her as she took his beloved fire and froze it like nothing but rain. She knew he could feel it too.

"*I told you I would help stop you*," she said.

Bandim replied only with a raging bellow, every scale of his neck pulsing, his tail whipping, and he pushed more power toward her than Emmy had ever felt before, not even from Bomsoi.

"*Bomsoi, where are you?*" she cried, though she knew it was in vain. Even if the Stranger was with them, she couldn't intervene, couldn't raise a hand against her mother.

Bandim's fire hurtled forward fast, her ice dwindling and splintering and cracking in its path. This was it. She was going to die.

But then there were hands upon her own, strong talons twining with hers.

"*Mantos?*"

It couldn't have been anyone else. A strange sensation came over her, a reversal of power as Mantos, no longer drawing power from her, willed his own through her.

"*We need to end this*," he said.

"*Yes*," Emmy replied, breathless with effort yet refreshed with new determination.

"*Yes*."

The third voice Emmy hadn't heard before, yet she knew it. Nunako, the one who had gifted her with her Heart.

All three joined together becoming one being of mind, hand and heart, working in tandem, sharing their memories and experiences, morphing, and changing. The ice pushed forward, and Bandim's fire receded.

As soon as the touch of coldness reached him, Bandim released another scream, different from before, pained, haunted. His fire extinguished like a snuffed candle, and he fell.

When his body hit the ground, Emmy was herself again. Mantos' hands were still upon hers at first, but at the sight of his brother's crumpled body lying in the churn of torn-up stone and the ship's wreckage, he released her and sucked in a breath. He ran forward, but Emmy looked back, aware now of the silence that had descended in the Masvam palace's vast arena. There was no fighting. Everyone had ceased.

"Emmy?"

She'd recognize that voice anywhere. Heart surging, Emmy turned to see Zecha charging toward her, his arms outstretched. She broke into a run, stumbling over debris until he wrapped her in his arms. Somehow, he lifted her off her feet, even though she was the taller of the two.

"Zecha, why are you here?"

Her best friend pulled back and swept some fronds from her face. "You're welcome."

Bruised and bleeding from the battle, somehow Zecha still smiled and jested. Emmy pressed a kiss to one of his filthy cheeks, laughing at his sarcasm.

Then she wasn't laughing as she turned to show Mantos that Zecha was okay. Mantos sat on the ground, cradling his brother's head in his lap. Johrann Maa stood nearby, her mouth covered by her hands, tears streaming down her face as her shoulders shook.

As soon as she saw Bandim's dead body, Emmy knew this wasn't what was meant to be. They'd thought, what seemed like cycles ago, that to bring balance to the world meant Bandim's destruction. But another piece of the puzzle in her head fell into place as Emmy realized to destroy one goddess wouldn't bring any more balance than only having one in the world.

"*Bomsoi?*" she called out. "*Grandmother? We're here now, all four of us together. What do you need?*"

A bellowing cry sounded from above them. All heads turned to see a huge, gleaming creature perched on one of the lilting towers of the palace, his glittering wings spread. It was Neiruk. Upon his back was a rider. Bomsoi.

The Stranger urged the Prago into flight for a short moment, landing in a swirl of dust. Emmy raised a hand to protect her eyes as Bomsoi slipped from Neiruk's back. She walked a few paces in silence, taking in the scene before her, her face impassive. Her gaze came to rest upon Bandim's crumpled form and Mantos' agonizing grief.

"Bomsoi," Emmy started, "I don't understand what we're supposed to do, but the Grandmother came to us, Johrann and I, and told us we needed the Hands and Hearts of Nunako and Dorai together. She said that you'd tell us what to do. So what do we do?"

"You aren't all four together," Bomsoi replied, her tone flat. "Bandim Tiboli is dead."

Though she'd already known it, Johrann Maa let out a wail of grief, sinking to her knees. Emmy didn't know if it was for losing Bandim, or because if he was dead, it meant the Grandmother couldn't do what it was Johrann had worked toward for her whole life.

"Then bring him back," Mantos blurted. "You did it for me." He jerked his head toward Johrann. "You did it too. So bring him back."

Crushing guilt fell on Emmy at the desperation in Mantos' voice. Despite everything, he still wanted his brother back. There was love when there shouldn't be. Even though Bandim had killed Mantos for his own gain, Mantos still wanted to bring his brother back to life. Mantos hadn't killed Bandim. It had been Emmy.

"Mantos, I'm so sorry," she started.

Before she could continue her apology, something shimmered in the air between them all. The stench of burning and charred skin filled Emmy's nostrils as a blackened figure appeared, tendrils of smoke writhing around it. Emmy's chest heaved. She'd seen this figure before, back in the Uloni temple.

Bomsoi reached outward and waved a hand at the tall figure that glinted with red and gold. The stench disappeared and, in a flash of light, the disfigurement lifted from them. Among all of those watching, Phen of House Yru stood, smiling down at her sons.

"Mother!"

Mantos' cry was at once pained and joyous.

"Mantos," Phen replied, her voice as clear as it had been the day she'd visited Emmy in the Uloni temple.

Mantos lifted Bandim's slack head and presented him to her like a youngling with a broken toy. "I didn't mean for him to die. At first, I did but then I didn't. It's not the right thing. It's never been the right thing."

Phen kneeled in front of her two sons, wood splintering beneath her, and shook her head. "No. It's never been the right thing."

Emmy's heart ached as if clutched by a hand, squeezing tighter with every one of Mantos' desperate words.

"Bring him back, Mother. Please."

Phen first touched Mantos' cheek, caressing the armor. Then she withdrew her touch and plucked up a jagged shard of wood from the ship's hull and held it out. Emmy followed the line of her gesture. It was to Bomsoi.

The Stranger took up the offered wood and nodded, understanding what Emmy didn't. Then she said, "Open your palm to me."

With no hesitation, Phen unfurled her talons. Emmy gasped as in one swift motion, Bomsoi sliced the ragged fragment of wood across Phen's fleshy palm. Bright red blood blossomed and pooled in her palm.

With Bandim's head still cradled in Mantos' lap, Phen brought her hand to rest on her dead son's forehead, just under his first horn. She anointed his two cheeks, then slid her bloodied hand across his lips. She'd done this before, Emmy realized. This was what she'd done to help bring Mantos back from the dead.

Only the creaking of debris and the snapping of half-destroyed banners broke the silence as Phen moved aside, Bomsoi taking her place. The Stranger closed her eyes for a moment, lifting her hands. When she opened them again, her eyes glowed blue. When she spoke, the entire arena filled with her strange words.

"*Gou wèm. Gou wèm ga bàm, ga bàm, yoyominkos.*"

Emmy recognized the language straight away as Khinish. From Mantos' face, she knew he did too.

The air chilled, as if time ran backwards and the worst of Vhaun returned. Ice cracked and rose around them, encircling the gathered in fractal patterns as Bomsoi's words came faster and louder, her voice lifting until it was the only sound in the entire world. Icy trails tracked Bandim's prone form, winding around him like ropes.

Bomsoi lifted her hands high, words melding and morphing as her eyes shone blue and she commanded, "*Rise!*"

There was a deep *clunk* from everywhere and nowhere. Emmy nailed her focus to Bandim, and they waited.

Then it happened.

Bandim Tiboli sat up straight, rising from the dead before them all. His eyes glowed with Bomsoi's power, not red but blue.

Mantos cried out in relief, wrapping his arms around his brother from behind. Bandim paid no attention. He only looked at the figure standing before him. His mother.

Phen smiled, a single tear escaping. "*I told you I would have done the same for you, my son.*" As she spoke, Emmy realized her body was no longer tangible, but was flickering and fading. "*I sacrifice myself this time for you, Bandim.*" Her voice wavered. "*My sons, I will never see you again. But please know that I love you.*" Emmy saw her move her gaze from one son to the other. "*I love you both. I will love you both* forever."

"*Mother?*" Bandim managed, leaning out of Mantos' gaze, one arm stretched to Phen's fading form.

"*I love you both. Love one another.*"

Phen's final words echoed around the arena as her body disappeared in a whirl of smoke and ash. Gone, the only thing that remained of her was the blood smeared on Bandim's face. Emmy dashed her hand across her eyes as grief played across the brothers' faces. Somehow, she understood what Phen had meant. Whatever power she'd had to return to the Arc in her ghostly form was gone.

"*I sacrifice myself this time for you.*"

Once, Phen of House Yru had given up her life to save Mantos. Now she had given up her afterlife for Bandim, and it was clear they would never see her again.

Bandim's expression was haunted as he fell against his brother. He touched the drying stickiness on his skin and armor with trembling hands.

"What?" was all he managed, shaking his head.

Mantos shifted into his brother's view, no longer touching him, but staying a little way off. They locked eyes and Emmy held her breath, feeling power well in anticipation of another explosion of conflict. Instead, Bandim and Mantos stared at each other, saying nothing.

Zecha appeared at Emmy's shoulder and touched a gentle hand to the small of her back. "It makes me realize my sisters could have been a lot worse," he whispered. "They might have turned me out of our home but at least they never tried to kill me."

Despite everything, Emmy was glad for the release in tension. She whispered, "Zecha, hush."

Johrann Maa approached them, her face wet with relief. "We're together now, all four. Two Hands, two Hearts." She gestured at Bomsoi. "Is that the one you spoke of? The one the Grandmother meant by 'she'?"

Emmy nodded. "That's Bomsoi. She's the one of balance. She's the one who created the Uloni—us."

Johrann's eyes widened, and she looked torn between her old instinct to lash out and a new feeling of supplication.

Bomsoi inclined her head. "I am your mother of long ago," she said. "I caused all this."

She raised a hand to gesture at the surrounding chaos. Johrann's eyeridges drew together, and Emmy frowned.

"You didn't cause all this," Emmy said.

The reply that came wasn't from Bomsoi's lips. It wasn't from anyone.

"I think you'll find, my dear, that Bomsoi did cause all this."

Just like Phen's, Emmy recognized that voice. And just like Phen, a figure materialized between them in a whirl. Not charred and smoking, this female was bent-backed and leaning on a cane, wizened claws and tail appearing from the cuffs and hem of her dark robe.

"The Grandmother of the World," Emmy breathed.

CHAPTER THIRTY-THREE

Bandim-Dorai

Bandim-Dorai couldn't take his eyes off his brother. One moment, Mantos had joined forces with his Heart to destroy him. The next, he was embracing Bandim-Dorai from behind, overjoyed. Then their mother was with them, her throat intact, her body unburned, and she was smiling at them.

"I sacrifice myself this time for you, Bandim. My sons, I will never see you again. But please know that I love you. I love you both."

Sacrifice? What had happened? His mother had disappeared then, like a shadow banished by too-bright light, leaving the rest of them behind. Mantos had looked at him then, his expression a strange mixture of fear and love and worry and wariness. All Bandim-Dorai did was stare back, giving the tiniest shake of his head.

"What?" was the only word he mustered.

Nothing made sense. Nothing felt right. Everything was off, as if he was no longer himself. It was worse than the sword-slice that Johrann's betrayal had been. It was as if the earth had lurched beneath him, tilting at an unnatural angle, forcing him to sway and struggle to maintain his balance.

He broke away from Mantos as Johrann and Emmy began talking, speaking of two Hands and two Hearts together, the way Johrann had before. He followed Johrann's gaze to a third Uloni figure, one Bandim-Dorai recognized all too well. Bomsoi. His daughter. Dorai's daughter.

Before he could speak, not knowing what he might say, a strange figure flickered into view between them, dressed in a cloak with a bent back and leaning on a stick, and though Bandim hadn't seen her before, Dorai knew her.

"I think you'll find, my dear," she said, in the unmistakable voice of the mother of Nunako and Dorai, "that Bomsoi did cause all this."

Emmy spoke her name with such reverence. "The Grandmother of the World."

It took all Bandim-Dorai's strength to suppress his scream. None of this made sense. They were in a battle. He'd been bent on killing Mantos once and for all, banishing Nunako's wretchedness from the world, showing everyone that he was the Sun Emperor, he was the rightful heir to the Masvams and the only one who mattered. Now things felt different. The urgency was no longer there. None of it mattered. All that did matter was that his mother had returned to him, even though he'd murdered her. He touched his face again, knowing, without knowing how, the stickiness was her blood, and it was all he had left of her. He knew, without knowing how, he would never see her again. Something rose in him, something strange.

Grief.

Overwhelmed, Bandim-Dorai clambered to his feet, seeking to escape. He knew his eyes were wide, he knew any of his watching soldiers would see his fear from clear across the speaker's bowl, yet he didn't care. It was all too much, too different, too painful. As he went to turn, a hand clamped on his arm, the grip like iron. Mantos shook his head, his yellow eyes reflecting the fear and uncertainty Bandim-Dorai felt himself. He should have struck out, willed whatever remained of his power through his hands and burned everyone assembled to nothing but ash. Yet he didn't. Within him, Dorai withheld something of herself, and a sudden rush of isolation came upon him like a great wave.

"I don't understand what's happening," he said, the words escaping with his grief.

His mother's voice—no, not his mother's, Dorai's mother's—sounded loud in the bowl. "I think it's time we had some explanations, don't you, granddaughter?"

Bomsoi, the one Dorai referred to as her daughter, inclined her head. Mantos loosened his hand, though he kept it on Bandim's arm. The Grandmother leaned on her cane with one hand as she lifted the other, casting a bright streak of power between them all. It crackled like lightning.

"I say that Bomsoi caused all this," she said, and as she spoke two figures appeared in her power, flickering as they nipped and bit at each other, "yet that isn't the full truth." Her gaze bored through the globe of her power, and she stared at Bandim-Dorai and Mantos. "Bomsoi is only here and only made her mistakes because my daughters decided to create her."

Guilt rose within him, though there was a distance to it that made Bandim-Dorai understand it wasn't his guilt but Dorai's. From Mantos' face, he was experiencing the same strangeness.

"And I suppose," the Grandmother continued, conjuring a third figure that loomed above the warring goddesses, "that Nunako and Dorai only made their mistakes because I made mine, which was creating them in the first place."

A stab of pain replaced the guilt. Bandim-Dorai glared at the Grandmother, the rejection of his beloved Dorai cutting him like it cut the goddess herself.

"I thought I was doing the right thing when I created my daughters," the Grandmother continued. She was either oblivious to or ignoring the pain she caused.

"From the very start, when Nunako and Dorai cleaved everything under my beloved Arc in two, dividing instead of sharing, I knew I'd made a mistake. And then," she added, incredulousness entering her tone as she brought another bright figure into view, "my daughters made the same mistake I made and created a life of their own. They did something they could never take back, this time mixing the divine and the mortal, blurring the lines between them."

Bomsoi, Emmy, and Johrann all wore matching expressions, masks of pain and rejection Bandim understood more than he wanted to.

When she spoke again, the Grandmother turned to Bomsoi. "Your creation was to balance the world between your mothers, but the strength of a god and the weakness of flesh could not balance themselves, never mind everything under the Arc."

"I'm sorry, Grandmother," Bomsoi said in a voice of utter pain. "I failed."

"You should never have had such a burden placed on your shoulders, Granddaughter, as we have spoken of before."

Emmy turned her head at that. "You have?"

"We have," the Grandmother said.

Bandim-Dorai slipped his arm from his brother's now loose grasp and stepped toward the glowing circle of power. He reached out but stilled his talons before they passed through the gleaming figures of the goddesses and Bomsoi. Mantos did the same.

"How did we not know about this?" he asked, following the lines of the Grandmother's power. "Bandim and I were educated with all the knowledge in the world, but I've never heard this story."

The Grandmother laughed. "The weakness of flesh. The arrogance of thinking you know everything."

Something shifted within him and Bandim-Dorai stumbled, the goddess's presence bursting to the fore.

Unable to hold herself back any longer, Dorai roared so loud and sudden it made the gathered mortals snap to their defenses. To hear her own mother-goddess decry her existence, and for her to blame the lack of knowledge of the folk on themselves and not the true culprit, was too much.

"Arrogance!" She prodded a talon at the vessel Nunako inhabited, this repulsive brother of Bandim's. Dorai rounded on her sister's fleshly body, seething with the fury of everything said. "The arrogance comes from Nunako. The Younglings lost this story because Nunako willed it to be so. So perfect, so unwilling to be seen as anything other than the beloved Lady of Light, she buried the tale to bury her mistake."

She jerked Bandim's arms upward and summoned her powers but the glory she wished to unleash never came. Something held her back. Johrann Maa, the one who'd taken the name of her Heart, held out both hands, clutching the air as if clutching Bandim's wrists.

"*Don't.*"

This half-breed of mortal and flesh was just as bad as the rest, infected with the rot of Nunako. Dorai struggled to release herself from the creature's grasp. Then more treacherous hands clamped the air. Dorai screeched at the other Uloni, Emmy, Nunako's wretched Heart. She writhed against their combined power with all her might, all sense fleeing her, knowing only betrayal, anger, and pain, until a pair of hands made of flesh and bone settled upon Bandim's arms, her arms, and all Dorai could see was Nunako.

"Sister, stop."

No matter what she did, Dorai couldn't twist herself from the combined power of the three, so she did what she could instead and spat into Nunako's face.

Her sister didn't release her to wipe the spittle away. For the first time, Dorai realized Nunako's eyes held tears. Tears. Nunako had never cried.

"I'm so sorry."

Dorai couldn't understand the sounds that came from the mortal vessel's lips, not until Nunako continued.

"I'm so sorry, sister. I did this. Grandmother blames both of us, but the fault doesn't lie with you, nor with our daughter. It lies with me. I was wrong. When the Younglings turned against us and we couldn't walk on the Arc any longer, I became greedy to have that power back. I set myself up as the only goddess. I pushed you aside, defiled your name, blamed everything on you, even though you were the one who sacrificed a part of yourself to protect the Younglings, not just from the storm but from me."

As her anger died like a snuffed candle, the two Hearts released her, leaving only Nunako's hands upon her. Dorai licked her lips, shaking her head. It wasn't possible that Nunako was saying these words. It was a lie. It was a trick, something impossible.

"You don't mean any of this," she said, trying to break away but Nunako held firm. "You've never apologized. You've never admitted wrongdoing."

"That in itself is my greatest wrongdoing," Nunako replied. "Mother is right. We shouldn't have divided the world. We should have shared everything, come together as sisters. I should never have tried to kill your good name. I'm sorry."

Nunako spoke the last two words in a tone that betrayed something bent and broken, a fundamental crushing from deep inside. Dorai licked her lips again, for it was in that moment that she knew her sister spoke the truth. That was enough. It was all Dorai wanted. Her sister acknowledged her. She accepted her wrongs. It didn't make the past disappear, nor the hurt. But it stopped it for the future.

"I accept your apology," Dorai whispered, inclining her head. "Let's finish this."

* * *

When Bandim-Dorai regained control of his body, the loneliness had dissipated. The goddess was still within him, but she was calm, quelled. From within himself, he had borne witness to everything that had happened. Nunako, arrogant, traitorous Nunako, had admitted she was wrong. It didn't atone for the cycle upon cycle of betrayal, but he knew Dorai was sated.

The eyes that looked at him were now his brother's, not Nunako's, a mirror of his own. Dorai twisted within him, not coursing through his veins but turning as if nudging him forward, suggesting something. Bandim-Dorai let out a shuddering breath as he understood.

"Do you think," he started in a quavering voice, "that we might learn something from the goddesses?" *Not we*, he thought. *I*. "I'm sorry, Mantos. I'm sorry for everything I've done. All my life I hated you because you took Mother away from me. But that was never your intention. I understand that now. You were innocent. I was the one who was wrong."

The Grandmother's voice cut across Mantos' reply. "Your wrongdoing wasn't for nothing, I assure you."

Bandim brought his eyeridges low in a question. The Grandmother gestured at her circling power again, conjuring two new figures: two princes vying for a crown.

"Your actions have always been your own but the influences upon you have often been out of your control. Johrann Maa didn't come to you by accident. I influenced her actions. And while the choices she made, that you made, in bringing Dorai back into the world were yours alone, you might not have come upon those choices without my influence." She pulled the figure of Bomsoi forward, hovering over the others. "It's all led to today." When she spoke again, the figure of Bomsoi quivered in her grasp. "*What is made cannot be unmade. But what has been made can be destroyed.*"

CHAPTER THIRTY-FOUR

Emmy

There was that phrase she'd heard so many times.

"*What is made cannot be unmade. But what has been made can be destroyed.*"

Emmy had pondered long and hard on those words, trying to come to some understanding. But it had always eluded her, whatever this complex meaning was. Yet when the Grandmother spoke and Emmy saw the stricken, haunted expression on Bomsoi's face, the suspicions that had churned in Emmy's stomach ever since the Grandmother had come to her and Johrann roiled anew. She'd known it wouldn't be something good. But this?

Realization worked her tongue. "No."

The word was soft, yet certain. It couldn't be. It couldn't be. Emmy shook her head at Bomsoi, her throat growing dry. Bomsoi's voice failed her, and all she could do in reply was to nod, mute.

"How could you lie to me?"

With Bomsoi still unable to answer, the Grandmother waved a hand and dismissed her glowing orb. "Emmy, when we first met, do you remember what I called you?"

Emmy blinked as she replied. "You said I was the best of all Bomsoi's work."

"I said perhaps you were that," the Grandmother clarified, "but yes. And that is why Bomsoi never told you her ultimate goal. She hasn't lied to you, young thing. She's simply withheld some of her story."

"That's not much different," Emmy snapped.

Beside her, Zecha shook his head, looking from Emmy to Bomsoi to the Grandmother. "Someone needs to explain what's going on, because I don't understand."

Emmy thought she heard the Grandmother mutter something about mortals, and ignorance, but she ignored it.

"Zecha," she said, trying to force her voice to be steady, "Bomsoi was created to balance the world, but she didn't. She couldn't. It would never have worked, and it even made things worse. All this time I thought we were working together to stop Bandim and Dorai, to balance the power of one goddess with another. But that's not it. That's not enough."

"So what is?" Zecha asked.

Emmy willed the crushing sense of treachery to leave her as she settled her gaze on Bomsoi. "'What has been made can be destroyed,'" she repeated. "Bomsoi is what's been made. Bomsoi is what needs to be destroyed."

Zecha's jaw slackened as he turned his head. "No."

"Yes," the Grandmother countered.

Her throat now so tight she didn't trust herself to speak, Emmy pressed her lips together, unable to look away from Bomsoi. The one of balance, the daughter of gods, Emmy's creator, the one who'd revealed to her the truth of her heritage, the one who'd helped unleash and nurture her power. The one who'd helped her realize she was worth something.

Two Hands, two Hearts together at last. All in the name of death.

Mantos and Bandim stood beside one another with twin looks of sorrow. Johrann Maa's face pulled not with grief but with sympathy, and she looked not at Bomsoi but at Emmy.

Anger rising, Emmy wheeled on the Grandmother and found her voice.

"How will killing Bomsoi return balance to the world? If her creation was to bring balance, she didn't cause the problem. It was them." She thrust one talon at Mantos and Bandim, though she didn't mean them. "Bomsoi didn't ask to be made. She didn't ask for the burden her mothers had put upon her. You said that yourself." Her voice wavered. "So why does she have to die?"

"Yes," the Grandmother crooned despite Emmy's ire, "you are perhaps the best of all Bomsoi's work." She shook her head. "Bomsoi's creation tied the godly with the fleshly in a way I never intended. It should never have been. It drove my daughters further apart, rather than bringing them back together. If things continue as they are, everything under the Arc of the Sky will burn, just like I showed you before."

With a click of her talons, the Grandmother brought forth the terrifying vision of the world burned and ashen once again. Emmy flinched from it. She thought it had been a glimpse of a future where Bandim's power reigned unchecked, but it wasn't as simple as that, just as the Grandmother had said.

"This future will come about because the power of the goddesses will always be abused. Look at what Bandim chose to do. All it takes is one heart full of corruption to destroy the world."

With another click of her talons, the scene disappeared, and the ruins of the Masvam arena loomed again.

"We must cleanse this world of our mistakes," the Grandmother continued. "That means we must purge the world. I will no longer allow my daughters to interfere in the lives of those they named the Younglings."

"Why bring the goddesses back?" Emmy asked. None of this made sense. "They were already powerless. By bringing them back, you've given them more power."

"More power but for a reason," the Grandmother replied.

Emmy turned as Bomsoi cleared her throat, regaining some composure Emmy knew well. "When I turned away from my mothers and didn't do as they asked me, I created another problem." She inclined her head. "You. My folk. The Uloni."

Emmy caught Johrann's gaze. She shared the distraught look Emmy knew painted her own face. "Do you mean to kill us?"

The Grandmother shook her head. "No. I have already killed enough of your kind."

Emmy whirled on her again. "Why? Why did you kill our folk?"

"It was the start of things," the Grandmother replied. "It stopped the spread of godly blood through the world. The more the blood spread, the more potential there was for that corrupt heart I spoke of to wreak destruction. For what I needed to do, I only needed two. Johrann was one of them. You were the other, which was why I allowed your mother to free you from the fire."

No longer able to stem the flow of sorrow, Emmy's eyes overflowed. "How can you call yourself a goddess? How can you be so cruel?"

"Gods are not all good. You understand that. We do not know everything, and sometimes even we need to atone for our mistakes."

Bomsoi reached for her, offering comfort. Emmy backed away, stumbling over the uneven ground. Bomsoi let her arms drop once again in defeat.

"Destroying me will not destroy you," she said, her voice breaking again, "but it will strip you of your power, you and all the others who share my blood. That's what the Grandmother means when she says we must purge the world. As long as my blood carries the power of the goddesses, Nunako and Dorai will never break from the world. But only my mothers can destroy what they created. You know I can't die by mortal means. That's why the Grandmother and I sought to return Nunako and Dorai to the world."

Mantos' words were pained. "Why us? Why Bandim and I?"

It was Bandim who responded. "Nunako and Dorai were two together, and so were we. Laid together, hatched together."

The Grandmother nodded. "It seemed only fitting. And the time had come."

The unfairness of everything rose like a swelling tide, and Emmy shook her head. "I didn't even know I had the blood of the goddesses within me before you told me.

If you'd never pulled me into this, I'd never have known. I wasn't powerful. I couldn't abuse something I didn't even know was there. How is that the goddesses interfering? How is ignorance a threat?"

Bomsoi tilted her head to the side. "You might not have known, but you still had power. We spoke before of the coldness you felt, of the uncanny ability you had to heal those around you better than any mere apothecary's assistant should have been able. The power of the goddesses has always been within you, and it runs in the veins of those half-Uloni who exist in the world."

"Like Rel and Jishu, the one who brought us here on the ship," Zecha said.

"Yes, like them. I tried for many cycles to gather all my folk back to me," Bomsoi continued, "but it was never possible. I couldn't keep the Uloni in the mountains like prisoners, and some left. Some of those folk never returned, and they sired half-blooded younglings. Not even the Grandmother knows how many exist."

"And while they hold their power," the Grandmother said, "the world will never be free from my daughters' influences. And as long as the power of the goddesses flows through the veins of the folk, there is potential for abuse. I burned the village to stop the spread of Bomsoi's blood, but I can't find and kill all of her descendants. If I miss even one, there's still the potential for the world to fall to ruin."

Emmy's fury burst forth again. "You didn't have to kill any of them! My parents, they didn't have to die! You could have let all the Uloni live and still have gone through with your plan, if killing Bomsoi will strip the power from us."

"I didn't have to," the Grandmother agreed, "but I did, because in a few generations the strangeness of Bomsoi's creations, with their odd coloring that brings so much persecution, will disappear, and there will be no more suffering on her account. Had I allowed them to live, even powerless, to breed and spread, the taint of Bomsoi's actions would always be upon the Arc."

Bomsoi flinched. Emmy shook her head again, more violent this time. "That's evil."

"I prefer pragmatic," the Grandmother said with a wave of her hand, "but call it what you must."

Emmy tried to reply again but the expression on Bomsoi's face stopped her. For a moment she pushed through her fury and looked at the Stranger's face. There was untold agony there, cycle upon cycle of guilt weighing upon her.

"Emmy," Bomsoi said, her eyes unbearably tired, "please try to comprehend what it feels like to know you exist for a single purpose, to fulfill the will of others, not for yourself. Then try to understand what it's like to carry the burden of failure all your long life, knowing there's nothing you can do to put things right, knowing that everything you've done is wrong. Knowing that your very existence is an abomination. Remember, I was there in the temple when the Grandmother had it burned. I was there, was powerless to stop it because it was her will. Even then I couldn't do what the Grandmother required. Only one Uloni should have survived. It was your mother's strength of will, the power of her love, that meant the Grandmother allowed you to live. But Rel was there, and I couldn't let her die, and I abused my power to save her, even though she should have died along with the rest. I keep making mistakes. I keep doing things wrong. Please" —her voice became pleading— "understand that this is what I want. I need to be free from this agony inside. I need to put everything right. My destruction is the only way. But I need you, and Johrann Maa, and Mantos and Bandim, all four of you together, to do it. Once I'm gone, you'll all be free. I'll be free."

A baying cry made every head jerk upward. A dark silhouette circled around them, growing closer, its wings wide and glimmering. Through her sorrow, Bomsoi managed a laugh as Neiruk landed and perched upon one of the thickest shattered boards of the ruined ship's hull.

"Neiruk will be free, too," she said, reaching for the creature. He slid from his perch and padded forward, nuzzling into her outstretched hand. "He's waited for so long for his release, Emmy. I created him, but in doing so I did what my mothers had done to me. I made him for my purpose, not to be himself, and he's always been alone. He needs to rest. We both do."

Emmy pushed the back of her hand across her eyes again, sucking in a breath as she pushed aside her agitation. "How can we," she started; then, unable to finish, asked, "how?"

Bomsoi turned to Mantos, whose eyes brightened with understanding. He took off, returning to the place where he'd sheltered from the onslaught of Bandim's power, and ducked down. When he rose again, something long and silver sparkled in his hand. Emmy shook her head, new grief budding in her eyes.

Haelo. They would kill her with Haelo.

CHAPTER THIRTY-FIVE

Mantos

He'd understood Bomsoi's expression as soon as it fell on him. When he laid his claws on the sword's great hilt, its weight no longer unbearable as it allowed him to wield it. Rel's words when she'd handed it to him returned.

"*You might need Haelo's strength.*"

He remembered too Neiruk's strange reaction, his fearful whine, and Bomsoi's odd explanation.

"*He fears what it means.*"

Mantos had wondered if she had meant that it was a weapon and it signaled conflict and death. But Neiruk hadn't feared death as an abstract. The Prago had known this particular sword would bring about his own demise. Bomsoi said Neiruk wanted the release but Mantos supposed that didn't mean death wasn't frightening.

When he turned to face the gathered, he swallowed hard, looking at them one by one. The devastation of what they were about to do was destroying Emmy. He could see it. The idea of it brought pain that spread like rot. Bomsoi's death meant Emmy would lose her friend and mentor, the one she'd grown to care for like a mother. Mantos understood it all because of what they'd shared. His heart shattered along with hers.

Zecha was beside Emmy, his presence a comfort, holding himself together in the face of so much strangeness, trying to be strong for his friend. Johrann Maa stood on Emmy's other side, and for the first time Mantos could see her with no hate in his heart. She'd killed him but he couldn't keep the anger burning within any longer. The Grandmother had played her just like the rest of them.

Lastly, Mantos' gaze came to Bandim. His brother, his face still covered in the cracking remnants of their mother's dried blood. His brother who, after everything they'd been through, everything they had done, had spoken the words, "*I'm sorry*," and Mantos knew he meant them. He thought of their father then, wondered if he would be proud if he had lived to see his sons reconcile, or at least attempt to do so.

Words are words, Bandim had said to him as they stood at their dying father's bedside, before any of the tumult of the last cycle had happened. Whether his heart was in them remained to be seen.

As Bomsoi beckoned him forward, part of Mantos longed to remain rooted to the spot. Their actions would change the world. Nothing would be the same again. Even more pressing was Emmy's grief, the horror that churned within her at the thought of what they must do. She didn't deserve it, and all Mantos wanted was to protect her from it. Emmy was too good, too pure to suffer such agony.

But inaction wouldn't solve anything. His soldier's mindset clicked into place with the smoothness of withdrawing a sword from a sheath, and Mantos bowed his head to Bomsoi, stepping toward her.

A sudden sob escaped Emmy, though she attempted to push down her distress. She schooled herself with the help of a comforting touch from Zecha. Mantos gripped the sword's handle in one hand, Nunako helping to bear its weight.

"How do we do this?" he asked.

Bomsoi touched her chestplate. "All four of you together must use Haelo to pierce my heart. I forged the sword, and thus the sword is part of me. That, together with the power of my mothers, will do it."

Haelo pulled on his arm but Mantos knew it was dread, and not the sword itself, that caused the weight. This creature, this Stranger, had brought him back to life. She'd brought his brother back to life. She'd given him the pleasure and power of feeling a goddess within him. Could he be a part of her demise?

Nunako turned inside him. Her sorrow was piercing but her determination more so. *Is this the right thing to do*? he asked her. The goddess sent a ripple of power through his sword arm, a tingle reached the tips of his talons, and he *knew* her answer was *'yes.'*

He couldn't let the moment go unmarked. This heavy burden was only the first he would bear as the Masvam Emperor. No matter whether Bandim was genuine in his apology, no matter how he might seek to change, Mantos was the first hatched. Mantos was the rightful heir. Though Bandim still lived, he would never be emperor again.

Pulling on every lesson Old Master Abe had given him on the duties of a prince and every thread of advice his father had given him on being the ruler of an empire, Mantos straightened his back and spoke, knowing his voice would carry all around the bowl.

"This duty we perform now is painful, but necessary. The first act I carry out as the emperor isn't a killing, but a release." He cast his gaze around the gathered faces and beyond them, to the Masvam soldiers with their stilled weapons. Chaata and her crew watched. "Bomsoi, the one known as the Stranger to the Althemerians, the one we now know to be the daughter of gods, offspring of Nunako and Dorai, has asked that we free her from the burden placed upon her by her mothers. It's an act of courage to ask such a thing. It's a great responsibility to do it. Before all of you here, myself, my brother, and two daughters of Bomsoi herself will remove the shackles of mortality from this great creature, who has given us so much. We do this with heavy hearts, but we temper our sorrow knowing this is the will of Bomsoi, Nunako, Dorai, and the Grandmother of the World."

He inclined his head to Bomsoi, then went to one knee. In his peripheral vision, he saw the rest of the gathered do the same. All except the Grandmother, who leaned on her stick and bowed her chin to her chest. She didn't look at Bomsoi as she did it. She looked at Mantos.

"The return of Bomsoi to her godly mothers also means the removal of the power of Nunako and Dorai from my brother and myself. I am thankful for the opportunity I've had to experience the truth of the goddesses, and the opportunity to find the truth of myself." Mantos sucked in a deep breath, willing the truth of his feelings to pour forth. "Before, I didn't want the mantle of leadership. While my death was not my doing, the choices I made afterward were. My one regret from this past cycle is that it took me so long to realize the truth of myself, and what it means to be Masvam. Although," he added, shooting Chaata a look, "I am grateful to the acquaintances I met on my journey back to myself." Chaata raised one eyeridge, gesturing to the debris of her ship, and Mantos added, "And of course, I am in their debt."

The captain tipped him a wink, and Mantos couldn't help but smile. Then the weight of Haelo in his hand sobered him once more. As he rose to his feet, and the others followed, Bomsoi clasped her talons together and nodded at him.

"I am grateful for your words, Mantos of House Tiboli. I too am thankful for those I have met on my journey home. Especially you, Emmy. And Rel. Please tell her I love her, and that I'm sorry." To her credit, Emmy maintained her composure, giving Bomsoi a tight nod. "I hope that you, and the rest of you, remember that true power and meaning comes not from godly power, but from within yourselves. I leave this world now, knowing I will never again set foot upon the earth of the Arc of the Sky. I would like to leave one final imprint for you to share with the folk: be kind to one another. Apologize for your wrongdoings. Remember that no mistake is terminal." She glanced from Mantos to Bandim. "Family is everything." She looked to Emmy and Zecha. "Family is more than those who share your blood. It is who you choose to love."

A serenity came upon Bomsoi's face as she unbuttoned the front of her tunic. She exposed the pattern of armor there, and the softer flesh between her chestplates through which Haelo would pass. Emmy burst forward at that, throwing her arms around Bomsoi.

"I'll miss you," she sobbed, and not only did Mantos' heart break, but Nunako's did too.

"I'll always be with you," Bomsoi murmured into Emmy's fronds. "Never forget that. And never forget, my dear daughter, that you are and always have been more than you think you are. You are the best of my work."

A snuffling snort came from the side. Mantos allowed himself a lopsided smile as Neiruk butted his head at the two as they embraced. Bomsoi barked a laugh that filled the bowl. "Joint best, then. Does that please you, Master Prago?"

Even Emmy managed a chuckle as Neiruk preened and shuffled his feet. Then the huge iridescent creature lay down on the ground, curling his great body in an arc around Bomsoi. The Stranger held Emmy at arm's length for another long moment before she let go, beckoning Mantos forward.

"Let's finish this," she said.

Mantos' reply was a silent nod, and he gestured for the others to join him.

Haelo's handle was long, and Mantos held it firm just under the guard. He looked back as Bandim settled his hand underneath, and the brothers, the godly sisters, withstood the sword's weight. Johrann Maa settled her hand atop Bandim's, and the two shared a look that Mantos couldn't read. He had no time to contemplate it as Emmy brought her trembling talons to rest over Mantos,' completing the four that the Grandmother had spoken of. Two Hands, Two Hearts, now together for one final gesture.

Bomsoi faced them with no fear. She bowed one final time and closed her eyes, awaiting her fate.

"Are you ready?" Mantos asked.

The answer that came back was threefold. "Yes."

After a moment he realized it hadn't been threefold, but fivefold. Nunako and Dorai were with them, and they were ready to take their daughter home.

There was no ceremony. There was no count. All of them, Emmy and Johrann, Mantos and Bandim, Nunako and Dorai, moved as one being, and in a motion as swift and steady as the movement of the sun and the moons across the Arc of the Sky, they brought Haelo forward, and it was done.

As the blade slid into Bomsoi's chest, the world exploded. Color and light and music and ethereal song came from everywhere and nowhere at once. Mantos' eyes widened as brightness enveloped him, power circling them like satellites, welding their hands to Haelo's hilt.

Within him, Nunako shifted and turned and somehow, he felt she was smiling, and then he knew she was smiling, because her presence pulled from his body and swirled to Bomsoi's side, just like her sister's. Both she and Dorai, freed from Mantos and Bandim, freed from the world, grasped Bomsoi's hands, supporting their daughter as Haelo cut the thread of her mortal life. The sword shimmered and blinked, and the hilt disappeared from within Mantos' grasp. At Bomsoi's feet, Neiruk shifted, seemed to grin, as he too flickered in and out of sight. When Mantos looked at Bomsoi's face, he saw the same pleasure there as light and her mothers embraced her.

"*Thank you, my friends*," Bomsoi breathed.

At her side, the two goddesses, impossible in their strength and beauty, inclined their heads. When Nunako spoke to him without moving her lips, Mantos' eyes filled with tears.

"*Thank you, Mantos Tiboli.*"

From the cut-off sob that escaped from his brother, Mantos knew Dorai had delivered a message much the same.

Bomsoi's face was a sculpture in serenity as the three disappeared, leaving only her final words behind. "*I will never forget you.*"

With that, the daughter of gods, her godly mothers, and the things she had created left the Arc of the Sky forever. Once more, the speaker's bowl was silent, except for the cracking of tattered banners on the wind.

Mantos closed his eyes, sensing everything in his own body. For the first time since Bomsoi had brought Nunako into him, he felt himself. There was no tingling power within. There was no nudging, turning influence inside. He was Mantos Tiboli again, incumbent emperor of the Masvam Empire, yet he didn't feel the same as he had before Nunako had come to him. He wasn't the same male who'd stood on the balcony above the speaker's bowl, waiting to be seen in his mourning whites. Nor was he the same as the one who'd awoken in the Althemerian palace, twice returned from the dead. He wasn't the same as when he had fled that same palace and his one true love. He wasn't the one who'd escaped across the Sea of Souls to kill his brother's troops in Metakala, the one who'd saved Tero and Zrazashi, then learned a valuable lesson from the humble Metakalan family. Nor was he the same as when he'd returned to Althemer on the *Water Prago*, accepting his fate.

He was none of these things. Mantos Tiboli, twice dead and twice revived, was more than the sum of them, better for all of them, and somehow more himself than he had ever been before.

CHAPTER THIRTY-SIX

Bandim

He sat on the edge of the bed, listening to the revelry outside. Bandim, no longer Bandim-Dorai, pressed his bare feet into the fine flat-woven rug under his soles, tracing the geometric Belfoni pattern. The window, though now barred, still allowed light to spill inside along with the sounds of celebration. It was Midsummer's Eve again. Within the walls of the now repaired Seat of the Empire, celebrations were underway. Noble and common folk alike flooded the city for not only tomorrow's festival, but also for the crowning and wedding to take place too. It was a celebration Bandim would receive no invitation to, but he could bear no grudge against that. Four weeks was time enough to accept he would never feel the power of Dorai course through him. He'd never manipulate fire or sense emotions again. It was time enough to accept that for the rest of his life, he'd be locked away in the Grieving Tower. He'd never again be free.

That morning servants had freshened his sheets, just like every other morning in the four weeks that had passed since everything changed. A guard remained in the room the whole time the servants changed the linens. The chores complete, the door was locked from the outside. One servant was Yameteth, who Mantos told him asked to attend to the prisoner. Dearest Yameteth, Bandim thought. Beautiful little thing.

She was the only one who'd stayed loyal. They'd taken Johrann as a prisoner alongside him. Since the conflict in the speaker's bowl, Tesselica hadn't shown his face. Bandim didn't know if he was free or even alive. He ran his feet along the rug again. Part of him wanted to care, because he had loved Tess, but a bigger part of him couldn't bring himself to stir any emotion. Emotion in himself served to remind him of what he'd lost. He couldn't imbibe the feelings of others any longer, and while he'd held that power for only one cycle of his twenty-two of life, its loss was like losing a limb. With it, he hadn't needed to guess at others' emotions. He knew the power of his own intimidation, and he'd never worried about betrayal. Not that his power mattered in the end. The one who'd betrayed him had held her feelings distant from him at all times. Now he was imprisoned in a tower, able to listen to the joy and hope of those outside, but to feel nothing of it.

Bandim curled his claws into fists. Captivity in the Grieving Tower hadn't been his preference for his sentencing, but Mantos had refused his request.

"I will not execute you, brother," he'd said, "although I understand you mean it when you ask, and it's what many folk call for. But there's been enough death. One more will not atone for those that came before."

Thus Mantos, ever-perfect Mantos, decided that a life of isolation and reflection was due for his brother, and Bandim could only nod and submit. What choice did he have? He accepted the constant guard. He accepted the bars on the window, understanding the silent implication there. They were in place to stop Bandim from fleeing the same way one dowager empress had escaped her grief, and it would be a lie to say he hadn't considered taking his death into his own hands.

A new chorus of singing erupted far below, this time very different. It was more lyrical, more beautiful than the rowdy revels of the Masvam court. It was a sound Bandim remembered well from his youth on excursions across the sea with his father. Althemerian chanting. He allowed himself a wry smile. His brother's husband, the soon-to-be Emperor Consort, had arrived.

Curiosity almost moved Bandim to the window to peer at the comings and goings and preparations below, but a heavier reluctance kept him in place on the edge of the bed, his feet flat on the floor. This was why he'd said Mantos should take his head. Bandim didn't want to die. It was more that living was a reminder of everything he'd done and everything he'd lost, although that was, he knew, why Mantos wanted him to live. His brother had sentenced Bandim Tiboli to life, not death, a life of remembrance to reflect on everything he'd done.

Bandim unclenched his fists and stared at his hands as they rested in his lap. How much destruction had those hands brought? He turned them over, examining their armored backs and their pale palms. They were hands that once held power. Not just the strength of the empire, but the power of a goddess too. Dorai had lived within him, been him, and it had seemed as if he was only himself when her presence guided him.

He stopped himself then, shaking his head. She'd only guided him in part. Part of Mantos' plan of repentance was to accept that Bandim's actions as Hand of Dorai had little to do with the goddess. While her hate for her sister had been burning and justified, it hadn't controlled his actions. Bandim's own hate did that, powered by what the goddess gave him or what he took from her. It wasn't Dorai who had stoked the fire of his anger since he was nothing but an ungendered youngling, learning the truth of why his mother wasn't with him. That was his own doing.

Johrann had been there throughout, steered by the Grandmother's master plan, but she hadn't started him down his path of hatred. She'd helped to pave it with her words of power and glory and giving Bandim what was his. However, he was the one who'd not only walked it, but decided its direction. He was the one who'd ignored Old Master Abe and his father's lessons in goodness and compassion and what it meant to be a leader. He might try to blame Dorai, try to blame Johrann, even the Grandmother, but his actions had been his own.

Such as when he'd made good on his promise and killed his mother.

Bandim sank his head into his hands. The irony of his current situation wasn't lost on him. In some ways, he thought it was poetic. Empress Phen had been shut away in the Grieving Tower, an embarrassment to her husband. Bandim knew his father thought it better if she'd been dead. He'd acted in many ways as if she was. It fit that Bandim would now call this place his home for the rest of his days, however long that might be. Cycles, decates, who knew? He would dwell within these walls, in a prison of his own making, surrounded by stone upon stone laid by his actions not just over the past cycle, but his entire life. However long he lived, it wouldn't be long enough to contemplate the death and destruction he had brought to the world.

While that was true, another part of him couldn't help but reflect on the parting words Dorai had spoken to him. They were the only direct words the goddess had ever gifted him. As she stood at Bomsoi's side as her mortality slipped away, Dorai had looked Bandim in the eye and spoken to him without moving her lips.

"Dedicate the rest of your life to love, Bandim Tiboli. Do not rest on anger. It will bring pain upon pain."

Those words cut Bandim deeper than he thought possible, wrenching a sob from his chest before he could stop it. Dorai was right. He'd built his whole life on anger, resting upon it as his foundation, and all it had brought was as she said: pain upon pain. His own pain, self-inflicted day after day. The pain he'd inflicted on his mother not just in the short time he'd had her in his grasp, but at his hands when he'd killed her with one red slice across her neck.

Bandim swallowed another sob. Despite what he'd done to her, his mother had come back for him. Just as she'd always maintained she would, she sacrificed herself for him just as she had for Mantos. All the cycles Bandim had dwelled in hatred were for nothing, all lies. Phen hadn't favored Mantos over Bandim because he was the first-hatched. She'd saved him because he was her youngling, and though he'd slit her throat, she'd still done the same for Bandim when the time came. That knowledge shifted everything Bandim thought he knew. He'd despised his mother all his life for abandoning him, but now he realized she never had. It was he who'd rejected her.

The sound of a key turning in a lock jolted his head from his hands. The door swung open. Bandim rose to his feet as a figure entered, flanked by a guard.

"Johrann."

His first instinct was to command the guard to leave. Four weeks couldn't break the habits he'd come into as emperor. The guard stayed at the door, which he left open. Bandim knew there was another guard outside, posted to monitor him every hour of every day. They taunted him with their presence, their impassive faces, and his inability to sense how they felt. Before, he understood the emotions of all those around him. Now he barely understood himself.

The last time Bandim had seen Johrann Maa was in the speaker's bowl, once Bomsoi's mission was complete. The one who had been his Heart had been bound in chains, with manacles on her wrists and ankles, dragged away to the underpalace cells. Now she was free of any constraint, bar the guard. Johrann took a few steps forward, clasping her talons in front of her. Bandim remained as he was, standing at the edge of the bed.

They remained silent for some time. Four weeks apart seemed long, but after an entire lifetime together it was nothing. No longer were they powerful, plotting their rise. Now they were two prisoners with nothing but their lives.

"I came to say goodbye," Johrann said.

Bandim remained silent. What could he say?

There was plenty to say. Even if he lived until the sun no longer traveled across the Arc, he would never have enough time to apologize for his cruelty. She might have used him as part of her plan, been used herself by the Grandmother, but no one had forced him to strike her or burn her. Bandim swallowed, unable to look away from the circular scarring that would forever mark the touch of his talons on her neck.

"I'm going to the Khinish mountains," Johrann went on, though Bandim asked for no explanation. "I'll live the rest of my days in the place where I committed my greatest wrong. I'll dedicate my life to worshiping the Grandmother of the World, hoping when I die, she accepts me into her embrace."

That comment loosened Bandim's tongue. "Why do you want her forgiveness? She was the one who lied to you. Everything you did, you did because of her."

With a humorless chuckle, Johrann shrugged one shoulder. "You're right. That's not my real reason. I just wanted to see if I could still hold things from you, power or not."

Habitual anger at her lie made Bandim's claws flex in the desire to lash out, but he stopped himself. That was his old life, and he couldn't be angry at Johrann for her actions.

"I can't stand to be here any longer. Everywhere I look, I see the shadows of what I've done. Emperor Mantos has been kind enough to release me into King Khitarian's custody. I'm to live with the soldiers who guard the Uloni temple there. I'll serve them in the mountains. I'm leaving on a ship tomorrow, returning with the Khinish delegation after the coronation and the wedding."

Wedding. Bandim's chest tightened, and bile rose in his throat. That was something he had planned. It was something he had truly wanted. "I need to tell you," he said before he could control his mouth, "that I loved you. Love you. And that I wanted to marry you."

For a hovering moment it seemed like Johrann would step toward him, but she remained in place. "I know, Bandim. And for what it's worth, I loved you too. Until I realized it wasn't Dorai who guided me all my life, marrying you was all I wanted. But," she continued, taking in a steadying breath, "I don't love you now. All you are to me is a reminder of all the ills I've committed. All you are is a reminder of the pain you caused me." The scars on her throat bobbed as she swallowed her emotions. "If you stay here, I can't. That's another reason I want to leave. I can't be near you any longer."

Everything she said was right and justified. Despite knowing this, Bandim sank onto the bed. He lowered his gaze to the floor, tracing the geometric Belfoni shapes again.

"Goodbye, Bandim."

Johrann turned with a swish of skirts on rushes. The sound startled a memory within Bandim of his mother's ragged form passing over this very floor. He lurched to his feet.

"Johrann, wait."

She half-turned, peering with suspicion over one shoulder. "Yes?"

"I'm sorry."

He owed her more than that. He needed to clarify why, what for, to list all the evils he did to her, but his voice died.

Johrann turned and inclined her head. "I'm sorry too."

With another swish of skirts against the floor, she was gone. The guard turned the key in the heavy lock, and Bandim was alone once more.

CHAPTER THIRTY-SEVEN

Emmy

The chambers Mantos had given her were luxurious, but Emmy couldn't stay inside them. Something drove her out, something she didn't understand. The world seemed changed, everything she looked at a frond's width different from before. It took time to realize it wasn't the world that had changed. It was Emmy herself. She now saw the world without her Uloni power. It was strange, disconcerting, uneasy.

She took to roaming the halls of the palace or, more often, walking in the gardens blooming in Merish. It was the middle of the season again, the day before Middlemerish on what the Masvams called Midsummer's Eve.

The sound of preparations for the celebration of Midsummer, the coronation of the new emperor and the impending wedding, made the city come alive. It was a pulsing, breathing being that enveloped her. That was part of why Emmy retreated to the safety of the winding gardens. It was quieter, the trees and blooming plants bringing welcome shelter and a barrier to the noise.

Emmy perched on a Daxo-wood bench and leaned forward, lacing her talons together. She pressed her feet into the gravel path, no longer clad in heavy Vhaun boots but in supple shoes of leather. They were beautiful, far finer than anything she'd ever owned. She'd long since abandoned her Khinish furs and skins in favor of lighter fabrics. Mantos had provided her with whatever she wished, though he couldn't give her what she wanted. No one could.

Bomsoi was gone. She was never coming back. Every time that reality settled upon Emmy's shoulders, her throat grew tight with sorrow. Everything she had done in the last cycle, from listening to Rel's stories of her 'friend' Bomsoi, to Emmy agreeing to meet her, then taking on the Heart of Nunako and fighting back against Bandim's tyranny, it had all been for a purpose kept from her. She'd been working not to free the world, but to bring about Bomsoi's death. Though she knew it was what Bomsoi wanted, and knew it was for the best, Emmy still burned with betrayal.

Bomsoi should have told her the truth. But unless Rel was as much a liar as Bomsoi, the Stranger hadn't even told her. That said much about how Bomsoi desired her death.

Emmy scuffed her fine shoe along the path, sending up a tiny cloud of dust. Her internal burning, she mused, might not have been because of betrayal alone. Her entire body ran hot now, as if her Uloni powers had cooled her from within her whole life. With Bomsoi gone, Emmy's power had gone too. Now she was as ordinary as she'd always thought, save for her colors. Bomsoi's death had trapped her in blue and purple. While Emmy hadn't held the ability to mask her heritage for long, she still mourned its loss. Normality had opened a refuge that might have saved her from taunts and mocking for the rest of her life. That refuge was closed to her now.

She stopped and shook her head. No. That was the old Emmy. She wasn't like that any longer.

Bomsoi's final words to her echoed in her ears. "*And never forget, my dear daughter, that you are and always have been more than you think you are. You are the best of my work.*"

She might've had strange colors, like a bruise, but Emmy was no longer bruised. She had overcome so much in a single cycle. She had learned more about herself in that short time than Krodge had ever taught her. A smile rose unbidden on her face when she remembered Neiruk's indignation at Emmy being named the best of Bomsoi's work. She would miss the Prago but knew he would be in the sky.

Would Bomsoi look down on her too? Would Nunako and Dorai, or the Grandmother? Or did their departure from the world mean they had abandoned the Younglings altogether? Emmy sighed, the smile slipping from her face. They would never find out.

A quiet cough drew her attention, and she glanced down the garden path. When she recognized what she saw, Emmy jumped to her feet and bounded toward the three figures, launching herself into the arms of the largest.

"*Rel!*"

When Rel's washed-out blue and purple arms wound around her, Emmy never wanted them to let her go. The Bonebreaker's presence was a welcome comfort amid loss. Emmy drew back at that. Did Rel understand what had happened? She hadn't been here when Bomsoi had passed from life. She might not know.

Rel's smile was soft, though her pale eyes looked strained. She still looked tired, but it was a different tiredness. No longer was she wracked with the extent of her injuries. Beneath her whitened skin and the scars of her burns, she was stronger. It wasn't pain that burdened her now. It was grief.

Another cough made Emmy turn. Charo stood beside Rel, her hands planted on her hips. She too looked stronger, and it took Emmy a moment to realize it was because she no longer bore a burden inside her.

"You laid?" Emmy asked as she embraced her friend.

"I did, in the Kingdom of Khin. We just arrived with the guests for the wedding. I brought the egg with me," Charo hastened to add. "I want to be there when it hatches. Zecha does too."

"How do you feel?"

"Terrified," Charo replied with a thin laugh, "but anyone would be."

Emmy kept her friend at arm's length for a moment, drinking in every detail. In a year, Charo had gone from a scarred waif with a plucked head to a strong and healthy female with reddish-brown fronds that shone glossy in the sunlight. Still only fifteen cycles old, too young for the burdens she bore, she seemed older. Happier.

Rel spoke, her voice soft. "We have much to talk about."

Emmy nodded. "Let's take a walk."

As she told the story of all that had happened since the Masvam had captured her in the Khinish mountains, her companions remained silent. Charo's shoulders grew tighter as Emmy spoke of her captivity in a Masvam cell, and at one point she snapped off half a bush in her rage. Emmy had to laugh at that, and when she realized what she'd done, Charo did the same, casting the broken branch aside.

Her friend's ire cooled a little as she spoke of Johrann Maa and everything Emmy had learned.

"How could you trust her?" Charo asked, attacking another plant.

Emmy sighed. She'd asked herself that question many times. "It was the right thing to do. It was what the Grandmother wanted."

"Even though she killed your parents?"

"Yes," Emmy replied. "What she did was wrong, but she thought it was right. I can't hold a grudge against her for believing what a goddess told her. It just turned out it wasn't the goddess she thought it was."

Charo snapped a thick branch over her knee. "Don't you feel betrayed? Aren't you angry at everything? The Grandmother, from what you've said, has played all of you for fools. Aren't gods supposed to be good?"

"Gods are not all good," Emmy replied, using the Grandmother's words. "And I am angry, but I'm angrier at Bomsoi than at the Grandmother." She looked at Rel. "Did she ever tell you the truth? Did you know everything was about her death?"

Rel's pale face looked ashen. "No, she didn't. I never knew the true extent of her plans. When I told you, back in the Althemerian camp, that I didn't understand why I was waiting for you, that was true. Bomsoi told me to find an Uloni. She told me of the need for a Hand and a Heart of Nunako to counter the force of Dorai, but I never knew her ultimate goal was to bring about her own death. She always knew more than I did, always kept her secrets. After so long being by her side and carrying out her wishes, I stopped questioning them. Perhaps I should have pressed harder, but I didn't. I trusted her, and I suppose she never lied to me. She simply didn't tell the full truth."

Charo shook her head but said nothing. Emmy sighed.

"You didn't seem surprised to hear Bomsoi was gone," she said to Rel, leaning in to smell the fresh scent of a pink bloom. It was a plant the Masvams called nuvi, beautiful but with no medicinal use. Now that her work as Heart of Nunako was done, she supposed she would need to call on her apothecary's knowledge again. She needed some purpose in the world.

"I knew she was gone from the world the moment my power disappeared," Rel replied. "One moment I was myself, and the next I wasn't. I couldn't raise the winds, I couldn't change my colors. And I knew then that she was gone. I wish Bomsoi had come to me at her end, given me some message. But she didn't. We were too far away, I suppose."

Emmy turned and shook her head. "She spoke of you right at the end, Rel. She left a message for you." Rel's eyes widened. Her throat bobbed in anticipation of Emmy's next words. "She told me to tell you she loves you, and that she was sorry."

Her eyes growing glassy, Rel blinked her sorrow away. "It's good to hear she remembered me."

"She loved you, Rel," Emmy said. "She told us something else, when we heard the whole story between her and the Grandmother. Only one Uloni should have survived the fire in the temple, but Bomsoi couldn't do it."

Rel's eyeridges crinkled with confusion. "What do you mean?"

"You should have died in the fire, Rel, but Bomsoi saved you. She couldn't let you die. That's how much she loved you."

This time Rel couldn't blink her sadness away. Tears traced her armored cheeks. "Oh. I never knew that." She managed a thick laugh. "Bomsoi's secrets never end, eh?"

Emmy nodded. "She also said family is everything, even family you choose. We're family now, Rel. I hope—" Her voice faltered. "I'll never be able to give you the same friendship that you had with Bomsoi, but I hope we can live together as a family."

Rel scooped her into another embrace, nodding into Emmy's shoulder. "I would love that, Emmy." She loosened one arm to draw Charo into the hug. "You too, Charo, and Zecha and your little one, when it comes. I want to choose you all as my family."

"It would be an honor," Charo replied, and Emmy knew she was smiling.

Something occurred to her as they released one another that pulled Emmy's face into a tight frown. "We've lost our powers, which means we can't disguise our colors any longer. How many others like us are there? Even if Johrann and I are the last full-blooded Uloni, there must be more half-Uloni. What are they going to do now they can't hide their identities, if they were doing it before?"

Rel scowled, remembering her own tortured upbringing as a so-called 'half-breed.' "Things will be very difficult for them. In places like Belfon, they'll be persecuted. Killed."

"They're our family too," Emmy said, "and they won't understand what's happened." Fervor burned within her, replacing the anger of before. Perhaps this would be her new purpose. "We have a duty to look after them, don't you think?"

"I do," Rel replied, following the path of Emmy's thoughts. "When the ceremonies are finished, perhaps we should consider finding those that remain."

Emmy nodded. "We can at least try to help where we can."

Charo nodded her approval, though her voice was crestfallen. "I wish I could go with you. Zecha and I have to stay here, or wherever Mantos sends us, if not here in the palace. We'll soon have a hatchling to care for. Traveling in search of your kind isn't an option for us."

"Family is more than being near others," Emmy replied. "All of us, even Zecha, understand that living in the same place as someone doesn't make them your family. And Mantos will let you stay in the palace or give you a nice home somewhere else if that's what you'd prefer. He will if I ask him to," she added with a wink. "It pays to be friends with an emperor."

When she thought about him, she remembered what was to happen that night. Before the next day's celebration, a commemoration would take place. "Were you told about the burning tonight?"

"Zecha told us," Charo replied. "If Mantos will have us there, we'd be honored to attend."

The three turned back up the path they'd wandered down, past the bench Emmy had sat upon, and back toward the palace. The bustle of preparations grew loud again. Bidding her friends farewell, Emmy padded back to her chambers. Sure enough, when she returned a new outfit waited for her, just as Mantos said. It was crisp and made of white fabric, the color Masvams wore to celebrate life. Emmy fingered the edge of the fine garment, nodding to herself.

Tomorrow they would celebrate the crowning of a new emperor, but tonight, they would commemorate the life of an empress. For everything she had done, Phen of House Yru deserved nothing less.

CHAPTER THIRTY-EIGHT

Mantos

As he ascended to the top of the Grieving Tower, Mantos pondered. The last time he'd been here, he hadn't known his mother. She'd been nothing but a husk, something half-dead and half-alive, and he didn't even know the sound of her voice. He nodded to the guard outside Bandim's door, who bowed before opening it. How much things had changed. He'd known his mother and learned even more about her after her death. If he could learn to wield half as much compassion as she had during and after her life, Mantos knew he would be a benevolent emperor. He owed it to her to try.

Bandim was at the barred window, perched on the inside ledge. He turned as Mantos entered, the movement languid, though he slid to his feet in respect.

"Brother," Mantos said.

"My Emperor," Bandim replied.

Mantos shook his head. "Tomorrow, yes. Today, not yet."

The air was still between them. The sun was setting and the moons rising, the light frozen in dusk. Unlike this time last cycle, the moons weren't upon each other. Dato, Rafa, and Akata lingered near one another in a graceful curve, but did not touch.

Bandim leaned against the window bars and waited as Mantos cast his gaze around the chamber. It was clean and barren, scented with rushes and with enough candles that Bandim would never be without light if that was what he wished. He couldn't light the wicks himself and had to ask a guard to do it for him. The logic was flawed, Mantos knew, for if Bandim intended to set the place alight, he could do it with a naked flame as much as a flint box. No matter. Mantos was reluctant to give his brother unfettered access to the substance he'd once wielded mastery over. It was paranoia. Mantos knew that too. His brother was as powerless now over flames as Mantos was over rock and stone. But it was a show of the reversal between them, a reinforcement of the new way. Mantos was now in charge.

"I'm holding a ceremonial burning for Mother in the Temple of Light this evening," he said.

Bandim nodded. If he held any surprise, he didn't show it. "I hope it's everything you want it to be. She deserves to be remembered."

"I'll make sure she is."

Another moment of silence stretched between them, the only sounds those drifting upward from the courtyard below.

"I wanted to tell you," Mantos continued, "but I also wanted to offer you the chance to attend, if you so wish."

Bandim showed surprise at that, stiffening against the window bars. "Why would you let me do that?" he asked, incredulous. "I killed her."

Unable to stop himself, Mantos let out a soft laugh. "Even in death, nothing could stop Mother. She came back to us." He sobered. "I'll let you attend if you want to because that's what she would have wanted. Mother was a vessel of compassion. Her last words to us were 'love one another.' I'm showing you that love."

The curve of Bandim's throat bobbed in the failing light. He turned to stare at the palace below and shook his head. "Thank you for your kindness, brother, but no. I won't attend."

A flash of hurt came from within Mantos. How could Bandim refuse such an offer? He wanted to demand an answer but didn't need to. Bandim supplied it himself.

"I don't deserve a place at a celebration of her life. I took that life from her twice. Once when I cut her throat, and again when she gave up whatever strange afterlife she gained to save me. Only those who showed her love should be present at the commemoration. I never did."

"Yet she loved you," Mantos said softly.

"I suppose that's what mothers do. Love without condition." Bandim shook his head and leaned it against the bars. "I can't go. But," he added, turning a little, "will you light a candle in the temple for her from me?"

Mantos nodded. "Why? You've never cleaved to any of the tradition of the Light. Or at least, what we once called the Light."

Bandim lifted one shoulder and allowed it to drop again. "I suppose it can't hurt. Will you do it for me?"

"I will."

The brothers remained in the stillness for some time, Bandim turning to stare out the window once more and Mantos staring at Bandim. The gulf between them stretched, filled with nothing but silence. Bandim had apologized. While Mantos knew he meant it, that didn't make up for everything they had been through all their lives. It wouldn't take back the hurt that Bandim had caused. It wouldn't take back the fact that he'd had his own brother killed. While Mantos had accepted the apology, their whole history was more difficult to come to terms with than a few words and four weeks could amend. As much as he would try to show love to his brother in their mother's memory, Mantos knew in his heart he could never forgive.

The sincerity of Bandim's apology was part of what had saved his life. Had it not been for that, Mantos would have strung his brother up on the walls of the palace just as Bandim had done to many folk, including their uncle Solseo. He would have hung a sign from his neck that said 'TRAITOR.' But he didn't; not only because of Bandim's apology, but because it wasn't what their mother would have wanted.

"*Love one another.*"

Mantos would never forget those words.

Shutting Bandim in the Grieving Tower as his prison was as much for his brother's protection as it was his punishment. There he was safe from assassins. Many refused to forgive the former so-called Sun Emperor's actions, and others refused to understand the emperor-incumbent's insistence to preserve his brother's life. There was one such presence who had just entered the city, to attend her brother's wedding. Mantos would never forget Valaria's words either, or his reply.

"*When I get my claws on your brother, I will choke him with these two hands. When he's on the cusp of oblivion, I'll release his neck enough to bring one final sweet breath into his chest, and then I will clamp down again until he's dead.*"

"*I'll not stand in your way.*"

She hadn't yet mentioned fulfilling that desire, but that didn't mean she had no intention of carrying out her threat.

Mantos broke the silence between them after a while. "If you change your mind, send word to me."

"I won't," Bandim replied, half-turning his head again, "but thank you. And good luck for tomorrow. I'm sure Father would be proud."

He turned away again. Mantos knew his brother wouldn't look back until long after he'd left the chamber.

* * *

Despite the cloak of darkness that had fallen upon the Arc, the Temple of Light was bright as day inside. Candles burned on every surface, and the swirling patterns of flame on the floor were cleared. The assembled congregation now each held one of those candles in their hands, awaiting the beginning of the ceremony. High upon a pyre, underneath the open, vaulted temple roof, lay an intricate carved effigy of Phen of House Yru. It wore one of her finest white gowns, decates out of fashion, and upon its head rested the crown and horn jewelry the empress had worn during her reign. The destruction of the palace in Kubodinnu had reduced her body to ash.

Mantos grieved to think her bones might lie in the foundations of their new seat of power forever, yet perhaps it was a sign. As Fonbir would be at his side as Emperor Consort, a symbol of the newfound peace between the Masvams and the Althemerians, so too would his mother be with Queen Valentia on Althemer, at the root of her rise to power.

Fonbir was at his side now, holding onto one arm with a reassuring tightness as they waited to process through the crowd to the base of the pyre. They were dressed in white, just like the rest of the gathered.

Fonbir, sensing his nerves, patted his hand. "You'll be fine, Toketa. I have faith in you, and all those in this temple love you."

Mantos wasn't sure if love was the right word, but he allowed the reassurance to wash over him. It was idiocy to be so nervous. The next day the folk would crown him emperor of the largest empire under the Arc of the Sky. He would have to bear that heavy burden for the rest of his life, the first of many cycles of his reign dedicated to undoing the damage of what his brother had done. He couldn't stand over the decisions Bandim had made. He couldn't keep the lands Bandim had claimed during his reign. Mantos had already given Althemer back to Valaria and the Althemerians. What of Metakala? Would he go back further than that? What of Selama, conquered under his father's reign, the throat of their queen cut by Mantos himself? If they asked for the return of their sovereignty, could he refuse it?

In the eye of this, Mantos wasn't nervous. But at the thought of lighting his mother's funeral rites, his legs quaked. It wasn't until he took one final steadying breath and began the procession toward the high pyre that he realized it wasn't nervousness he felt at all.

It was fear.

As he approached the center of the temple, under its open roof, Mantos wondered what it was fear of. Saying goodbye? His mother had been gone for long enough he could believe it true, if not come to terms with it. It wasn't fear of seeing her dead body either, for it wasn't present, and he'd seen her as the light disappeared from her eyes.

Priests and acolytes of what the folk still called the Light inclined their heads as he passed. It was neither of those things, he decided as he reached the bottom of the high pyre. It was the fear of not doing her memory justice. But he had to. He must.

He released Fonbir's arm and turned to take in the faces of those who had gathered. Nearest to him were those who'd been closest and dearest to him for the past cycle. Emmy held a candle to her chest, giving him a compassionate half-smile. Beside her was Rel, still marked and scarred by his brother's actions, but standing tall and strong and beautiful in the flickering light. With them were Charo and Zecha, the latter wearing an incubating pouch on his front. Their egg nestled inside, and Mantos inclined his head at them.

Elsya was there too, bedecked in white but holding a House Yru banner high above the crowd. The blue and yellow shone like azure and gold, the sigil of a gargon fluttering proud, signaling Phen's release. Beside him was Queen Valaria of the Island of Althemer, her face an unreadable mask, a crown of twisted metal on her head, and with her was King Khitarian, silent and strong as their rocky kingdom.

Close too, at Mantos' insistence, were Uzet and Zrazashi. The younger of the two looked bewildered at the ceremony's pomp. Zrazashi's face was solemn, but not sad. He inclined his head to Mantos, touching his sibling's shoulder. Tero's younglings would remain close to Mantos for the rest of his life, as long as he had his way. He'd made a promise to Tero to keep them safe, and until they were old enough to make their own choices, Uzet and Zrazashi would remain in the Masvam palace as Mantos' wards. Mantos had vowed to himself to treat them like his own offspring. *It's what Tero would have done.*

The High Priest approached Mantos with a lit torch, offering it to him with a bow. Mantos stilled at first but urged himself into action and took it in his claws. Then, turning to the candlelit congregation, he spoke words he hoped would honor his mother and make her proud.

"Phen of House Yru was a great female. She sacrificed more in her lifetime than anyone should. Wife and empress to my father, Braslen Tiboli, and mother to myself and my brother, she was good, and true, and strong, and loving to the very end." He turned to the pyre, holding the flaming torch aloft. "In the name of the goddesses, both Nunako and Dorai, I commit her memory to the sky. May her soul fly free."

There was a murmur when he spoke the names of both goddesses, but Mantos didn't care. He lowered the torch and walked around the pyre, lighting it at intervals, allowing the flames to take hold. As they did, ethereal chanting rose from the edges of the temple. An Althemerian choir had circled the gathered, offering up their haunting song. Mantos turned and first looked to Fonbir, who pointed to his sister. Valaria's hard mask slipped, and she pressed two talons to her lips as she bowed her head. Mantos mouthed 'thank you' in her native tongue before returning his attention to the pyre.

The flames took hold, racing upward until they consumed the effigy. Smoke billowed upward and out of the open temple roof, and Mantos knew that across the city, the streets and houses too would fill with light to guide Phen's spirit to the afterlife, whatever and wherever that was. Once, they had called it the Light. Now, he wasn't sure what to call it. He was certain of one thing, though. Whatever it was, Phen was already there.

CHAPTER THIRTY-NINE

Fonbir

His wedding robe hung from the end of the bed, its elaborate length running from the bar between the posts to pool on the floor. Fonbir couldn't take his eyes from it, not even when Othelan commanded his attention.

"Stop staring at the thing and let me take care of those fronds of yours! If I don't get the oil in now, they'll never sit right for tomorrow. It's bad enough I'm starting as late as I am."

Fonbir stepped back, still drinking in the details of the garment. It was Althemerian blue embroidered with silver serpents, and at the hem and cuffs were golden Tiboli lightning strikes. At Mantos' request, there was no chain. Fonbir was not to be chained again.

He stumbled as Oth snagged his arm and all but dragged him to the stool at the dressing table, making him sit with a firm push on his shoulders.

"Fon, it's beautiful. You'll look wonderful in it, but only from the neck down if we don't sort out this mess."

Othelan tapped Fonbir on the head with his last word, knocking the soon-to-be Emperor Consort into sense again.

"Yes, sorry. Go ahead."

With a tut, Othelan uncorked the bottle of oil and set to work sliding it along each of Fonbir's short red fronds. It smelled of home, like sea salt and iron and flowers all at once. With a sigh, Fonbir stared into the polished silver plate, watching Oth's clever dark hands at work.

"I can't believe it's happening tomorrow."

"And I can't believe your emperor scheduled his mother's ceremonial burning for the night before the wedding. Who has time for that? We have preparations to carry out."

Fonbir swiped a hand at Oth. "Don't be cruel."

The attendant clicked his tongue and poured more oil into the palm of his hand. "I'm just saying, he's had ample time. Why the night before?"

"To put his mother's memory to rest at last. Tomorrow marks the start of things. Tonight is an end."

Othelan stilled his hands for a moment. "Well, if you insist on being so sensible and sensitive about it, I suppose you're right."

Fonbir chuckled at Oth's tone, which verged on apologetic but didn't quite make it. As he continued his work, Fonbir sighed again, luxuriating in the feel of Othelan's clever touch.

"I know I've asked you a thousand times," Othelan started.

Fonbir grinned, eyes still closed. "Yes, I'm sure about this. I've wanted this for cycles. And you might not like him, but Mantos is a good male. And this is a chance to bring peace and an alliance between our folk again."

After wiping his hands with a fine cloth, Othelan settled his hands onto Fonbir's shoulders.

"Whatever you want, I'll be here with you. And not just because I have to be, because you're a high and mighty prince turned emperor consort and I'm a servant. I just want you to remember you'll always have a friend here."

Fonbir brought a hand up to rest on Oth's and caught his eyes in the plate. "I thank you for it."

Othelan withdrew his touch, smiling. "Just remember that when you're drawing up my pension. Your thanks can come in bickles, crom, and cren."

"No pips?" Fonbir joked.

"No pips," Othelan replied. "From now on I deal in real coinage only, none of that small nonsense. Now, let's do another trial run of your face for tomorrow."

Fonbir groaned and rolled his eyes. "Again?"

"Yes, again," Oth said, reaching for the covered palette of pigments the Masvams used to paint their faces. "I'm not satisfied I got the lightning strikes right."

Though he'd rather spend more time staring at the beauty of his wedding robe, Fonbir sat still for Othelan and allowed him to practice the elaborate make-up again. Masvams were curious folk in their insistence that on both formal occasions and in war, faces were painted with the ciphers of their houses. Fonbir wondered if marriage was like a battle two folk engaged in for the rest of their lives. It would be full of fights and alliances and treaties, knowing when to concede and when to fight your ground. *I wonder if Mother and Father's marriage was like that. I don't remember.*

However it might be, he hoped theirs *would* be a successful one. Mantos, for all his faults, was good. He made mistakes, but he made up for them. He wasn't the same as the male Fonbir had fallen in love with through cryptic messages and infrequent visits. He was better.

A knock sounded at the door as Othelan finished the final flourish on Fonbir's face. He huffed in irritation. "I hope that's not your emperor. He's not to see you until tomorrow."

He bustled to the door and opened it a crack, though he pulled it the full way after the shortest beat. He fell into a bow.

"Your Highness."

Fonbir rose from his stool as the impressive figure of Valaria entered. "Sister."

"Brother."

Othelan withdrew to the side of the room as Valaria approached, her hands open to welcome Fonbir in an embrace. She held him tight, her many bracelets clinking and shifting. Fonbir returned the gesture, pressing the side of his face to hers.

"I'm so glad you're here."

Valaria released him and raised an eyeridge. "It's not every day your big brother gets married. Even if it is to him."

The playfulness in her tone told Fonbir to take no offense. In his heart he knew Valaria would never accept Mantos as a friend, but if she considered him an uneasy ally, that was good enough for now.

"I see you're going with Masvam tradition for your face. Will you wear a veil?"

Fonbir pressed his lips together before he answered. "I wasn't going to. But if you want, I will."

She waved off his offer. "Do what you wish. I think veils are pointless anyway, especially when a certain brother of mine insists on wearing ones that are transparent. What's the point?" They shared a laugh, but hers died before his. "I see there's no chain on that robe. Will you abandon all our traditions for your Masvam?"

There was more venom in her voice. The chain, it seemed, was not as easy to discard as the veil.

Fonbir shook his head. "I won't wear a chain any longer, Valaria. I'm tired of it. I have scars on my hips from the weight of the damn things. Mantos doesn't want me to wear one, and I don't want to either. But I'm still an Althemerian. The sea flows through my veins as much as in yours."

Valaria pursed her lips, the expression on her face unreadable. Then she let the matter drop. "You must know, I'm here only for tomorrow. I leave first thing the day after."

"So soon?" Fonbir cursed the sorrow in his voice.

"I can't leave the island for long."

Though it pained him, Fonbir nodded. "I understand."

He took a moment to memorize the detail of his sister's appearance, as he knew it might be cycles before they saw one another face to face again. He traced the pattern of brown skin and black armor on her face. He drank in the deep green of her eyes, ringed with black. She had changed from the white garments she had worn to

Phen's burning, now wearing a sober quilted doublet of blue silk. On her head was a circlet of dark metal wrought in the shape of two twined serpents. Fonbir hadn't seen it before, yet he knew where the metal came from.

"That's from the ruins of Kubodinnu."

Valaria raised a hand to touch the circlet and nodded. "Yes. So is my crown."

"You must send me a sketch," Fonbir said, trying to lighten his sudden despair. "I hear it's very regal, especially for something made from scraps."

"The best things are those that mean something," his sister replied. "Precious metal comes in many forms. Speaking of which," she continued, delving into the pocket of her trousers, "this is for you."

She withdrew a clinking object. It was a bracelet, the links made from the same dark metal of her circlet. From it hung a square charm embossed with their beloved twin serpents.

"It's traditional to wear a bracelet owned by your mother or father, but everything Mother owned was destroyed. So I had this made for you. She owned all of Kubodinnu and everything in it. I hope it will serve as a suitable alternative."

Fonbir let her pool the bracelet in his hand. The metal was warm from its closeness to her body.

"I should have put it in a box, I suppose," she said, rubbing at her neck scales in uncharacteristic uncertainty. Her own bracelets, numerous on both left and right, clanked as she moved. "But I've never been good at such things. I didn't think."

Fonbir slipped the bracelet on his left wrist, admiring it as it glinted in the candlelight. Having never killed nor saved anyone, this was the first bracelet he had earned. Grinning, he pulled his sister into another embrace. "It's perfect. Thank you."

Valaria patted his back. "You're very welcome."

When they drew apart, his sister burst into sudden laughter that made Fonbir pale. At his distress, she pointed to his face.

"I've smudged your damned paint." Her levity disappeared as one hand went to her own cheek. "Is it on me?"

It was Fonbir's turn to laugh as he nodded. "Yes."

"Ugh!"

Turning to Othelan for help, Fonbir shrugged. His attendant made a strangled sound as he bustled forward, distraught at the destruction of his work. He handed the siblings wet cloths to clean themselves. He gave Valaria a respectful bow, but Fonbir a scowl. "You didn't get to see how perfect those lightning strikes were."

"I'll see them tomorrow, Oth," Fonbir replied with a chuckle.

It took longer to clean his face than hers, and as she waited, Valaria crossed to the bed to admire the wedding robe hanging there. Fonbir discarded the cloth and joined her.

"It's stunning," Valaria said, unable to stop herself fingering the fine embroidery. "I approve of the Althemerian blue and silver, but these gold squiggles I could take or leave."

"They're lightning strikes, not squiggles," Fonbir groused, though he kept his tone playful. He knew Valaria knew that, and he knew she was trying to make light. "I thought it was symbolic, like the twining of two great powers."

When his sister spoke again, her voice was low and serious. "I hope you appreciate what you're doing. I understand you love him, but the Althemerian folk don't love the Masvams. It's taken a lot of threats to stop the dissent of some of my new court. They don't like this marriage, and for good reason. Bandim Tiboli invaded us, stole our island, plundered our resources. It will take cycles to regain all we've lost. And while I appreciate the efforts Mantos has gone to, to return what's ours, he can't bring the dead back to life."

Fonbir's heart lurched. That included their mother and Fylica, two figures who wouldn't be at his twining. "It'll take a long time for easiness to come between our folk. But if we don't try, things will never improve. We might not have an easy peace within our lifetimes, but we can achieve it. I want to help start it. Every great wave starts as a ripple."

"I'll try for as long as the Masvams try," Valaria said.

Fonbir offered a smile. "And I'll make sure Mantos keeps trying."

Valaria didn't return the expression. "That leaves us with the issue of Bandim."

At the darkness in his sister's tone, Fonbir turned toward her. "He'll be a prisoner for the rest of his life. He'll never be free."

"Not good enough for me," Valaria replied. "He killed our mother."

"And he killed Mantos' mother too," Fonbir countered. "What will another death achieve?"

Valaria remained silent and turned her attention back to the wedding robe. "I still think you should unpick all of this gold stitching. I'm sure Othelan would do it for you without hesitation."

The change of topic signaled the conversation was over. Though his sister tried for levity, a chill still pervaded her words.

"I'm sure he would," Fonbir replied, sliding an arm around his sister's, "but I don't want him to." He steered Valaria away from the wedding robe and toward a small table with two carved chairs. "Will you have a drink with me before you go?"

With a visible effort, Valaria shook herself from the haze of her hatred for Bandim and tightened her grip on Fonbir.

"I'd be honored, brother."

CHAPTER FORTY

Mantos

The procession was to begin at the city gates. A long serpent of nobles, lords, and guests, all arranged according to their rank and privilege, snaked back along the road to the city of Masvam for miles. Mantos, astride a great dappled vaemar, waited under the cover and shade of the gate's archway in the thick walls, anticipation churning inside him. From here he could see the palace standing stoic in the distance, waiting to crown its new emperor. Stretched out before him was a great band of musicians to herald him on his journey, and undulating crowds lined the streets. They bore Tiboli banners, the lightning strikes riding high on fields of red.

On a vaemar at his side, Elsya gave Mantos a grin. "How are you feeling? You look like you might bolt at any moment."

Mantos shook his head at the jibe. "I feel fine."

Resplendent in his Yru colors, Elsya shook his head. "I don't believe you."

"Perhaps I feel a little nervous," Mantos conceded with a half-smile, "but not at the coronation. There's a dreadful fear in the back of my mind that Fonbir won't be there for the wedding."

"Pfft," Elsya waved a hand, "don't be ridiculous. He'll be there."

Though he knew it was as ridiculous a fear as Elsya said, Mantos' insides still wavered. This was it, the day he'd hoped for in secret for so long. At last he and Fonbir could be together, not hiding their love as members of warring countries, but displaying it for all to see. If Fonbir didn't arrive at the wedding, it would cut Mantos deeper than any knife. But he would be there. He would be there. All Mantos needed to do was process through the city, receive his crown, and then he and Fonbir would be together for the rest of their lives.

They would belong to one another.

The retainer in charge of proceedings approached Mantos and Elsya, bowing and clasping his hands in deference. "Are you ready to proceed, Your Grace?"

With one last supportive glance from Elsya, Mantos nodded his acquiescence. "Let's begin."

A grin on his face, the retainer scurried away to pass on the word. A few beats later the band of musicians standing before Mantos burst into a great herald. The commander of the color guard that surrounded the incumbent emperor and his heir shouted his orders.

"Stand ready!"

The music swelled further.

"Make way for the Emperor! March!"

In an eruption of music and joy, the procession began, and the wave of adoration swept Mantos' nerves away. The Midsummer sun streamed down upon the scene as if the goddesses were smiling upon them. If they could see the world, Mantos hoped they were. The folk screamed for him, cheered both his and the Tiboli name, waving their red banners against the blue sky.

Mantos' vaemar held steady in the face of the crowds and bore him through the streets with pride. His bright red silken robes flowed down the creature's sides and back, fanning out to show a storm of golden lightning strikes interspersed with the outlines of Yru gargons. His horn jewelry jingled and flashed in the sunlight and would soon give way to the weight of a crown Mantos had never wanted, but knew he had to bear upon his head.

The crowds grew ever thicker as they drew closer to the palace, the procession fanning out and riding along the wide cobbled roads. The musicians never paused in their playing, moving from one rousing tune to another, their marching in perfect sync with that of the soldiers who flanked both them and the emperor. Elsya grinned the way Mantos remembered from the cycles when they were young and as free as a royal youngling could be, back before they understood how cruel the world and its inhabitants could be. In the absence of any other family, Mantos appreciated Elsya's proximity.

That thought made his gaze rise to the line of towers of the palace. His eyes settled on the Grieving Tower, and Mantos wondered if its sole inhabitant was watching the proceedings.

He forced himself to turn away from the consideration of his brother and back to the surrounding joyousness. The folk continued to scream their happiness as the procession traveled across the wide blackblood and redbark drawbridge leading to the palace walls. Mantos knew their cheering wasn't all for him. They lauded the return of normality and the casting off of the upheaval of Bandim's reign. So too did they cheer for the end of the conflict between nations, stopped before it could soak the land in blood. Masvams were conquerors, not the conquered, and the attack on the city of Masvam from all sides had shaken the beliefs of the folk even more than Bandim's insistence on their worship of the so-called Dark.

Dark, Light, Mantos mused as he waved to the crowd, *it means nothing. Everything is gray.*

They reached the palace walls. From them hung more grand-Tiboli banners and Yru flags, something Mantos had insisted on. It wasn't only to honor his mother. It was as much to remember her brother Solseo too, and when Elsya saw them, his eyes brimmed but he sat a little straighter at the honor.

"Thank you," he mouthed, and Mantos inclined his head in reply.

Passing through the portcullis, the procession continued through the courtyards until they reached the speaker's bowl. It swelled with music and was full of great tiered seating areas for the lords and nobles. A high stage was raised, upon which Mantos would receive his crown. Again, at his insistence, it was built in part from the wreckage of the *Water Prago*. He knew Chaata would be in the crowd somewhere. She wouldn't have gone without saying goodbye, or without collecting her debt. Mantos intended to make good on his promise as soon as it was ready.

The musicians took their places on a raised platform below the stage as Mantos and Elsya dismounted their vaemar. With the cheers of the crowds soaring around the bowl, Mantos inhaled, long and deep, and began his ascendance.

When he reached the top of the steps, his eyes went straight for one figure in the small crowd. Standing beside the emperor's crown, which rested on a stone column alongside two others, was Fonbir. He was resplendent in Althemerian blue and silver, and to Mantos' astonishment, he had the most beautiful painted lightning strikes upon his face Mantos had ever seen. There were further golden strikes at his wrists. In that moment, Mantos' heart swelled, and he knew he could never love his Nabi more.

Queen Valaria stood beside her brother, and on the other side of the platform stood King Khitarian. To both other monarchs, Mantos gave respectful bows. Without them, he would never have regained his crown. That was something he would never forget.

Mantos approached the stone column and bowed to the High Priest of the Temple of Light, who in the absence of either of his parents would place the crown upon his head. A moment of sorrow passed through Mantos as the High Priest held his hands up for silence. It should have been his mother's hands that crowned him emperor.

No, Mantos thought. *No sorrow today. Let's invite new beginnings.* Fonbir caught his gaze, concern flashing across his face. Mantos gave him a reassuring smile.

"Before you all today," the High Priest began, his voice carrying around the bowl, "the Masvam Empire will crown its next emperor. Goddess Nunako, Lady of Light," he intoned, and then added with some reluctance, "and her sister goddess Dorai, please give to Mantos of House Tiboli the virtues of temperance and patience, and give him the wisdom to make the best choices for our great empire, and the strength with which to carry them out."

No one uttered a word as the High Priest turned to the stone column and lifted the emperor's crown. The last time Mantos had seen the splendid golden furls with their moonpearls and gemstones, it had been atop his father's head. In one slow and controlled movement, he inclined his head, and the High Priest settled the weight of the entire Masvam Empire upon his head.

As Mantos rose and turned to show the crowd his splendor, the High Priest called out Mantos' new title, "His Imperial Majesty, Sole Ruler of the Masvam Empire, Protector of the Realm, One Blessed by the Goddesses, son of Braslen Tiboli, grandson of Maram Tiboli, Emperor Mantos Tiboli!"

The bowl rang with his words, and the jubilation of the crowd swelled, along with more invigorating music. The crown was heavy, but Mantos knew he could bear it. He waved his appreciation for the crowd's love and when he stopped, the High Priest signaled for further quiet.

"Emperor Mantos has decreed that his is not to be the only coronation today."

Mantos grinned at Elsya, who was smiling at Fonbir. But Mantos bade his cousin look at the stone column again. For the first time Elsya realized *two* crowns, not one, remained. His brown face paled as his jaw slackened. All Mantos could do was smile.

"Today, we not only crown our new emperor," the High Priest continued, "but we recognize the emperor's cousin Elsya of House Yru as heir to the throne."

When the High Priest plucked up the crown, Elsya remained rooted to the spot, frowning. Mantos gave his cousin a push, forcing him forward. Once the crown settled on Elsya's head, the High Priest declared, "Henceforth, we shall know him as Imperial Prince Elsya."

Stunned, Elsya stared as the crowd roared their appreciation, only waving his thanks when Mantos lifted his arm upward. As he waved, Elsya spoke into Mantos' ear.

"Cousin, you didn't need to do that. I'm older than you, for the goddess' sake. And what of your own younglings? You and Fonbir might take an egg. What of your house?"

Mantos raised Elsya's hand higher. "It's time for a new house to rule after me. If that's not you, then it will be your descendant. As for my younglings, I already have two wards whom I intend to love as their father. But they will not rule. I won't lumber them with that responsibility."

"But you'll lumber me and my younglings with it," Elsya said in a voice of half-laughter and half-incredulousness.

"You can handle it," Mantos replied, clapping him on the back.

Again, the High Priest signaled for silence. There was a third crown to award. Mantos' mouth grew dry as the moment he had wanted more than anything else arrived. The High Priest beckoned him forward and Fonbir fell in beside him, their red and blue robes lifting and gleaming in the sun and wind. Valaria stood at Fonbir's side and Elsya at Mantos,' and the wedding ceremony began.

It was a mixture of Masvam and Althemerian traditions, and the merging of belief in Ethay and Apago and Nunako and Dorai. Mantos wondered, were the pairs of gods the same? Where the religions of 'Dark' and 'Light' were influenced by Nunako's jealous separation of herself from her sister, the Althemerians and their fellow believers had resisted such interpretations and kept the two gods together, albeit under different names. Perhaps that was why the Althemerians had welcomed Bomsoi as the Stranger. Now they would never know.

The first part was the Althemerian twining ceremony. The High Priest stepped back and allowed Valaria to take one of her brother's hands, then one of Mantos' hands, and intone the lore of Ethay and Apago. To her credit, Mantos thought, she didn't glare at him once through the whole story.

She brought their two hands toward each other, pressing each of their matching claws together with each of the five blessings she gave to perform the twining. Her many Althemerian bracelets jangled as she moved. As she spoke the words, Mantos had eyes for Fonbir alone, who looked up at him with utter joy.

"May you be blessed with happiness all your lives. May you be blessed with good health. May you remain loyal to one another alone. May you share each other's burdens. And may you stay together forever, in this life and the next."

The joining of their talons signaled their twining and required no words. Valaria released their hands, and Mantos was sure he saw the flash of a tear, but it disappeared before he could look again. She stepped back, allowing the High Priest to begin the second stage of the ceremony. An acolyte handed him two candles, which he gave to Mantos and Fonbir. They held them in their free hands, keeping their others together. The High Priest held a third.

"We hold the belief that marriage is a bond to last a lifetime. Do you both accept this condition?"

Grinning at each other, Mantos and Fonbir answered, "We do."

"We hold that marriage is a sacred thing, not to be squandered or forced. Do you both come to this joining in seriousness and of your own free will?"

"We do," they answered in tandem again.

"And finally, we hold that in marriage, the partners will love and cherish one another, no matter the cost. Are you both willing to sacrifice all else for each other in the name of love?"

There was no hesitation. "We do."

"Then light this candle from your two flames, signaling to those present and the goddess" —he stumbled for a moment, then clarified— "*goddesses*, that from this moment onward, the two of you become one heart, one soul, one breath, for the rest of your days."

The flame trembled with Mantos' hand as he brought it forward, lighting the wick along with Fonbir. When they withdrew their individual candles, the High Priest retrieved them, blowing out the flames and handing them back to the acolyte, before bidding the couple to raise their single candle high, declaring to everyone that they were married.

They were greeted with more cheering and joy, and when the High Priest placed the final crown upon Fonbir's head, declaring him Emperor Consort, they cheered all the louder. Then, above it all, rose the ethereal beauty of the Althemerian choir.

Mantos leaned in to claim a kiss from the now-crowned Fonbir, and he held it for as long as he could. The sun shone down upon them, they held each other close, and everything was perfect.

CHAPTER FORTY-ONE

Bandim

Though he'd tried to remain in bed all day, the strain in his back became too much. Lingering inside the Grieving Tower was sending his body into atrophy. Bandim remembered the stick-thin waif his mother had become and wondered if that was what awaited him too. Different circumstances, but perhaps the same outcome. *I'll ask Mantos if, at some point, he'll allow me to take some exercise when no one will see. The dead of night would suit well.*

The sun had set, sending the three moons high into the sky. Bandim leaned on the stone ledge at the window and stared at each one. Rafa. Dato. Akata. Now the goddesses were gone from the world, were the moons still Nunako's faces? Did she still peer down at her creation, or had she and Dorai closed their eyes to the world?

The sounds of revelry brought his eyes down again. This dual celebration, crowning and wedding, would last long into the night. Bandim pressed his lips together as crowds of folk churned in the courtyards and the speaker's bowl, their clumsy processions lit with endless lanterns. At the end of Vhaun, four armies had converged on this city: the rebels, the Mellul, the Khinish, and the Althemerians. Countless numbers had died in the fighting before word of Bandim's fall and Mantos' rise had reached them. It was no wonder the folk wanted something to celebrate. Bandim had changed everything they had known to be right, only for Mantos to twist it back, though things would never be the same. They couldn't be, not now that the goddesses were gone forever.

As always, when Bandim thought about the loss of Dorai, his insides ached. He clenched his talons hard on the stone ledge, closing his eyes to the carousing below. The world outside had changed. The world inside Bandim had changed too. The goddess had disappeared and, with her, had taken more than herself. She'd taken Bandim's long-held beliefs, his misconceptions, his dreams. The foundation on which Bandim had built his life was gone. It was no wonder he submitted to imprisonment, even welcomed death. Society might recover, but Bandim didn't think he ever would. As cycles passed and his actions became those of history, tales told at firesides, the folk would find their distance from him. Bandim would never have that. He would never be separate from himself and what he had done. Perhaps even death wouldn't grant him that relief.

Another chorus of joy rose from below, with shouts of "Long live the Emperor!" sounding loudest of all. *Yes, long life to you, brother*, Bandim thought, *and I hope I die before you, because the only one interested in preserving my life is you. If you die, I'll be at the mercy of Elsya, and he won't forgive what I did to Uncle Solseo. How could he? Why should he?*

A noise from across the room made Bandim spin on his heel. It was the sound of the key in the lock. His eye ridges drew low. Only Mantos would visit at this hour. But why would his brother take from not only his coronation night, but his wedding night, to visit Bandim? Something cold tracked down Bandim's spine as the door swung open with painful slowness.

A figure stepped inside alone, permitting no guard to enter. Bandim's mouth went dry, and he pressed his back against the window bars. The figure locked the door from the inside and pocketed the keys in her embroidered blue over-tunic. A striking brown-skinned, black-armored face grinned at him.

"Hello, Bandim."

"Valaria," he whispered. "Why are you here?"

Bandim couldn't breathe as the now-crowned Althemerian queen took steps toward him with deliberate slowness. He didn't need to sense her emotions to know them. The smile that graced her face was like a blade.

"I came along to see my brother become Emperor Consort," she said. Her voice was low, but her words were clear. "It was a beautiful ceremony, and Fonbir has never been happier. It was heartwarming. You should have been there."

With nowhere to go, Bandim's back screamed against the bars. "Why are you here?"

Valaria's grin widened, but her black-ringed green eyes narrowed. "I've come to claim what's mine." Bandim tried to shout, but before he could utter a sound, Valaria held up a dark talon. "No, no, Bandim Tiboli. Don't scream. And even if you do," she added with a self-satisfied laugh, "your little guard won't come running. One, he can't get in because I have the keys." She tapped the pocket of her blue over-tunic, the truth jingling within. "And two, I've paid him enough to guarantee his silence for the rest of his life."

Bandim's heart thundered and blood roared in his ears, worsening as a soft *hiss* sounded, and a long, hooded serpent wound its way from underneath Valaria's tunic. It coiled around her neck.

She turned to kiss its snub snout, touching under its jaws with the indulgence of a mother. "This is little Fylica. She has a terrible temperament, so the name suits her well. I keep her with me all the time. Do you remember her namesake, Bandim?" Her tone turned cold. "Do you remember what you did to both her and my mother?"

All he could do was remain silent. There was no right way to answer. He remembered. He remembered the burning power of Dorai within him, the fire, blood, and destruction. He remembered the thin curve of Fylica's neck in his hand, the stench of her skin as it burned at his fingertips, the terror on her face. He remembered her wide-eyed shock as he loosened his grip. He remembered Queen Valentia's scream, "*Fylica!*" And he remembered how the mother caught her daughter as they fell, wrapping her arms around her in death.

"This Fylica," Valaria said, extending an arm for the serpent to snake along, "is much like my sister. Untrained and venomous. She doesn't often listen or do as she's bid." Bandim remained rooted to the spot as Valaria reached out her arm toward him and the serpent slithered from her onto his shoulder. "But sometimes she does. *Tight.*"

At the queen's command, the serpent moved with incredible speed, wrapping itself around Bandim's neck and squeezing, just as its master instructed. Bandim choked under its grip, stars blurring at the edge of his vision. His claws scrabbled to pry the serpent off, but it was futile. The creature wound tighter and tighter.

"I told your brother that I would take your life," Valaria continued. "You took everything from my folk. You plundered our island, killed thousands, murdered my sister and my mother." Her face swirled out of focus as consciousness began to fade. "And for what, Bandim? What did your sins achieve? It's all been for nothing."

Just as blackness encroached, Valaria commanded, "*Loose.*" The serpent released his neck and Bandim sucked in a whooping breath, clutching at his throat as the creature abandoned his neck, slithering back up the queen's outstretched arm. Bandim fell to his knees as the world bucked and turned around him.

"Don't bother getting up," Valaria said. She sent a boot into his ribs for good measure and he collapsed onto the rushes. "Stay down where you belong."

Humiliation swept over Bandim in a wave, but the fire that had once dwelt within him was gone, and he remained on the stone floor.

Valaria loomed over him, her white teeth glinting like knives. "I told your brother I would choke you with my own hands, but then I thought it might be more fitting to allow Fylica to do it, considering her namesake. But I wondered, was that too easy? Would it be painful enough? And I decided that yes, it was too easy, and no, it wouldn't be painful enough. My sister and mother must have died in absolute terror, and all I can hope is that they fell so far, their deaths were immediate. But they were bloody, Bandim. Oh, so bloody. I think you deserve a bloody end too, no?"

His fear ebbed toward sorrow, and Bandim spluttered a reply. "Do whatever you want to me. I don't *care.*" He rolled onto his back and saw confusion and frustration pass over Valaria's beautiful face. He pressed on. "I wanted Mantos to execute me. I asked for it because I have to live with everything I've done every day for the rest of my life, and I can't atone for any of it. I can't apologize enough. I can't explain or justify. What I did to you, your island, your family, is unforgivable. So do whatever you want. Flay me. Cut my throat. Cut off my head, I don't care." The exertion of such honesty brought new despair to his eyes. "I don't care."

Queen Valaria stared at him, her chest rising and falling with anger. It was clear she wanted him to writhe and beg and plead for mercy. She wanted him to supplicate himself before her, to kiss her boots. But he couldn't do that. Not because of pride; it was simpler than that. He didn't have the will to save his own life. He didn't deserve it.

"*Get up,*" Valaria commanded. When he stayed where he was, she kicked him again. "*Get up.*"

She wrenched him to his feet and sent him spinning across the floor. He stumbled into the bedpost, scrabbling for purchase so he didn't fall again. Valaria crossed to him, not stalking but walking with deliberate steps. She stopped a pace away from him, Fylica hissing at her neck.

"The last thing I desire is to give you what you want." Her green eyes were unbearably cold. "If you want death, I wish you a long, long life."

Bandim swallowed against her bitterness. Valaria reached inside her tunic, the embroidered silver serpents on her chest dancing with the movement, and for a moment Bandim thought she might give him the keys to his cell. Instead, she withdrew a long dagger with an elaborate handle in the shape of two twined serpents. One side of its blade gleamed silver in the moons' light. The other flickered gold in the light from his candles.

"However," Valaria continued, running one talon along the flat edge of the blade, "never let it be said I am a cruel queen." She flipped the blade in her hand and offered it to him, handle first. "Take this."

Bandim hesitated but reached for the blade as Valaria's expression flashed with anger again. The weapon was heavy in his hands. The serpents' gemstone eyes winked in the light.

Valaria spoke with a voice of iron. "Keep this blade in this chamber as a reminder not only of what you've done to my folk, but of me. Hide it where no one will find it, but don't forget about it. Think about it every day. Remember Fylica. Remember my mother." She paused and placed a firm finger on his chestplate, right above his heart. "On the day you can't live with the burden of what you've done any longer, use that blade and cut yourself open. Bleed yourself to death. At that point, you'll have my forgiveness for all your sins."

Bandim couldn't take his eyes from the silver-cast serpents and their glinting green eyes. Green, just like Valaria's.

Footsteps broke his concentration, and he looked up in time to see the queen unlock the door and close it behind her without a final glance. The key turned in the lock again, and the sound of bolts being drawn clanked loud and sinister. With the queen gone, the sounds of revelry rose loud once more. Outside, everything was the same.

Bandim stared at the dagger, tested its weight, passed the pad of one thumb over the relief of the serpents. The finish of the blade was elaborate, beautiful. He glanced around the chamber, eyes roving for some secret place to hide it away. If a servant found it, they would take it from him. His brother would want to know where it came from, though its serpentine nature made that clear.

Bandim knew there was nowhere to hide the weapon, however. The chamber in the Grieving Tower had no secret compartments or floorboards to pry loose. There was only one place for it. Bandim knew that too.

* * *

Yameteth

The morning after the celebrations, Yameteth Tiboli ascended the many stairs to the chamber at the top of the Grieving Tower, as she did every morning. She bore a tray of food and drink, a little more elaborate than usual since her emperor cousin Mantos had asked her to bring Bandim some leftovers from the feasting the evening before. It was still nothing compared to what she'd brought Bandim when she'd been his cupbearer, but it brought her some pleasure to think he might get a share of happiness from eating something different from bread and cheese. He had been cruel to her. He had almost burned her to death in a hearth. But he had saved her from the Lurking Death.

In the time she'd served Bandim, that was the main thing she had learned of him. He was a dichotomy, two beings living in one body. He could be cruel, but some of his actions were good. He had killed, but he had also saved. That was why she served him. She couldn't forgive him, but she couldn't abandon him either.

The guard unlocked the chamber door for her, and Yameteth entered on silent feet. Bandim was still in bed. Unusual. When she brought his breakfast, she often found him staring out the barred window of the tower or sitting in the single chair, pondering whatever it was former goddesses and emperors pondered.

Yameteth placed the tray on the bedside table. She went to call him but didn't. As soon as she saw his face, her heart stopped. He was pale and still. She knew what that meant. She'd seen it before, faced it herself. Peeling back the covers, she saw scarlet, and a flash of silver still clutched in his hands, even in death.

She didn't scream. She didn't cry for the guard. Yameteth Tiboli inclined her head and sent a silent prayer to Nunako. And Dorai.

Please have mercy on his soul.

Then, wiping the tears from her eyes, she called for the guard.

CHAPTER FORTY-TWO

Emmy

A few weeks passed before they were ready to depart. It was nearing the end of Merish, and although Emmy knew she and Rel needed to set out before the high temperatures of Decos made travel uncomfortable, she was glad they lingered. As she stared down at the little bundle of sharp claws and a stubby tail in her arms, she couldn't stop smiling.

"They are beautiful," she cooed.

She sat in the shade of one of the larger Daxo trees in the palace gardens, enjoying the quiet of early morning and cradling the hatchling of her two closest friends. The little creature stirred in their sleep and a roll of panic rose in Emmy when it seemed they might cry. Charo chuckled at Emmy's discomfort.

"You're more afraid of Kurero than anyone else you've met in this past cycle."

Kurero, Emmy thought, *meaning joy*. As the hatchling stirred again, she handed them over to their father. Zecha hushed and rocked tiny Kurero to calmness once more. Emmy shook her head. "You're a natural."

"I don't know about natural," Zecha replied. "Just determined to try."

Emmy grinned. That was Zecha, through and through. "I'm glad I got to see them before I go."

Charo's smile fell. "How long will you and Rel be gone?"

"I don't know. It could be a season. It could be a cycle, maybe longer. It depends on what we find. Mantos has gathered some leads for us to follow, but whether they come to anything is as much your guess as mine."

A warm breeze wafted through the garden, bringing the scent of petals. Zecha settled Kurero in their woven basket. "I wish we could go with you," he said, "but it's not safe."

"Kurero is your priority now," Emmy said with a nod. "It's not like we'll never see one another again. And anyway, it's in your interests to stay here. Hasn't Mantos offered to have you both trained alongside the sons of the nobility? That's what you always wanted, Zecha, to fight."

"It is," Zecha said with some reluctance, "but I never considered not having you around."

Emmy touched his head. "You're a soft thing."

"When do you leave?" Charo asked.

"Tomorrow morning. Mantos has chartered a ship to take us east." Emmy's voice wavered. "I'll miss you both so much."

Charo and Zecha drew her into an embrace in response, and Emmy bit back her tears.

"It's not goodbye forever," Charo murmured. "It's just goodbye for now."

Emmy drew back and nodded, and the fact her friends' eyes were wet too made her feel less foolish.

"Thank you, both of you," she said, "for everything."

"Thank you, Emmy," Zecha said, pulling her in for another tighter hug. "We'll be waiting for you to come back. Don't forget about us."

Emmy laughed at that. "How could I forget about you two?" She bent to give Kurero the lightest touch to their face. "Be good for your moi and poi, little one."

As Emmy left the gardens, the gravel path crunching under her new boots, she didn't look back. She told herself she could see her friends again before tomorrow but knew she couldn't do much more than wave. If she embraced them again, she might never let go.

Emmy disappeared back into the palace and made her way to one of the royal receiving chambers. Mantos had asked her to meet the captain of the ship he'd sourced for their journey, and it wouldn't do to disobey an emperor in his own palace.

It still seemed unreal, she thought as she approached the chamber. Mantos, the prince who had fled under the weight of his responsibility, was now the rightful emperor of his country. But then, they had all changed. None of them were the same folk they'd been just one cycle before. Entering the luxury of the Masvam emperor's chamber, with its beautiful woven wall hangings and luscious rugs, it struck Emmy how far she'd come from sweeping the floors of Krodge's Apothecary in Bellim.

Mantos rose as she entered and beckoned her with open arms and a wide smile. Now crowned and married, despite the pressure that came with his duties, he seemed happier. Perhaps he was more at peace.

"Emmy, please take a seat," he said, gesturing to one of the gilded chairs clustered around a low table covered in maps. "This is Captain Ngili Chaata, who'll be taking you and Rel on your journey."

This was the first time Emmy had seen the captain up close. She'd had glances during the battle of the speaker's bowl, but now the female's youth struck her hard.

As if reading her thoughts, Chaata shrugged her shoulders. "What can I say? I'm just that good."

The laugh was out before Emmy realized, eliciting chuckles from the others. Mantos and Chaata talked her though the route they would take, south across the Sea of Souls to Mellul.

"Queen Tayu and King Nannu of the Mellul provided intelligence of a small band of traveling folk in their lands, sometimes described as blue and purple in colors," Mantos explained as he tapped Mellul on the map. "They never stayed in one place for long but were known for their strange abilities. I appreciate it's not much. However, it's at least a beginning to your journey." He exchanged a look with Chaata that spoke of something more than her position as the captain of her sea journey. "There's one more detail, too, and I won't take no for an answer."

"Oh?" Emmy replied, crossing her arms, and raising an eyeridge.

"Chaata isn't just going to transport you and Rel across the sea. She and her crew will stay with you for as long as you need."

Chaata slapped one knee. "As you might have noticed, we can hold our own in a battle. It isn't safe for two strange creatures to travel alone."

Emmy barked another laugh. "You've never seen Rel fight. Uloni powers or not, she's a match for anyone."

"That may be the case," Mantos continued, his face now cloaked with seriousness, "but I won't let you do this alone. It's take Chaata's protection and her ship or have nothing at all."

Indignant, Emmy's neck scales fluttered, but she let the feeling ebb as fast as it came. Mantos wasn't being a meddling emperor. He was being a concerned friend. She looked from him to Chaata, who wiggled her eyeridges—what an odd creature—and back at Mantos again.

"All right, I accept. It's not like I have much choice."

"No, you don't," Mantos replied with a grin, "but I'm glad I didn't have to force the issue. And Chaata is excited to begin a new life as private protection sailing under Masvam colors."

The captain wagged a talon. "We'll only sail under Masvam colors when it's prudent, Your Gloriousness. There are many parts of this world where the name 'Masvam' is worse than the worst swear any Linvarran sailor such as myself might exclaim. Like—"

Mantos jerked up a hand to still her mouth, and Chaata let out a wicked laugh. Emmy's mouth widened with a grin as Mantos nodded in supplication.

"I'll take your word for it."

"You didn't take my word. You didn't let me say it," Chaata replied with a pout.

Emmy shook her head. "What kind of captain are you?"

Chaata wiggled her eyeridges again. "The best kind. Now, if you'll excuse me," she said, bending to grasp the maps and sea charts in one crinkled armful that made Mantos wince. As she did, a gleaming gold pendant slipped from her collar. Emmy recognized it as the crossed lightning strike cipher of House Tiboli. "I have to make ready. The *Stranger* won't check herself."

She strode off without a goodbye or a bow to the emperor. Emmy watched in disbelief. "You allow her to speak to you that way?"

Mantos shrugged. "She knew me before I was an emperor, before she even knew I was a prince."

"And she wears your cipher?"

"That was part of the price I paid for my first passage with her," he replied, one side of his mouth tugging upward in remembrance.

"She called her ship the *Stranger*," Emmy added, the familiar twinge of sorrow rising in her throat.

"I named the ship," Mantos said, "in honor of Bomsoi. I owed Chaata a great debt not just for allowing me to destroy the *Water Prago*, but for bringing her into the middle of a conflict that had nothing to do with her. But I never said I'd let her name her new ship. I thought you'd appreciate it."

Emmy placed her hand on top of one of Mantos.' "I do, very much."

"We've come a long way, you and I," the emperor replied, turning his hand to take Emmy's in his strong grip. "Whatever you need, I'll always be here for you. We might not be Hand and Heart of Nunako, but we're part of each other." He gave her a lopsided smile. "I'll miss you, little sister."

Emmy swallowed at the sentiment and leaned to give him a brief hug. "I'll miss you too," she hesitated before she added, "big brother. And don't think I've forgotten your promise about dessert. I expect you to keep that promise."

Mantos grinned. "When you get back, whenever that may be, I'll have a dessert banquet waiting for you. You have my word."

"Goodbye, Mantos."

"Goodbye, Emmy."

As she left the chamber and walked back to her own rooms to gather her belongings, a messenger hurried past. Emmy looked back as he exchanged harried words with the guard posted on Mantos' door before being permitted entry. Whatever that news was, it wasn't good. Emmy turned and continued on her way, her footsteps ringing against the smooth stone.

* * *

The *Stranger*, an impressive ship in both size and firepower, sailed out of the harbor of the city of Masvam under the rising sun. Masvam flags flew from her three masts, though Emmy knew they'd come down as soon as it was no longer prudent to fly them. She and Rel stood at the rail, watching the city grow smaller.

"A fine vessel with an even finer name," Rel said, running her talons along the smooth wood. "May she bear us with the strength of her namesake."

"But perhaps with fewer surprises," Emmy added.

Rel's laugh, so loud and bright, made Emmy's heart sing. Her strong, unwavering friend was back. Emmy leaned against Rel's arm, relishing the warmth slung around her shoulders.

"Do you think we'll find what we're looking for?" she asked.

Rel glanced over her shoulder. "Well, we've already found one other fellow part-Uloni," she said, referring to the pale blue and purple of Jishu, who danced about the deck as if the power of the wind was still within her. "Let's hope that's a good omen."

Emmy nodded and set her face into a determined smile. Together they watched as the city of Masvam disappeared, and the *Stranger* took them forward on their next adventure.

###

Thank you for reading The World Breaker by LMR Clarke. If you enjoyed this book, would you please leave a review?

ABOUT L. M. R. CLARKE

L.M.R. CLARKE IS A WRITER from Northern Ireland who writes Young Adult fiction, primarily in the Fantasy genre.

She writes with inclusion in mind, especially LGBT+, and explores themes such as sectarianism, racism, and other forms of discrimination in her books. She does not believe in shying away from difficult issues in YA. In fact, LMR thinks it's vitally important that young people are given access to difficult topics through fiction in order for them to see the consequences of actions as well as the ability for characters to conquer adversity.

CONNECT WITH L. M. R. CLARKE

Find me on my publisher's website:
www.castrumpress.com/authors/lmr-clarke

BOOKS BY L. M. R. CLARKE

NOVELS
ARC OF THE SKY (3 BOOK SERIES)

The Moon Rogue, book 1
The Sun Emperor, book 2
The World Breaker, book 3

Most books available in ebook, paperback and audiobook.

Visit castrumpress.com for more.

YOU

MAY ALSO LIKE

Following is an excerpt from:

DAWN OF PURPLE & GRAY

Hyllethan Gifts, book 1

Caroline Sciriha

Cover designed by The Gilded Quill

Caroline Sciriha
Visit my website at www.castrumpress.com/caroline-sciriha

Printed in the United Kingdom

First Printing: Oct 2019

castrum PRESS

ISBN-13 978-1-9123274-2-3

CHAPTER ONE

No more.

No more would Ma fuss and scold and care. No more would she smile away a tear and stitch away a hurt.

Taking in a shuddering breath, her wide trousers and cloak dragging in the swish of the morning swell, Shael touched the side of the Zy'el boat. It drifted away from under her fingers, carrying Ma's body towards Hylletha, land of the enemy.

As Ma had wished.

"There are mages and monsters there. Even dragons." Andrey's words came barely more than a whisper.

Shael tore her gaze from the boat and drew Andrey to her. "Those stories might not be true."

She swallowed the ache of unshed tears and tucked an unruly lock of hair behind his ear. "Ma's in the arms of Zy'el now. He'll keep her safe."

Bastian, their eldest brother, had carved a watching eye on the boat's prow intended to invoke the death god's protection. Perhaps they all needed to wear the ivory tooth of Ay'el beneath their clothing as this choice of funeral would doubtlessly lead to talk, and talk could lead to questions and a hangman's noose for all the family.

A seagull's squawk drew Shael's eye away from Andrey, the bird's caw, caw, caw, echoing her unvoiced cry. With black-tipped wings outspread, the gull glided over the silvery water. The gull headed towards the sun rising above the Hyllethan isle. If she could, she'd call the gull back before it reached that shore. Hyllethan mages experimented on animals, people said, transforming them into the monsters Andrey had mentioned.

Yet on her deathbed, Ma had insisted on returning to the Hyllethans.

Jana, the draper's daughter, walked down to the water's edge to stand by her side, the wind billowing her cloak like a poorly rigged sail.

"It was a beautiful ceremony," Jana said. "Father said he hasn't been to a passing-over-the-water for at least five years."

Zy'el's teeth. The funeral had already set tongues clacking. "Do people think it strange?"

Shael peeked at the handful of neighbors who had accompanied them down the short track from Merecastle to the beach. To honor Ma, most of the women wore their best kaftans and the men their headscarves. Ma had been loved, respected. But the worst enemies would be those posing as friends.

"There's been talk," Jana said. "It's not too unexpected, considering it's you."

A cold finger strummed chords down Shael's back. "What do you mean?" She asked pulling Andrey closer to her, as if holding him would shield him from what was to come. But Jana wouldn't be standing so tranquilly by her side if she suspected what Shael truly was.

"Well, just look at the way you dress. And you and your mother never uncover your hair. I mean, who else at Merecastle clings to the old ways?"

"Ma considered it a sign of modesty."

Shael forced a smile and hid her thoughts. Today, she wore her coming-of-age kaftan which Ma had painstakingly decorated with seeds. It had taken more castellions than they could afford. But trust a draper's daughter to comment on the shapeless clothing and headscarf.

Shael adjusted the strip of cloth wound round her head, then lowered her hand. Don't draw attention to it, Ma had cautioned repeatedly. She had known very well what would happen if anyone caught sight of Shael's silver hair.

Ma had cuddled and shushed her when she had sobbed that she wanted hair like Jana's, straight like water falling over a cliff, the color of ripe blackberries on a sunny day. Like Ma's had been. Like her brothers' and all Merecastlians'.

"The wind's picking up," Jana said.

Shael nodded. The flat-bottomed vessel should be sturdy enough to withstand the rising squall and reach the Hyllethan shore intact. The current had already pushed it so far out into the strait it was now little more than a black speck on gray waves.

People began to leave the beach and walk up the narrow path hewn into the cliff. Jana's parents and brother Markus were the last to draw away from the water's edge. They clasped the hands of Bastian and Eszter, his wife.

Markus walked over to where Shael and Jana stood. He was one of the few men at Merecastle as tall as Shael.

At least he had that in his favor.

Markus took her hands in his. His palms were smooth, unlike Bastian's and Andrey's, but then Markus worked in his family's drapery shop and not in a pottery like her brothers.

"Shael, I know this is a terrible time for you. If you need anything, anything at all, let me know." He squeezed her fingers.

"Thank you." You can't give me my family.

"I know this is not the right time, but..." A flush darkened Markus's pock-marked face. "When you can, think about my proposal. And there's ample space, even for Andrey, if you wish him to live with us." He winked at her brother and ruffled his hair.

Andrey twisted his head away from Markus's assault and grinned for the first time in days.

Blinking eyes that had become gritty and hot, Shael nodded and slipped her hands out of Markus's. He's a good man, Ma had said. She had looked so anxious when they had discussed him. You are only sixteen. There's no need to hurry making a decision. Ma's passing now meant she had to decide, and soon.

Jana kissed Shael's cheek, then walked away with Markus and their parents. A sudden gust of wind flapped Shael's cloak against her kaftan and whistled through the vegetation clinging to the cliff behind her. Despite her resolve not to glance up, hollow thumps drew her gaze above the cliff to the gray walls of Merecastle. The breeze had set the group of five corpses hanging there swaying and bumping against the bastions. The smallest corpse was that of a child no older than Andrey. Shael shivered and drew her cloak closer. The family's crime had been that of helping the wife's brother—a man wanted for stealing from the lord's keep.

Her own family would be meted the same fate if anyone realized Shael's secret.

"Shael, Andrey." Bastian tucked Eszter's hand into the crook of his arm. "It's over. Let's go home."

Shael ripped her gaze from the hanging figures above taking one last look at the white-crested waves. She had never felt so alone. And so frightened. Marriage to Markus would give her a secure future, yet she'd be placing a noose around his neck.

* * *

On their trudge along the spiral fortifications of Merecastle up to the third tier, Shael adjusted her stride to reflect Bastian's and Eszter's slower pace. Many of the people they met stopped to offer sympathy. Shael tucked her impatience out of sight and instead shaped a weak smile. They didn't seem to realize all she wanted was to be alone to mourn.

By the time they reached Artisan's Way and Shael caught sight of the splash of red against the gray stone of their house, the sun's beams had already slid over Third Wall. Ma had always said she'd planted the geraniums in the huge clay pots Pa had made to draw them all back home if they ever lost their way. Perhaps Pa and Tomas had made similar pots in Zy'el's realm and filled them with geraniums to help Ma find them.

Once inside the house, Shael rushed up the stairs to her room. Situated above the pottery, it was just large enough to contain two beds, a wooden chest at the foot of each, and a washstand. Her gaze went to the empty bed next to hers, covered with Ma's colorful crochet throw. Ma had worked on it every evening last winter, one square a night. She'd been so angry when Andrey had taken a skein, painstakingly dyed the color of wet grass in spring, to practice making slingshots. She'd run after him with a raised wooden spoon round and round the kitchen table.

Who would have thought Ma wouldn't see another winter? In the last days of her illness, the throw had kept her warm when nothing else would stop the shivering, and all you could see was her pale face peeping out of the crochet folds.

Shael's shallow breaths turned into shuddering sobs. First Pa, then Tomas, and now Ma. She leaned against the door, fighting for control. Ma had been the spindle round which their lives spun, and even more so after Pa and then Tomas disappeared. And now...

The family was slipping away from her like sand from the beach. Bastian had Eszter and their unborn child—they would be Bastian's priority. She and Andrey had each other, but Andrey needed a mother's love.

The downstairs window shutters thudded and scraped against the outside wall. Bastian must have taken off his jerkin, sash, and headwear before opening the pottery to do some work.

Even today.

Shael sniffed, wiping her face with the back of her hand. She had best see to her chores. Crying solved nothing. Ma had known that well.

Undressing she wrapped her kaftan in a swathe of linen, careful not to crease the cuffs and high collar with their intricate scallops of seeds. Ma had spent weeks sewing the tiny sunflower seeds with the light of a candle.

The gray trousers however needed a soak. The sea water had left salt stains along the bottom.

Gray and Purple. The colors of the sky at dawn, Ma had said.

"Llyntrellcastle colors." Bastian's lips had curled as if the colors offended him.

The next time she'd wear the kaftan would be to marry Markus, most likely. Not the cheeriest of thoughts.

Reaching for the old clothes she wore in the house Shael paused. She couldn't slide back into the familiar routine as if nothing had changed, at least not today.

From the chest she pulled out Tomas's homespun trousers, jerkin and belt. The trousers were short, but she tucked them into her boots before placing her slingshot in the trouser pocket. Tomas's hunting knife went down the side of her boot. A run in Mere Wood with Fluff, her pet wolf, would keep her mind off Ma. And she hadn't dyed her hair in days—she'd been too busy caring for Ma. Now she had to think about protecting the living.

After retying her headscarf around her head, Shael hurried down the stairs, slowing as she caught sight of Eszter sat on a stool by the long table in the center of the downstairs room, with a small heap of vegetables before her. Bunches of Ma's herbs hung from the rafters above her, filling the kitchen with a fragrance of mint and rosemary. A fire crackled in the grate, and Eszter had hung a pot over it to boil water.

Eszter looked up from the onion she was peeling. "Don't tell me you're going out, today of all days?" Storm clouds gathered in her gaze. "What will the neighbors think?"

Eszter's words, more than her sensibility, cut through Shael. She hadn't considered that. The vegetables on the table multiplied her remorse. She should stay to help. The baby was due soon, and Eszter needed more rest. And there were the pottery pieces Bastian had asked her to decorate with the leafy design she'd drawn for him.

Neither task would fill the hollow within.

Shael swung her cloak over her shoulders and tied it at the neck. "I'm off. I'll get some rabbits or birds for supper."

Without waiting for Eszter's answer, Shael pulled the door closed behind her. The pale fall sunshine shimmering on the gray stone and red flowers warmed by the morning air. Shael zigzagged between the carts and peddlers and shoppers that filled Artisan's Way. The hubbub of humans and animals in the narrow road, so normal on any other day, pounded at her.

Shael lengthened her stride. She had to get away, before the high walls and the crowds smothered her. Jana passed by carrying a wrapped bundle. Shael nodded to her but kept on going. Hopefully, Jana would understand and not think her rude, but she couldn't take any more empty words of sympathy or meaningless chatter.

A brisk walk halfway round Second Way brought Shael to the vaulted gateway leading into First Way. Passing through it, she moved aside to let a posse of armed riders clatter and clop past her before the arched main entrance with its heavy iron portcullis came into sight.

A trader from a neighboring castle leading a string of donkeys and two young journeymen obstructed the entrance. Perfect. The guards would have better things to do than bother her. Shael pulled up her hood and straightened her cloak to position the embroidered Merecastlian emblem on her left shoulder. Rounding her shoulders to reduce her height, she slipped past the donkeys. The two sentries, busy checking the trader's documents, looked up but spared her only a fleeting glance.

Shael crossed the barren space in front of the castle, conscious of the gaze of the sentries patrolling along the four bastions and the roof of the keep. She forced her pace not to falter, to tread neither too fast, nor too slow, as one who had nothing to hide, until the leafy canopy of the wood hid her from their view.

At last. Inhaling deeply, she let the pulpy smell loosen her muscles. Straightening her shoulders, Shael threw back her hood, and whistled long and loud.

In her mind Shael built up an image of Fluff, his goofy face and muscular body. A faint howl answered. Her smile deepened. Fluff always responded to her call, notwithstanding where he was.

The wolf hadn't sounded too far away. Taking out her sling she picked small stones off the forest floor. Twigs and dried leaves crunched beneath her boots. A tiny mouse scurried away from under a clump of rock and moss. Another followed. A streaking flash of gray behind the trunk of an oak tree made her look up. Fluff came to a standstill by her side.

He rubbed his snout against her legs.

"Hi, Fluffball." The heaviness weighing down her shoulders eased off. Fluff did not need the gift of speech to offer comfort, or to be told when it was needed. Sinking her hands into the thick fur at his neck she massaged one of his favorite spots. Fluff was already as tall as her hip, despite being only eighteen months old. A deep rumble of contentment vibrated within his chest. Shael squatted and hugged him—she'd never be alone for as long as she had Andrey and Fluff. "It's just me today. Andrey's at home."

The wolf yipped and tugged at her cloak.

"Hungry, huh?" She had been right to come to the woods. And Ma would have agreed and understood. Ma had never stopped her coming here, understanding that the trees and wilderness were more home to Shael than the confining closeness of a castle's walls. You are nature's child, Ma used to say.

Shael stood, clicking her tongue at Fluff, advancing into the undergrowth. All was quiet, except for normal forest rustling and creaking. No Outcasts were close by. The desperate men and women who had been banished from the castles, or were on the run, were even more frightening than the wolves. But she had Fluff, and he would alert her if anyone approached.

Some rabbit droppings dotted their path. Shael kneeled by them. Fresh. Fluff sniffed out the trail, and she followed him. A leaf trembled, and a brown rabbit raced across the trail. Place. Whirl. Release. The stone, flung from her sling, found its mark. One down.

A few moments later, she bagged a second rabbit. Shael hung their dinner to her belt—one rabbit for Fluff; one for the family. But Bastian's appetite being what it was, it would be best to catch another. She clicked her tongue. "Come, Fluff."

Fluff's ears twitched, and he stood still. Shael's gaze darted around them. Nothing stirred, however the wolf's hearing and eyesight were superior to hers. She motioned to move back into a thicket behind them. Fluff slunk down and belly-crawled under the dense foliage. Shael followed, moving backwards erasing their tracks with a long twig. If the approaching menace was a group of Outcasts, that should throw them off their trail.

She slithered into the thicket and eased Tomas's knife out of her boot, the sigh of iron against leather loud in her ears. Now all she could do was wait.

Her clothing soaked up the moisture in the ground from last night's rain. If Ma could see her, she'd scold and nag about catching a cold.

If only.

Fluff's breath warmed the back of her neck. That, and the heat of his body stretched along her side, helped to dissipate the cold. Whatever was out there was taking its time.

The musky, earthy smell of wet soil tickled her nose. Shael switched the knife from one hand to the other to rub her palms against her trousers. Perhaps what Fluff had sensed was waiting for the right moment to pounce.

A rustle of leaves. A squirrel scampered away in the undergrowth. Shael glanced at Fluff. A squirrel wouldn't have alarmed him, and he had not relaxed his tense stance. His perked-up ears twitched.

The ground vibrated beneath her. Galloping horses. More than one horse could mean armed men.

She eased her grip on her knife. She couldn't fight horsemen.

Birds took off with a flurry of leaves, and twigs snapped as small creatures scuttled away into the warren of burrows beneath the soil. Then the bushes in front of her swayed. A short man appeared, stumbling over an exposed root, an arrow shaft protruding from his chest. He pressed his hands against his ribs and blood dripped from between his fingers.

"What—?" Shael half rose, then froze. She should help him but what about the danger to herself?

The stranger wore the blue livery and badge of a messenger. Messengers were held in high esteem, and attacks on them were severely punished, but appearances could be deceptive. Messengers didn't travel on foot. And who were the approaching horsemen?

The man faltered, then fell, paces from her hiding place. His gaze locked onto hers. Her breath missed a beat, her insides churned, she tightened her grip on the knife.

Not taking his eyes off her, the man crawled towards her, leaving a trail of blood-stained leaves and loam.

So much for not leaving tracks.

Her legs jittered. A wounded animal, or a desperate man, was always the most dangerous.

The man caught sight of Fluff, causing him to still. Shael eased her grip on the knife, conscious of the tremble in her hand. The messenger couldn't harm her; his injury was too severe, and she had Fluff. The wolf was a big baby to her, but his size and bared teeth made him terrifying to others.

"Hide me." The man's voice cracked, and relief flooded her. He didn't consider her the enemy. He was scared—of her? Of Fluff?

Shael placed her hand over Fluff's neck, stilling his growl. Someone had attacked the man. And whoever it was remained out there. Her searching gaze swept the surrounding trees. Nothing moved for as far as she could see. Which didn't mean much.

The man crawled into the thicket. His tunic and cloak were torn but not too worn or dirty. It didn't seem as if he'd been living rough. Not an Outcast on the run, then. Perhaps he was just what he seemed. "Who are you? Who's following you?" She asked.

"Shush, boy." The man closed his eyes fighting for breath.

Boy! Well, she could pass for a boy in Tomas's clothes and her long hair wrapped up out of sight.

The man had used an authoritative, curt voice, like one expecting instant obedience—just as a castle official would, the type of person she avoided at all costs.

Whoever he was, he was hurt, and she couldn't just abandon him to his fate.

The ground thundered. The horses were heading towards them. Metal clinked.

"They're almost upon us," the man hissed.

Who's they?

The sound of hooves rumbled closer and closer, multiplying the beat of her heart. Whatever their quarrel was, she would be caught in the middle.

Shael darted out of the thicket and scattered leaves and twigs over the bloodstains.

Fluff growled a warning, and she scurried back sliding in between the wounded man and Fluff. Throwing her arm around the wolf, she peered out between the branches.

A rider less horse appeared. Its hooves hammering the ground by their hiding place; the dangling reins swiped off twigs above her head. She squeezed Fluff harder. If those hooves slammed into them, they'd be killed. The horse raced away, its coat sheathed in lather, eyes rolling wildly.

More horses approached, closer and closer. Three armed riders tore past, their bat-black cloaks marking them as strangers. No castle emblem on the cloaks. However, all three riders had swords hanging from their waists and bows and quivers on their backs.

They didn't have the haunted, scruffy look of Outcasts.

Shael briefly caught sight of one grim face beneath the wide hood of a cloak. The man looked young—perhaps in his late teens—his glacial expression turned her skin clammy. Hiding had been the right decision.

The sound of hooves faded away, and the man beside her moaned. A splash of blood spread beneath him. Whatever his quarrel with the armed riders, now was not the time to ask about it. She had to stop the bleeding.

Her stomach roiling, Shael pulled out her shirt and slit a strip off the edge with her knife. "I need to remove the arrow and bind the wound," she said.

The man reached out and clutched her arm. Shael gasped and jerked away, for one in the arms of Zy'el, his grip was hard, and he did not release her. Instead, using her as a prop, he struggled to sit up. Blood spurted from the wound.

The messenger fell back, his chest rising and falling rapidly.

His fingers tightened around her wrist. "What's your name?"

What? She stopped struggling to free her arm—this was not the time for idle talk. "Shael. What's yours?"

"Shael... so you're a girl." His nails dug into her wrist, and she winced. "It's an unusual name... for an Inlander."

Heat drained from her cheeks. This was not the first time her name had attracted suspicion. After years of raised eyebrows and questions, Shael had her answer falling from her lips without thought.

"My parents were servants in a Hyllethan castle before the war freed them. My mother's Hyllethan mistress wanted her to name me so—she said it would bring me luck."

"And has it? Brought you luck, I mean?" The man's tone was ironic, derisive. Bitter.

Shael shrugged, wary. Choosing her words with care, she said, "We are free from our Hyllethan masters. Praise be to the king and queen."

His grip on her arm lessened; his breath rattled in his throat.

Shael's shoulders relaxed. Hoping she'd dispelled his suspicions. "Sir, I need to remove the arrow and get you to the healers at the castle. Or I can run for help. The guards can bring horses—"

The man shook his head. "I'm dying... I will not reach... your castle. I need you to listen carefully. I have a pouch... for Queen Neis. I want you... to give it to Lord Jothan.... Tell him to guard it... well."

Queen Neis! And Lord Jothan! She couldn't get involved in this. She'd avoided the Lord of Merecastle all her life. She couldn't let this man endanger her and the family.

The man coughed and blood flecked his lips. "Tell your lord the pouch has... to be delivered... at once... to Queen Neis."

His voice was so low, Shael strained to catch his words.

"There is no time to lose." The man seized her wrist again. "Neither you, nor Lord Jothan... must open the bag. Tell him... I was... followed... attacked... by Hyllethans."

CHAPTER TWO

The riders she'd seen were Hyllethans! Shael's gaze darted to the path the riders had taken, her grip on her knife tightening. No Hyllethans had roamed the Inner Lands for fourteen years. And now they were back. Searching for the man dying before her.

Thank Ay'el she hadn't brought Andrey with her.

This man was no mere messenger, if his task involved the Queen and the Hyllethans. She didn't remember the battle the Inlanders had fought against their previous overlords, she'd only been two years old at the time, but everyone said they were now much better off without the Hyllethans. Everyone, except Ma.

The man groped beneath his cloak and withdrew a soft leather bag with the drawstring wrapped around the opening. He thrust the pouch into Shael's hands.

It was heavier than one would expect from its size, and whatever was inside had irregular shapes. A tiny rent in the material caught her eye. The arrowhead could have caused that. Blood smeared onto her fingers, and her stomach cringed. The leather pouch had soaked in the man's blood. Her hands had been bloody countless times after a hunt, but this was different. This was a man's blood—his lifeblood, dripping on her fingers.

"Promise me... pro... mise..." The man fell back. His grip on Shael's hand loosened.

Fluff whined as Shael took in a shaky breath. The man had passed. He probably had a family somewhere who would wonder all their lives what had become of him, like she did about Pa and Tomas. Hopefully, they had not died on their own, either, and someone had paid them the respect due to the departed. Shael reached up and closed the man's eyes.

Now what? She couldn't just leave the man's body here for the predators to get to. She had to tell the guards at the castle gate about him. But that would mean mentioning the Hyllethans.

She of all people couldn't be associated with the Hyllethans. 'Keep your head down and keep away from the lords.' Ma's warning reverberated in her head. But the man had bled to death next to her, and he expected her to do as he had asked.

Whatever was in the bag could be very important, perhaps involving the safety of the land.

But her life and her family's safety were important, too.

She could leave the bag by the body. After all, if she hadn't been there, who would the man have given it to? Getting rid of the pouch might be the best solution.

However, it might be wiser to find out what was in it first.

Don't open it, the man had said. What would happen if she did? Would she trigger some spell? The man could be a mage for all she knew. She had never seen a mage before. Would he look so ordinary?

If she had seen the messenger in the castle, she wouldn't have given him a second glance. He was just a man. His graying hair neatly cut, but his clothing was plain and his hands rough. Perhaps he was just what he seemed—a castle servant. Why should she obey his instructions, putting herself and her family in danger? Yet she couldn't just leave him under a bush.

Fluff whined again. Shael ran her hand down his back, soothing him. Zy'el's wings must be over her today—first Ma's funeral, and now this. The messenger's errand could just as likely earn her a hangman's noose as Ma's funeral. And all because of what Ma's Hyllethan witch of a mistress had done sixteen years before.

She'd best get back to the castle, then decide what to do. If she used the route round the peninsula rather than the inland way the three horsemen had taken, with a bit of luck, she wouldn't cross the Hyllethans' path.

Shael motioned to Fluff and he bounded out of the thicket. They loped through the undergrowth, the rabbit carcasses swinging and knocking against her legs. To their left, a brook gurgled and meandered between the tree trunks and they raced along its bank.

Fluff slowed when they reached the bush-hidden hollow in the hillside where Shael kept a spare sling and a torn blanket. There was no time to check if something had disturbed the tiny cave. She clicked her tongue. The quicker she returned to the castle, the better. Fluff darted away, and they raced on until they reached the edge of the wood, where the ground fell away and the brook poured straight into the sea.

Shael exhaled in relief. They were close to her favorite hideout. The entrance to the cave was halfway down the cliff and appeared to be little more than a gash, hidden by the small waterfall that tumbled over the ledge. The split in the rock was just wide enough for a person to edge in, but it widened up into a large space. Water from the brook dripped into a small pool at the back of the cave. If she ever needed to hide from the Lord of Merecastle, that cave was where she would go. She had all that she needed there—a constant supply of water, a stock of dried food and blankets, a few odds and ends she'd got from home to make it comfortable, and the henna and sage concoction she used to dye her hair.

Fluff snarled as an arrow impaled the ground by his paws. A bearded man leaped out from behind a tree, again pulling taut his bowstring.

Outcasts!

Too shocked to cry out, Shael could only stare. A teenage boy in a dirty white smock and dark leggings rose out of the undergrowth behind the man rushing towards her, a butcher's knife in his hand.

Fluff hurled himself onto the boy. Another shaft winged past Shael, goading her into action. Reaching for her sling while her other hand dug into her other pocket for her supply of stones. She twirled, let fly. The bearded archer fell to the ground.

The boy grappling with Fluff shrieked. The wolf had latched onto the boy's forearm, immobilizing the hand holding the knife with his teeth. Blood dripped, splattering onto soil.

Fluff would tear the boy's arm off if he didn't let go of the knife. The Outcast clawed Fluff's shoulder. She had to stop them, or they'd both get hurt. Shael placed another stone into the leather cradle of her sling, then hesitated. She could hit Fluff.

The boy and Fluff, a jumble of fur and limbs, rolled closer to the edge. If they fell over the cliff, the height and jagged rocks would kill them. Shael inhaled to yell a warning. Movement to her left caused her to spin round. A third Outcast, a shaggy-haired teenage girl, leaped onto her.

Shael cried out in pain as she hit the ground, plowing sharp rock and loose stones into her back. Blood pounded in her head. Digging her fingers into the ground, she gouged out a fistful of soil and threw it into the girl's eyes. The Outcast snarled. Finger nails slashed across Shael's face.

Pain, like a hot iron, blurred her sight. She had to get away. She had to see, or she'd end up another dead body in the woods.

"Give me your clothes." The girl yanked at Shael's cloak.

The ties dug into Shael's airways. She couldn't breathe. Frantically, she groped for the hilt of the knife in her boot. The comforting touch of wood in her grasp, Shael slashed.

Yelping, the girl let go of the material, a line of blood trickling down her arm.

Shael gulped in air, sweat stinging her eyes as she pulled herself away from under the girl's weight, the asphyxiating smell of unwashed clothing and stale sweat making her head spin even more.

The Outcast girl drove a knee into Shael's stomach.

White hot agony paralyzed her limbs, cramped her lungs, pummeled her temples. Shael doubled over. Her vision swam, dimmed. A guard's cuff had never hurt as much.

The girl wrenched the knife out of Shael's hand and pulled it back, the blade aimed at Shael's throat.

Shael opened her mouth to scream. No sound came out. Their eyes locked and Shael gazed up at the flames burning in the Outcast's eyes. Time seemed to slow down, to stop. A ball of acid burst in Shael's stomach, raced up her throat. She was going to die. It would be days before she'd be found. She'd promised Ma she'd take care of Andrey, but Eszter would be all he'd have now.

The blade dove down.

Shael's scream rent the air, her heart stuttered, kicking against her chest.

The blade clipped her lip, cutting through the cloak ties at her neck. The iron taste of blood filled Shael's mouth. She was alive. Zy'el had given her a second chance.

The Outcast hacked through the ties attaching the rabbit carcasses to Shael's belt. Then she tugged at the cloak, but Shael's weight held it pinned to the ground.

Fluff bounded towards them. Hackles raised; the wolf was twice the size of other wolves. He snarled, deep and low, baring red-stained teeth that could slice through flesh and bone with a jerk of his head.

The girl shrieked and backed away off Shael grabbing the rabbits before bolting. The boy Fluff had mauled staggered to his feet and fled into the trees too, holding his bleeding arm against his body.

Fluff made to follow.

"No, boy." The words came out in a raw croak.

Twigs snapped, swished, then settled. The bearded archer Shael had stunned also fleeing. He must have crept away in the confusion. The wood listened with them to the sounds of the Outcasts' flight. Then a bird chirped, and branches breathed and sighed. All clear.

She'd been such a fool. No one was safe in the wood, but she had let worry about the dead man and his pouch distract her. Nor had she realized that the breeze was blowing from the sea, driving the scent of any predator or Outcast away from them, away from Fluff.

The wolf trotted back to her. His hot breath and his tongue on her face helped to slow the hammering of her heart, the panic snatching at her breath and veiling her sight. Legs shaking, Shael got to her feet and shook the dust off her clothing and cloak. She could repair the tears at home. Apart from a few scratches, she and Fluff were not injured. They had lost their dinner, but it could have been much worse. The Outcasts had likely only wanted warm clothing for the winter—even her threadbare cloak would stave off some of the cold.

She'd have willingly let the girl take the messenger's pouch. It would have solved that problem. Shael groped inside her tunic where she had tucked the bag. Fingering the leather, three irregularly shaped items, each about five inches long, rolled between her fingers. Another tiny object settled at the bottom of the bag. Its edge poked out of the rent in the material and she pulled it out.

Her breath hitched.

Clay had been molded into a slim human arm. A delicately shaped hand protruded from the cuff of a sleeve, each tiny finger perfectly proportioned. The attention to detail was remarkable. Only an artist could have sculpted that arm.

Shael ran her finger along the top. It was jagged. If the bag contained a set of statuettes for Queen Neis, she'd broken one of them in the scuffle.

Well done, Shael!

Pa had once made a clay miniature of her. It had been perfect in so many ways, just like this arm. But Ma had forced him to destroy it.

She'd never understood why Ma had feared that tiny statue so much. Pa had also made tiny animals for them, but Ma hadn't made him destroy those. Over the years, a paw or a head had got broken, and Pa or Bastian had mended them. She knew what had to be done to repair the statuette, but first she had to open the bag and take out the rest of the contents, and that was best done elsewhere. The Outcasts could come back and bring others with them. She wouldn't be so lucky to escape unscathed next time.

Stuffing the leather pouch back beneath her shirt she whistled to Fluff. She'd go to the hideout. The cave was close and the safest place she knew.

Getting to her feet, she walked along the edge of the cliff on legs that still shook, till she reached the path leading to the beach. Fluff scrambled down the slippery slope ahead of her. Tiny pebbles rolled and bounced, dislodged by their descent. Shael forced herself to move slowly. Plummeting down the cliff would be a great way to end the worst day of her life. Her legs were still wobbly from the fight, and she'd also better pay extra care where she placed her feet as the overhanging rock-face threw deep shadows over the wet ground.

The waterfall splashed spray onto her. It was freezing, but it cleared her head.

Reaching the fissure in the rock behind the cascade, Shael looked around one last time to check that no one was watching before slipping into the cave behind Fluff.

The coldness of the rock against her back eased the tension within her, and she sagged against the rock. She was safe here. No one could get to her.

Fluff went to the back of the cave to lap water from the pool, but she remained near the opening, the cool breeze fanning her face and the rhythmic swish of the sea soothing her. Inhaling deeply, she straightened and pulled the leather bag from beneath her clothing.

To open, or not to open? She could just lob the pouch out of the cave, and it would drop into the sea, lost forever. As if it had never been. But she'd live all her life wondering what had been in the pouch.

And if the Inner Lands were attacked, and something within the pouch could have averted it, she'd have to live knowing that she might have prevented a massacre.

Shael reached up to a natural ledge in the cave wall and pulled down one of the blankets she kept there. Unrolling it where a narrow window of sunlight warmed the ground, she kneeled on it and picked at the knot tying the drawstrings of the bag. A few careful tugs, and the knot gave way.

Shael glowered at the bag. This could be the moment she'd be transformed into a frog, or something. She'd have to hop all the way to Merecastle where Andrey could be counted on to smuggle her into his closet of a room and keep her out of Eszter's sight.

Wiping her sweating palms down her trousers, Shael jerked the thin leather cords apart.

No sparks or smoke burst out of the messenger's pouch. Chuckling at the absurdity of her fear, Shael opened the bag as wide as it would go and drew out three clay figures.

Just as the little arm had been beautifully sculpted, the figures were superb. Three lanky males, dressed in finery and in a fashion, she had never seen in Merecastle—not even when Lord Jothan's daughter had married, and guests had arrived from all over the Inner Lands.

The figures were too beautiful, too perfect to represent real people. Shael rubbed at the blood staining the paintwork. The miniatures didn't represent Inlanders. The silvery-white paint of the hair and the long graceful legs made their race unmistakable. Had the Hyllethans been this beautiful? She'd never met any, and with Ay'el's help never would.

Shael rose and headed for the back of the cave. The dead man's blood had dried on the figurines, but a little water would remove it. She unwound her headscarf and shook her hair down. It was always such a relief to do so, but she could only do it here or in her room at night, as Bastian insisted, she kept her hair hidden even in the house. Too many people came to the workshop during the day, and even when freshly dyed, the color never came close to the Merecastlian blackness.

Shael dipped the tail of the long strip of material into the pool. After squeezing out the excess water, she went back to the miniatures. Gingerly rubbing at the blood stains, the intricate etching and paintwork emerged.

Each figure was dressed in patterned brocades over clay lace that flowed from the wrists. The figurine with the broken arm brandished a sword.

Shael slid her finger along the smooth length of the weapon. It sliced into her.

Inhaling sharply, she sucked her finger while a drop of blood trickled down the sword blade. How strange. Baked clay was not usually razor sharp. Shael wiped the blood off the sword and lifted the miniature closer to her eyes. The sword was not made of clay but of some hard creamy-white material

Bone or horn. Perhaps.

Shael put the swordsman down and took up the figurine of a well-built man with a bird of prey perched on his arm. A wipe-down with her headscarf revealed feathers and talons as delicately crafted as the man's body. The bird's beak was made from the same creamy-white matter as the sword.

The third miniature was of a gangly male who held a creamy-white reed pipe to his mouth.

A musician, a falconer and a swordsman. It was an odd combination.

Something about the miniatures niggled at a memory. She had seen something similar a long time ago but couldn't place where. It could wait. The broken arm was the more pressing problem. A little maneuvering, and the tiny limb fitted neatly into the rest of the swordsman's forearm.

Mending the arm would not be a problem. She just needed the tools in Bastian's workshop. Hiding the break, however, would be more difficult. Still, she'd had loads of practice painting Bastian's pots and plates. Some play with paint and shadowing would hide the worst of the damage.

Shael returned the figurines to the leather bag, tucking it inside her shirt before retying her headscarf. Dyeing her hair would have to wait for another day. The quicker she returned home, the better.

After rolling up the blanket and storing it in its usual place on the ledge, she whistled to Fluff and slipped out of the cave.

With the wolf in the lead, they picked their way down to the rocks and sand below the cave. Fluff jumped down from one ledge to another, but Shael took her time, knowing a false step would send her to the bottom of the cliff quicker than she'd prefer.

Her boots finally touched sand, Shael gave one final look around. A bird twitted somewhere above her. Surf swished up to her boots and a dry leaf or two floated down to the beach from the overhanging trees. Nothing else moved or made a sound. Fluff wagged his tail. They were alone and no Hyllethans lay in wait.

"Race you to the castle?" Shael said, patting the wolf.

Fluff yipped and took off.

"Cheater!" Her feet squelching in the wet sand, she loped after him.

The breeze smeared her cheeks with sea spray, and she licked the salt off her lips. No air tasted fresher or more invigorating.

Skirting the foot of the cliff, Fluff waited till she'd almost caught up before dashing off again. Gulls swooped and shrieked overhead. Shael scanned the sky for some stray pigeon. Bastian did not like the taste of gull meat, so those birds couldn't replace the rabbits she'd lost. Taking out her sling she brought down a couple. Fluff raced back to gobble them down. The wolf at least would have a full belly. And she could take the lead in the race.

Yipping, Fluff loped to catch up with her, then he slowed to keep pace. They jogged on, side by side. Over the water, the looming dark mass of Hylletha, seen from this angle, looked like a crouching wolf.

Unfortunately, not all wolves had Fluff's friendly disposition. The three riders had most likely come from that island, but they had needed a boat to cross—a large boat, since they had horses. The small natural harbor the Merecastlians used lay about a mile away. Two guards were always stationed there, and a stable boy who looked after the mounts of travelers and merchants who preferred to travel by sea rather than overland. The guards on the top tiers of Merecastle, or those stationed at the harbor, would have seen a large craft approaching from Hylletha.

Shael shuddered and hugged her cloak closer around her. This return of the Hyllethans could signal the beginning of another war. Being so close to the enemy, Merecastle would be the first castle the Hyllethans assailed. And all the Merecastlian men, women and children would be roped in to defend it. Even Andrey. He'd be old enough to help the archers on the battlements.

Pity a wolf wasn't welcome inside the castle. If the Hyllethans breached their walls, Fluff would be more lethal than any of Lord Jothan's men.

The wolf halted and bristled.

Shael's lungs faltered as she reached for her knife and swept the flow of sand and water with narrow eyes. Something had alerted Fluff. But there was nowhere to hide. Which also meant whatever had alerted Fluff couldn't be hidden, unless —

Shael peered up at the sheer rock face soaring above her. A honey-colored lizard scurried over an outcrop and disappeared beneath one of the hardy shrubs dotting the wind-eroded stone. If someone was at the top of the cliff, he couldn't jump down without killing himself.

Shael tightened her grip on her knife. No normal man could, that is. A Hyllethan might, if he used magic. Or had wings.

Did Hyllethans fly? Only on dragons, she'd heard.

But mages could appear out of thin air.

Crouching low, Fluff slunk towards some driftwood lying on the sand, an arrow's reach away from them. Then he pounced.

###

Thank you for reading an excerpt of The Dawn of Purple & Gray by Caroline Sciriha.
If you enjoyed this read, you can grab the book here.